DOVER·THRI

Family Happiness
and Other Stories

LEO TOLSTOY

DOVER PUBLICATIONS, INC.
Mineola, New York

DOVER THRIFT EDITIONS

GENERAL EDITOR: MARY CAROLYN WALDREP
EDITOR OF THIS VOLUME: T. N. R. ROGERS

Bibliographical Note

This Dover edition, first published in 2005, is a new compilation of six unabridged stories, reprinted from standard editions: "Family Happiness" (Семейное счастье, 1859), "Three Deaths" (Три смерти, 1859), "The Three Hermits" (Три старца, 1886), "The Devil" (Дьявол, written 1889–1890; first published 1911), "Father Sergius" (Отец Сергий, written 1890–1898; first published 1911), and "Master and Man" (Хозяин и работник, 1895). Spelling has been made consistent and Americanized, and the editor has written a new Introduction and a few footnotes specially for the Dover edition.

Library of Congress Cataloging-in-Publication Data

Tolstoy, Leo, graf, 1828–1910.
　　[Short stories. English. Selections]
　　Family happiness and other stories / Leo Tolstoy.
　　　　p. cm. — (Dover thrift editions)
　　1st work originally published: 1859. 2nd work originally published: 1859. 3rd word originally published: 1886. 4th work originally published: 1911. 5th work originally published: 1911. 6th work originally published: 1895. With new introd.
　　Contents: Family happiness—Three deaths—The three hermits—The devil—Father Sergius—Master and man.
　　ISBN 0-486-44081-8 (pbk.)
　　1. Tolstoy, Leo, graf, 1828–1910—Translations into English. I. Title. II. Series.

PG3366.A13 2005
891.73'3—dc22

2005045420

Manufactured in the United States of America
Dover Publications, Inc., 31 East 2nd Street, Mineola, N.Y. 11501

Introduction

LEV NIKOLAYEVICH TOLSTOY (1828–1910) will of course always be best known for *War and Peace* and *Anna Karenina*. But before and after those monumental novels, he produced many short stories, essays, and short novels (or long stories—a particularly Russian form known as *povesti*). This volume, which contains four of his long stories and two shorter ones, spans almost his entire writing life and displays well his unique, uneasy temperament and intelligence.

"Family Happiness," the longest, richest, and most novelistic (though not the most powerful) of the stories presented here, comes from his early period—the period, that is, before his marriage and before his great novels. As he does in much of his best fiction, Tolstoy makes substantial use of the facts of his life—especially those that have left him wracked with guilt. In 1856, after the death of her father, he was appointed the tutor to a young woman named Valeriya Arseneva, who lived on a nearby estate. He became deeply involved with her, but could not bring himself to marry her. "I never loved her with real love," he admitted later. "I was carried away by the reprehensible desire to inspire love. This gave me a delight I had never before experienced. . . . I have behaved very badly."[1] His impeccable artistry and sensitivity led him to imagine the story from the point of view of the young woman, and thus it took on its own life, its own truth. But the bad behavior continued to haunt him; after the story was done and was set to be published, he wrote to a friend that it was a vile, loathsome work, and begged him to burn the manuscript.

At that time, still unmarried, he had not yet personally experienced the tortuous ups and downs of family happiness. He married only a few years later, in 1862, when he was thirty-four. His bride was the eighteen-year-old Sofya Andreyevna Bers, with whom he would live almost fifty years and who would bear thirteen of his children. Because he wanted

---

[1] *Introduction to Tolstoy's Writings*, by Ernest J. Simmons (Chicago: University of Chicago Press, 1968).

their relationship to be completely honest, he invited her to read his diaries before their wedding. Such a dose of the truth was more than she really wanted. She was in love, and was able, she thought, to forgive Tolstoy his past affairs—but his diaries made them so vivid that they festered in her all the rest of her life.

The hardest to deal with were his fevered words about a married young peasant woman named Aksinya, who had borne him a son and with whom he had had a deep, passionate affair till two years before his marriage. That affair was part of the genesis of "The Devil." But according to Aylmer Maude, Tolstoy's friend and translator, the story was also based on an incident from 1880, when Tolstoy asked a tutor at Yasnaya Polyana, his estate, to accompany him on his daily walks to keep him from acting on a temptation. As he confessed to the tutor, he had arranged an assignation with the servants' cook, which had only been prevented when one of his children called out to him as he was setting out to meet her. Tolstoy's daughter Aleksandra said that he had dashed off a draft of "The Devil" in the fall of 1889 and then put it aside for twenty years before revising it.[2] He kept it hidden from Sofya in order to keep her jealousy of Aksinya, which had never ceased to torment her, from flaring up again.

Right up to the end, "The Devil" is vital, genuine, and impassioned—"real," as Mark Van Doren says, "in the same awful way in which Tolstoi at his best was always real—and in a way that the term 'realism,' incidentally, cannot illuminate."[3] It is well worth reading, but the ending—or lack of one—is a terrible disappointment. Tolstoy wrote two different endings, both of which are included here, but neither fits well with what has gone before, and it is unlikely that either was satisfying to him. And that is certainly at least one reason why the story was not published till after his death.

Another of the stories not published till after his death was "Father Sergius." In the late 1870s Tolstoy had gone through a spiritual crisis (detailed in A Confession, 1882) that had left him almost suicidal and had led him to embrace a Christianity of self-denial. In his earlier fiction, he had approached the world with artistry and an open mind. In his later work the artistry is still there, but it is sometimes at war with the spiritual message he wants to convey. As in most of Tolstoy's fiction, the twists and turns of "Father Sergius" are as unpredictable as those of life. But once again the ending feels forced.

Some literary historians have suggested that Tolstoy avoided publishing "Father Sergius" and several other stories in order to minimize fric-

[2] From Tolstoy: A Life of My Father (New York: Harper & Brothers, 1953).
[3] "First Glance" by Mark Van Doren, The Nation, 23 June 1926.

tion with his wife. It's true that he had given up the copyrights of all of his later work, and that Sofya disagreed with this decision, as she disagreed with so much of the way he was living. So perhaps it was because he wanted to avoid quarreling with her about publication rights that he did not publish "Father Sergius" or "The Devil." But it also seems likely that he wasn't completely satisfied with them.

Tolstoy was, after all, his own harshest critic. Even when he felt good about his work, he often remained uncertain about whether it was worth publishing. For instance, when he had finished "Master and Man"[4]—the most powerful of the stories included here—Tolstoy needed to be reassured, and sent the manuscript to a friend, saying "It is so long since I've written anything artistic that I truly do not know whether it ought to be printed." "My God!" his friend wrote back, "how splendid, priceless it is . . ."[5] His friend was right. It may have been Tolstoy's religious beliefs that moved him to write the story, but the story remains deeply human and moving in every detail. And yes—priceless.

The remaining two stories are much shorter, and both are charming and unusual. The first, "Three Deaths," is from his early period. He wrote it long before his spiritual crisis and conversion, and it has almost a Taoist feeling. This is what he had to say about it in a letter to his cousin Alexandra before the story was published:

> My idea was this: three creatures died . . . . [One] is pitiful and loathsome because she has lied all her life, and lies when on the point of death. . . . [Another] dies peacefully just because he is not a Christian. His religion is different, even though by force of habit he has observed the Christian ritual: his religion is nature, which he has lived with. . . . [The third] dies peacefully, honestly, and beautifully. Beautifully—because it doesn't lie, doesn't put on airs, isn't afraid, and has no regrets. There you have my idea, and of course you don't agree with it; but it can't be disputed—it is in my soul, and in yours too.[6]

The other, "The Three Hermits," from almost three decades later, is one of a group of stories Tolstoy took from folk tales. A decade or so later, in *What Is Art?* (1897), he gave his opinion that such folk art—tales or jokes that might delight millions of people—was much more valuable than novels written for the bored delectation of the leisured classes. According to his son Ilya, Tolstoy heard many such tales from a

---

[4] This translation of the title seems to have a religious connotation that is not present in the Russian. A more accurate translation would be "Master and Worker."

[5] Quoted in *Introduction to Tolstoy's Writings*, by Ernest J. Simmons (Chicago: University of Chicago Press, 1968).

[6] From a translated letter of 1 May 1858 included in *Tolstoy's Short Fiction*, edited by Michael R. Katz (New York: W. W. Norton & Company, 1991).

wandering minstrel named Shchegolenkov, who stayed with them in the summer of 1879:

> His endless stories delighted me and I loved to sit and gaze at his long gray beard, which hung in twisted locks. These tales were imbued with remote antiquity, and one felt in them the accumulation of centuries of sound wisdom. Papa used to listen to him with great interest, every day making him recite something new, and Petrovich never failed to comply. He was inexhaustible. Later Father borrowed several of these subjects for his popular tales.[7]

So "The Three Hermits" might be called "found art." What makes it Tolstoy's is its neat illustration of one of his core beliefs: that the poor and the unlearned are the natural children of God. Most of the stories in this book are enriched by that philosophy.

T. N. R. ROGERS

---

[7] From *Tolstoy, My Father* (Chicago: Cowles Book Company, 1971).

Contents

Family Happiness

PART I

Chapter I

WE were in mourning for my mother, who had died in the autumn, and I spent all that winter alone in the country with Katya and Sonya.

Katya was an old friend of the family, our governess who had brought us all up, and I had known and loved her since my earliest recollections. Sonya was my younger sister. It was a dark and sad winter which we spent in our old house of Pokrovskoye. The weather was cold and so windy that the snowdrifts came higher than the windows; the panes were almost always dimmed by frost, and we seldom walked or drove anywhere throughout the winter. Our visitors were few, and those who came brought no addition of cheerfulness or happiness to the household. They all wore sad faces and spoke low, as if they were afraid of waking someone; they never laughed, but sighed and often shed tears as they looked at me and especially at little Sonya in her black frock. The feeling of death clung to the house; the air was still filled with the grief and horror of death. My mother's room was kept locked; and whenever I passed it on my way to bed, I felt a strange uncomfortable impulse to look into that cold empty room.

I was then seventeen; and in the very year of her death my mother was intending to move to Petersburg, in order to take me into society. The loss of my mother was a great grief to me; but I must confess to another feeling behind that grief—a feeling that though I was young and pretty (so everybody told me), I was wasting a second winter in the solitude of the country. Before the winter ended, this sense of dejection, solitude, and simple boredom increased to such an extent that I refused to leave my room or open the piano or take up a book. When Katya urged me to find some occupation, I said that I did not feel able for it; but in my heart I said, "What is the good of it? What is the good of doing anything, when the best part of my life is being wasted like this?" And to this question, tears were my only answer.

1

I was told that I was growing thin and losing my looks; but even this failed to interest me. What did it matter? For whom? I felt that my whole life was bound to go on in the same solitude and helpless dreariness, from which I had myself no strength and even no wish to escape. Towards the end of winter Katya became anxious about me and determined to make an effort to take me abroad. But money was needed for this, and we hardly knew how our affairs stood after my mother's death. Our guardian, who was to come and clear up our position, was expected every day.

In March he arrived.

"Well, thank God!" Katya said to me one day, when I was walking up and down the room like a shadow, without occupation, without a thought, and without a wish. "Sergey Mikhaylych has arrived; he has sent to inquire about us and means to come here for dinner. You must rouse yourself, dear Mashechka," she added, "or what will he think of you? He was so fond of you all."

Sergey Mikhaylych was our near neighbor, and, though a much younger man, had been a friend of my father's. His coming was likely to change our plans and to make it possible to leave the country; and also I had grown up in the habit of love and regard for him; and when Katya begged me to rouse myself, she guessed rightly that it would give me especial pain to show to disadvantage before him, more than before any other of our friends. Like everyone in the house, from Katya and his goddaughter Sonya down to the helper in the stables, I loved him from old habit; and also he had a special significance for me, owing to a remark which my mother had once made in my presence. "I should like you to marry a man like him," she said. At the time this seemed to me strange and even unpleasant. My ideal husband was quite different: he was to be thin, pale, and sad; and Sergey Mikhaylych was middle-aged, tall, robust, and always, as it seemed to me, in good spirits. But still my mother's words stuck in my head; and even six years before this time, when I was eleven, and he still said "thou" to me, and played with me, and called me by the pet-name of "violet"—even then I sometimes asked myself in a fright, "What *shall* I do, if he suddenly wants to marry me?"

Before our dinner, to which Katya made an addition of sweets and a dish of spinach, Sergey Mikhaylych arrived. From the window I watched him drive up to the house in a small sleigh; but as soon as it turned the corner, I hastened to the drawing room, meaning to pretend that his visit was a complete surprise. But when I heard his tramp and loud voice and Katya's footsteps in the hall, I lost patience and went to meet him myself. He was holding Katya's hand, talking loud, and smiling. When he saw me, he stopped and looked at me for a time without bowing. I was uncomfortable and felt myself blushing.

"Can this be really you?" he said in his plain decisive way, walking towards me with his arms apart. "Is so great a change possible? How grown-up you are! I used to call you 'violet,' but now you are a rose in full bloom!"

He took my hand in his own large hand and pressed it so hard that it almost hurt. Expecting him to kiss my hand, I bent towards him, but he only pressed it again and looked straight into my eyes with the old firmness and cheerfulness in his face.

It was six years since I had seen him last. He was much changed—older and darker in complexion; and he now wore whiskers which did not become him at all; but much remained the same—his simple manner, the large features of his honest open face, his bright intelligent eyes, his friendly, almost boyish, smile.

Five minutes later he had ceased to be a visitor and had become the friend of us all, even of the servants, whose visible eagerness to wait on him proved their pleasure at his arrival.

He behaved quite unlike the neighbors who had visited us after my mother's death. They had thought it necessary to be silent when they sat with us, and to shed tears. He, on the contrary, was cheerful and talkative, and said not a word about my mother, so that this indifference seemed strange to me at first and even improper on the part of so close a friend. But I understood later that what seemed indifference was sincerity, and I felt grateful for it. In the evening Katya poured out tea, sitting in her old place in the drawing room, where she used to sit in my mother's lifetime; Sonya and I sat near him; our old butler Grigori had hunted out one of my father's pipes and brought it to him; and he began to walk up and down the room as he used to do in past days.

"How many terrible changes there are in this house, when one thinks of it all!" he said, stopping in his walk.

"Yes," said Katya with a sigh; and then she put the lid on the samovar and looked at him, quite ready to burst out crying.

"I suppose you remember your father?" he said, turning to me.

"Not clearly," I answered.

"How happy you would have been together now!" he added in a low voice, looking thoughtfully at my face above the eyes. "I was very fond of him," he added in a still lower tone, and it seemed to me that his eyes were shining more than usual.

"And now God has taken her too!" said Katya; and at once she laid her napkin on the teapot, took out her handkerchief, and began to cry.

"Yes, the changes in this house are terrible," he repeated, turning away. "Sonya, show me your toys," he added after a little and went off to the parlor. When he had gone, I looked at Katya with eyes full of tears.

"What a splendid friend he is!" she said. And, though he was no relation, I did really feel a kind of warmth and comfort in the sympathy of this good man.

I could hear him moving about in the parlor with Sonya, and the sound of her high childish voice. I sent tea to him there; and I heard him sit down at the piano and strike the keys with Sonya's little hands.

Then his voice came—"Marya Aleksandrovna, come here and play something."

I liked his easy behavior to me and his friendly tone of command; I got up and went to him.

"Play this," he said, opening a book of Beethoven's music at the *adagio* of the "Moonlight Sonata." "Let me hear how you play," he added, and went off to a corner of the room, carrying his cup with him.

I somehow felt that with him it was impossible to refuse or to say beforehand that I played badly: I sat down obediently at the piano and began to play as well as I could; yet I was afraid of criticism, because I knew that he understood and enjoyed music. The *adagio* suited the remembrance of past days evoked by our conversation at tea, and I believe that I played it fairly well. But he would not let me play the *scherzo*. "No," he said, coming up to me; "you don't play that right; don't go on; but the first movement was not bad; you seem to be musical." This moderate praise pleased me so much that I even reddened. I felt it pleasant and strange that a friend of my father's, and his contemporary, should no longer treat me like a child but speak to me seriously. Katya now went upstairs to put Sonya to bed, and we were left alone in the parlor.

He talked to me about my father, and about the beginning of their friendship and the happy days they had spent together, while I was still busy with lesson-books and toys; and his talk put my father before me in quite a new light, as a man of simple and delightful character. He asked me too about my tastes, what I read and what I intended to do, and gave me advice. The man of mirth and jest who used to tease me and make me toys had disappeared; here was a serious, simple, and affectionate friend, for whom I could not help feeling respect and sympathy. It was easy and pleasant to talk to him; and yet I felt an involuntary strain also. I was anxious about each word I spoke: I wished so much to earn for my own sake the love which had been given me already merely because I was my father's daughter.

After putting Sonya to bed, Katya joined us and began to complain to him of my apathy, about which I had said nothing.

"So she never told me the most important thing of all!" he said, smiling and shaking his head reproachfully at me.

"Why tell you?" I said. "It is very tiresome to talk about, and it will pass off." (I really felt now, not only that my dejection would pass off, but that it had already passed off, or rather had never existed.)

"It is a bad thing," he said, "not to be able to stand solitude. Can it be that you are a young lady?"

"Of course, I am a young lady," I answered, laughing.

"Well, I can't praise a young lady who is alive only when people are admiring her, but as soon as she is left alone, collapses and finds nothing to her taste—one who is all for show and has no resources in herself."

"You have a flattering opinion of me!" I said, just for the sake of saying something.

He was silent for a little. Then he said: "Yes; your likeness to your father means something. There is something in you . . . ," and his kind attentive look again flattered me and made me feel a pleasant embarrassment.

I noticed now for the first time that his face, which gave one at first the impression of high spirits, had also an expression peculiar to himself—bright at first and then more and more attentive and rather sad.

"You ought not to be bored and you cannot be," he said; "you have music, which you appreciate, books, study; your whole life lies before you, and now or never is the time to prepare for it and save yourself future regrets. A year hence it will be too late."

He spoke to me like a father or an uncle, and I felt that he kept a constant check upon himself, in order to keep on my level. Though I was hurt that he considered me as inferior to himself, I was pleased that for me alone he thought it necessary to try to be different.

For the rest of the evening he talked about business with Katya.

"Well, good-bye, dear friends," he said. Then he got up, came towards me, and took my hand.

"When shall we see you again?" asked Katya.

"In spring," he answered, still holding my hand. "I shall go now to Danilovka" (this was another property of ours), "look into things there and make what arrangements I can; then I go to Moscow on business of my own; and in summer we shall meet again."

"Must you really be away so long?" I asked, and I felt terribly grieved. I had really hoped to see him every day, and I felt a sudden shock of regret, and a fear that my depression would return. And my face and voice must have made this plain.

"You must find more to do and not get depressed," he said; and I thought his tone too cool and unconcerned. "I shall put you through an examination in spring," he added, letting go my hand and not looking at me.

When we saw him off in the hall, he put on his fur coat in a hurry and still avoided looking at me. "He is taking a deal of trouble for nothing!" I thought. "Does he think me so anxious that he should look at me? He is a good man, a very good man; but that's all."

That evening, however, Katya and I sat up late, talking, not about him but about our plans for the summer, and where we should spend next winter and what we should do then. I had ceased to ask that terrible question—what is the good of it all? Now it seemed quite plain and simple: the proper object of life was happiness, and I promised myself much happiness ahead. It seemed as if our gloomy old house had suddenly become full of light and life.

Chapter II

Meanwhile spring arrived. My old dejection passed away and gave place to the unrest which spring brings with it, full of dreams and vague hopes and desires. Instead of living as I had done at the beginning of winter, I read and played the piano and gave lessons to Sonya; but also I often went into the garden and wandered for long alone through the avenues, or sat on a bench there; and Heaven knows what my thoughts and wishes and hopes were at such times. Sometimes at night, especially if there was a moon, I sat by my bedroom window till dawn; sometimes, when Katya was not watching, I stole out into the garden wearing only a wrapper and ran through the dew as far as the pond; and once I went all the way to the open fields and walked right round the garden alone at night.

I find it difficult now to recall and understand the dreams which then filled my imagination. Even when I *can* recall them, I find it hard to believe that my dreams were just like that: they were so strange and so remote from life.

Sergey Mikhaylych kept his promise: he returned from his travels at the end of May.

His first visit to us was in the evening and was quite unexpected. We were sitting in the veranda, preparing for tea. By this time the garden was all green, and the nightingales had taken up their quarters for the whole of St. Peter's Fast in the leafy borders. The tops of the round lilac bushes had a sprinkling of white and purple—a sign that their flowers were ready to open. The foliage of the birch avenue was all transparent in the light of the setting sun. In the veranda there was shade and freshness. The evening dew was sure to be heavy on the grass. Out of doors beyond the garden the last sounds of day were audible, and the noise of the sheep and cattle, as they were driven home. Nikon, the half-witted boy, was driving his water-cart along the path outside the veranda, and a cold stream of water from the sprinkler made dark circles on the mould round the stems and supports of the dahlias. In our veranda the polished samovar shone and hissed on the white table-cloth; there were cracknels and biscuits and cream on the table. Katya was busy washing the cups with her plump hands. I was too hungry after bathing to wait for tea, and was eating bread with thick fresh cream. I was wearing a gingham blouse with loose sleeves, and my hair, still wet, was covered with a kerchief. Katya saw him first, even before he came in.

"You, Sergey Mikhaylych!" she cried. "Why, we were just talking about you."

I got up, meaning to go and change my dress, but he caught me just by the door.

"Why stand on such ceremony in the country?" he said, looking with a smile at the kerchief on my head. "You don't mind the presence of your butler, and I am really the same to you as Grigori is." But I felt just then that he was looking at me in a way quite unlike Grigori's way, and I was uncomfortable.

"I shall come back at once," I said, as I left them.

"But what is wrong?" he called out after me; "it's just the dress of a young peasant woman."

"How strangely he looked at me!" I said to myself as I was quickly changing upstairs. "Well, I'm glad he has come; things will be more lively." After a look in the glass I ran gaily downstairs and into the veranda; I was out of breath and did not disguise my haste. He was sitting at the table, talking to Katya about our affairs. He glanced at me and smiled; then he went on talking. From what he said it appeared that our affairs were in capital shape: it was now possible for us, after spending the summer in the country, to go either to Petersburg for Sonya's education, or abroad.

"If only you would go abroad with us—" said Katya; "without you we shall be quite lost there."

"Oh, I should like to go round the world with you," he said, half in jest and half in earnest.

"All right," I said; "let us start off and go round the world."

He smiled and shook his head.

"What about my mother? What about my business?" he said. "But that's not the question just now: I want to know how you have been spending your time. Not depressed again, I hope?"

When I told him that I had been busy and not bored during his absence, and when Katya confirmed my report, he praised me as if he had a right to do so, and his words and looks were kind, as they might have been to a child. I felt obliged to tell him, in detail and with perfect frankness, all my good actions, and to confess, as if I were in church, all that he might disapprove of. The evening was so fine that we stayed in the veranda after tea was cleared away; and the conversation interested me so much that I did not notice how we ceased by degrees to hear any sound of the servants indoors. The scent of flowers grew stronger and came from all sides; the grass was drenched with dew; a nightingale struck up in a lilac bush close by and then stopped on hearing our voices; the starry sky seemed to come down lower over our heads.

It was growing dusk, but I did not notice it till a bat suddenly and silently flew in beneath the veranda awning and began to flutter round my white shawl. I shrank back against the wall and nearly cried out; but the bat as silently and swiftly dived out from under the awning and disappeared in the half-darkness of the garden.

"How fond I am of this place of yours!" he said, changing the conversation; "I wish I could spend all my life here, sitting in this veranda."

"Well, do then!" said Katya.

"That's all very well," he said, "but life won't sit still."

"Why don't you marry?" asked Katya; "you would make an excellent husband."

"Because I like sitting still?" and he laughed. "No, Katerina Karlovna, too late for you and me to marry. People have long ceased to think of me as a marrying man, and I am even surer of it myself; and I declare I have felt quite comfortable since the matter was settled."

It seemed to me that he said this in an unnaturally persuasive way.

"Nonsense!" said Katya; "a man of thirty-six makes out that he is too old!"

"Too old indeed," he went on, "when all one wants is to sit still. For a man who is going to marry that's not enough. Just you ask her," he added, nodding at me; "people of her age should marry, and you and I can rejoice in their happiness."

The sadness and constraint latent in his voice were not lost upon me. He was silent for a little, and neither Katya nor I spoke.

"Well, just fancy," he went on, turning a little on his seat; "suppose that by some mischance I married a girl of seventeen, Masha, if you like—I mean, Marya Aleksandrovna. The instance is good; I am glad it turned up; there could not be a better instance."

I laughed; but I could not understand why he was glad, or what it was that had turned up.

"Just tell me honestly, with your hand on your heart," he said, turning as if playfully to me, "would it not be a misfortune for you to unite your life with that of an old worn-out man who only wants to sit still, whereas Heaven knows what wishes are fermenting in that heart of yours?"

I felt uncomfortable and was silent, not knowing how to answer him.

"I am not making you a proposal, you know," he said, laughing; "but am I really the kind of husband you dream of when walking alone in the avenue at twilight? It would be a misfortune, would it not?"

"No, not a misfortune," I began.

"But a bad thing," he ended my sentence.

"Perhaps; but I may be mistaken . . ." He interrupted me again.

"There, you see! She is quite right, and I am grateful to her for her frankness, and very glad to have had this conversation. And there is something else to be said"—he added: "for me too it would be a very great misfortune."

"How odd you are! You have not changed in the least," said Katya, and then left the veranda, to order supper to be served.

When she had gone, we were both silent and all was still around us, but for one exception. A nightingale, which had sung last night by fitful snatches, now flooded the garden with a steady stream of song, and was soon answered by another from the dell below, which had not sung till that evening. The nearer bird stopped and seemed to listen for a moment, and then broke out again still louder than before, pouring out his song in piercing long-drawn cadences. There was a regal calm in the birds' voices, as they floated through the realm of night which belongs to those birds and not to man. The gardener walked past to his sleeping-quarters in the greenhouse, and the noise of his heavy boots grew fainter and fainter along the path. Someone whistled twice sharply at the foot of the hill; and then all was still again. The rustling of leaves could just be heard; the veranda awning flapped; a faint perfume, floating in the air, came down on the veranda and filled it. I felt silence awkward after what had been said, but what to say I did not know. I looked at him. His eyes, bright in the half-darkness, turned towards me.

"How good life is!" he said.

I sighed, I don't know why.

"Well?" he asked.

"Life is good," I repeated after him.

Again we were silent, and again I felt uncomfortable. I could not help fancying that I had wounded him by agreeing that he was old; and I wished to comfort him but did not know how.

"Well, I must be saying good-bye," he said, rising; "my mother expects me for supper; I have hardly seen her all day."

"I meant to play you the new sonata," I said.

"That must wait," he replied; and I thought that he spoke coldly. "Good-bye."

I felt still more certain that I had wounded him, and I was sorry. Katya and I went to the steps to see him off and stood for a while in the open, looking along the road where he had disappeared from view. When we ceased to hear the sound of his horse's hoofs, I walked round the house to the veranda, and again sat looking into the garden; and all I wished to see and hear, I still saw and heard for a long time in the dewy mist filled with the sounds of night.

He came a second time, and a third; and the awkwardness arising from that strange conversation passed away entirely, never to return. During that whole summer he came two or three times a week; and I grew so accustomed to his presence, that, when he failed to come for some time, I missed him and felt angry with him, and thought he was behaving badly in deserting me. He treated me like a boy whose company he liked, asked me questions, invited the most cordial frankness on my part, gave me advice and encouragement, or sometimes scolded and checked me. But in spite of his constant effort to keep on my level, I was aware that behind the part of him which I could understand there remained an entire region of mystery, into which he did not consider it necessary to admit me; and this fact did much to preserve my respect for him and his attraction for me. I knew from Katya and from our neighbors that he had not only to care for his old mother with whom he lived, and to manage his own estate and our affairs, but was also responsible for some public business which was the source of serious worries; but what view he took of all this, what were his convictions, plans, and hopes, I could not in the least find out from him. Whenever I turned the conversation to his affairs, he frowned in a way peculiar to himself and seemed to imply, "Please stop! That is no business of yours"; and then he changed the subject. This hurt me at first; but I soon grew accustomed to confining our talk to my affairs, and felt this to be quite natural.

There was another thing which displeased me at first and then became pleasant to me. This was his complete indifference and even contempt for my personal appearance. Never by word or look did he imply that I was pretty; on the contrary, he frowned and laughed, whenever the word was applied to me in his presence. He even liked to find fault with my looks and tease me about them. On special days Katya liked to dress me out in fine clothes and to arrange my hair effectively; but my finery met only with mockery from him, which pained kind-hearted Katya and at first disconcerted me. She had made up her mind that he admired me; and she could not understand how a man could help wishing a woman whom he admired to appear to the utmost advantage. But I soon understood what he wanted. He wished to make sure that I had not a trace of affectation. And when I understood this I was really quite free from affectation in the clothes I wore, or the arrangement of my hair, or my movements; but a very obvious form of affectation took its place—an affectation of simplicity, at a time when I could not yet be really simple. That he loved me, I knew; but I did not yet ask myself whether he loved me as a child or as a woman. I valued his love; I felt that he thought me better than all other young women in the world, and I could not help wishing him to go on being deceived about me. Without wishing to deceive him, I did deceive him, and I became better myself while deceiving him. I felt it a better and worthier course to show him the good points of my heart and mind than of my body. My hair, hands, face, ways—all these, whether good or bad, he had appraised at once and knew so well, that I could add nothing to my external appearance except the wish to deceive him. But my mind and heart he did not know, because he loved them, and because they were in the very process of growth and development; and on this point I could and did deceive him. And how easy I felt in his company, once I understood this clearly! My causeless bashfulness and awkward movements completely disappeared. Whether he saw me from in front, or in profile, sitting or standing, with my hair up or my hair down, I felt that he knew me from head to foot, and I fancied, was satisfied with me as I was. If, contrary to his habit, he had suddenly said to me as other people did, that I had a pretty face, I believe that I should not have liked it at all. But, on the other hand, how light and happy my heart was when, after I had said something, he looked hard at me and said, hiding emotion under a mask of raillery:

"Yes, there *is* something in you! you are a fine girl—that I must tell you."

And for what did I receive such rewards, which filled my heart with pride and joy? Merely for saying that I felt for old Grigori in his love for his little granddaughter; or because the reading of some poem or novel moved me to tears; or because I liked Mozart better than Schulhof. And I was surprised at my own quickness in guessing what was good and worthy of love, when I certainly did not know then what *was* good and worthy to be loved. Most of my former tastes and habits did not please him; and a mere look of his, or a twitch of his eyebrow was enough to show that he did not like what I was trying to say; and I felt at once that my own standard was changed. Sometimes, when he was about to give me a piece of advice, I seemed to know beforehand what he would say. When he looked in my face and asked me a question, his very look would draw out of me the answer he wanted. All my thoughts and feelings of that time were not really mine: they were his thoughts and feelings, which had suddenly become mine and passed into my life and lighted it up. Quite unconsciously I began to look at everything with different eyes—at Katya and the servants and Sonya and myself and my occupations. Books, which I used to read merely to escape boredom, now became one of the chief pleasures of my life, merely because he brought me the books and we read and discussed them together. The lessons I gave to Sonya had been a burdensome obligation which I forced myself to go through from a sense of duty; but, after he was present at a lesson, it became a joy to me to watch Sonya's progress. It used to seem to me an impossibility to learn a whole piece of music by heart; but now, when I knew that he would hear it and might praise it, I would play a single movement forty times over without stopping, till poor Katya stuffed her ears with cotton-wool, while I was still not weary of it. The same old

sonatas seemed quite different in their expression, and came out quite
changed and much improved. Even Katya, whom I knew and loved like
a second self, became different in my eyes. I now understood for the first
time that she was not in the least bound to be the mother, friend, and
slave that she was to us. Now I appreciated all the self-sacrifice and devotion of this affectionate creature, and all my obligations to her; and I
began to love her even better. It was he too who taught me to take quite
a new view of our serfs and servants and maids. It is an absurd confession
to make—but I had spent seventeen years among these people and yet
knew less about them than about strangers whom I had never seen; it had
never once occurred to me that they had their affections and wishes and
sorrows, just as I had. Our garden and woods and fields, which I had
known so long, became suddenly new and beautiful to me. He was right
in saying that the only certain happiness in life is to live for others. At
the time his words seemed to me strange, and I did not understand them;
but by degrees this became a conviction with me, without thinking
about it. He revealed to me a whole new world of joys in the present,
without changing anything in my life, without adding anything except
himself to each impression in my mind. All that had surrounded me from
childhood without saying anything to me, suddenly came to life. The
mere sight of him made everything begin to speak and press for admit-
tance to my heart, filling it with happiness.

Often during that summer, when I went upstairs to my room and lay
down on my bed, the old unhappiness of spring with its desires and
hopes for the future gave place to a passionate happiness in the present.
Unable to sleep, I often got up and sat on Katya's bed, and told her how
perfectly happy I was, though I now realize that this was quite unneces-
sary, as she could see it for herself. But she told me that she was quite
content and perfectly happy, and kissed me. I believed her—it seemed to
me so necessary and just that everyone should be happy. But Katya could
think of sleep too; and sometimes, pretending to be angry, she drove me
from her bed and went to sleep, while I turned over and over in my mind
all that made me so happy. Sometimes I got up and said my prayers over
again, praying in my own words and thanking God for all the happiness
he had given me.

All was quiet in the room; there was only the even breathing of Katya
in her sleep, and the ticking of the clock by her bed, while I turned from
side to side and whispered words of prayer, or crossed myself and kissed
the cross round my neck. The door was shut and the windows shuttered;
perhaps a fly or gnat hung buzzing in the air. I felt a wish never to leave
that room—a wish that dawn might never come, that my present frame
of mind might never change. I felt that my dreams and thoughts and
prayers were live things, living there in the dark with me, hovering about

my bed, and standing over me. And every thought was his thought, and every feeling his feeling. I did not know yet that this was love; I thought that things might go on so for ever, and that this feeling involved no consequences.

Chapter III

One day when the corn was being carried, I went with Katya and Sonya to our favorite seat in the garden, in the shade of the lime trees and above the dell, beyond which the fields and woods lay open before us. It was three days since Sergey Mikhaylych had been to see us; we were expecting him, all the more because our bailiff reported that he had promised to visit the harvest field. At two o'clock we saw him ride on to the rye field. With a smile and a glance at me, Katya ordered peaches and cherries, of which he was very fond, to be brought; then she lay down on the bench and began to doze. I tore off a crooked flat lime tree branch, which made my hand wet with its juicy leaves and juicy bark. Then I fanned Katya with it and went on with my book, breaking off from time to time, to look at the field-path along which he must come. Sonya was making a dolls' house at the root of an old lime tree. The day was sultry, windless, and steaming; the clouds were packing and growing blacker; all morning a thunderstorm had been gathering, and I felt restless, as I always did before thunder. But by afternoon the clouds began to part, the sun sailed out into a clear sky, and only in one quarter was there a faint rumbling. A single heavy cloud, lowering above the horizon and mingling with the dust from the fields, was rent from time to time by pale zigzags of lightning which ran down to the ground. It was clear that for today the storm would pass off, with us at all events. The road beyond the garden was visible in places, and we could see a procession of high creaking carts slowly moving along it with their load of sheaves, while the empty carts rattled at a faster pace to meet them, with swaying legs and shirts fluttering in them. The thick dust neither blew away nor settled down—it stood still beyond the fence, and we could see it through the transparent foliage of the garden trees. A little farther off, in the stack-yard, the same voices and the same creaking of wheels were audible; and the same yellow sheaves that had moved slowly past the fence were now flying aloft, and I could see the oval stacks gradually rising higher, and their conspicuous pointed tops, and the laborers swarming upon them. On the dusty field in front more carts were moving and more yellow sheaves were visible; and the noise of the carts, with the sound of talking and singing, came to us from a distance. At one side the bare stubble, with strips of fallow covered with wormwood, came more and more into view. Lower down, to the right, the gay dresses of the women were visible, as they bent down and swung their arms to bind the sheaves. Here the bare stubble looked untidy; but the disorder was cleared by degrees, as the pretty sheaves were ranged at close intervals. It seemed as if summer had suddenly turned to autumn before my eyes. The dust and heat were everywhere, except in our favorite nook in the garden; and everywhere, in this heat and dust and under the burning sun, the laborers carried on their heavy task with talk and noise.

Meanwhile Katya slept so sweetly on our shady bench, beneath her white cambric handkerchief, the black juicy cherries glistened so temptingly on the plate, our dresses were so clean and fresh, the water in the jug was so bright with rainbow colors in the sun, and I felt so happy! "How can I help it?" I thought; "am I to blame for being happy? And how can I share my happiness? How and to whom can I surrender all myself and all my happiness?"

By this time the sun had sunk behind the tops of the birch avenue, the dust was settling on the fields, the distance became clearer and brighter in the slanting light. The clouds had dispersed altogether; I could see through the trees the thatch of three new corn stacks. The laborers came down off the stacks; the carts hurried past, evidently for the last time, with a loud noise of shouting; the women, with rakes over their shoulders and straw bands in their belts, walked home past us, singing loudly; and still there was no sign of Sergey Mikhaylych, though I had seen him ride down the hill long ago. Suddenly he appeared upon the avenue, coming from a quarter where I was not looking for him. He had walked round by the dell. He came quickly towards me, with his hat off and radiant with high spirits. Seeing that Katya was asleep, he bit his lip, closed his eyes, and advanced on tiptoe; I saw at once that he was in that peculiar mood of causeless merriment which I always delighted to see in him, and which we called "wild ecstasy." He was just like a schoolboy playing truant; his whole figure, from head to foot, breathed content, happiness, and boyish frolic.

"Well, young violet, how are you? All right?" he said in a whisper, coming up to me and taking my hand. Then, in answer to my question, "Oh, I'm splendid today, I feel like a boy of thirteen—I want to play at horses and climb trees."

"Is it wild ecstasy?" I asked, looking into his laughing eyes, and feeling that the "wild ecstasy" was infecting me.

"Yes," he answered, winking and checking a smile. "But I don't see why you need hit Katerina Karlovna on the nose."

With my eyes on him I had gone on waving the branch, without noticing that I had knocked the handkerchief off Katya's face and was now brushing her with the leaves. I laughed.

"She will say she was awake all the time," I whispered, as if not to awake Katya; but that was not my real reason—it was only that I liked to whisper to him.

He moved his lips in imitation of me, pretending that my voice was too low for him to hear. Catching sight of the dish of cherries, he pretended to steal it, and carried it off to Sonya under the lime tree, where he sat down on her dolls. Sonya was angry at first, but he soon made his peace with her by starting a game, to see which of them could eat cherries faster.

"If you like, I will send for more cherries," I said; "or let us go ourselves."

He took the dish and set the dolls on it, and we all three started for the orchard. Sonya ran behind us, laughing and pulling at his coat, to make him surrender the dolls. He gave them up and then turned to me, speaking more seriously.

"You really are a violet," he said, still speaking low, though there was no longer any fear of waking anybody; "when I came to you out of all that dust and heat and toil, I positively smelt violets at once. But not the sweet violet—you know, that early dark violet that smells of melting snow and spring grass."

"Is harvest going on well?" I asked, in order to hide the happy agitation which his words produced in me.

"First-rate! Our people are always splendid. The more you know them, the better you like them."

"Yes," I said; "before you came I was watching them from the garden, and suddenly I felt ashamed to be so comfortable myself while they were hard at work, and so . . ."

He interrupted me, with a kind but grave look: "Don't talk like that, my dear; it is too sacred a matter to talk of lightly. God forbid that you should use fine phrases about that!"

"But it is only to *you* I say this."

"All right, I understand. But what about those cherries?"

The orchard was locked, and no gardener to be seen: he had sent them all off to help with the harvest. Sonya ran to fetch the key. But he would not wait for her: climbing up a corner of the wall, he raised the net and jumped down on the other side.

His voice came over the wall—"If you want some, give me the dish."

"No," I said; "I want to pick for myself. I shall fetch the key; Sonya won't find it."

But suddenly I felt that I must see what he was doing there and what he looked like—that I must watch his movements while he supposed that no one saw him. Besides I was simply unwilling just then to lose sight of him for a single minute. Running on tiptoe through the nettles to the other side of the orchard where the wall was lower, I mounted on an empty cask, till the top of the wall was on a level with my waist, and then leaned over into the orchard. I looked at the gnarled old trees, with their broad dented leaves and the ripe black cherries hanging straight and heavy among the foliage; then I pushed my head under the net, and from under the knotted bough of an old cherry tree I caught sight of Sergey Mikhaylych. He evidently thought that I had gone away and that no one was watching him. With his hat off and his eyes shut, he was sitting on the fork of an old tree and carefully rolling into a ball a lump of cherry tree gum. Suddenly he shrugged his shoulders, opened his eyes, muttered something, and smiled. Both words and smile were so unlike him that I felt ashamed of myself for eavesdropping. It seemed to me that he had said, "Masha!" "Impossible," I thought. "Darling Masha!" he said again, in a lower and more tender tone. There was no possible doubt about the two words this time. My heart beat hard, and such a passionate joy—illicit joy, as I felt—took hold of me, that I clutched at the wall, fearing to fall and betray myself. Startled by the sound of my movement, he looked round—he dropped his eyes instantly, and his face turned red, even scarlet, like a child's. He tried to speak, but in vain; again and again his face positively flamed up. Still he smiled as he looked at me, and I smiled too. Then his whole face grew radiant with happiness. He had ceased to be the old uncle who spoiled or scolded me; he was a man on my level, who loved and feared me as I loved and feared him. We looked at one another without speaking. But suddenly he frowned; the smile and light in his eyes disappeared, and he resumed his cold paternal tone, just as if we were doing something wrong and he was repenting and calling on me to repent.

"You had better get down, or you will hurt yourself," he said; "and do put your hair straight; just think what you look like!"

"What makes him pretend? what makes him want to give me pain?" I thought in my vexation. And the same instant brought an irresistible desire to upset his composure again and test my power over him.

"No," I said; "I mean to pick for myself." I caught hold of the nearest branch and climbed to the top of the wall; then, before he had time to catch me, I jumped down on the other side.

"What foolish things you do!" he muttered, flushing again and trying to hide his confusion under a pretence of annoyance; "you might really have hurt yourself. But how do you mean to get out of this?"

He was even more confused than before, but this time his confusion frightened rather than pleased me. It infected me too and made me blush; avoiding his eye and not knowing what to say, I began to pick cherries though I had nothing to put them in. I reproached myself, I repented of what I had done, I was frightened; I felt that I had lost his good opinion for ever by my folly. Both of us were silent and embarrassed.

From this difficult situation Sonya rescued us by running back with the key in her hand. For some time we both addressed our conversation to her and said nothing to each other. When we returned to Katya, who assured us that she had never been asleep and was listening all the time, I calmed down, and he tried to drop into his fatherly patronizing manner again, but I was not taken in by it. A discussion which we had had some days before came back clear before me.

Katya had been saying that it was easier for a man to be in love and declare his love than for a woman.

"A man may say that he is in love, and a woman can't," she said.

"I disagree," said he; "a man has no business to say, and can't say, that he is in love."

"Why not?" I asked.

"Because it never can be true. What sort of a revelation is that, that a man is in love? A man seems to think that whenever he says the word, something will go pop!—that some miracle will be worked, signs and wonders, with all the big guns firing at once! In my opinion," he went on, "whoever solemnly brings out the words 'I love you' is either deceiving himself or, which is even worse, deceiving others."

"Then how is a woman to know that a man is in love with her, unless he tells her?" asked Katya.

"That I don't know," he answered; "every man has his own way of telling things. If the feeling exists, it will out somehow. But when I read novels, I always fancy the crestfallen look of Lieut. Strelsky or Alfred, when he says, 'I love you, Eleanora,' and expects something wonderful to happen at once, and no change at all takes place in either of them—their eyes and their noses and their whole selves remain exactly as they were."

Even then I had felt that this banter covered something serious that had reference to myself. But Katya resented his disrespectful treatment of the heroes in novels.

"You are never serious," she said; "but tell me truthfully, have you never yourself told a woman that you loved her?"

"Never, and never gone down on one knee," he answered, laughing; "and never will."

This conversation I now recalled, and I reflected that there was no need for him to tell me that he loved me. "I know that he loves me," I thought, "and all his endeavors to seem indifferent will not change my opinion."

He said little to me throughout the evening, but in every word he said to Katya and Sonya and in every look and movement of his I saw love and felt no doubt of it. I was only vexed and sorry for him, that he thought it necessary still to hide his feelings and pretend coldness, when it was all so clear, and when it would have been so simple and easy to be boundlessly happy. But my jumping down to him in the orchard weighed on me like a crime. I kept feeling that he would cease to respect me and was angry with me.

After tea I went to the piano, and he followed me.

"Play me something—it is long since I heard you," he said, catching me up in the parlor.

"I was just going to," I said. Then I looked straight in his face and said quickly, "Sergey Mikhaylych, you are not angry with me, are you?"

"What for?" he asked.

"For not obeying you this afternoon," I said, blushing.

He understood me: he shook his head and made a grimace, which implied that I deserved a scolding but that he did not feel able to give it.

"So it's all right, and we are friends again?" I said, sitting down at the piano.

"Of course!" he said.

In the drawing room, a large lofty room, there were only two lighted candles on the piano, the rest of the room remaining in half-darkness. Outside the open windows the summer night was bright. All was silent, except when the sound of Katya's footsteps in the unlighted parlor was heard occasionally, or when his horse, which was tied up under the window, snorted or stamped his hoof on the burdocks that grew there. He sat behind me, where I could not see him; but everywhere—in the half-darkness of the room, in every sound, in myself—I felt his presence. Every look, every movement of his, though I could not see them, found an echo in my heart. I played a sonata of Mozart's which he had brought me and which I had learnt in his presence and for him. I was not thinking at all of what I was playing, but I believe that I played it well, and I thought that he was pleased. I was conscious of his pleasure, and conscious too, though I never looked at him, of the gaze fixed on me from behind. Still moving my fingers mechanically, I turned round quite involuntarily and looked at him. The night had grown brighter, and his head stood out on a background of darkness. He was sitting with his head propped on his hands, and his eyes shone as they gazed at me. Catching his look, I smiled and stopped playing. He smiled too and shook his head reproachfully at the music, for me to go on. When I stopped, the moon had grown brighter and was riding high in the heavens; and the faint light of the candles was supplemented by a new silvery light which came in through the windows and fell on the floor. Katya called out that it was really too bad—that I had stopped at the best part of the piece, and that I was playing badly. But he declared that I had never played so well; and then he began to walk about the rooms—through the drawing room to the unlighted parlor and back again to the drawing room, and each time he looked at me and smiled. I smiled too; I wanted even to laugh with no reason; I was so happy at something that had happened that very day. Katya and I were standing by the piano; and each time that he vanished through the drawing room door, I started kissing her in my favorite place, the soft part of her neck under the chin; and each time he came back, I made a solemn face and refrained with difficulty from laughing.

"What is the matter with her today?" Katya asked him.

He only smiled at me without answering; he knew what was the matter with me.

"Just look what a night it is!" he called out from the parlor, where he had stopped by the open French window looking into the garden.

We joined him; and it really was such a night as I have never seen since. The full moon shone above the house and behind us, so that we could not see it, and half the shadow, thrown by the roof and pillars of the house and by the veranda awning, lay slanting and foreshortened on the gravel-path and the strip of turf beyond. Everything else was bright and saturated with the silver of the dew and the moonlight. The broad garden path, on one side of which the shadows of the dahlias and their supports lay aslant, all bright and cold, and shining on the inequalities of the gravel, ran on till it vanished in the mist. Through the trees the roof of the greenhouse shone bright, and a growing mist rose from the dell. The lilac bushes, already partly leafless, were all bright to the center. Each flower was distinguishable apart, and all were drenched with dew. In the avenues light and shade were so mingled that they looked, not like paths and trees but like transparent houses, swaying and moving. To our right, in the shadow of the house, everything was black, indistinguishable, and uncanny. But all the brighter for the surrounding darkness was the top of a poplar, with a fantastic crown of leaves, which for some strange reason remained there close to the house, towering into the bright light, instead of flying away into the dim distance, into the retreating dark blue of the sky.

"Let us go for a walk," I said.

Katya agreed, but said I must put on galoshes.

"I don't want them, Katya," I said; "Sergey Mikhaylych will give me his arm."

As if that would prevent me from wetting my feet! But to us three this seemed perfectly natural at the time. Though he never used to offer me his arm, I now took it of my own accord, and he saw nothing strange in it. We all went down from the veranda together. That whole world, that sky, that garden, that air, were different from those that I knew.

We were walking along an avenue, and it seemed to me, whenever I looked ahead, that we could go no farther in the same direction, that the world of the possible ended there, and that the whole scene must remain fixed for ever in its beauty. But we still moved on, and the magic wall kept parting to let us in; and still we found the familiar garden with trees and paths and withered leaves. And we were really walking along the paths, treading on patches of light and shade; and a withered leaf was really crackling under my foot, and a live twig brushing my face. And that was really he, walking steadily and slowly at my side, and carefully supporting my arm; and that was really Katya walking beside us with her creaking shoes. And that must be the moon in the sky, shining down on us through the motionless branches.

But at each step the magic wall closed up again behind us and in front, and I ceased to believe in the possibility of advancing farther—I ceased to believe in the reality of it all.

"Oh, there's a frog!" cried Katya.

"Who said that? and why?" I thought. But then I realized it was Katya, and that she was afraid of frogs. Then I looked at the ground and saw a little frog which gave a jump and then stood still in front of me, while its tiny shadow was reflected on the shining clay of the path.

"You're not afraid of frogs, are you?" he asked.

I turned and looked at him. Just where we were there was a gap of one tree in the lime avenue, and I could see his face clearly—it was so handsome and so happy!

Though he had spoken of my fear of frogs, I knew that he meant to say, "I love you, my dear one!" "I love you, I love you" was repeated by his look, by his arm; the light, the shadow, and the air all repeated the same words.

We had gone all round the garden. Katya's short steps had kept up with us, but now she was tired and out of breath. She said it was time to go in; and I felt very sorry for her. "Poor thing!" I thought; "why does not she feel as we do? why are we not all young and happy, like this night and like him and me?"

We went in, but it was a long time before he went away, though the cocks had crowed, and everyone in the house was asleep, and his horse, tethered under the window, snorted continually and stamped his hoof on the burdocks. Katya never reminded us of the hour, and we sat on talking of the merest trifles and not thinking of the time, till it was past two. The cocks were crowing for the third time and the dawn was breaking when he rode away. He said good-bye as usual and made no special allusion; but I knew that from that day he was mine, and that I should never lose him now. As soon as I had confessed to myself that I loved him, I took Katya into my confidence. She rejoiced in the news and was touched by my telling her; but she was actually able—poor thing!—to go to bed and sleep! For me, I walked for a long, long time about the veranda; then I went down to the garden where, recalling each word, each movement, I walked along the same avenues through which I had walked with him. I did not sleep at all that night, and saw sunrise and early dawn for the first time in my life. And never again did I see such a night and such a morning. "Only why does he not tell me plainly that he loves me?" I thought; "what makes him invent obstacles and call himself old, when all is so simple and so splendid? What makes him waste this golden time which may never return? Let him say 'I love you'—say it in plain words; let him take my hand in his and bend over it and say 'I love you.' Let him blush and look down before me; and then I will tell him all. No! not tell him, but throw my arms round him and press close to him and weep." But then a thought came to me—"What if I am mistaken and he does not love me?"

I was startled by this fear—God knows where it might have led me. I recalled his embarrassment and mine, when I jumped down to him in the orchard; and my heart grew very heavy. Tears gushed from my eyes, and I began to pray. A strange thought occurred to me, calming me and bringing hope with it. I resolved to begin fasting on that day, to take the Communion on my birthday, and on that same day to be betrothed to him.

How this result would come to pass I had no idea; but from that moment I believed and felt sure it would be so. The dawn had fully come and the laborers were getting up when I went back to my room.

Chapter IV

The Fast of the Assumption falling in August, no one in the house was surprised by my intention of fasting.

During the whole of the week he never once came to see us; but, far from being surprised or vexed or made uneasy by his absence, I was glad of it—I did not expect him until my birthday. Each day during the week I got up early. While the horses were being harnessed, I walked in the garden alone, turning over in my mind the sins of the day before, and considering what I must do today, so as to be satisfied with my day and not spoil it by a single sin. It seemed so easy to me then to abstain from sin altogether; only a trifling effort seemed necessary. When the horses came round, I got into the carriage with Katya or one of the maids, and we drove to the church two miles away. While entering the church, I always recalled the prayer for those who "come unto the Temple in the fear of God," and tried to get just that frame of mind when mounting the two grass-grown steps up to the building. At that hour there were not more than a dozen worshippers—household servants or peasant women keeping the fast. They bowed to me, and I returned their bows with studied humility. Then, with what seemed to me a great effort of courage, I went myself and got candles from the man who kept them, an old soldier and an elder; and I placed the candles before the icons. Through the central door of the altar screen I could see the altar cloth which my mother had worked; on the screen were the two angels which had seemed so big to me when I was little, and the dove with a golden halo which had fascinated me long ago. Behind the choir stood the old battered font, where I had been christened myself and stood godmother to so many of the servants' children. The old priest came out, wearing a cope made of the pall that had covered my father's coffin, and began to read in the same voice that I had heard all my life—at services held in our house, at Sonya's christening, at memorial services for my father, and at my mother's funeral. The same old quavering voice of the deacon rose in the choir; and the same old woman, whom I could remember at every service in that church, crouched by the wall, fixing her streaming eyes on an icon in the choir, pressing her folded fingers against her faded kerchief, and muttering with her toothless gums. And these objects were no longer merely curious to me, merely interesting from old recollections—each had become important and sacred in my eyes and seemed charged with profound meaning. I listened to each word of the prayers and tried to suit my feeling to it; and if I failed to understand, I prayed silently that God would enlighten me, or made up a prayer of my own in place of what I had failed to catch. When the penitential prayers were repeated, I recalled my past life, and that innocent childish past seemed to me so black when compared to the present brightness of my soul, that I wept and was horrified at myself; but I felt too that all those sins would be forgiven, and that if my sins had been even greater, my repentance would be all the sweeter. At the end of the service when the priest said, "The blessing of the Lord be upon you!" I seemed to feel an immediate sensation of physical well-being, of a mysterious light and warmth that instantly filled my heart. The service over, the priest came and asked me whether he should come to our house to say mass, and what hour would suit me; and I thanked him for the suggestion, intended, as I thought, to please me, but said that I would come to church instead, walking or driving.

"Is that not too much trouble?" he asked. And I was at a loss for an answer, fearing to commit a sin of pride.

After the mass, if Katya was not with me, I always sent the carriage home and walked back alone, bowing humbly to all who passed, and trying to find an opportunity of giving help or advice. I was eager to sacrifice myself for someone, to help in lifting a fallen cart, to rock a child's cradle, to give up the path to others by stepping into the mud. One evening I heard the bailiff report to Katya that Simon, one of our serfs, had come to beg some boards to make a coffin for his daughter, and a ruble to pay the priest for the funeral; the bailiff had given what he asked.

"Are they as poor as that?" I asked. "Very poor, Miss," the bailiff answered; "they have no salt to their food." My heart ached to hear this, and yet I felt a kind of pleasure too. Pretending to Katya that I was merely going for a walk, I ran upstairs, got out all my money (it was very little but it was all I had), crossed myself, and started off alone, through the veranda and the garden, on my way to Simon's hut. It stood at the end of the village, and no one saw me as I went up to the window, placed the money on the sill, and tapped on the pane. Someone came out, making the door creak, and hailed me; but I hurried home, cold and shaking with fear like a criminal. Katya asked where I had been and what was the matter with me; but I did not answer, and did not even understand what she was saying. Everything suddenly seemed to me so petty and insignificant. I locked myself up in my own room, and walked up and down alone for a long time, unable to do anything, unable to think, unable to understand my own feelings. I thought of the joy of the whole family, and of what they would say of their benefactor; and I felt sorry that I had not given them the money myself. I thought too of what Sergey Mikhaylych would say, if he knew what I had done; and I was glad to think that no one would ever find out. I was so happy, and I felt myself and everyone else so bad, and yet was so kindly disposed to myself and to all the world, that the thought of death came to me as a dream of happiness. I smiled and prayed and wept, and felt at that moment a burning passion of love for all the world, myself included. Between services I used to read the Gospel; and the book became more and more intelligible to me, and the story of that divine life simpler and more touching; and the depths of thought and feeling I found in studying it became more awful and impenetrable. On the other hand, how clear and simple everything seemed to me when I rose from the study of this book and looked again on life around me and reflected on it! It was so difficult, I felt, to lead a bad life, and so simple to love everyone and be loved. All were so kind and gentle to me; even Sonya, whose lessons I had not broken off, was quite different—trying to understand and please me and not to vex me. Everyone treated me as I treated them. Thinking over my enemies, of whom I must ask pardon before confession, I could only remember one—one of our neighbors, a girl whom I had made fun of in company a year ago, and who had ceased to visit us. I wrote to her, confessing my fault and asking her forgiveness. She replied that she forgave me and wished me to forgive her. I cried for joy over her simple words, and saw in them, at the time, a deep and touching feeling. My old nurse cried, when I asked her to forgive me. "What makes them all so kind to me? what have I done to deserve their love?" I asked myself. Sergey Mikhaylych would come into my mind, and I thought for long about him. I could not help it, and I did not consider these thoughts sinful. But my thoughts of him were quite different from what they had been on the night when I first realized that I loved him: he seemed to me now like a second self, and became a part of every plan for the future. The inferiority which I had always felt in his presence had vanished entirely: I felt myself his equal, and could understand him thoroughly from the moral elevation I had reached. What had seemed strange in him was now quite clear to me. Now I could see what he meant by saying that to live for others was the only true happiness, and I agreed with him perfectly. I believed that our life together would be endlessly happy and untroubled. I looked forward, not to foreign tours or fashionable society or display, but to a quite different scene—a quiet family life in the country, with constant self-sacrifice, constant mutual love, and constant recognition in all things of the kind hand of Providence.

I carried out my plan of taking the Communion on my birthday. When I came back from church that day, my heart was so swelling with happiness that I was afraid of life, afraid of any feeling that might break in on that happiness. We had hardly left the carriage for the steps in front of the house, when there was a sound of wheels on the bridge, and I saw Sergey Mikhaylych drive up in his well-known trap. He congratulated me,[1] and we went together to the parlor. Never since I had known him had I been so much at my ease with him and so self-possessed as on that morning. I felt in myself a whole new world out of his reach and beyond his comprehension. I was not conscious of the slightest embarrassment in speaking to him. He must have understood the cause of this feeling; for he was tender and gentle beyond his wont and showed a kind of reverent consideration for me. When I made for the piano, he locked it and put the key in his pocket.

"Don't spoil your present mood," he said, "you have the sweetest of all music in your soul just now."

I was grateful for his words, and yet I was not quite pleased at his understanding too easily and clearly what ought to have been an exclusive secret in my heart. At dinner he said that he had come to congratulate me and also to say good-bye; for he must go to Moscow tomorrow. He looked at Katya as he spoke; but then he stole a glance at me, and I saw that he was afraid he might detect signs of emotion on my face. But I was neither surprised nor agitated; I did not even ask whether he would be long away. I knew he would say this, and I knew that he would not go. How did I know? I cannot explain that to myself now; but on that memorable day it seemed that I knew everything that had been and that would be. It was like a delightful dream, when all that happens seems to

---

[1]It is the custom in Russia to congratulate anyone on his or her birthday, and also on receiving Communion.

have happened already and to be quite familiar, and it will all happen over again, and one knows that it will happen.

He meant to go away immediately after dinner; but, as Katya was tired after church and went to lie down for a little, he had to wait until she woke up in order to say good-bye to her. The sun shone into the drawing room, and we went out to the veranda. When we were seated, I began at once, quite calmly, the conversation that was bound to fix the fate of my heart. I began to speak, no sooner and no later, but at the very moment when we sat down, before our talk had taken any turn or color that might have hindered me from saying what I meant to say. I cannot tell myself where it came from—my coolness and determination and preciseness of expression. It was as if something independent of my will was speaking through my lips. He sat opposite me with his elbows resting on the rails of the veranda; he pulled a lilac branch towards him and stripped the leaves off it. When I began to speak, he let go the branch and leaned his head on one hand. His attitude might have shown either perfect calmness or strong emotion.

"Why are you going?" I asked, significantly, deliberately, and looking straight at him.

He did not answer at once.

"Business!" he muttered at last and dropped his eyes.

I realized how difficult he found it to lie to me, and in reply to such a frank question.

"Listen," I said; "you know what today is to me, how important for many reasons. If I question you, it is not to show an interest in your doings (you know that I have become intimate with you and fond of you)—I ask you this question, because I *must* know the answer. Why are you going?"

"It is very hard for me to tell you the true reason," he said. "During this week I have thought much about you and about myself, and have decided that I must go. You understand why; and if you care for me, you will ask no questions." He put up a hand to rub his forehead and cover his eyes. "I find it very difficult . . . But you will understand."

My heart began to beat fast.

"I cannot understand you," I said; "I *cannot! you* must tell me; in God's name and for the sake of this day tell me what you please, and I shall hear it with calmness," I said.

He changed his position, glanced at me, and again drew the lilac-twig towards him.

"Well!" he said, after a short silence and in a voice that tried in vain to seem steady, "it is a foolish business and impossible to put into words, and I feel the difficulty, but I will try to explain it to you," he added, frowning as if in bodily pain.

"Well?" I said.

"Just imagine the existence of a man—let us call him A—who has left youth far behind, and of a woman whom we may call B, who is young and happy and has seen nothing as yet of life or of the world. Family circumstances of various kinds brought them together, and he grew to love her as a daughter, and had no fear that his love would change its nature."

He stopped, but I did not interrupt him.

"But he forgot that B was so young, that life was still all a May-game to her," he went on with a sudden swiftness and determination and without looking at me, "and that it was easy to fall in love with her in a different way, and that this would amuse her. He made a mistake and was suddenly aware of another feeling, as heavy as remorse, making its way into his heart, and he was afraid. He was afraid that their old friendly relations would be destroyed, and he made up his mind to go away before that happened." As he said this, he began again to rub his eyes, with a pretense of indifference, and to close them.

"Why was he afraid to love differently?" I asked very low; but I restrained my emotion and spoke in an even voice. He evidently thought that I was not serious; for he answered as if he were hurt.

"You are young, and I am not young. You want amusement, and I want something different. Amuse yourself, if you like, but not with me. If you do, I shall take it seriously; and then I shall be unhappy, and you will repent. That is what A said," he added; "however, this is all nonsense; but you understand why I am going. And don't let us continue this conversation. Please not!"

"No! no!" I said, "we must continue it," and tears began to tremble in my voice. "Did he love her, or not?"

He did not answer.

"If he did not love her, why did he treat her as a child and pretend to love her?" I asked.

"Yes, A behaved badly," he interrupted me quickly; "but it all came to an end and they parted friends."

"This is horrible! Is there no other ending?" I said with a great effort and then felt afraid of what I had said.

"Yes, there is," he said, showing a face full of emotion and looking straight at me. "There are two different endings. But, for God's sake, listen to me quietly and don't interrupt. Some say"—here he stood up and smiled with a smile that was heavy with pain—"some say that A went off his head, fell passionately in love with B, and told her so. But she only laughed. To her it was all a jest, but to him a matter of life and death."

I shuddered and tried to interrupt him—tried to say that he must not dare to speak for me; but he checked me, laying his hand on mine.

"Wait!" he said, and his voice shook. "The other story is that she took pity on him, and fancied, poor child, from her ignorance of the world, that she really could love him, and so consented to be his wife. And he, in his madness, believed it—believed that his whole life could begin anew; but she saw herself that she had deceived him and that he had deceived her. . . . But let us drop the subject finally," he ended, clearly unable to say more; and then he began to walk up and down in silence before me.

Though he had asked that the subject should be dropped, I saw that his whole soul was hanging on my answer. I tried to speak, but the pain at my heart kept me dumb. I glanced at him—he was pale and his lower lip trembled. I felt sorry for him. With a sudden effort I broke the bonds of silence which had held me fast, and began to speak in a low inward voice, which I feared would break every moment.

"There is a third ending to the story," I said, and then paused, but he said nothing; "the third ending is that he did not love her, but hurt her, hurt her, and thought that he was right; and he left her and was actually proud of himself. You have been pretending, not I; I have loved you since the first day we met, loved you," I repeated, and at the word "loved" my low inward voice changed, without intention of mine, to a wild cry which frightened me myself.

He stood pale before me, his lip trembled more and more violently, and two tears came out upon his cheeks.

"It is wrong!" I almost screamed, feeling that I was choking with angry unshed tears. "Why do you do it?" I cried and got up to leave him.

But he would not let me go. His head was resting on my knees, his lips were kissing my still trembling hands, and his tears were wetting them. "My God! if I had only known!" he whispered.

"Why? why?" I kept on repeating, but in my heart there was happiness, happiness which had now come back, after so nearly departing for ever.

Five minutes later Sonya was rushing upstairs to Katya and proclaiming all over the house that Masha intended to marry Sergey Mikhaylych.

Chapter V

There were no reasons for putting off our wedding, and neither he nor I wished for delay. Katya, it is true, thought we ought to go to Moscow, to buy and order wedding clothes; and his mother tried to insist that, before the wedding, he must set up a new carriage, buy new furniture, and repaper the whole house. But we two together carried our point, that all these things, if they were really indispensable, should be done afterwards, and that we should be married within a fortnight after my birthday, quietly, without wedding clothes, without a party, without best men and supper and champagne, and all the other conventional features of a wedding. He told me how dissatisfied his mother was that there should be no band, no mountain of luggage, no renovation of the whole house—so unlike her own marriage which had cost thirty thousand rubles; and he told of the solemn and secret confabulations which she held in her storeroom with her housekeeper, Maryushka, rummaging the chests and discussing carpets, curtains, and salvers as indispensable conditions of our happiness. At our house Katya did just the same with my old nurse, Kuzminichna. It was impossible to treat the matter lightly with Katya. She was firmly convinced that he and I, when discussing our future, were merely talking the sentimental nonsense natural to people in our position; and that our real future happiness depended on the hemming of tablecloths and napkins and the proper cutting out and stitching of underclothing. Several times a day secret information passed between the two houses, to communicate what was going forward in each; and though the external relations between Katya and his mother were most affectionate, yet a slightly hostile though very subtle diplomacy was already perceptible in their dealings. I now became more intimate with Tatyana Semyonovna, the mother of Sergey Mikhaylych, an old-fashioned lady, strict and formal in the management of her household. Her son loved her, and not merely because she was his mother: he thought her the best, cleverest, kindest, and most affectionate woman in the world. She was always kind to us and to me especially, and was glad that her son should be getting married; but when I was with her after our engagement, I always felt that she wished me to understand that, in her opinion, her son might have looked higher, and that it would be as well for me to keep that in mind. I understood her meaning perfectly and thought her quite right.

During that fortnight he and I met every day. He came to dinner regularly and stayed on till midnight. But though he said—and I knew he was speaking the truth—that he had no life apart from me, yet he never spent the whole day with me, and tried to go on with his ordinary occupations. Our outward relations remained unchanged to the very day of our marriage: we went on saying "you" and not "thou" to each other; he did not even kiss my hand; he did not seek, but even avoided, opportunities of being alone with me. It was as if he feared to yield to the harmful excess of tenderness he felt. I don't know which of us had changed; but I now felt myself entirely his equal; I no longer found in him the pretence of simplicity which had displeased me earlier; and I often delighted to see in him, not a grown man inspiring respect and awe but a loving and wildly happy child. "How mistaken I was about him!" I often thought; "he is just such another human being as myself!" It seemed to me now, that his whole character was before me and that I thoroughly understood it. And how simple was every feature of his character, and how congenial to my own! Even his plans for our future life together were just my plans, only more clearly and better expressed in his words.

The weather was bad just then, and we spent most of our time indoors. The corner between the piano and the window was the scene of our best intimate talks. The candlelight was reflected on the blackness of the window near us; from time to time drops struck the glistening pane and rolled down. The rain pattered on the roof; the water splashed in a puddle under the spout; it felt damp near the window; but our corner seemed all the brighter and warmer and happier for that.

"Do you know, there is something I have long wished to say to you," he began one night when we were sitting up late in our corner; "I was thinking of it all the time you were playing."

"Don't say it, I know all about it," I replied.

"All right! mum's the word!"

"No! what is it?" I asked.

"Well, it is this. You remember the story I told you about A and B?"

"I should just think I did! What a stupid story! Lucky that it ended as it did!"

"Yes, I was very near destroying my happiness by my own act. You saved me. But the main thing is that I was always telling lies then, and I'm ashamed of it, and I want to have my say out now."

"Please don't! you really mustn't!"

"Don't be frightened," he said, smiling. "I only want to justify myself. When I began then, I meant to argue."

"It is always a mistake to argue," I said.

"Yes, I argued wrong. After all my disappointments and mistakes in life, I told myself firmly when I came to the country this year, that love was no more for me, and that all I had to do was to grow old decently. So for a long time, I was unable to clear up my feeling towards you, or to make out where it might lead me. I hoped, and I didn't hope: at one time I thought you were trifling with me; at another I felt sure of you but could not decide what to do. But after that evening, you remember, when we walked in the garden at night, I got alarmed: the present happiness seemed too great to be real. What if I allowed myself to hope and then failed? But of course I was thinking only of myself, for I am disgustingly selfish."

He stopped and looked at me.

"But it was not all nonsense that I said then. It was possible and right for me to have fears. I take so much from you and can give so little. You are still a child, a bud that has yet to open; you have never been in love before, and I . . ."

"Yes, do tell me the truth . . ." I began, and then stopped, afraid of his answer. "No, never mind," I added.

"Have I been in love before? is that it?" he said, guessing my thoughts at once. "That I can tell you. No, never before—nothing at all like what I feel now." But a sudden painful recollection seemed to flash across his mind. "No," he said sadly; "in this too I need your compassion, in order to have the right to love you. Well, was I not bound to think twice before saying that I loved you? What do I give you? love, no doubt."

"And is that little?" I asked, looking him in the face.

"Yes, my dear, it is little to give *you,*" he continued; "you have youth and beauty. I often lie awake at night from happiness, and all the time I think of our future life together. I have lived through much, and now I think I have found what is needed for happiness. A quiet secluded life in the country, with the possibility of being useful to people to whom it is easy to do good, and who are not accustomed to have it done to them; then work which one hopes may be of some use; then rest, nature, books, music, love for one's neighbor—such is my idea of happiness. And then, on the top of all that, you for a mate, and children, perhaps—what more can the heart of man desire?"

"It should be enough," I said.

"Enough for me whose youth is over," he went on, "but not for you. Life is still before you, and you will perhaps seek happiness, and perhaps find it, in something different. You think now that this is happiness, because you love me."

"You are wrong," I said; "I have always desired just that quiet domestic life and prized it. And you only say just what I have thought."

He smiled.

"So you think, my dear; but that is not enough for you. You have youth and beauty," he repeated thoughtfully.

But I was angry because he disbelieved me and seemed to cast my youth and beauty in my teeth.

"Why do you love me then?" I asked angrily; "for my youth or for myself?"

"I don't know, but I love you," he answered, looking at me with his attentive and attractive gaze.

I did not reply and involuntarily looked into his eyes. Suddenly a strange thing happened to me: first I ceased to see what was around me; then his face seemed to vanish till only the eyes were left, shining over against mine; next the eyes seemed to be in my own head, and then all became confused—I could see nothing and was forced to shut my eyes, in order to break loose from the feeling of pleasure and fear which his gaze was producing in me . . .

The day before our wedding day, the weather cleared up towards evening. The rains which had begun in summer gave place to clear weather, and we had our first autumn evening, bright and cold. It was a wet, cold, shining world, and the garden showed for the first time the spaciousness and color and bareness of autumn. The sky was clear, cold, and pale. I went to bed happy in the thought that tomorrow, our wedding day, would be fine. I awoke with the sun, and the thought that this very day . . . seemed alarming and surprising. I went out into the garden. The sun had just risen and shone fitfully through the meager yellow leaves of the lime avenue. The path was strewn with rustling leaves, clusters of mountain-ash berries hung red and wrinkled on the boughs, with a sprinkling of frost-bitten crumpled leaves; the dahlias were black and wrinkled. The first rime lay like silver on the pale green of the grass and on the broken burdock plants round the house. In the clear cold sky there was not, and could not be, a single cloud.

"Can it possibly be today?" I asked myself, incredulous of my own happiness. "Is it possible that I shall wake tomorrow, not here but in that strange house with the pillars? Is it possible that I shall never again wait for his coming and meet him, and sit up late with Katya to talk about him? Shall I never sit with him beside the piano in our drawing room? never see him off and feel uneasy about him on dark nights?" But I remembered that he promised yesterday to pay a last visit, and that Katya had insisted on my trying on my wedding dress, and had said "For tomorrow." I believed for a moment that it was all real, and then doubted again. "Can it be that after today I shall be living there with a mother-in-law, without Nadezhda or old Grigori or Katya? Shall I go to bed without kissing my old nurse good night and hearing her say, while she signs me with the cross from old custom, 'Good night, Miss'? Shall I never again teach Sonya and play with her and knock through the wall to her in the morning and hear her hearty laugh? Shall I become from today someone that I myself do not know? and is a new world, that will realize my hopes and desires, opening before me? and will that new world last for ever?" Alone with these thoughts I was depressed and impatient for his arrival. He came early, and it required his presence to convince me that I should really be his wife that very day, and the prospect ceased to frighten me.

Before dinner we walked to our church, to attend a memorial service for my father.

"If only he were living now!" I thought as we were returning and I leant silently on the arm of him who had been the dearest friend of the object of my thoughts. During the service, while I pressed my forehead against the cold stone of the chapel floor, I called up my father so vividly; I was so convinced that he understood me and approved my choice, that I felt as if his spirit were still hovering over us and blessing me. And my recollections and hopes, my joy and sadness, made up one solemn and satisfied feeling which was in harmony with the fresh still air, the silence, the bare fields and pale sky, from which the bright but powerless rays, trying in vain to burn my cheek, fell over all the landscape. My companion seemed to understand and share my feeling. He walked slowly and silently; and his face, at which I glanced from time to time, expressed the same serious mood between joy and sorrow which I shared with nature.

Suddenly he turned to me, and I saw that he intended to speak. "Suppose he starts some other subject than that which is in my mind?" I thought. But he began to speak of my father and did not even name him.

"He once said to me in jest, 'you should marry my Masha,'" he began.

"He would have been happy now," I answered, pressing closer the arm which held mine.

"You were a child then," he went on, looking into my eyes; "I loved those eyes then and used to kiss them only because they were like his, never thinking they would be so dear to me for their own sake. I used to call you Masha then."

"I want you to say 'thou' to me," I said.

"I was just going to," he answered; "I feel for the first time that *thou art* entirely mine"; and his calm happy gaze that drew me to him rested on me.

We went on along the footpath over the beaten and trampled stubble; our voices and footsteps were the only sounds. On one side the brownish stubble stretched over a hollow to a distant leafless wood; across it at some distance a peasant was noiselessly ploughing a black strip which grew wider and wider. A drove of horses scattered under the hill seemed close to us. On the other side, as far as the garden and our house peeping through the trees, a field of winter corn, thawed by the sun, showed black with occasional patches of green. The winter sun shone over everything, and everything was covered with long gossamer spider's webs, which floated in the air round us, lay on the frost-dried stubble, and got into our eyes and hair and clothes. When we spoke, the sound of our voices hung in the motionless air above us, as if we two were alone in the whole world—alone under that azure vault, in which the beams of the winter sun played and flashed without scorching.

I too wished to say "thou" to him, but I felt ashamed.

"Why *dost thou* walk so fast?" I said quickly and almost in a whisper; I could not help blushing.

He slackened his pace, and the gaze he turned on me was even more affectionate, gay, and happy.

At home we found that his mother and the inevitable guests had arrived already, and I was never alone with him again till we came out of church to drive to Nikolskoye.

The church was nearly empty: I just caught a glimpse of his mother standing up straight on a mat by the choir and of Katya wearing a cap with purple ribbons and with tears on her cheeks, and of two or three of our servants looking curiously at me. I did not look at him, but felt his presence there beside me. I attended to the words of the prayers and repeated them, but they found no echo in my heart. Unable to pray, I looked listlessly at the icons, the candles, the embroidered cross on the priest's cope, the screen, and the window, and took nothing in. I only felt that something strange was being done to me. At last the priest turned to us with the cross in his hand, congratulated us, and said, "I christened you and by God's mercy have lived to marry you." Katya and his mother kissed us, and Grigori's voice was heard, calling up the carriage. But I was only frightened and disappointed: all was over, but nothing extraordinary, nothing worthy of the Sacrament I had just received, had taken place in myself. He and I exchanged kisses, but the kiss seemed strange and not expressive of our feeling. "Is this all?" I thought. We went out of church, the sound of wheels reverberated under the vaulted roof, the fresh air blew on my face, he put on his hat and handed me into the carriage. Through the window I could see a frosty moon with a halo round it. He sat down beside me and shut the door after him. I felt a sudden pang. The assurance of his proceedings seemed to me insulting. Katya called out that I should put something on my head; the wheels rumbled on the stone and then moved along the soft road, and we were off. Huddling in a corner, I looked out at the distant fields and the road flying past in the cold glitter of the moon. Without looking at him, I felt his presence beside me. "Is this all I have got from the moment, of which I expected so much?" I thought; and still it seemed humiliating and insulting to be sitting alone with him, and so close. I turned to him, intending to speak; but the words would not come, as if my love had vanished, giving place to a feeling of mortification and alarm.

"Till this moment I did not believe it was possible," he said in a low voice in answer to my look.

"But I am afraid somehow," I said.

"Afraid of me, my dear?" he said, taking my hand and bending over it. My hand lay lifeless in his, and the cold at my heart was painful.

"Yes," I whispered.

But at that moment my heart began to beat faster, my hand trembled and pressed his, I grew hot, my eyes sought his in the half-darkness, and all at once I felt that I did not fear him, that this fear was love—a new love still more tender and stronger than the old. I felt that I was wholly his, and that I was happy in his power over me.

PART II

Chapter I

DAYS, weeks, two whole months of seclusion in the country slipped by unnoticed, as we thought then; and yet those two months comprised feelings, emotions, and happiness, sufficient for a lifetime. Our plans for the regulation of our life in the country were not carried out at all in the way that we expected; but the reality was not inferior to our ideal. There was none of that hard work, performance of duty, self-sacrifice, and life for others, which I had pictured to myself before our marriage; there was, on the contrary, merely a selfish feeling of love for one another, a wish to be loved, a constant causeless gaiety and entire oblivion of all the world. It is true that my husband sometimes went to his study to work, or drove to town on business, or walked about attending to the management of the estate; but I saw what it cost him to tear himself away from me. He confessed later that every occupation, in my absence, seemed to him mere nonsense in which it was impossible to take any interest. It was just the same with me. If I read, or played the piano, or passed my time with his mother, or taught in the school, I did so only because each of these occupations was connected with him and won his approval; but whenever the thought of him was not associated with any duty, my hands fell by my sides and it seemed to me absurd to think that anything existed apart from him. Perhaps it was a wrong and selfish feeling, but it gave me happiness and lifted me high above all the world. He alone existed on earth for me, and I considered him the best and most faultless man in the world; so that I could not live for anything else than for him, and my one object was to realize his conception of me. And in his eyes I was the first and most excellent woman in the world, the possessor of all possible virtues; and I strove to be that woman in the opinion of the first and best of men.

He came to my room one day while I was praying. I looked round at him and went on with my prayers. Not wishing to interrupt me, he sat down at a table and opened a book. But I thought he was looking at me and looked round myself. He smiled, I laughed, and had to stop my prayers.

"Have you prayed already?" I asked.

"Yes. But you go on; I'll go away."

"You do say your prayers, I hope?"

He made no answer and was about to leave the room when I stopped him.

"Darling, for my sake, please repeat the prayers with me!" He stood up beside me, dropped his arms awkwardly, and began, with a serious face and some hesitation. Occasionally he turned towards me, seeking signs of approval and aid in my face.

When he came to an end, I laughed and embraced him. "I feel just as if I were ten! And you do it all!" he said, blushing and kissing my hands.

Our house was one of those old-fashioned country houses in which several generations have passed their lives together under one roof, respecting and loving one another. It was all redolent of good sound family traditions, which as soon as I entered it seemed to become mine too. The management of the household was carried on by Tatyana Semyonovna, my mother-in-law, on old-fashioned lines. Of grace and beauty there was not much; but, from the servants down to the furniture and food, there was abundance of everything, and a general cleanliness, solidity, and order, which inspired respect. The drawing-room furniture was arranged symmetrically; there were portraits on the walls, and the floor was covered with home-made carpets and mats. In the morning-room there was an old piano, with chiffoniers of two different patterns, sofas, and little carved tables with bronze ornaments. My sitting room, specially arranged by Tatyana Semyonovna, contained the best furniture in the house, of many styles and periods, including an old pier glass, which I was frightened to look into at first, but came to value as an old friend. Though Tatyana Semyonovna's voice was never heard, the whole household went like a clock. The number of servants was far too large (they all wore soft boots with no heels, because Tatyana Semyonovna had an intense dislike for stamping heels and creaking soles); but they all seemed proud of their calling, trembled before their old mistress, treated my husband and me with an affectionate air of patronage, and performed their duties, to all appearance, with extreme satisfaction. Every Saturday the floors were scoured and the carpets beaten without fail; on the first of every month there was a religious service in the house and holy water was sprinkled; on Tatyana Semyonovna's name day and on her son's (and on mine too, beginning from that autumn) an entertainment was regularly provided for the whole neighborhood. And all this had gone on without a break ever since the beginning of Tatyana Semyonovna's life.

My husband took no part in the household management, he attended only to the farm-work and the laborers, and gave much time to this. Even in winter he got up so early that I often woke to find him gone. He generally came back for early tea, which we drank alone together; and at that time, when the worries and vexations of the farm were over, he was almost always in that state of high spirits which we called "wild ecstasy." I often made him tell me what he had been doing in the morning, and he gave such absurd accounts that we both laughed till we cried. Sometimes I insisted on a serious account, and he gave it, restraining a smile. I watched his eyes and moving lips and took nothing in: the sight of him and the sound of his voice was pleasure enough.

"Well, what have I been saying? repeat it," he would sometimes say. But I could repeat nothing. It seemed so absurd that *he* should talk to *me* of any other subject than ourselves. As if it mattered in the least what went on in the world outside! It was at a much later time that I began to some extent to understand and take an interest in his occupations. Tatyana Semyonovna never appeared before dinner: she breakfasted alone and said good morning to us by deputy. In our exclusive little world of frantic happiness a voice from the staid orderly region in which she dwelt was quite startling: I often lost self-control and could only laugh without speaking, when the maid stood before me with folded hands and made her formal report: "The mistress bade me inquire how you slept after your walk yesterday evening; and about her I was to report that she had pain in her side all night, and a stupid dog barked in the village and kept her awake; and also I was to ask how you liked the bread this morning, and to tell you that it was not Taras who baked today, but Nikolashka who was trying his hand for the first time; and she says his baking is not at all bad, especially the cracknels: but the tea rusks were overbaked." Before dinner we saw little of each other: he wrote or went out again while I played the piano or read; but at four o'clock we all met in the drawing room before dinner. Tatyana Semyonovna sailed out of her own room, and certain poor and pious maiden ladies, of whom there were always two or three living in the house, made their appearance also. Every day without fail my husband by old habit offered his arm to his mother, to take her in to dinner; but she insisted that I should take the other, so that every day, without fail, we stuck in the doors and got in each other's way. She also presided at dinner, where the conversation, if rather solemn, was polite and sensible. The commonplace talk between my husband and me was a pleasant interruption to the formality of those entertainments. Sometimes there were squabbles between mother and son and they bantered one another; and I especially enjoyed those scenes, because they were the best proof of the strong and tender love which united the two. After dinner Tatyana Semyonovna went to the parlor, where she sat in an armchair and ground her snuff or cut the leaves of new books, while we read aloud or went off to the piano in the morning room. We read much together at this time, but music was our favorite and best enjoyment, always evoking fresh chords in our hearts and as it were revealing each afresh to the other. While I played his favorite pieces, he sat on a distant sofa where I could hardly see him. He was ashamed to betray the impression produced on him by the music; but often, when he was not expecting it, I rose from the piano, went up to him, and tried to detect on his face signs of emotion—the unnatural brightness and moistness of the eyes, which he tried in vain to conceal. Tatyana Semyonovna, though she often wanted to take a look at us there, was also anxious to put no constraint upon us. So she always passed through the room with an air of indifference and a pretence of being busy; but I knew that she had no real reason for going to her room and returning so soon. In the evening I poured out tea in the large drawing room, and all the household met again. This solemn ceremony of distributing cups and glasses before the solemnly shining samovar made me nervous for a long time. I felt myself still unworthy of such a distinction, too young and frivolous to turn the tap of such a big samovar, to put glasses on Nikita's salver, saying "For Peter Ivanovich," "For Marya Minichna," to ask "Is it sweet enough?" and to leave out lumps of sugar for Nurse and other deserving persons. "Capital! capital! Just like a grown-up person!" was a frequent comment from my husband, which only increased my confusion.

After tea Tatyana Semyonovna played patience or listened to Marya Minichna telling fortunes by the cards. Then she kissed us both and signed us with the cross, and we went off to our own rooms. But we generally sat up together till midnight, and that was our best and pleasantest time. He told me stories of his past life; we made plans and sometimes even talked philosophy; but we tried always to speak low, for fear we should be heard upstairs and reported to Tatyana Semyonovna, who insisted on our going to bed early. Sometimes we grew hungry; and then we stole off to the pantry, secured a cold supper by the good offices of Nikita, and ate it in my sitting room by the light of one candle. He and I lived like strangers in that big old house, where the uncompromising spirit of the past and of Tatyana Semyonovna ruled supreme. Not she only, but the servants, the old ladies, the furniture, even the pictures, inspired me with respect and a little alarm, and made me feel that he and I were a little out of place in that house and must always be very careful and cautious in our doings. Thinking it over now, I see that many things—the pressure of that unvarying routine, and that crowd of idle and inquisitive servants—were uncomfortable and oppressive; but at the time that very constraint made our love for one another still keener. Not I only, but he also, never grumbled openly at anything; on the contrary he shut his eyes to what was amiss. Dmitri Sidorov, one of the footmen, was a great smoker; and regularly every day, when we two were in the morning room after dinner, he went to my husband's study to take tobacco from the jar; and it was a sight to see Sergey Mikhaylych creeping on tiptoe to me with a face between delight and terror, and a wink and a warning forefinger, while he pointed at Dmitri Sidorov, who was quite unconscious of being watched. Then, when Dmitri Sidorov had gone away without having seen us, in his joy that all had passed off successfully, he declared (as he did on every other occasion) that I was a darling, and kissed me. At times his calm connivance and apparent indifference to everything annoyed me, and I took it for weakness, never noticing that I acted in the same way myself. "It's like a child who dares not show his will," I thought.

"My dear! my dear!" he said once when I told him that his weakness surprised me; "how can a man, as happy as I am, be dissatisfied with anything? Better to give way myself than to put compulsion on others; of that I have long been convinced. There is no condition in which one cannot be happy; but our life is such bliss! I simply cannot be angry; to me now nothing seems bad, but only pitiful and amusing. Above all—*le mieux est l'ennemi du bien*.[2] Will you believe it, when I hear a ring at the bell, or receive a letter, or even wake up in the morning, I'm frightened. Life must go on, something may change; and nothing can be better than the present."

I believed him but did not understand him. I was happy; but I took that as a matter of course, the invariable experience of people in our position, and believed that there was somewhere, I knew not where, a different happiness, not greater but different.

So two months went by and winter came with its cold and snow; and, in spite of his company, I began to feel lonely, that life was repeating itself, that there was nothing new either in him or in myself, and that we were merely going back to what had been before. He began to give more time to business which kept him away from me, and my old feeling returned, that there was a special department of his mind into which he was unwilling to admit me. His unbroken calmness provoked me. I loved him as much as ever and was as happy as ever in his love; but my love, instead of increasing, stood still; and another new and disquieting sensation began to creep into my heart. To love him was not enough for me after the happiness I had felt in falling in love. I wanted movement and not a calm course of existence. I wanted excitement and danger and the chance to sacrifice myself for my love. I felt in myself a superabundance of energy which found no outlet in our quiet life. I had fits of depression which I was ashamed of and tried to conceal from him, and fits of excessive tenderness and high spirits which alarmed him. He realized my state of mind before I did, and proposed a visit to Petersburg; but I begged him to give this up and not to change our manner of life or spoil our happiness. Happy indeed I was; but I was tormented by the thought that this happiness cost me no effort and no sacrifice, though I was even painfully conscious of my power to face both. I loved him and saw that I was all in all to him; but I wanted everyone to see our love; I wanted to love him in spite of obstacles. My mind, and even my senses, were fully occupied; but there was another feeling of youth and craving for move-

---

[2] "The better is the enemy of the good."

ment, which found no satisfaction in our quiet life. What made him say that, whenever I liked, we could go to town? Had he not said so I might have realized that my uncomfortable feelings were my own fault and dangerous nonsense, and that the sacrifice I desired was there before me, in the task of overcoming these feelings. I was haunted by the thought that I could escape from depression by a mere change from the country; and at the same time I felt ashamed and sorry to tear him away, out of selfish motives, from all he cared for. So time went on, the snow grew deeper, and there we remained together, all alone and just the same as before, while outside I knew there was noise and glitter and excitement, and hosts of people suffering or rejoicing without one thought of us and our remote existence. I suffered most from the feeling that custom was daily petrifying our lives into one fixed shape, that our minds were losing their freedom and becoming enslaved to the steady passionless course of time. The morning always found us cheerful; we were polite at dinner, and affectionate in the evening. "It is all right," I thought, "to do good to others and lead upright lives, as he says; but there is time for that later; and there are other things, for which the time is now or never." I wanted, not what I had got, but a life of struggle; I wanted feeling to be the guide of life, and not life to guide feeling. If only I could go with him to the edge of a precipice and say, "One step, and I shall fall over— one movement, and I shall be lost!" then, pale with fear, he would catch me in his strong arms and hold me over the edge till my blood froze, and then carry me off whither he pleased.

This state of feeling even affected my health, and I began to suffer from nerves. One morning I was worse than usual. He had come back from the estate office out of sorts, which was a rare thing with him. I noticed it at once and asked what was the matter. He would not tell me and said it was of no importance. I found out afterwards that the police inspector, out of spite against my husband, was summoning our peasants, making illegal demands on them, and using threats to them. My husband could not swallow this at once; he could not feel it merely "pitiful and amusing." He was provoked, and therefore unwilling to speak of it to me. But it seemed to me that he did not wish to speak to me about it because he considered me a mere child, incapable of understanding his concerns. I turned from him and said no more. I then told the servant to ask Marya Minichna, who was staying in the house, to join us at breakfast. I ate my breakfast very fast and took her to the morning room, where I began to talk loudly to her about some trifle which did not interest me in the least. He walked about the room, glancing at us from time to time. This made me more and more inclined to talk and even to laugh; all that I said myself, and all that Marya Minichna said, seemed to me laughable. Without a word to me he went off to his study and shut

the door behind him. When I ceased to hear him, all my high spirits vanished at once; indeed Marya Minichna was surprised and asked what was
the matter. I sat down on a sofa without answering, and felt ready to cry.
"What has he got on his mind?" I wondered; "some trifle which he
thinks important; but, if he tried to tell it me, I should soon show him it
was mere nonsense. But he must needs think that I won't understand,
must humiliate me by his majestic composure, and always be in the right
as against me. But I too am in the right when I find things tiresome and
trivial," I reflected; "and I do well to want an active life rather than to
stagnate in one spot and feel life flowing past me. I want to move forward, to have some new experience every day and every hour, whereas
he wants to stand still and to keep me standing beside him. And how easy
it would be for him to gratify me! He need not take me to town; he need
only be like me and not put compulsion on himself and regulate his feelings, but live simply. That is the advice he gives me, but he is not simple
himself. That is what is the matter."

I felt the tears rising and knew that I was irritated with him. My irritation frightened me, and I went to his study. He was sitting at the table,
writing. Hearing my step, he looked up for a moment and then went on
writing; he seemed calm and unconcerned. His look vexed me: instead
of going up to him, I stood beside his writing table, opened a book, and
began to look at it. He broke off his writing again and looked at me.

"Masha, are you out of sorts?" he asked.

I replied with a cold look, as much as to say, "You are very polite, but
what is the use of asking?" He shook his head and smiled with a tender
timid air; but his smile, for the first time, drew no answering smile from me.

"What happened to you today?" I asked; "why did you not tell me?"

"Nothing much—a trifling nuisance," he said. "But I might tell you
now. Two of our serfs went off to the town . . ."

But I would not let him go on.

"Why would you not tell me, when I asked you at breakfast?"

"I was angry then and should have said something foolish."

"I wished to know then."

"Why?"

"Why do you suppose that I can never help you in anything?"

"Not help me!" he said, dropping his pen. "Why, I believe that without you I could not live. You not only help me in everything I do, but
you do it yourself. You are very wide of the mark," he said, and laughed.
"My life depends on you. I am pleased with things, only because you are
there, because I need you . . ."

"Yes, I know; I am a delightful child who must be humored and kept
quiet," I said in a voice that astonished him, so that he looked up as if
this was a new experience; "but I don't want to be quiet and calm; that

is more in your line, and too much in your line," I added.

"Well," he began quickly, interrupting me and evidently afraid to let me continue, "when I tell you the facts, I should like to know your opinion."

"I don't want to hear them now," I answered. I did want to hear the story, but I found it so pleasant to break down his composure. "I don't want to play at life," I said, "but to live, as you do yourself."

His face, which reflected every feeling so quickly and so vividly, now expressed pain and intense attention.

"I want to share your life, to . . . ," but I could not go on—his face showed such deep distress. He was silent for a moment.

"But what part of my life do you not share?" he asked; "is it because I, and not you, have to bother with the inspector and with tipsy laborers?"

"That's not the only thing," I said.

"For God's sake try to understand me, my dear!" he cried. "I know that excitement is always painful; I have learnt that from the experience of life. I love you, and I can't but wish to save you from excitement. My life consists of my love for you; so you should not make life impossible for me."

"You are always in the right," I said without looking at him.

I was vexed again by his calmness and coolness while I was conscious of annoyance and some feeling akin to penitence.

"Masha, what is the matter?" he asked. "The question is not, which of us is in the right—not at all; but rather, what grievance have you against me? Take time before you answer, and tell me all that is in your mind. You are dissatisfied with me: and you are, no doubt, right; but let me understand what I have done wrong."

But how could I put my feeling into words? That he understood me at once, that I again stood before him like a child, that I could do nothing without his understanding and foreseeing it—all this only increased my agitation.

"I have no complaint to make of you," I said; "I am merely bored and want not to be bored. But you say that it can't be helped, and, as always, you are right."

I looked at him as I spoke. I had gained my object: his calmness had disappeared, and I read fear and pain in his face.

"Masha," he began in a low troubled voice, "this is no mere trifle: the happiness of our lives is at stake. Please hear me out without answering. Why do you wish to torment me?"

But I interrupted him.

"Oh, I know you will turn out to be right. Words are useless; of course you are right." I spoke coldly, as if some evil spirit were speaking with my voice.

"If you only knew what you are doing!" he said, and his voice shook. I burst out crying and felt relieved. He sat down beside me and said nothing. I felt sorry for him, ashamed of myself, and annoyed at what I had done. I avoided looking at him. I felt that any look from him at that moment must express severity or perplexity. At last I looked up and saw his eyes: they were fixed on me with a tender gentle expression that seemed to ask for pardon. I caught his hand and said,

"Forgive me! I don't know myself what I have been saying."

"But I do; and you spoke the truth."

"What do you mean?" I asked.

"That we must go to Petersburg," he said; "there is nothing for us to do here just now."

"As you please," I said.

He took me in his arms and kissed me.

"You must forgive me," he said; "for I am to blame."

That evening I played to him for a long time, while he walked about the room. He had a habit of muttering to himself; and when I asked him what he was muttering, he always thought for a moment and then told me exactly what it was. It was generally verse, and sometimes mere nonsense, but I could always judge of his mood by it. When I asked him now, he stood still, thought an instant, and then repeated two lines from Lermontov:

> He in his madness prays for storms,
> And dreams that storms will bring him peace.

"He is really more than human," I thought; "he knows everything. How can one help loving him?"

I got up, took his arm, and began to walk up and down with him, trying to keep step.

"Well?" he asked, smiling and looking at me.

"All right," I whispered. And then a sudden fit of merriment came over us both: our eyes laughed, we took longer and longer steps, and rose higher and higher on tiptoe. Prancing in this manner, to the profound dissatisfaction of the butler and astonishment of my mother-in-law, who was playing patience in the parlor, we proceeded through the house till we reached the dining room; there we stopped, looked at one another, and burst out laughing.

A fortnight later, before Christmas, we were in Petersburg.

Chapter II

The journey to Petersburg, a week in Moscow, visits to my own relations and my husband's, settling down in our new quarters, travel, new towns and new faces—all this passed before me like a dream. It was all so new, various, and delightful, so warmly and brightly lighted up by his presence and his love, that our quiet life in the country seemed to me something very remote and unimportant. I had expected to find people in society proud and cold; but to my great surprise, I was received everywhere with unfeigned cordiality and pleasure, not only by relations, but also by strangers. I seemed to be the one object of their thoughts, and my arrival the one thing they wanted, to complete their happiness. I was surprised too to discover in what seemed to me the very best society a number of people acquainted with my husband, though he had never spoken of them to me; and I often felt it odd and disagreeable to hear him now speak disapprovingly of some of these people who seemed to me so kind. I could not understand his coolness towards them or his endeavors to avoid many acquaintances that seemed to me flattering. Surely, the more kind people one knows, the better; and here everyone was kind.

"This is how we must manage, you see," he said to me before we left the country; "here we are little Croesuses, but in town we shall not be at all rich. So we must not stay after Easter, or go into society, or we shall get into difficulties. For your sake too I should not wish it."

"Why should we go into society?" I asked; "we shall have a look at the theaters, see our relations, go to the opera, hear some good music, and be ready to come home before Easter."

But these plans were forgotten the moment we got to Petersburg. I found myself at once in such a new and delightful world, surrounded by so many pleasures and confronted by such novel interests, that I instantly, though unconsciously, turned my back on my past life and its plans. "All that was preparatory, a mere playing at life; but here is the real thing! And there is the future too!" Such were my thoughts. The restlessness and symptoms of depression which had troubled me at home vanished at once and entirely, as if by magic. My love for my husband grew calmer, and I ceased to wonder whether he loved me less. Indeed I could not doubt his love: every thought of mine was understood at once, every feeling shared, and every wish gratified by him. His composure, if it still existed, no longer provoked me. I also began to realize that he not only loved me but was proud of me. If we paid a call, or made some new acquaintance, or gave an evening party at which I, trembling inwardly from fear of disgracing myself, acted as hostess, he often said when it was over: "Bravo, young woman! capital! you needn't be frightened; a real success!" And his praise gave me great pleasure. Soon after our arrival he wrote to his mother and asked me to add a postscript, but refused to let me see his letter; of course I insisted on reading it; and he had said: "You would not know Masha again, I don't myself. Where does she get that charming graceful self-confidence and ease, such social gifts with such simplicity and charm and kindliness? Everybody is delighted with her. I can't admire her enough myself, and should be more in love with her than ever, if that were possible."

"Now I know what I am like," I thought. In my joy and pride I felt that I loved him more than before. My success with all our new acquaintances was a complete surprise to me. I heard on all sides, how this uncle had taken a special fancy for me, and that aunt was raving about me; I was told by one admirer that I had no rival among the Petersburg ladies, and assured by another, a lady, that I might, if I cared, lead the fashion in society. A cousin of my husband's, in particular, a Princess D—, middle-aged and very much at home in society, fell in love with me at first sight and paid me compliments which turned my head. The first time that she invited me to a ball and spoke to my husband about it, he turned to me and asked if I wished to go; I could just detect a sly smile on his face. I nodded assent and felt that I was blushing.

"She looks like a criminal when confessing what she wishes," he said with a good-natured laugh.

"But you said that we must not go into society, and you don't care for it yourself," I answered, smiling and looking imploringly at him.

"Let us go, if you want to very much," he said.

"Really, we had better not."

"Do you want to? very badly?" he asked again.

I said nothing.

"Society in itself is no great harm," he went on; "but unsatisfied social aspirations are a bad and ugly business. We must certainly accept, and we will."

"To tell you the truth," I said, "I never in my life longed for anything as much as I do for this ball."

So we went, and my delight exceeded all my expectations. It seemed to me, more than ever, that I was the center round which everything revolved, that for my sake alone this great room was lighted up and the band played, and that this crowd of people had assembled to admire me. From the hairdresser and the lady's maid to my partners and the old gentlemen promenading the ballroom, all alike seemed to make it plain that they were in love with me. The general verdict formed at the ball about me and reported by my cousin, came to this: I was quite unlike the other women and had a rural simplicity and charm of my own. I was so flattered by my success that I frankly told my husband I should like to attend two or three more balls during the season, and "so get thoroughly sick of them," I added; but I did not mean what I said.

He agreed readily; and he went with me at first with obvious satisfaction. He took pleasure in my success, and seemed to have quite forgotten his former warning or to have changed his opinion.

But a time came when he was evidently bored and wearied by the life we were leading. I was too busy, however, to think about that. Even if I sometimes noticed his eyes fixed questioningly on me with a serious attentive gaze, I did not realize its meaning. I was utterly blinded by this sudden affection which I seemed to evoke in all our new acquaintances, and confused by the unfamiliar atmosphere of luxury, refinement, and novelty. It pleased me so much to find myself in these surroundings not merely his equal but his superior, and yet to love him better and more independently than before, that I could not understand what he could object to for me in society life. I had a new sense of pride and self-satisfaction when my entry at a ball attracted all eyes, while he, as if ashamed to confess his ownership of me in public, made haste to leave my side and efface himself in the crowd of black coats. "Wait a little!" I often said in my heart, when I identified his obscure and sometimes woebegone figure at the end of the room—"Wait till we get home! Then you will see and understand for whose sake I try to be beautiful and brilliant, and what it is I love in all that surrounds me this evening!" I really believed that my success pleased me only because it enabled me to give it up for his sake. One danger I recognized as possible—that I might be carried away by a fancy for some new acquaintance, and that my husband might grow jealous. But he trusted me so absolutely, and seemed so undisturbed and indifferent, and all the young men were so inferior to him, that I was not alarmed by this one danger. Yet the attention of so many people in society gave me satisfaction, flattered my vanity, and made me think that there was some merit in my love for my husband. Thus I became more offhand and self-confident in my behavior to him.

'Oh, I saw you this evening carrying on a most animated conversation with Mme N—,' I said one night on returning from a ball, shaking my finger at him. He had really been talking to this lady, who was a well-known figure in Petersburg society. He was more silent and depressed than usual, and I said this to rouse him up.

"What is the good of talking like that, for *you* especially, Masha?" he said with half-closed teeth and frowning as if in pain. "Leave that to others; it does not suit you and me. Pretense of that sort may spoil the true relation between us, which I still hope may come back."

I was ashamed and said nothing.

"Will it ever come back, Masha, do you think?" he asked.

"It never was spoilt and never will be," I said; and I really believed this then.

"God grant that you are right!" he said; "if not, we ought to be going home."

But he only spoke like this once—in general he seemed as satisfied as I was, and I was so gay and so happy! I comforted myself too by thinking, "If he is bored sometimes, I endured the same thing for his sake in the country. If the relation between us has become a little different, everything will be the same again in summer, when we shall be alone in our house at Nikolskoye with Tatyana Semyonovna."

So the winter slipped by, and we stayed on, in spite of our plans, over Easter in Petersburg. A week later we were preparing to start; our packing was all done; my husband, who had bought things—plants for the garden and presents for people at Nikolskoye, was in a specially cheerful and affectionate mood. Just then Princess D— came and begged us to stay till the Saturday, in order to be present at a reception to be given by Countess R—. The countess was very anxious to secure me, because a foreign prince, who was visiting Petersburg and had seen me already at a ball, wished to make my acquaintance; indeed this was his motive for attending the reception, and he declared that I was the most beautiful woman in Russia. All the world was to be there; and, in a word, it would really be too bad, if I did not go too.

My husband was talking to someone at the other end of the drawing room.

"So you will go, won't you, Mary?" said the princess.

"We meant to start for the country the day after tomorrow," I answered undecidedly, glancing at my husband. Our eyes met, and he turned away at once.

"I must persuade him to stay," she said, "and then we can go on Saturday and turn all heads. All right?"

"It would upset our plans; and we have packed," I answered, beginning to give way.

"She had better go this evening and make her curtsey to the prince," my husband called out from the other end of the room; and he spoke in a tone of suppressed irritation which I had never heard from him before.

"I declare he's jealous, for the first time in his life," said the lady, laughing. "But it's not for the sake of the prince I urge it, Sergey Mikhaylych, but for all our sakes. The countess was so anxious to have her."

"It rests with her entirely," my husband said coldly, and then left the room.

I saw that he was much disturbed, and this pained me. I gave no positive promise. As soon as our visitor left, I went to my husband. He was walking up and down his room, thinking, and neither saw nor heard me when I came in on tiptoe.

Looking at him, I said to myself: "He is dreaming already of his dear Nikolskoye, our morning coffee in the bright drawing room, the land

and the laborers, our evenings in the music room, and our secret midnight suppers." Then I decided in my own heart: "Not for all the balls and all the flattering princes in the world will I give up his glad confusion and tender cares." I was just about to say that I did not wish to go to the ball and would refuse, when he looked round, saw me, and frowned. His face, which had been gentle and thoughtful, changed at once to its old expression of sagacity, penetration, and patronizing composure. He would not show himself to me as a mere man, but had to be a demigod on a pedestal.

"Well, my dear?" he asked, turning towards me with an unconcerned air.

I said nothing. I was provoked, because he was hiding his real self from me, and would not continue to be the man I loved.

"Do you want to go to this reception on Saturday?" he asked.

"I did, but you disapprove. Besides, our things are all packed," I said.

Never before had I heard such coldness in his tone to me, and never before seen such coldness in his eye.

"I shall order the things to be unpacked," he said, "and I shall stay till Tuesday. So you can go to the party, if you like. I hope you will; but I shall not go."

Without looking at me, he began to walk about the room jerkily, as his habit was when perturbed.

"I simply can't understand you," I said, following him with my eyes from where I stood. "You say that you never lose self-control" (he had never really said so); "then why do you talk to me so strangely? I am ready on your account to sacrifice this pleasure, and then you, in a sarcastic tone which is new from you to me, insist that I should go."

"So you make a *sacrifice*!" he threw special emphasis on the last word. "Well, so do I. What could be better? We compete in generosity—what an example of family happiness!"

Such harsh and contemptuous language I had never heard from his lips before. I was not abashed, but mortified by his contempt; and his harshness did not frighten me but made me harsh too. How could *he* speak thus, he who was always so frank and simple and dreaded insincerity in our speech to one another? And what had I done that he should speak so? I really intended to sacrifice for his sake a pleasure in which I could see no harm; and a moment ago I loved him and understood his feelings as well as ever. We had changed parts: now he avoided direct and plain words, and I desired them.

"You are much changed," I said, with a sigh. "How am I guilty before you? It is not this party—you have something else, some old count against me. Why this insincerity? You used to be so afraid of it yourself. Tell me plainly what you complain of." "What will he say?" thought I, and reflected with some complacency that I had done nothing all winter which he could find fault with.

I went into the middle of the room, so that he had to pass close to me, and looked at him. I thought, "He will come and clasp me in his arms, and there will be an end of it." I was even sorry that I should not have the chance of proving him wrong. But he stopped at the far end of the room and looked at me.

"Do you not understand yet?" he asked.

"No, I don't."

"Then I must explain. What I feel, and cannot help feeling, positively sickens me for the first time in my life." He stopped, evidently startled by the harsh sound of his own voice.

"What do you mean?" I asked, with tears of indignation in my eyes.

"It sickens me that the prince admired you, and you therefore run to meet him, forgetting your husband and yourself and womanly dignity; and you wilfully misunderstand what your want of self-respect makes your husband feel for you: you actually come to your husband and speak of the 'sacrifice' you are making, by which you mean—'To show myself to His Highness is a great pleasure to me, but I "sacrifice" it.'"

The longer he spoke, the more he was excited by the sound of his own voice, which was hard and rough and cruel. I had never seen him, had never thought of seeing him, like that. The blood rushed to my heart and I was frightened; but I felt that I had nothing to be ashamed of, and the excitement of wounded vanity made me eager to punish him.

"I have long been expecting this," I said. "Go on. Go on!"

"What you expected, I don't know," he went on; "but I might well expect the worst, when I saw you day after day sharing the dirtiness and idleness and luxury of this foolish society, and it has come at last. Never have I felt such shame and pain as now—pain for myself, when your friend thrusts her unclean fingers into my heart and speaks of my jealousy!—jealousy of a man whom neither you nor I know; and you refuse to understand me and offer to make a sacrifice for me—and what sacrifice? I am ashamed for you, for your degradation! . . . Sacrifice!" he repeated again.

"Ah, so this is a husband's power," thought I: "to insult and humiliate a perfectly innocent woman. Such may be a husband's rights, but I will not submit to them." I felt the blood leave my face and a strange distension of my nostrils, as I said, "No! I make no sacrifice on your account. I shall go to the party on Saturday without fail."

"And I hope you may enjoy it. But all is over between us two!" he cried out in a fit of unrestrained fury. "But you shall not torture me any longer! I was a fool, when I . . .", but his lips quivered, and he refrained with a visible effort from ending the sentence.

I feared and hated him at that moment. I wished to say a great deal to him and punish him for all his insults; but if I had opened my mouth, I should have lost my dignity by bursting into tears. I said nothing and left the room. But as soon as I ceased to hear his footsteps, I was horrified at what we had done. I feared that the tie which had made all my happiness might really be snapped forever; and I thought of going back. But then I wondered: "Is he calm enough now to understand me, if I mutely stretch out my hand and look at him? Will he realize my generosity? What if he calls my grief a mere pretence? Or he may feel sure that he is right and accept my repentance and forgive me with unruffled pride. And why, oh why, did he whom I loved so well insult me so cruelly?"

I went not to him but to my own room, where I sat for a long time and cried. I recalled with horror each word of our conversation, and substituted different words, kind words, for those that we had spoken, and added others; and then again I remembered the reality with horror and a feeling of injury. In the evening I went down for tea and met my husband in the presence of a friend who was staying with us; and it seemed to me that a wide gulf had opened between us from that day. Our friend asked me when we were to start; and before I could speak, my husband answered:

"On Tuesday," he said; "we have to stay for Countess R—'s reception." He turned to me: "I believe you intend to go?" he asked.

His matter-of-fact tone frightened me, and I looked at him timidly. His eyes were directed straight at me with an unkind and scornful expression; his voice was cold and even.

"Yes," I answered.

When we were alone that evening, he came up to me and held out his hand.

"Please forget what I said to you today," he began.

As I took his hand, a smile quivered on my lips and the tears were ready to flow; but he took his hand away and sat down on an armchair at some distance, as if fearing a sentimental scene. "Is it possible that he still thinks himself in the right?" I wondered; and, though I was quite ready to explain and to beg that we might not go to the party, the words died on my lips.

"I must write to my mother that we have put off our departure," he said; "otherwise she will be uneasy."

"When do you think of going?" I asked.

"On Tuesday, after the reception," he replied.

"I hope it is not on my account," I said, looking into his eyes; but those eyes merely looked—they said nothing, and a veil seemed to cover them from me. His face seemed to me to have grown suddenly old and disagreeable.

We went to the reception, and good friendly relations between us seemed to have been restored, but these relations were quite different from what they had been.

At the party I was sitting with other ladies when the prince came up to me, so that I had to stand up in order to speak to him. As I rose, my eyes involuntarily sought my husband. He was looking at me from the other end of the room, and now turned away. I was seized by a sudden sense of shame and pain; in my confusion I blushed all over my face and neck under the prince's eye. But I was forced to stand and listen, while he spoke, eyeing me from his superior height. Our conversation was soon over: there was no room for him beside me, and he, no doubt, felt that I was uncomfortable with him. We talked of the last ball, of where I should spend the summer, and so on. As he left me, he expressed a wish to make the acquaintance of my husband, and I saw them meet and begin a conversation at the far end of the room. The prince evidently said something about me; for he smiled in the middle of their talk and looked in my direction.

My husband suddenly flushed up. He made a low bow and turned away from the prince without being dismissed. I blushed too: I was ashamed of the impression which I and, still more, my husband must have made on the prince. Everyone, I thought, must have noticed my awkward shyness when I was presented, and my husband's eccentric behavior. "Heaven knows how they will interpret such conduct? Perhaps they know already about my scene with my husband!"

Princess D— drove me home, and on the way I spoke to her about my husband. My patience was at an end, and I told her the whole story of what had taken place between us owing to this unlucky party. To calm me, she said that such differences were very common and quite unimportant, and that our quarrel would leave no trace behind. She explained to me her view of my husband's character—that he had become very stiff and unsociable. I agreed, and believed that I had learned to judge him myself more calmly and more truly.

But when I was alone with my husband later, the thought that I had sat in judgment upon him weighed like a crime upon my conscience; and I felt that the gulf which divided us had grown still greater.

Chapter III

From that day there was a complete change in our life and our relations to each other. We were no longer as happy when we were alone together as before. To certain subjects we gave a wide berth, and conversation flowed more easily in the presence of a third person. When the talk turned on life in the country, or on a ball, we were uneasy and shrank from looking at one another. Both of us knew where the gulf between us lay, and seemed afraid to approach it. I was convinced that he was proud and irascible, and that I must be careful not to touch him on his weak point. He was equally sure that I disliked the country and was dying for social distraction, and that he must put up with this unfortunate taste of mine. We both avoided frank conversation on these topics, and each misjudged the other. We had long ceased to think each other the most perfect people in the world; each now judged the other in secret, and measured the offender by the standard of other people. I fell ill before we left Petersburg, and we went from there to a house near town, from which my husband went on alone, to join his mother at Nikolskoye. By that time I was well enough to have gone with him, but he urged me to stay on the pretext of my health. I knew, however, that he was really afraid we should be uncomfortable together in the country; so I did not insist much, and he went off alone. I felt it dull and solitary in his absence; but when he came back, I saw that he did not add to my life what he had added formerly. In the old days every thought and experience weighed on me like a crime till I had imparted it to him; every action and word of his seemed to me a model of perfection; we often laughed for joy at the mere sight of each other. But these relations had changed, so imperceptibly that we had not even noticed their disappearance. Separate interests and cares, which we no longer tried to share, made their appearance, and even the fact of our estrangement ceased to trouble us. The idea became familiar, and, before a year had passed, each could look at the other without confusion. His fits of boyish merriment with me had quite vanished; his mood of calm indulgence to all that passed, which used to provoke me, had disappeared; there was an end of those penetrating looks which used to confuse and delight me, an end of the ecstasies and prayers which we once shared in common. We did not even meet often: he was continually absent, with no fears or regrets for leaving me alone; and I was constantly in society, where I did not need him.

There were no further scenes or quarrels between us. I tried to satisfy him, he carried out all my wishes, and we seemed to love each other.

When we were by ourselves, which we seldom were, I felt neither joy nor excitement nor embarrassment in his company: it seemed like being alone. I realized that he was my husband and no mere stranger, a good man, and as familiar to me as my own self. I was convinced that I knew just what he would say and do, and how he would look; and if anything he did surprised me, I concluded that he had made a mistake. I expected nothing from him. In a word, he was my husband—and that was all. It seemed to me that things must be so, as a matter of course, and that no other relations between us had ever existed. When he left home, especially at first, I was lonely and frightened and felt keenly my need of support; when he came back, I ran to his arms with joy, though two hours later my joy was quite forgotten, and I found nothing to say to him. Only at moments which sometimes occurred between us of quiet undemonstrative affection, I felt something wrong and some pain at my heart, and I seemed to read the same story in his eyes. I was conscious of a limit to tenderness, which he seemingly would not, and I could not, overstep. This saddened me sometimes; but I had no leisure to reflect on anything, and my regret for a change which I vaguely realized I tried to drown in the distractions which were always within my reach. Fashionable life, which had dazzled me at first by its glitter and flattery of my self-love, now took entire command of my nature, became a habit, laid its fetters upon me, and monopolized my capacity for feeling. I could not bear solitude, and was afraid to reflect on my position. My whole day, from late in the morning till late at night, was taken up by the claims of society; even if I stayed at home, my time was not my own. This no longer seemed to me either gay or dull, but it seemed that so, and not otherwise, it always had to be.

So three years passed, during which our relations to one another remained unchanged and seemed to have taken a fixed shape which could not become either better or worse. Though two events of importance in our family life took place during that time, neither of them changed my own life. These were the birth of my first child and the death of Tatyana Semyonovna. At first the feeling of motherhood did take hold of me with such power, and produce in me such a passion of unanticipated joy, that I believed this would prove the beginning of a new life for me. But, in the course of two months, when I began to go out again, my feeling grew weaker and weaker, till it passed into mere habit and the lifeless performance of a duty. My husband, on the contrary, from the birth of our first boy, became his old self again—gentle, composed, and home-loving, and transferred to the child his old tenderness and gaiety. Many a night when I went, dressed for a ball, to the nursery, to sign the child with the cross before he slept, I found my husband there and felt his eyes fixed on me with something of reproof in their serious gaze. Then I was ashamed and even shocked by my own callousness, and asked myself if I was worse than other women. "But it can't be helped," I said to myself; "I love my child, but to sit beside him all day long would bore me; and nothing will make me pretend what I do not really feel."

His mother's death was a great sorrow to my husband; he said that he found it painful to go on living at Nikolskoye. For myself, although I mourned for her and sympathized with my husband's sorrow, yet I found life in that house easier and pleasanter after her death. Most of those three years we spent in town: I went only once to Nikolskoye for two months; and the third year we went abroad and spent the summer at Baden.

I was then twenty-one; our financial position was, I believed, satisfactory; my domestic life gave me all that I asked of it; everyone I knew, it seemed to me, loved me; my health was good; I was the best-dressed woman in Baden; I knew that I was good-looking; the weather was fine; I enjoyed the atmosphere of beauty and refinement; and, in short, I was in excellent spirits. They had once been even higher at Nikolskoye, when my happiness was in myself and came from the feeling that I deserved to be happy, and from the anticipation of still greater happiness to come. That was a different state of things; but I did very well this summer also. I had no special wishes or hopes or fears; it seemed to me that my life was full and my conscience easy. Among all the visitors at Baden that season there was no one man whom I preferred to the rest, or even to our old ambassador, Prince K——, who was assiduous in his attentions to me. One was young, and another old; one was English and fair, another French and wore a beard—to me they were all alike, but all indispensable. Indistinguishable as they were, they together made up the atmosphere which I found so pleasant. But there was one, an Italian marquis, who stood out from the rest by reason of the boldness with which he expressed his admiration. He seized every opportunity of being with me—danced with me, rode with me, and met me at the casino; and everywhere he spoke to me of my charms. Several times I saw him from my windows loitering round our hotel, and the fixed gaze of his bright eyes often troubled me, and made me blush and turn away. He was young, handsome, and well-mannered; and, above all, by his smile and the expression of his brow, he resembled my husband, though much handsomer than he. He struck me by this likeness, though in general, in his lips, eyes, and long chin, there was something coarse and animal which contrasted with my husband's charming expression of kindness and noble serenity. I supposed him to be passionately in love with me, and thought of him sometimes with proud commiseration. When I tried at times to soothe him and change his tone to one of easy, half-friendly confidence, he resented the suggestion with vehemence, and continued to disquiet me by a smoldering passion which was ready at any moment to burst forth. Though I would not own it even to myself, I feared him and often thought of him against my will. My husband knew him, and greeted him—even more than other acquaintances of ours who regarded him only as my husband—with coldness and disdain.

Towards the end of the season I fell ill and stayed indoors for a fortnight. The first evening that I went out again to hear the band, I learnt that Lady S——, an Englishwoman famous for her beauty, who had long been expected, had arrived in my absence. My return was welcomed, and a group gathered round me; but a more distinguished group attended the beautiful stranger. She and her beauty were the one subject of conversation around me. When I saw her, she was really beautiful, but her self-satisfied expression struck me as disagreeable, and I said so. That day everything that had formerly seemed amusing, seemed dull. Lady S— arranged an expedition to the ruined castle for the next day; but I declined to be of the party. Almost everyone else went; and my opinion of Baden underwent a complete change. Everything and everybody seemed to me stupid and tiresome; I wanted to cry, to break off my cure, to return to Russia. There was some evil feeling in my soul, but I did not yet acknowledge it to myself. Pretending that I was not strong, I ceased to appear at crowded parties; if I went out, it was only in the morning by myself, to drink the waters; and my only companion was Mme M—, a Russian lady, with whom I sometimes took drives in the surrounding country. My husband was absent: he had gone to Heidelberg for a time, intending to return to Russia when my cure was over, and only paid me occasional visits at Baden.

One day when Lady S— had carried off all the company on a hunting expedition, Mme M— and I drove in the afternoon to the castle. While our carriage moved slowly along the winding road, bordered by ancient chestnut trees and commanding a vista of the pretty and pleasant country round Baden, with the setting sun lighting it up, our conversation took a more serious turn than had ever happened to us before. I had known my companion for a long time; but she appeared to me now in a new light, as a well-principled and intelligent woman, to whom it was possible to speak without reserve, and whose friendship was worth having. We spoke of our private concerns, of our children, of the emptiness of life at Baden, till we felt a longing for Russia and the Russian countryside. When we entered the castle we were still under the impression of this serious feeling. Within the walls there was shade and coolness; the sunlight played from above upon the ruins. Steps and voices were audible. The landscape, charming enough but cold to a Russian eye, lay before us in the frame made by a doorway. We sat down to rest and watched the sunset in silence. The voices now sounded louder, and I thought I heard my own name. I listened and could not help overhearing every word. I recognized the voices: the speakers were the Italian marquis and a French friend of his whom I knew also. They were talking of me and of Lady S—, and the Frenchman was comparing us as rival beauties. Though he said nothing insulting, his words made my pulse quicken. He explained in detail the good points of us both. I was already a mother, while Lady S— was only nineteen; though I had the advantage in hair, my rival had a better figure. "Besides," he added, "Lady S— is a real *grande dame,* and the other is nothing in particular, only one of those obscure Russian princesses who turn up here nowadays in such numbers." He ended by saying that I was wise in not attempting to compete with Lady S—, and that I was completely buried as far as Baden was concerned.

"I am sorry for her—unless indeed she takes a fancy to console herself with you," he added with a hard ringing laugh.

"If she goes away, I follow her"—the words were blurted out in an Italian accent.

"Happy man! he is still capable of a passion!" laughed the Frenchman.

"Passion!" said the other voice and then was still for a moment. "It is a necessity to me: I cannot live without it. To make life a romance is the one thing worth doing. And with me romance never breaks off in the middle, and this affair I shall carry through to the end."

"*Bonne chance, mon ami!*"[3] said the Frenchman.

They now turned a corner, and the voices stopped. Then we heard them coming down the steps, and a few minutes later they came out upon us by a side door. They were much surprised to see us. I blushed when the marquis approached me, and felt afraid when we left the castle and he offered me his arm. I could not refuse, and we set off for the carriage, walking behind Mme M— and his friend. I was mortified by what the Frenchman had said of me, though I secretly admitted that he had only put in words what I felt myself; but the plain speaking of the Italian had surprised and upset me by its coarseness. I was tormented by the thought that, though I had overheard him, he showed no fear of me. It was hateful to have him so close to me; and I walked fast after the other couple, not looking at him or answering him and trying to hold his arm in such a way as not to hear him. He spoke of the fine view, of the unexpected pleasure of our meeting, and so on; but I was not listening. My thoughts were with my husband, my child, my country; I felt ashamed, distressed, anxious; I was in a hurry to get back to my solitary room in the Hôtel de Bade, there to think at leisure of the storm of feeling that had just risen in my heart. But Mme M— walked slowly, it was still a long way to the carriage, and my escort seemed to loiter on purpose as if he wished to detain me. "None of that!" I thought, and resolutely quickened my pace. But it soon became unmistakable that he was detaining me and even pressing my arm. Mme M— turned a corner, and we were quite alone. I was afraid.

"Excuse me," I said coldly and tried to free my arm; but the lace of my sleeve caught on a button of his coat. Bending towards me, he began to unfasten it, and his ungloved fingers touched my arm. A feeling new to me, half horror and half pleasure, sent an icy shiver down my back. I

---

[3] "Good luck, my friend!"

looked at him, intending by my coldness to convey all the contempt I felt
for him; but my look expressed nothing but fear and excitement. His
liquid blazing eyes, right up against my face, stared strangely at me, at my
neck and breast; both his hands fingered my arm above the wrist; his
parted lips were saying that he loved me, and that I was all the world to
him; and those lips were coming nearer and nearer, and those hands were
squeezing mine harder and harder and burning me. A fever ran through
my veins, my sight grew dim, I trembled, and the words intended to
check him died in my throat. Suddenly I felt a kiss on my cheek.
Trembling all over and turning cold, I stood still and stared at him.
Unable to speak or move, I stood there, horrified, expectant, even de-
sirous. It was over in a moment, but the moment was horrible! In that
short time I saw him exactly as he was—the low straight forehead (that
forehead so like my husband's!) under the straw hat; the handsome regular nose and dilated nostrils; the long waxed mustache and short beard;
the close-shaved cheeks and sunburned neck. I hated and feared him; he
was utterly repugnant and alien to me. And yet the excitement and passion of this hateful strange man raised a powerful echo in my own heart;
I felt an irresistible longing to surrender myself to the kisses of that
coarse handsome mouth, and to the pressure of those white hands with
their delicate veins and jewelled fingers; I was tempted to throw myself
headlong into the abyss of forbidden delights that had suddenly opened
up before me.

"I am so unhappy already," I thought; "let more and more storms of
unhappiness burst over my head!"

He put one arm round me and bent towards my face. "Better so!" I
thought: "let sin and shame cover me ever deeper and deeper!"

"*Je vous aime!*"[4] he whispered in the voice which was so like my husband's. At once I thought of my husband and child, as creatures once
precious to me who had now passed altogether out of my life. At that
moment I heard Mme M—'s voice; she called to me from round the corner. I came to myself, tore my hand away without looking at him, and almost ran after her: I only looked at him after she and I were already
seated in the carriage. Then I saw him raise his hat and ask some commonplace question with a smile. He little knew the inexpressible aversion I felt for him at that moment.

My life seemed so wretched, the future so hopeless, the past so black!
When Mme M— spoke, her words meant nothing to me. I thought that
she talked only out of pity, and to hide the contempt I aroused in her. In
every word and every look I seemed to detect this contempt and insulting pity. The shame of that kiss burned my cheek, and the thought of

---

[4] "I love you."

my husband and child was more than I could bear. When I was alone in my own room, I tried to think over my position; but I was afraid to be alone. Without drinking the tea which was brought me, and uncertain of my own motives, I got ready with feverish haste to catch the evening train and join my husband at Heidelberg.

I found seats for myself and my maid in an empty carriage. When the train started and the fresh air blew through the window on my face, I grew more composed and pictured my past and future to myself more clearly. The course of our married life from the time of our first visit to Petersburg now presented itself to me in a new light, and lay like a reproach on my conscience. For the first time I clearly recalled our start at Nikolskoye and our plans for the future; and for the first time I asked myself what happiness had my husband had since then. I felt that I had behaved badly to him. "But why," I asked myself, "did he not stop me? Why did he make pretenses? Why did he always avoid explanations? Why did he insult me? Why did he not use the power of his love to influence me? Or did he not love me?" But whether he was to blame or not, I still felt the kiss of that strange man upon my cheek. The nearer we got to Heidelberg, the clearer grew my picture of my husband, and the more I dreaded our meeting. "I shall tell him all," I thought, "and wipe out everything with tears of repentance; and he will forgive me." But I did not know myself what I meant by "everything"; and I did not believe in my heart that he would forgive me.

As soon as I entered my husband's room and saw his calm though surprised expression, I felt at once that I had nothing to tell him, no confession to make, and nothing to ask forgiveness for. I had to suppress my unspoken grief and penitence.

"What put this into your head?" he asked. "I meant to go to Baden tomorrow." Then he looked more closely at me and seemed to take alarm. "What's the matter with you? What has happened?" he said.

"Nothing at all," I replied, almost breaking down. "I am not going back. Let us go home, tomorrow if you like, to Russia."

For some time he said nothing but looked at me attentively. Then he said, "But do tell me what has happened to you."

I blushed involuntarily and looked down. There came into his eyes a flash of anger and displeasure. Afraid of what he might imagine, I said with a power of pretence that surprised myself:

"Nothing at all has happened. It was merely that I grew weary and sad by myself; and I have been thinking a great deal of our way of life and of you. I have long been to blame towards you. Why do you take me abroad, when you can't bear it yourself? I have long been to blame. Let us go back to Nikolskoye and settle there for ever."

"Spare us these sentimental scenes, my dear," he said coldly. "To go back to Nikolskoye is a good idea, for our money is running short; but the notion of stopping there 'for ever' is fanciful. I know you would not settle down. Have some tea, and you will feel better," and he rose to ring for the waiter.

I imagined all he might be thinking about me; and I was offended by the horrible thoughts which I ascribed to him when I encountered the dubious and shamefaced look he directed at me. "He will not and cannot understand me." I said I would go and look at the child, and I left the room. I wished to be alone, and to cry and cry and cry . . .

Chapter IV

The house at Nikolskoye, so long unheated and uninhabited, came to life again; but much of the past was dead beyond recall. Tatyana Semyonovna was no more, and we were now alone together. But far from desiring such close companionship, we even found it irksome. To me that winter was the more trying because I was in bad health, from which I only recovered after the birth of my second son. My husband and I were still on the same terms as during our life in Petersburg: we were coldly friendly to each other; but in the country each room and wall and sofa recalled what he had once been to me, and what I had lost. It was if some unforgiven grievance held us apart, as if he were punishing me and pretending not to be aware of it. But there was nothing to ask pardon for, no penalty to deprecate; my punishment was merely this, that he did not give his whole heart and mind to me as he used to do; but he did not give it to anyone or to anything; as though he had no longer a heart to give. Sometimes it occurred to me that he was only pretending to be like that, in order to hurt me, and that the old feeling was still alive in his breast; and I tried to call it forth. But I always failed: he always seemed to avoid frankness, evidently suspecting me of insincerity, and dreading the folly of any emotional display. I could read in his face and the tone of his voice, "What is the good of talking? I know all the facts already, and I know what is on the tip of your tongue, and I know that you will say one thing and do another." At first I was mortified by his dread of frankness, but I came later to think that it was rather the absence, on his part, of any need of frankness. It would never have occurred to me now, to tell him of a sudden that I loved him, or to ask him to repeat the prayers with me or listen while I played the piano. Our intercourse came to be regulated by a fixed code of good manners. We lived our separate lives: he had his own occupations in which I was not needed, and which I no longer wished to share, while I continued my idle life which no longer vexed or grieved him. The children were still too young to form a bond between us.

But spring came round and brought Katya and Sonya to spend the summer with us in the country. As the house at Nikolskoye was under repair, we went to live at my old home at Pokrovskoye. The old house was unchanged—the veranda, the folding table and the piano in the sunny drawing room, and my old bedroom with its white curtains and the dreams of my girlhood which I seemed to have left behind me there. In that room there were two beds: one had been mine, and in it now my plump little Kokosha lay sprawling, when I went at night to sign him with the cross; the other was a crib, in which the little face of my baby, Vanya, peeped out from his swaddling clothes. Often, when I had made the sign over them and remained standing in the middle of the quiet room, suddenly there rose up from all the corners, from the walls and curtains, old forgotten visions of youth. Old voices began to sing the songs of my girlhood. Where were those visions now? where were those dear old sweet songs? All that I had hardly dared to hope for had come to pass. My vague confused dreams had become a reality, and the reality had become an oppressive, difficult, and joyless life. All remained the same—the garden visible through the window, the grass, the path, the very same bench over there above the dell, the same song of the nightingale by the pond, the same lilacs in full bloom, the same moon shining above the house; and yet, in everything such a terrible inconceivable change! Such coldness in all that might have been near and dear! Just as in old times, Katya and I sit quietly alone together in the parlor and talk, and talk of him. But Katya has grown wrinkled and pale; and her eyes no longer shine with joy and hope, but express only sympathy, sorrow, and regret. We do not go into raptures as we used to, we judge him coolly; we do not wonder what we have done to deserve such happiness, or long to proclaim our thoughts to all the world. No! we whisper together like conspirators and ask each other for the hundredth time why all has changed so sadly. Yet he was still the same man, save for the deeper furrow between his eyebrows and the whiter hair on his temples; but his serious attentive look was constantly veiled from me by a cloud. And I am the same woman, but without love or desire for love, with no longing for work and not content with myself. My religious ecstasies, my love for my husband, the fullness of my former life—all these now seem utterly remote and visionary. Once it seemed so plain and right that to live for others was happiness; but now it has become unintelligible. Why live for others, when life had no attraction even for oneself?

I had given up my music altogether since the time of our first visit to Petersburg; but now the old piano and the old music tempted me to begin again.

One day I was not well and stayed indoors alone. My husband had taken Katya and Sonya to see the new buildings at Nikolskoye. Tea was laid; I went downstairs and while waiting for them sat down at the piano. I opened the "Moonlight Sonata" and began to play. There was no one within sight or sound, the windows were open over the garden, and the familiar sounds floated through the room with a solemn sadness. At the end of the first movement I looked round instinctively to the corner where he used once to sit and listen to my playing. He was not there; his chair, long unmoved, was still in its place; through the window I could see a lilac bush against the light of the setting sun; the freshness of evening streamed in through the open windows. I rested my elbows on the piano and covered my face with both hands; and so I sat for a long time, thinking. I recalled with pain the irrevocable past, and timidly imagined the future. But for me there seemed to be no future, no desires at all and no hopes. "Can life be over for me?" I thought with horror; then I looked up, and, trying to forget and not to think, I began playing the same movement over again. "O God!" I prayed, "forgive me if I have sinned, or restore to me all that once blossomed in my heart, or teach me what to do and how to live now." There was a sound of wheels on the grass and before the steps of the house; then I heard cautious and familiar footsteps pass along the veranda and cease; but my heart no longer replied to the sound. When I stopped playing the footsteps were behind me and a hand was laid on my shoulder.

"How clever of you to think of playing that!" he said.

I said nothing.

"Have you had tea?" he asked.

I shook my head without looking at him—I was unwilling to let him see the signs of emotion on my face.

"They'll be here immediately," he said; "the horse gave trouble, and they got out on the high road to walk home."

"Let us wait for them," I said, and went out to the veranda, hoping that he would follow; but he asked about the children and went upstairs to see them. Once more his presence and simple kindly voice made me doubt if I had really lost anything. What more could I wish? "He is kind and gentle, a good husband, a good father; I don't know myself what more I want." I sat down under the veranda awning on the very bench on which I had sat when we became engaged. The sun had set, it was growing dark, and a little spring rain cloud hung over the house and garden, and only behind the trees the horizon was clear, with the fading glow of twilight, in which one star had just begun to twinkle. The landscape, covered by the shadow of the cloud, seemed waiting for the light spring shower. There was not a breath of wind; not a single leaf or blade of grass stirred; the scent of lilac and bird cherry was so strong in the garden and veranda that it seemed as if all the air was in flower; it came in wafts, now stronger and now weaker, till one longed to shut both eyes and ears and drink in that fragrance only. The dahlias and rose bushes, not yet in flower, stood motionless on the black mould of the border, looking as if they were growing slowly upwards on their white-shaved props; beyond the dell, the frogs were making the most of their time before the rain drove them to the pond, croaking busily and loudly. Only the high continuous note of water falling at some distance rose above their croaking. From time to time the nightingales called to one another, and I could hear them flitting restlessly from bush to bush. Again this spring a nightingale had tried to build in a bush under the window, and I heard her fly off across the avenue when I went into the veranda. From there she whistled once and then stopped; she, too, was expecting the rain.

I tried in vain to calm my feelings: I had a sense of anticipation and regret.

He came downstairs again and sat down beside me.

"I am afraid they will get wet," he said.

"Yes," I answered; and we sat for long without speaking.

The cloud came down lower and lower with no wind. The air grew stiller and more fragrant. Suddenly a drop fell on the canvas awning and seemed to rebound from it; then another broke on the gravel path; soon there was a splash on the burdock leaves, and a fresh shower of big drops came down faster and faster. Nightingales and frogs were both dumb; only the high note of the falling water, though the rain made it seem more distant, still went on; and a bird, which must have sheltered among the dry leaves near the veranda, steadily repeated its two unvarying notes. My husband got up to go in.

"Where are you going?" I asked, trying to keep him; "it is so pleasant here."

"We must send them an umbrella and galoshes," he replied.

"Don't trouble—it will soon be over."

He thought I was right, and we remained together in the veranda. I rested one hand upon the wet slippery rail and put my head out. The fresh rain wetted my hair and neck in places. The cloud, growing lighter and thinner, was passing overhead; the steady patter of the rain gave place to occasional drops that fell from the sky or dripped from the trees. The frogs began to croak again in the dell; the nightingales woke up and began to call from the dripping bushes from one side and then from another. The whole prospect before us grew clear.

"How delightful!" he said, seating himself on the veranda rail and passing a hand over my wet hair.

This simple caress had on me the effect of a reproach: I felt inclined to cry.

"What more can a man need?" he said; "I am so content now that I want nothing; I am perfectly happy!"

He told me a different story once, I thought. He had said that, however great his happiness might be, he always wanted more and more. Now he is calm and contented; while my heart is full of unspoken repentance and unshed tears.

"I think it delightful too," I said; "but I am sad just because of the beauty of it all. All is so fair and lovely outside me, while my own heart is confused and baffled and full of vague unsatisfied longing. Is it possible that there is no element of pain, no yearning for the past, in your enjoyment of nature?"

He took his hand off my head and was silent for a little.

"I used to feel that too," he said, as though recalling it, "especially in spring. I used to sit up all night too, with my hopes and fears for company, and good company they were! But life was all before me then. Now it is all behind me, and I am content with what I have. I find life capital," he added with such careless confidence, that I believed, whatever pain it gave me to hear it, that it was the truth.

"But is there nothing you wish for?" I asked.

"I don't ask for impossibilities," he said, guessing my thoughts. "You go and get your head wet," he added, stroking my head like a child's and again passing his hand over the wet hair; "you envy the leaves and the grass their wetting from the rain, and you would like yourself to be the grass and the leaves and the rain. But I am content to enjoy them and everything else that is good and young and happy."

"And do you regret nothing of the past?" I asked, while my heart grew heavier and heavier.

Again he thought for a time before replying. I saw that he wished to reply with perfect frankness.

"Nothing," he said shortly.

"Not true! not true!" I said, turning towards him and looking into his eyes. "Do you really not regret the past?"

"No!" he repeated; "I am grateful for it, but I don't regret it."

"But would you not like to have it back?" I asked.

He turned away and looked out over the garden.

"No; I might as well wish to have wings. It is impossible."

"And would you not alter the past? do you not reproach yourself or me?"

"No, never! It was all for the best."

"Listen to me!" I said, touching his arm to make him look round. "Why did you never tell me that you wished me to live as you really wished me to? Why did you give me a freedom for which I was unfit? Why did you stop teaching me? If you had wished it, if you had guided me differently, none of all this would have happened!" said I in a voice that increasingly expressed cold displeasure and reproach, in place of the love of former days.

"What would not have happened?" he asked, turning to me in surprise. "As it is, there is nothing wrong. Things are all right, quite all right," he added with a smile.

"Does he really not understand?" I thought; "or still worse, does he not wish to understand?"

Then I suddenly broke out. "Had you acted differently, I should not now be punished, for no fault at all, by your indifference and even contempt, and you would not have taken from me unjustly all that I valued in life!"

"What do you mean, my dear one?" he asked—he seemed not to understand me.

"No! don't interrupt me! You have taken from me your confidence, your love, even your respect; for I cannot believe, when I think of the past, that you still love me. No! don't speak! I must once for all say out what has long been torturing me. Is it my fault that I knew nothing of life, and that you left me to learn experience for myself? Is it my fault that now, when I have gained the knowledge and have been struggling for nearly a year to come back to you, you push me away and pretend not to understand what I want? And you always do it so that it is impossible to reproach you, while I am guilty and unhappy. Yes, you wish to drive me out again to that life which might rob us both of happiness."

"How did I show that?" he asked in evident alarm and surprise.

"No later than yesterday you said, and you constantly say, that I can never settle down here, and that we must spend this winter too at Petersburg; and I hate Petersburg!" I went on. "Instead of supporting me, you avoid all plain speaking, you never say a single frank affectionate word to me. And then, when I fall utterly, you will reproach me and rejoice in my fall."

"Stop!" he said with cold severity. "You have no right to say that. It only proves that you are ill-disposed towards me, that you don't . . ."

"That I don't love you? Don't hesitate to say it!" I cried, and the tears began to flow. I sat down on the bench and covered my face with my handkerchief.

"So that is how he understood me!" I thought, trying to restrain the sobs which choked me. "Gone, gone is our former love!" said a voice at my heart. He did not come close or try to comfort me. He was hurt by what I had said. When he spoke, his tone was cool and dry.

"I don't know what you reproach me with," he began. "If you mean that I don't love you as I once did . . ."

"Did love!" I said, with my face buried in the handkerchief, while the bitter tears fell still more abundantly.

"If so, time is to blame for that, and we ourselves. Each time of life has its own kind of love." He was silent for a moment. "Shall I tell you the whole truth, if you really wish for frankness? In that summer when I first knew you, I used to lie awake all night, thinking about you, and I made that love myself, and it grew and grew in my heart. So again, in Petersburg and abroad, in the course of horrible sleepless nights, I strove to shatter and destroy that love, which had come to torture me. I did not destroy it, but I destroyed that part of it which gave me pain. Then I grew calm; and I feel love still, but it is a different kind of love."

"You call it love, but I call it torture!" I said. "Why did you allow me to go into society, if you thought so badly of it that you ceased to love me on that account?"

"No, it was not society, my dear," he said.

"Why did you not exercise your authority?" I went on; "why did you not lock me up or kill me? That would have been better than the loss of all that formed my happiness. I should have been happy, instead of being ashamed."

I began to sob again and hid my face.

Just then Katya and Sonya, wet and cheerful, came out to the veranda, laughing and talking loudly. They were silent as soon as they saw us, and went in again immediately.

We remained silent for a long time. I had had my cry out and felt relieved. I glanced at him. He was sitting with his head resting on his hand; he intended to make some reply to my glance, but only sighed deeply and resumed his former position.

I went up to him and removed his hand. His eyes turned thoughtfully to my face.

"Yes," he began, as if continuing his thoughts aloud, "all of us, and especially you women, must have personal experience of all the nonsense of life, in order to get back to life itself; the evidence of other people is no good. At that time you had not got near the end of that charming nonsense which I admired in you. So I let you go through it alone, feeling that I had no right to put pressure on you, though my own time for that sort of thing was long past."

"If you loved me," I said, "how could you stand beside me and suffer me to go through it?"

"Because it was impossible for you to take my word for it, though you would have tried to. Personal experience was necessary, and now you have had it."

"There was much calculation in all that," I said, "but little love."

Again we were silent.

"What you said just now is severe, but it is true," he began, rising suddenly and beginning to walk about the veranda. "Yes, it is true. I was to blame," he added, stopping opposite me; "I ought either to have kept myself from loving you at all, or to have loved you in a simpler way."

"Let us forget it all," I said timidly.

"No," he said; "the past can never come back, never"; and his voice softened as he spoke.

"It is restored already," I said, laying a hand on his shoulder.

He took my hand away and pressed it.

"I was wrong when I said that I did not regret the past. I do regret it; I weep for that past love which can never return. Who is to blame, I do not know. Love remains, but not the old love; its place remains, but it is all wasted away and has lost all strength and substance; recollections are still left, and gratitude; but . . ."

"Do not say that!" I broke in. "Let all be as it was before! Surely that is possible?" I asked, looking into his eyes; but their gaze was clear and calm, and did not look deeply into mine.

Even while I spoke, I knew that my wishes and my petition were impossible. He smiled calmly and gently; and I thought it the smile of an old man.

"How young you are still!" he said, "and I am so old. What you seek in me is no longer there. Why deceive ourselves?" he added, still smiling.

I stood silent opposite to him, and my heart grew calmer.

"Don't let us try to repeat life," he went on. "Don't let us make pretences to ourselves. Let us be thankful that there is an end of the old emotions and excitements. The excitement of searching is over for us; our quest is done, and happiness enough has fallen to our lot. Now we must stand aside and make room—for him, if you like," he said, pointing to the nurse who was carrying Vanya out and had stopped at the veranda door. "That's the truth, my dear one," he said, drawing down my head and kissing it, not a lover any longer but an old friend.

The fragrant freshness of the night rose ever stronger and sweeter from the garden; the sounds and the silence grew more solemn; star after star began to twinkle overhead. I looked at him, and suddenly my heart grew light; it seemed that the cause of my suffering had been removed like an aching nerve. Suddenly I realized clearly and calmly that the past feeling, like the past time itself, was gone beyond recall, and that it would be not only impossible but painful and uncomfortable to bring it back. And after all, was that time so good which seemed to me so happy? And it was all so long, long ago!

"Time for tea!" he said, and we went together to the parlour. At the door we met the nurse with the baby. I took him in my arms, covered his bare little red legs, pressed him to me, and kissed him with the lightest touch of my lips. Half asleep, he moved the parted fingers of one creased little hand and opened dim little eyes, as if he was looking for something or recalling something. All at once his eyes rested on me, a spark of consciousness shone in them, the little pouting lips, parted before, now met and opened in a smile. "Mine, mine, mine!" I thought, pressing him to my breast with such an impulse of joy in every limb that I found it hard to restrain myself from hurting him. I fell to kissing the cold little feet, his stomach and hand and head with its thin covering of down. My husband came up to me, and I quickly covered the child's face and uncovered it again.

"Ivan Sergeich!" said my husband, tickling him under the chin. But I made haste to cover Ivan Sergeich up again. None but I had any business to look long at him. I glanced at my husband. His eyes smiled as he looked at me; and I looked into them with an ease and happiness which I had not felt for a long time.

That day ended the romance of our marriage; the old feeling became a precious irrecoverable remembrance; but a new feeling of love for my children and the father of my children laid the foundation of a new life and a quite different happiness; and that life and happiness have lasted to the present time.

Three Deaths

I

IT WAS AUTUMN. Two vehicles were going along the highway at a quick trot. In the first sat two women: a lady, thin and pale, and a maidservant, plump and rosy and shining. The maid's short dry hair escaped from under her faded bonnet and her red hand in its torn glove kept pushing it back by fits and starts; her full bosom, covered by a woollen shawl, breathed health, her quick black eyes now watched the fields as they glided past the window, now glanced timidly at her mistress, and now restlessly scanned the corners of the carriage. In front of her nose dangled her mistress's bonnet, pinned to the luggage carrier, on her lap lay a puppy, her feet were raised on the boxes standing on the floor and just audibly tapped against them to the creaking of the coach-springs and the clatter of the window-panes.

Having folded her hands on her knees and closed her eyes, the lady swayed feebly against the pillows placed at her back, and, frowning slightly, coughed inwardly. On her head she had a white nightcap, and a blue kerchief was tied round her delicate white throat. A straight line receding under the cap parted her light brown, extremely flat, pomaded hair, and there was something dry and deathly about the whiteness of the skin of that wide parting. Her features were delicate and handsome, but her skin was flabby and rather sallow, though there was a hectic flush on her cheeks. Her lips were dry and restless, her scanty eyelashes had no curl in them, and her cloth travelling coat fell in straight folds over a sunken breast. Though her eyes were closed her face bore an expression of weariness, irritation, and habitual suffering.

A footman, leaning on the arms of his seat, was dozing on the box. The mail-coach driver, shouting lustily, urged on his four big sweating horses, occasionally turning to the other driver who called to him from the caleche behind. The broad parallel tracks of the tires spread themselves evenly and fast on the muddy, chalky surface of the road. The sky was grey and cold and a damp mist was settling on the fields and road. It was stuffy in the coach and there was a smell of eau de cologne and dust. The invalid drew back her head and slowly opened her beautiful dark eyes, which were large and brilliant.

"Again," she said, nervously pushing away with her beautiful thin hand an end of her maid's cloak which had lightly touched her foot, and her mouth twitched painfully. Matryosha gathered up her cloak with both hands, rose on her strong legs, and seated herself farther away, while her fresh face grew scarlet. The lady, leaning with both hands on the seat, also tried to raise herself so as to sit up higher, but her strength failed her. Her mouth twisted, and her whole face became distorted by a look of impotent malevolence and irony. "You might at least help me! . . . No, don't bother! I can do it myself, only don't put your bags or anything behind me, for goodness' sake! . . . No, better not touch me since you don't know how to!" The lady closed her eyes and then, again quickly raising her eyelids, glared at the maid. Matryosha, looking at her, bit her red nether lip. A deep sigh rose from the invalid's chest and turned into a cough before it was completed. She turned away, puckered her face, and clutched her chest with both hands. When the coughing fit was over she once more closed her eyes and continued to sit motionless. The carriage and caleche entered a village. Matryosha stretched out her thick hand from under her shawl and crossed herself.

"What is it?" asked her mistress.

"A post station, madam."

"I am asking why you crossed yourself."

"There's a church, madam."

The invalid turned to the window and began slowly to cross herself, looking with large wide-open eyes at the big village church her carriage was passing.

The carriage and caleche both stopped at the post-station and the invalid's husband and doctor stepped out of the caleche and went up to the coach.

"How are you feeling?" asked the doctor, taking her pulse.

"Well, my dear, how are you—not tired?" asked the husband in French. "Wouldn't you like to get out?"

Matryosha, gathering up the bundles, squeezed herself into a corner so as not to interfere with their conversation.

"Nothing much, just the same," replied the invalid. "I won't get out."

Her husband after standing there a while went into the station house, and Matryosha, too, jumped out of the carriage and ran on tiptoe across the mud and in at the gate.

"If I feel ill, it's no reason for you not to have lunch," said the sick woman with a slight smile to the doctor, who was standing at her window.

"None of them has any thought for me," she added to herself as soon as the doctor, having slowly walked away from her, ran quickly up the steps to the station house. "They are well, so they don't care. Oh, my God!"

"Well, Edward Ivanovich?" said the husband, rubbing his hands as he met the doctor with a merry smile. "I have ordered the lunch basket to be brought in. What do you think about it?"

"A capital idea," replied the doctor.

"Well, how is she?" asked the husband with a sigh, lowering his voice and lifting his eyebrows.

"As I told you: it is impossible for her to reach Italy—God grant that she gets even as far as Moscow, especially in this weather."

"But what are we to do? Oh, my God, my God!" and the husband hid his eyes with his hand. "Bring it here!" he said to the man who had brought in the lunch basket.

"She ought to have stayed at home," said the doctor, shrugging his shoulders.

"But what could I do?" rejoined the husband. "You know I used every possible means to get her to stay. I spoke of the expense, of our children whom we had to leave behind, and of my business affairs, but she would not listen to anything. She is making plans for life abroad as if she were in good health. To tell her of her condition would be to kill her."

"But she is killed already—you must know that, Vasili Dmitrich. A person can't live without lungs, and new lungs won't grow. It is sad and hard, but what is to be done? My business and yours is to see that her end is made as peaceful as possible. It's a priest who is needed for that."

"Oh, my God! Think of my condition, having to remind her about her will. Come what may I can't tell her that, you know how good she is . . ."

"Still, try to persuade her to wait till the roads are fit for sledging," said the doctor, shaking his head significantly, "or something bad may happen on the journey."

"Aksyusha, hello Aksyusha!" yelled the stationmaster's daughter, throwing her jacket over her head and stamping her feet on the muddy back porch. "Come and let's have a look at the Shirkin lady: they say she is being taken abroad for a chest trouble, and I've never seen what consumptive people look like!"

She jumped onto the threshold, and seizing one another by the hand the two girls ran out of the gate. Checking their pace, they passed by the coach and looked in at the open window. The invalid turned her head towards them but, noticing their curiosity, frowned and turned away.

"De-arie me!" said the stationmaster's daughter, quickly turning her head away. "What a wonderful beauty she must have been, and see what she's like now! It's dreadful. Did you see, did you, Aksyusha?"

"Yes, how thin!" Aksyusha agreed. "Let's go and look again, as if we were going to the well. See, she has turned away, and I hadn't seen her yet. What a pity, Masha!"

"Yes, and what mud!" said Masha, and they both ran through the gate.

"Evidently I look frightful," thought the invalid. "If only I could get abroad quicker, quicker. I should soon recover there."

"Well, my dear, how are you?" said her husband, approaching her and still chewing.

"Always the same question," thought the invalid, "and he himself is eating."

"So-so," she murmured through her closed teeth.

"You know, my dear, I'm afraid you'll get worse travelling in this weather, and Edward Ivanovich says so too. Don't you think we'd better turn back?"

She remained angrily silent.

"The weather will perhaps improve and the roads be fit for sledging; you will get better meanwhile, and we will all go together."

"Excuse me. If I had not listened to you for so long, I should now at least have reached Berlin, and have been quite well."

"What could be done, my angel? You know it was impossible. But now if you stayed another month you would get nicely better, I should have finished my business, and we could take the children with us."

"The children are well, but I am not."

"But do understand, my dear, that if in this weather you should get worse on the road. . . . At least you would be at home."

"What of being at home? . . . To die at home?" answered the invalid, flaring up. But the word "die" evidently frightened her, and she looked imploringly and questioningly at her husband. He hung his head and was silent. The invalid's mouth suddenly widened like a child's, and tears rolled down her cheeks. Her husband hid his face in his handkerchief and stepped silently away from the carriage.

"No, I will go on," said the invalid, and lifting her eyes to the sky she folded her hands and began whispering incoherent words: "Oh, my God, what is it for?" she said, and her tears flowed faster. She prayed long and fervently, but her chest ached and felt as tight as before; the sky, the fields, and the road were just as grey and gloomy, and the autumnal mist fell, neither thickening nor lifting, and settled on the muddy road, the roofs, the carriage, and the sheepskin coats of the drivers, who talking in their strong merry voices were greasing the wheels and harnessing the horses.

II

The carriage was ready but the driver still loitered. He had gone into the drivers' room at the station. It was hot, stuffy, and dark there, with an oppressive smell of baking bread, cabbage, sheepskin garments, and humanity. Several drivers were sitting in the room, and a cook was busy at the oven, on the top of which lay a sick man wrapped in sheepskins.

"Uncle Theodore! I say, Uncle Theodore!" said the young driver, entering the room in his sheepskin coat with a whip stuck in his belt, and addressing the sick man.

"What do you want Theodore for, lazybones?" asked one of the drivers. "There's your carriage waiting for you."

"I want to ask for his boots; mine are quite worn out," answered the young fellow, tossing back his hair and straightening the mittens tucked in his belt. "Is he asleep? I say, Uncle Theodore!" he repeated, walking over to the oven.

"What is it?" answered a weak voice, and a lean face with a red beard looked down from the oven, while a broad, emaciated, pale, and hairy hand pulled up the coat over the dirty shirt covering his angular shoulder.

"Give me a drink, lad. . . . What is it you want?"

The lad handed him up a dipper with water.

"Well, you see, Theodore," he said, stepping from foot to foot, "I expect you don't need your new boots now; won't you let me have them? I don't suppose you'll go about any more."

The sick man, lowering his weary head to the shiny dipper and immersing his sparse drooping moustache in the turbid water, drank feebly but eagerly. His matted beard was dirty, and his sunken clouded eyes had difficulty in looking up at the lad's face. Having finished drinking he tried to lift his hand to wipe his wet lips, but he could not do so, and rubbed them on the sleeve of his coat instead. Silently, and breathing heavily through his nose, he looked straight into the lad's eyes, collecting his strength.

"But perhaps you have promised them to someone else?" asked the lad. "If so, it's all right. The worst of it is, it's wet outside and I have to go about my work, so I said to myself: 'Suppose I ask Theodore for his boots; I expect he doesn't need them.' If you need them yourself—just say so."

Something began to rumble and gurgle in the sick man's chest; he doubled up and began to choke with an abortive cough in his throat.

"Need them indeed!" the cook snapped out unexpectedly so as to be heard by the whole room. "He hasn't come down from the oven for more than a month! Hear how he's choking—it makes me ache inside just to hear him. What does he want with boots? They won't bury him in new boots. And it was time long ago—God forgive me the sin! See how he chokes. He ought to be taken into the other room or some-where. They say there are hospitals in the town. Is it right that he should take up the whole corner?—there's no more to be said. I've no room at all, and yet they expect cleanliness!"

"Hullo, Sergey! Come along and take your place, the gentlefolk are waiting!" shouted the drivers' overseer, looking in at the door.

Sergey was about to go without waiting for a reply, but the sick man, while coughing, let him understand by a look that he wanted to give him an answer.

"Take my boots, Sergey," he said when he had mastered the cough and rested a moment. "But listen. . . . Buy a stone for me when I die," he added hoarsely.

"Thank you, uncle. Then I'll take them, and I'll buy a stone for sure."

"There, lads, you heard that?" the sick man managed to utter, and then bent double again and began to choke.

"All right, we heard," said one of the drivers. "Go and take your seat, Sergey, there's the overseer running back. The Shirkin lady is ill, you know."

Sergey quickly pulled off his unduly big, dilapidated boots and threw them under a bench. Uncle Theodore's new boots just fitted him, and having put them on he went to the carriage with his eyes fixed on his feet.

"What fine boots! Let me grease them," said a driver, who held some axle-grease in his hand, as Sergey climbed onto the box and gathered up the reins. "Did he give them to you for nothing?"

"Why, are you envious?" Sergey replied, rising and wrapping the skirts of his coat under his legs. "Off with you! Gee up, my beauties!" he shouted to the horses, flourishing the whip, and the carriage and caleche with their occupants, portmanteaux, and trunks rolled rapidly along the wet road and disappeared in the grey autumnal mist.

The sick driver was left on the top of the oven in the stuffy room and, unable to relieve himself by coughing, turned with an effort onto his other side and became silent.

Till late in the evening people came in and out of the room and dined there. The sick man made no sound. When night came, the cook climbed up onto the oven and stretched over his legs to get down her sheepskin coat.

"Don't be cross with me, Nastasya," said the sick man. "I shall soon leave your corner empty."

"All right, all right, never mind," muttered Nastasya. "But what is it that hurts you? Tell me, uncle."

"My whole inside has wasted away. God knows what it is!"

"I suppose your throat hurts when you cough?"

"Everything hurts. My death has come—that's how it is. Oh, oh, oh!" moaned the sick man.

"Cover up your feet like this," said Nastasya, drawing his coat over him as she climbed down from the oven.

A night-light burnt dimly in the room. Nastasya and some ten drivers slept on the floor or on the benches, loudly snoring. The sick man groaned feebly, coughed, and turned about on the oven. Towards morning he grew quite quiet.

"I had a queer dream last night," said Nastasya next morning, stretching herself in the dim light. "I dreamt that Uncle Theodore got down from the oven and went out to chop wood. 'Come, Nastasya,' he says, 'I'll help you!' and I say, 'How can you chop wood now?,' but he just seizes the axe and begins chopping quickly, quickly, so that the chips fly all about. 'Why,' I say, 'haven't you been ill?' 'No,' he says, 'I am well,' and he swings the axe so that I was quite frightened. I gave a cry and woke up. I wonder whether he is dead! Uncle Theodore! I say, Uncle Theodore!"

Theodore did not answer.

"True enough he may have died. I'll go and see," said one of the drivers, waking up.

The lean hand covered with reddish hair that hung down from the oven was pale and cold.

"I'll go and tell the stationmaster," said the driver. "I think he is dead."

Theodore had no relatives: he was from some distant place. They buried him next day in the new cemetery beyond the wood, and Nastasya went on for days telling everybody of her dream, and of having been the first to discover that Uncle Theodore was dead.

III

Spring had come. Rivulets of water hurried down the wet streets of the city, gurgling between lumps of frozen manure; the colors of the people's clothes as they moved along the streets looked vivid and their voices sounded shrill. Behind the garden fences the buds on the trees were swelling and their branches were just audibly swaying in the fresh breeze. Everywhere transparent drops were forming and falling. . . . The sparrows chirped, and fluttered awkwardly with their little wings. On the sunny side of the street, on the fences, houses, and trees, everything was in motion and sparkling. There was joy and youth everywhere in the sky, on the earth, and in the hearts of men.

In one of the chief streets fresh straw had been strewn on the road before a large, important house, where the invalid who had been in a hurry to go abroad lay dying.

At the closed door of her room stood the invalid's husband and an elderly woman. On the sofa a priest sat with bowed head, holding something wrapped in his stole. In a corner of the room the sick woman's old mother lay on an invalid chair weeping bitterly: beside her stood one maidservant holding a clean handkerchief, waiting for her to ask for it; while another was rubbing her temples with something and blowing under the old lady's cap onto her grey head.

"Well, may Christ aid you, dear friend," the husband said to the elderly woman who stood near him at the door. "She has such confidence in you and you know so well how to talk to her, so persuade her as well as you can, my dear—go to her." He was about to open the door, but her cousin stopped him, pressing her handkerchief several times to her eyes and giving her head a shake.

"Well, I don't think I look as if I had been crying now," said she and, opening the door herself, went in.

The husband was in great agitation and seemed quite distracted. He walked towards the old woman, but while still several steps from her turned back, walked about the room, and went up to the priest. The priest looked at him, raised his eyebrows to heaven, and sighed: his thick, greyish beard also rose as he sighed and then came down again.

"My God, my God!" said the husband.

"What is to be done?" said the priest with a sigh, and again his eyebrows and beard rose and fell.

"And her mother is here!" said the husband almost in despair. "She won't be able to bear it. You see, loving her as she does . . . I don't know! If you would only try to comfort her, Father, and persuade her to go away."

The priest got up and went to the old woman.

"It is true, no one can appreciate a mother's heart," he said—"but God is merciful."

The old woman's face suddenly twitched all over, and she began to hiccup hysterically.

"God is merciful," the priest continued when she grew a little calmer. "Let me tell you of a patient in my parish who was much worse than Mary Dmitrievna, and a simple tradesman cured her in a short time with various herbs. That tradesman is even now in Moscow. I told Vasili Dmitrich—we might try him. . . . It would at any rate comfort the invalid. To God all is possible."

"No, she will not live," said the old woman. "God is taking her instead of me," and the hysterical hiccuping grew so violent that she fainted.

The sick woman's husband hid his face in his hands and ran out of the room.

In the passage the first person he met was his six-year-old son, who was running full speed after his younger sister.

"Won't you order the children to be taken to their mamma?" asked the nurse.

"No, she doesn't want to see them—it would upset her."

The boy stopped a moment, looked intently into his father's face, then gave a kick and ran on, shouting merrily.

"She pretends to be the black horse, Papa!" he shouted, pointing to his sister.

Meanwhile in the other room the cousin sat down beside the invalid, and tried by skilful conversation to prepare her for the thought of death. The doctor was mixing a draught at another window.

The patient, in a white dressing gown, sat up in bed supported all round by pillows, and looked at her cousin in silence.

"Ah, my dear friend," she said, unexpectedly interrupting her, "don't prepare me! Don't treat me like a child. I am a Christian. I know it all. I know I have not long to live, and know that if my husband had listened to me sooner I should now have been in Italy and perhaps—no, certainly—should have been well. Everybody told him so. But what is to be done? Evidently this is God's wish. We have all sinned heavily. I know that, but I trust in God's mercy everybody will be forgiven, probably all will be forgiven. I try to understand myself. I have many sins to answer for, dear friend, but then how much I have had to suffer! I try to bear my sufferings patiently . . ."

"Then shall I call the priest, my dear? You will feel still more comfortable after receiving Communion," said her cousin.

The sick woman bent her head in assent.

"God forgive me, sinner that I am!" she whispered.

The cousin went out and signalled with her eyes to the priest.

"She is an angel!" she said to the husband, with tears in her eyes. The husband burst into tears; the priest went into the next room; the invalid's mother was still unconscious, and all was silent there. Five minutes later he came out again, and after taking off his stole, straightened out his hair.

"Thank God she is calmer now," she said, "and wishes to see you."

The cousin and the husband went into the sick-room. The invalid was silently weeping, gazing at an icon.

"I congratulate you, my dear,"[1] said her husband.

---

[1] It is customary in Russia to congratulate people who have received Communion.

"Thank you! How well I feel now, what inexpressible sweetness I feel!" said the sick woman, and a soft smile played on her thin lips. "How merciful God is! Is he not? Merciful and all powerful!" and again she looked at the icon with eager entreaty and her eyes full of tears.

Then suddenly, as if she remembered something, she beckoned to her husband to come closer.

"You never want to do what I ask . . ." she said in a feeble and dissatisfied voice.

The husband, craning his neck, listened to her humbly.

"What is it, my dear?"

"How many times have I not said that these doctors don't know anything; there are simple women who can heal, and who do cure. The priest told me . . . there is also a tradesman . . . Send!"

"For whom, my dear?"

"O God, you don't want to understand anything!" . . . And the sick woman's face puckered and she closed her eyes.

The doctor came up and took her hand. Her pulse was beating more and more feebly. He glanced at the husband. The invalid noticed that gesture and looked round in affright. The cousin turned away and began to cry.

"Don't cry, don't torture yourself and me," said the patient. "Don't take from me the last of my tranquillity."

"You are an angel," said the cousin, kissing her hand.

"No, kiss me here! Only dead people are kissed on the hand. My God, my God!"

That same evening the patient was a corpse, and the body lay in a coffin in the music room of the large house. A deacon sat alone in that big room reading the Psalms of David through his nose in a monotonous voice. A bright light from the wax candles in their tall silver candlesticks fell on the pale brow of the dead woman, on her heavy wax-like hands, on the stiff folds of the pall which brought out in awesome relief the knees and the toes. The deacon without understanding the words read on monotonously, and in the quiet room the words sounded strangely and died away. Now and then from a distant room came the sounds of children's voices and the patter of their feet.

"Thou hidest thy face, they are troubled," said the psalter. "Thou takest away their breath, they die and return to their dust. Thou sendest forth thy spirit, they are created: and thou renewest the face of the earth. The glory of the Lord shall endure for ever."

The dead woman's face looked stern and majestic. Neither in the clear cold brow nor in the firmly closed lips was there any movement. She seemed all attention. But had she even now understood those solemn words?

IV

A month later a stone chapel was being erected over the grave of the deceased woman. Over the driver's tomb there was still no stone, and only the light green grass sprouted on the mound which served as the only token of the past existence of a man.

"It will be a sin, Sergey," said the cook at the station house one day, "if you don't buy a stone for Theodore. You kept saying 'It's winter, it's winter!' but why don't you keep your word now? You know I witnessed it. He has already come back once to ask you to do it; if you don't buy him one, he'll come again and choke you."

"But why? I'm not backing out of it," replied Sergey. "I'll buy a stone as I said I would, and give a ruble and a half for it. I haven't forgotten it, but it has to be fetched. When I happen to be in town I'll buy one."

"You might at least put up a cross—you ought to—else it's really wrong," interposed an old driver. "You know you are wearing his boots."

"Where can I get a cross? I can't cut one out of a log."

"What do you mean, can't cut one out of a log? You take an axe and go into the forest early, and you can cut one there. Cut down a young ash or something like that, and you can make a cross of it . . . you may have to treat the forester to vodka; but one can't afford to treat him for every trifle. There now, I broke my splinter-bar and went and cut a new one, and nobody said a word."

Early in the morning, as soon as it was daybreak, Sergey took an axe and went into the wood.

A cold white cover of dew, which was still falling untouched by the sun, lay on everything. The east was imperceptibly growing brighter, reflecting its pale light on the vault of heaven still veiled by a covering of clouds. Not a blade of grass below, nor a leaf on the topmost branches of the trees, stirred. Only occasionally a sound of wings amid the brushwood, or a rustling on the ground, broke the silence of the forest. Suddenly a strange sound, foreign to Nature, resounded and died away at the outskirts of the forest. Again the sound was heard, and was rhythmically repeated at the foot of the trunk of one of the motionless trees. A treetop began to tremble in an unwonted manner, its juicy leaves whispered something, and the robin who had been sitting in one of its branches fluttered twice from place to place with a whistle, and jerking its tail sat down on another tree.

The axe at the bottom gave off a more and more muffled sound, sappy white chips were scattered on the dewy grass and a slight creaking was heard above the sound of the blows. The tree, shuddering in its whole body, bent down and quickly rose again, vibrating with fear on its roots. For an instant all was still, but the tree bent again, a crashing sound came from its trunk, and with its branches breaking and its boughs hanging down it fell with its crown on the damp earth.

The sounds of the axe and of the footsteps were silenced. The robin whistled and flitted higher. A twig which it brushed with its wings shook a little and then with all its foliage grew still like the rest. The trees flaunted the beauty of their motionless branches still more joyously in the newly cleared space.

The first sunbeams, piercing the translucent cloud, shone out and spread over earth and sky. The mist began to quiver like waves in the hollows, the dew sparkled and played on the verdure, the transparent cloudlets grew whiter, and hurriedly dispersed over the deepening azure vault of the sky. The birds stirred in the thicket and, as though bewildered, twittered joyfully about something; the sappy leaves whispered gladly and peacefully on the treetops, and the branches of those that were living began to rustle slowly and majestically over the dead and prostrate tree.

The Three Hermits

AN OLD LEGEND CURRENT IN THE VOLGA DISTRICT

And in praying use not vain repetitions, as the Gentiles do: for they think that they shall be heard for their much speaking. Be not therefore like unto them: for your Father knoweth what things ye have need of, before ye ask Him.—*Matt.* vi. 7, 8.

A BISHOP was sailing from Archangel to the Solovetsk Monastery, and on the same vessel were a number of pilgrims on their way to visit the shrines at that place. The voyage was a smooth one. The wind favorable and the weather fair. The pilgrims lay on deck, eating, or sat in groups talking to one another. The bishop, too, came on deck, and as he was pacing up and down he noticed a group of men standing near the prow and listening to a fisherman, who was pointing to the sea and telling them something. The bishop stopped, and looked in the direction in which the man was pointing. He could see nothing, however, but the sea glistening in the sunshine. He drew nearer to listen, but when the man saw him, he took off his cap and was silent. The rest of the people also took off their caps and bowed.

"Do not let me disturb you, friends," said the bishop. "I came to hear what this good man was saying."

"The fisherman was telling us about the hermits," replied one, a tradesman, rather bolder than the rest.

"What hermits?" asked the bishop, going to the side of the vessel and seating himself on a box. "Tell me about them. I should like to hear. What were you pointing at?"

"Why, that little island you can just see over there," answered the man, pointing to a spot ahead and a little to the right. "That is the island where the hermits live for the salvation of their souls."

"Where is the island?" asked the bishop. "I see nothing."

"There, in the distance, if you will please look along my hand. Do you see that little cloud? Below it and a bit to the left, there is just a faint streak. That is the island."

The bishop looked carefully, but his unaccustomed eyes could make out nothing but the water shimmering in the sun.

"I cannot see it," he said. "But who are the hermits that live there?"

"They are holy men," answered the fisherman. "I had long heard tell of them, but never chanced to see them myself till the year before last."

And the fisherman related how once, when he was out fishing, he had been stranded at night upon that island, not knowing where he was. In the morning, as he wandered about the island, he came across an earth hut, and met an old man standing near it. Presently two others came out, and after having fed him and dried his things, they helped him mend his boat.

"And what are they like?" asked the bishop.

"One is a small man and his back is bent. He wears a priest's cassock and is very old; he must be more than a hundred, I should say. He is so old that the white of his beard is taking a greenish tinge, but he is always smiling, and his face is as bright as an angel's from heaven. The second is taller, but he also is very old. He wears a tattered, peasant coat. His beard is broad, and of a yellowish-grey color. He is a strong man. Before I had time to help him, he turned my boat over as if it were only a pail. He too is kindly and cheerful. The third is tall, and has a beard as white as snow and reaching to his knees. He is stern, with overhanging eyebrows; and he wears nothing but a piece of matting tied round his waist."

"And did they speak to you?" asked the bishop.

"For the most part they did everything in silence, and spoke but little even to one another. One of them would just give a glance, and the others would understand him. I asked the tallest whether they had lived there long. He frowned, and muttered something as if he were angry; but the oldest one took his hand and smiled, and then the tall one was quiet. The oldest one only said: 'Have mercy upon us,' and smiled."

While the fisherman was talking, the ship had drawn nearer to the island.

"There, now you can see it plainly, if your Lordship will please to look," said the tradesman, pointing with his hand.

The bishop looked, and now he really saw a dark streak—which was the island. Having looked at it a while, he left the prow of the vessel, and going to the stern, asked the helmsman:

"What island is that?"

"That one," replied the man, "has no name. There are many such in this sea."

"Is it true that there are hermits who live there for the salvation of their souls?"

"So it is said, your Lordship, but I don't know if it's true. Fishermen say they have seen them; but of course they may only be spinning yarns."

"I should like to land on the island and see these men," said the bishop. "How could I manage it?"

"The ship cannot get close to the island," replied the helmsman, "but you might be rowed there in a boat. You had better speak to the captain."

The captain was sent for and came.

"I should like to see these hermits," said the bishop. "Could I not be rowed ashore?"

The captain tried to dissuade him.

"Of course it could be done," said he, "but we should lose much time. And if I might venture to say so to your Lordship, the old men are not worth your pains. I have heard say that they are foolish old fellows, who understand nothing, and never speak a word, any more than the fish in the sea."

"I wish to see them," said the bishop, "and I will pay you for your trouble and loss of time. Please let me have a boat."

There was no help for it; so the order was given. The sailors trimmed the sails, the steersman put up the helm, and the ship's course was set for the island. A chair was placed at the prow for the bishop, and he sat there, looking ahead. The passengers all collected at the prow, and gazed at the island. Those who had the sharpest eyes could presently make out the rocks on it, and then a mud hut was seen. At last one man saw the hermits themselves. The captain brought a telescope and, after looking through it, handed it to the bishop.

"It's right enough. There are three men standing on the shore. There, a little to the right of that big rock."

The Bishop took the telescope, got it into position, and he saw the three men: a tall one, a shorter one, and one very small and bent, standing on the shore and holding each other by the hand.

The captain turned to the bishop.

"The vessel can get no nearer in than this, your Lordship. If you wish to go ashore, we must ask you to go in the boat, while we anchor here."

The cable was quickly let out, the anchor cast, and the sails furled. There was a jerk, and the vessel shook. Then a boat having been lowered, the oarsmen jumped in, and the bishop descended the ladder and took his seat. The men pulled at their oars and the boat moved rapidly towards the island. When they came within a stone's throw, they saw three old men: a tall one with only a piece of matting tied round his waist: a shorter one in a tattered peasant coat, and a very old one bent with age and wearing an old cassock—all three standing hand in hand.

The oarsmen pulled in to the shore, and held on with the boathook while the bishop got out.

The old men bowed to him, and he gave them his blessing, at which they bowed still lower. Then the bishop began to speak to them.

"I have heard," he said, "that you, godly men, live here saving your own souls and praying to our Lord Christ for your fellow men. I, an unworthy servant of Christ, am called, by God's mercy, to keep and teach his flock. I wished to see you, servants of God, and to do what I can to teach you, also."

The old men looked at each other smiling, but remained silent.

"Tell me," said the bishop, "what you are doing to save your souls, and how you serve God on this island."

The second hermit sighed, and looked at the oldest, the very ancient one. The latter smiled, and said:

"We do not know how to serve God. We only serve and support ourselves, servant of God."

"But how do you pray to God?" asked the bishop.

"We pray in this way," replied the hermit. "Three are ye, three are we, have mercy upon us."

And when the old man said this, all three raised their eyes to heaven, and repeated:

"Three are ye, three are we, have mercy upon us!"

The bishop smiled.

"You have evidently heard something about the Holy Trinity," said he. "But you do not pray aright. You have won my affection, godly men. I see you wish to please the Lord, but you do not know how to serve him. That is not the way to pray; but listen to me, and I will teach you. I will teach you, not a way of my own, but the way in which God in the Holy Scriptures has commanded all men to pray to him."

And the bishop began explaining to the hermits how God had revealed himself to men; telling them of God the Father, and God the Son, and God the Holy Ghost.

"God the Son came down on earth," said he, "to save men, and this is how he taught us all to pray. Listen, and repeat after me: 'Our Father.'"

And the first old man repeated after him, "Our Father," and the second said, "Our Father," and the third said, "Our Father."

"Which art in heaven," continued the bishop.

The first hermit repeated, "Which art in heaven," but the second blundered over the words, and the tall hermit could not say them properly. His hair had grown over his mouth so that he could not speak plainly. The very old hermit, having no teeth, also mumbled indistinctly.

The bishop repeated the words again, and the old men repeated them after him. The bishop sat down on a stone, and the old men stood before him, watching his mouth, and repeating the words as he uttered them. And all day long the bishop labored, saying a word twenty, thirty, a hundred times over, and the old men repeated it after him. They blundered, and he corrected them, and made them begin again.

The bishop did not leave off till he had taught them the whole of the Lord's Prayer so that they could not only repeat it after him, but could say it by themselves. The middle one was the first to know it, and to repeat the whole of it alone. The bishop made him say it again and again, and at last the others could say it too.

It was getting dark, and the moon was appearing over the water, before the bishop rose to return to the vessel. When he took leave of the old men they all bowed down to the ground before him. He raised them, and kissed each of them, telling them to pray as he had taught them. Then he got into the boat and returned to the ship.

And as he sat in the boat and was rowed to the ship he could hear the three voices of the hermits loudly repeating the Lord's Prayer. As the boat drew near the vessel their voices could no longer be heard, but they could still be seen in the moonlight, standing as he had left them on the shore, the shortest in the middle, the tallest on the right, the middle one on the left. As soon as the bishop had reached the vessel and got on board, the anchor was weighed and the sails unfurled. The wind filled them and the ship sailed away, and the bishop took a seat in the stern and watched the island they had left. For a time he could still see the hermits, but presently they disappeared from sight, though the island was still visible. At last it too vanished, and only the sea was to be seen, rippling in the moonlight.

The pilgrims lay down to sleep, and all was quiet on deck. The bishop did not wish to sleep, but sat alone at the stern, gazing at the sea where the island was no longer visible, and thinking of the good old men. He thought how pleased they had been to learn the Lord's Prayer; and he thanked God for having sent him to teach and help such godly men.

So the bishop sat, thinking, and gazing at the sea where the island had disappeared. And the moonlight flickered before his eyes, sparkling, now here, now there, upon the waves. Suddenly he saw something white and shining, on the bright path which the moon cast across the sea. Was it a seagull, or the little gleaming sail of some small boat? The bishop fixed his eyes on it, wondering.

"It must be a boat sailing after us," thought he, "but it is overtaking us very rapidly. It was far, far away a minute ago, but now it is much nearer. It cannot be a boat, for I can see no sail; but whatever it may be, it is following us, and catching us up."

And he could not make out what it was. Not a boat, nor a bird, nor a fish! It was too large for a man, and besides a man could not be out there in the midst of the sea. The bishop rose, and said to the helmsman:

"Look there, what is that, my friend? What is it?" the bishop repeated, though he could now see plainly what it was—the three hermits running upon the water, all gleaming white, their grey beards shining, and approaching the ship as quickly as though it were not moving.

The steersman looked, and let go the helm in terror.

"Oh Lord! The hermits are running after us on the water as though it were dry land!"

The passengers, hearing him, jumped up and crowded to the stern. They saw the hermits coming along hand in hand, and the two outer ones beckoning the ship to stop. All three were gliding along upon the water without moving their feet. Before the ship could be stopped, the hermits had reached it, and raising their heads, all three as with one voice, began to say:

"We have forgotten your teaching, servant of God. As long as we kept repeating it we remembered, but when we stopped saying it for a time, a word dropped out, and now it has all gone to pieces. We can remember nothing of it. Teach us again."

The bishop crossed himself, and leaning over the ship's side, said:

"Your own prayer will reach the Lord, men of God. It is not for me to teach you. Pray for us sinners."

And the bishop bowed low before the old men; and they turned and went back across the sea. And a light shone until daybreak on the spot where they were lost to sight.

The Devil

But I say unto you, that every one that looketh on a woman to lust after her hath committed adultery with her already in his heart.

And if thy right eye causeth thee to stumble, pluck it out, and cast it from thee: for it is profitable for thee that one of thy members should perish, and not thy whole body be cast into hell.

And if thy right hand causeth thee to stumble, cut it off, and cast it from thee: for it is profitable for thee that one of thy members should perish, and not thy whole body go into hell.—*Matt.* v. 28, 29, 30

I

A BRILLIANT career lay before Eugene Irtenev. He had everything necessary to attain it: an admirable education at home, high honors when he graduated in law at Petersburg University, and connections in the highest society through his recently deceased father; he had also already begun service in one of the ministries under the protection of the minister. Moreover he had a fortune; even a large one, though insecure. His father had lived abroad and in Petersburg, allowing his sons, Eugene and Andrew (who was older than Eugene and in the Horse Guards), six thousand rubles a year each, while he himself and his wife spent a great deal. He only used to visit his estate for a couple of months in summer and did not concern himself with its direction, entrusting it all to an unscrupulous manager who also failed to attend to it, but in whom he had complete confidence.

After the father's death, when the brothers began to divide the property, so many debts were discovered that their lawyer even advised them to refuse the inheritance and retain only an estate left them by their grandmother, which was valued at a hundred thousand rubles. But a neighboring landed proprietor who had done business with old Irtenev, that is to say, who had promissory notes from him and had come to Petersburg on that account, said that in spite of the debts they could straighten out affairs so as to retain a large fortune (it would only be necessary to sell the forest and some outlying land, retaining the rich

Semyonov estate with four thousand desyatins[1] of black earth, the sugar factory, and two hundred desyatins of water meadows) if one devoted oneself to the management of the estate, settled there, and farmed it wisely and economically.

And so, having visited the estate in spring (his father had died in Lent), Eugene looked into everything, resolved to retire from the civil service, settle in the country with his mother, and undertake the management with the object of preserving the main estate. He arranged with his brother, with whom he was very friendly, that he would pay him either four thousand rubles a year, or a lump sum of eighty thousand, for which Andrew would hand over to him his share of his inheritance.

So he arranged matters and, having settled down with his mother in the big house, began managing the estate eagerly, yet cautiously.

It is generally supposed that Conservatives are usually old people, and that those in favor of change are the young. That is not quite correct. Usually Conservatives are young people: those who want to live but who do not think about how to live, and have not time to think, and therefore take as a model for themselves a way of life that they have seen.

Thus it was with Eugene. Having settled in the village, his aim and ideal was to restore the form of life that had existed, not in his father's time— his father had been a bad manager—but in his grandfather's. And now he tried to resurrect the general spirit of his grandfather's life—in the house, the garden, and in the estate management—of course with changes suited to the times—everything on a large scale—good order, method, and everybody satisfied. But to do this entailed much work. It was necessary to meet the demands of the creditors and the banks, and for that purpose to sell some land and arrange renewals of credit. It was also necessary to get money to carry on (partly by farming out land, and partly by hiring labor) the immense operations on the Semyonov estate, with its four hundred desyatins of ploughland and its sugar factory, and to deal with the garden so that it should not seem to be neglected or in decay.

There was much work to do, but Eugene had plenty of strength— physical and mental. He was twenty-six, of medium height, strongly built, with muscles developed by gymnastics. He was full-blooded and his whole neck was very red, his teeth and lips were bright, and his hair soft and curly though not thick. His only physical defect was short-sightedness, which he had himself developed by using spectacles, so that he could not now do without a pince-nez, which had already formed a line on the bridge of his nose.

Such he was physically. For his spiritual portrait it might be said that the better people knew him the better they liked him. His mother had

---

[1][A desyatin (more properly, desyatina) is about 2.7 acres.]

always loved him more than anyone else, and now after her husband's death she concentrated on him not only her whole affection but her whole life. Nor was it only his mother who so loved him. All his comrades at the high school and the university not merely liked him very much, but respected him. He had this effect on all who met him. It was impossible not to believe what he said, impossible to suspect any deception or falseness in one who had such an open, honest face and in particular such eyes.

In general his personality helped him much in his affairs. A creditor who would have refused another trusted him. The clerk, the village elder, or a peasant, who would have played a dirty trick and cheated someone else, forgot to deceive under the pleasant impression of intercourse with this kindly, agreeable, and above all candid man.

It was the end of May. Eugene had somehow managed in town to get the vacant land freed from the mortgage, so as to sell it to a merchant, and had borrowed money from that same merchant to replenish his stock, that is to say, to procure horses, bulls, and carts, and in particular to begin to build a necessary farmhouse. The matter had been arranged. The timber was being carted, the carpenters were already at work, and manure for the estate was being brought on eighty carts, but everything still hung by a thread.

II

Amid these cares something came about which though unimportant tormented Eugene at the time. As a young man he had lived as all healthy young men live, that is, he had had relations with women of various kinds. He was not a libertine but neither, as he himself said, was he a monk. He only turned to this, however, in so far as was necessary for physical health and to have his mind free, as he used to say. This had begun when he was sixteen and had gone on satisfactorily—in the sense that he had never given himself up to debauchery, never once been infatuated, and had never contracted a disease. At first he had had a seamstress in Petersburg, then she got spoilt and he made other arrangements, and that side of his affairs was so well secured that it did not trouble him.

But now he was living in the country for the second month and did not at all know what he was to do. Compulsory self-restraint was beginning to have a bad effect on him.

Must he really go to town for that purpose? And where to? How? That was the only thing that disturbed him; but as he was convinced that the thing was necessary and that he needed it, it really became a necessity, and he felt that he was not free and that his eyes involuntarily followed every young woman.

He did not approve of having relations with a married woman or a maid in his own village. He knew by report that both his father and grandfather had been quite different in this matter from other landowners of that time. At home they had never had any entanglements with peasant women, and he had decided that he would not do so either; but afterwards, feeling himself ever more and more under compulsion and imagining with horror what might happen to him in the neighboring country town, and reflecting on the fact that the days of serfdom were now over, he decided that it might be done on the spot. Only it must be done so that no one should know of it, and not for the sake of debauchery but merely for health's sake—as he said to himself. And when he had decided this he became still more restless. When talking to the village Elder, the peasants, or the carpenters, he involuntarily brought the conversation round to women, and when it turned to women he kept it on that theme. He noticed the women more and more.

III

To settle the matter in his own mind was one thing but to carry it out was another. To approach a woman himself was impossible. Which one? Where? It must be done through someone else, but to whom should he speak about it?

He happened to go into a watchman's hut in the forest to get a drink of water. The watchman had been his father's huntsman, and Eugene Ivanich chatted with him, and the man began telling some strange tales of hunting sprees. It occurred to Eugene Ivanich that it would be convenient to arrange matters in this hut, or in the wood, only he did not know how to manage it and whether old Daniel would undertake the arrangement. "Perhaps he will be horrified at such a proposal and I shall have disgraced myself, but perhaps he will agree to it quite simply." So he thought while listening to Daniel's stories. Daniel was telling how once when they had been stopping at the hut of the sexton's wife in an outlying field, he had brought a woman for Fyodor Zakharich Pryanishnikov.

"It will be all right," thought Eugene.

"Your father, may the kingdom of heaven be his, did not go in for nonsense of that kind."

"It won't do," thought Eugene. But to test the matter he said: "How was it you engaged on such bad things?"

"But what was there bad in it? She was glad, and Fyodor Zakharich was satisfied, very satisfied. I got a ruble. Why, what was he to do? He too is a lively limb apparently, and drinks wine."

"Yes, I may speak," thought Eugene, and at once proceeded to do so.

"And do you know, Daniel, I don't know how to endure it,"—he felt himself going scarlet.

Daniel smiled.

"I am not a monk—I have been accustomed to it."

He felt that what he was saying was stupid, but was glad to see that Daniel approved.

"Why of course, you should have told me long ago. It can all be arranged," said he: "only tell me which one you want."

"Oh, it is really all the same to me. Of course not an ugly one, and she must be healthy."

"I understand!" said Daniel briefly. He reflected.

"Ah! There is a tasty morsel," he began. Again Eugene went red. "A tasty morsel. See here, she was married last autumn." Daniel whispered—"and he hasn't been able to do anything. Think what that is worth to one who wants it!"

Eugene even frowned with shame.

"No, no," he said. "I don't want that at all. I want, on the contrary (what could the contrary be?), on the contrary I only want that she should be healthy and that there should be as little fuss as possible—a woman whose husband is away in the army or something of that kind."

"I know. It's Stepanida I must bring you. Her husband is away in town, just the same as a soldier. And she is a fine woman, and clean. You will be satisfied. As it is I was saying to her the other day—you should go, but she . . ."

"Well then, when is it to be?"

"Tomorrow if you like. I shall be going to get some tobacco and I will call in, and at the dinner hour come here, or to the bathhouse behind the kitchen garden. There will be nobody about. Besides after dinner everybody takes a nap."

"All right then."

A terrible excitement seized Eugene as he rode home. "What will happen? What is a peasant woman like? Suppose it turns out that she is hideous, horrible? No, she is handsome," he told himself, remembering some he had been noticing. "But what shall I say? What shall I do?"

He was not himself all that day. Next day at noon he went to the forester's hut. Daniel stood at the door and silently and significantly nodded towards the wood. The blood rushed to Eugene's heart, he was conscious of it and went to the kitchen garden. No one was there. He went to the bathhouse—there was no one about, he looked in, came out, and suddenly heard the crackling of a breaking twig. He looked round—and she was standing in the thicket beyond the little ravine. He rushed there across the ravine. There were nettles in it which he had not noticed. They stung him and, losing the pince-nez from his nose, he ran up the slope on the farther side. She stood there, in a white embroidered apron, a red-brown skirt, and a bright red kerchief, barefoot, fresh, firm, and handsome, and smiling shyly.

"There is a path leading round—you should have gone round," she said. "I came long ago, ever so long."

He went up to her and, looking her over, touched her.

A quarter of an hour later they separated; he found his pince-nez, called in to see Daniel, and in reply to his question: "Are you satisfied, master?" gave him a ruble and went home.

He was satisfied. Only at first had he felt ashamed, then it had passed off. And everything had gone well. The best thing was that he now felt at ease, tranquil and vigorous. As for her, he had not even seen her thoroughly. He remembered that she was clean, fresh, not bad-looking, and simple, without any pretence. "Whose wife is she?" said he to himself. "Pechnikov's, Daniel said. What Pechnikov is that? There are two households of that name. Probably she is old Michael's daughter-in-law. Yes, that must be it. His son does live in Moscow. I'll ask Daniel about it some time."

From then onward that previously important drawback to country life—enforced self-restraint—was eliminated. Eugene's freedom of mind was no longer disturbed and he was able to attend freely to his affairs.

And the matter Eugene had undertaken was far from easy: before he had time to stop up one hole a new one would unexpectedly show itself, and it sometimes seemed to him that he would not be able to go through with it and that it would end in his having to sell the estate after all, which would mean that all his efforts would be wasted and that he had failed to accomplish what he had undertaken. That prospect disturbed him most of all.

All this time more and more debts of his father's unexpectedly came to light. It was evident that towards the end of his life he had borrowed right and left. At the time of the settlement in May, Eugene had thought he at least knew everything, but in the middle of the summer he suddenly received a letter from which it appeared that there was still a debt of twelve thousand rubles to the widow Esipova. There was no promissory note, but only an ordinary receipt which his lawyer told him could be disputed. But it did not enter Eugene's head to refuse to pay a debt of his father's merely because the document could be challenged. He only wanted to know for certain whether there had been such a debt.

"Mamma! Who is Kaleriya Vladimirovna Esipova?" he asked his mother when they met as usual for dinner.

"Esipova? She was brought up by your grandfather. Why?"

Eugene told his mother about the letter.

"I wonder she is not ashamed to ask for it. Your father gave her so much!"

"But do we owe her this?"

"Well now, how shall I put it? It is not a debt. Papa, out of his unbounded kindness . . ."

"Yes, but did Papa consider it a debt?"

"I cannot say. I don't know. I only know it is hard enough for you without that."

Eugene saw that Mary Pavlovna did not know what to say, and was as it were sounding him.

"I see from what you say that it must be paid," said he. "I will go to see her tomorrow and have a chat, and see if it cannot be deferred."

"Ah, how sorry I am for you, but you know that will be best. Tell her she must wait," said Mary Pavlovna, evidently tranquilized and proud of her son's decision.

Eugene's position was particularly hard because his mother, who was living with him, did not at all realize his position. She had been so accustomed all her life long to live extravagantly that she could not even imagine to herself the position her son was in, that is to say, that today or tomorrow matters might shape themselves so that they would have nothing left and he would have to sell everything and live and support his mother on what salary he could earn, which at the very most would be two thousand rubles. She did not understand that they could only save themselves from that position by cutting down expense in everything, and so she could not understand why Eugene was so careful about trifles, in expenditure on gardeners, coachmen, servants—even on food. Also, like most widows, she nourished feelings of devotion to the memory of her departed spouse quite different from those she had felt for him while he lived, and she did not admit the thought that anything the departed had done or arranged could be wrong or could be altered.

Eugene by great efforts managed to keep up the garden and the conservatory with two gardeners, and the stables with two coachmen. And Mary Pavlovna naively thought that she was sacrificing herself for her son and doing all a mother could do, by not complaining of the food which the old man-cook prepared, of the fact that the paths in the park were not all swept clean, and that instead of footmen they had only a boy.

So, too, concerning this new debt, in which Eugene saw an almost crushing blow to all his undertakings, Mary Pavlovna only saw an incident displaying Eugene's noble nature. Moreover she did not feel much anxiety about Eugene's position, because she was confident that he would make a brilliant marriage which would put everything right. And he could make a very brilliant marriage: she knew a dozen families who would be glad to give their daughters to him. And she wished to arrange the matter as soon as possible.

IV

Eugene himself dreamt of marriage, but not in the same way as his mother. The idea of using marriage as a means of putting his affairs in order was repulsive to him. He wished to marry honorably, for love. He observed the girls whom he met and those he knew, and compared himself with them, but no decision had yet been taken. Meanwhile, contrary to his expectations, his relations with Stepanida continued, and even acquired the character of a settled affair. Eugene was so far from debauchery, it was so hard for him secretly to do this thing which he felt to be bad, that he could not arrange these meetings himself and even after the first one hoped not to see Stepanida again; but it turned out that after some time the same restlessness (due he believed to that cause) again overcame him. And his restlessness this time was no longer impersonal, but suggested just those same bright, black eyes, and that deep voice, saying, "ever so long," that same scent of something fresh and strong, and that same full breast lifting the bib of her apron, and all this in that hazel and maple thicket, bathed in bright sunlight.

Though he felt ashamed he again approached Daniel. And again a rendezvous was fixed for midday in the wood. This time Eugene looked her over more carefully and everything about her seemed attractive. He tried talking to her and asked about her husband. He really was Michael's son and lived as a coachman in Moscow.

"Well, then, how is it you . . ." Eugene wanted to ask how it was she was untrue to him.

"What about 'how is it'?" asked she. Evidently she was clever and quick-witted.

"Well, how is it you come to me?"

"There now," said she merrily. "I bet he goes on the spree there. Why shouldn't I?"

Evidently she was putting on an air of sauciness and assurance, and this seemed charming to Eugene. But all the same he did not himself fix a rendezvous with her. Even when she proposed that they should meet without the aid of Daniel, to whom she seemed not very well disposed, he did not consent. He hoped that this meeting would be the last. He liked her. He thought such intercourse was necessary for him and that there was nothing bad about it, but in the depth of his soul there was a stricter judge who did not approve of it and hoped that this would be the last time, or if he did not hope that, at any rate did not wish to participate in arrangements to repeat it another time.

So the whole summer passed, during which they met a dozen times and always by Daniel's help. It happened once that she could not be there because her husband had come home, and Daniel proposed another woman, but Eugene refused with disgust. Then the husband went away and the meetings continued as before, at first through Daniel, but afterwards he simply fixed the time and she came with another woman, Prokhorova—as it would not do for a peasant woman to go about alone.

Once at the very time fixed for the rendezvous a family came to call on Mary Pavlovna, with the very girl she wished Eugene to marry, and it was impossible for Eugene to get away. As soon as he could do so, he went out as though to the thrashing floor, and round by the path to their meeting place in the wood. She was not there, but at the accustomed spot everything within reach had been broken—the black alder, the hazeltwigs, and even a young maple the thickness of a stake. She had waited, had become excited and angry, and had skittishly left him a remembrance. He waited and waited, and then went to Daniel to ask him to call her for tomorrow. She came and was just as usual.

So the summer passed. The meetings were always arranged in the wood, and only once, when it grew towards autumn, in the shed that stood in her backyard.

It did not enter Eugene's head that these relations of his had any importance for him. About her he did not even think. He gave her money and nothing more. At first he did not know and did not think that the affair was known and that she was envied throughout the village, or that her relations took money from her and encouraged her, and that her conception of any sin in the matter had been quite obliterated by the influence of the money and her family's approval. It seemed to her that if people envied her, then what she was doing was good.

"It is simply necessary for my health," thought Eugene. "I grant it is not right, and though no one says anything, everybody, or many people, know of it. The woman who comes with her knows. And once she knows she is sure to have told others. But what's to be done? I am acting badly," thought Eugene, "but what's one to do? Anyhow it is not for long."

What chiefly disturbed Eugene was the thought of the husband. At first for some reason it seemed to him that the husband must be a poor sort, and this as it were partly justified his conduct. But he saw the husband and was struck by his appearance: he was a fine fellow and smartly dressed, in no way a worse man than himself, but surely better. At their next meeting he told her he had seen her husband and had been surprised to see that he was such a fine fellow.

"There's not another man like him in the village," said she proudly.

This surprised Eugene, and the thought of the husband tormented him still more after that. He happened to be at Daniel's one day and Daniel, having begun chatting, said to him quite openly:

"And Michael asked me the other day: 'Is it true that the master is living with my wife?' I said I did not know. 'Anyway,' I said, 'better with the master than with a peasant.'"

"Well, and what did he say?"

"He said: 'Wait a bit. I'll get to know and I'll give it her all the same.'"

"Yes, if the husband returned to live here I would give her up," thought Eugene.

But the husband lived in town and for the present their intercourse continued.

"When necessary I will break it off, and there will be nothing left of it," thought he.

And this seemed to him certain, especially as during the whole summer many different things occupied him very fully: the erection of the new farmhouse, and the harvest, and building, and above all meeting the debts and selling the wasteland. All these were affairs that completely absorbed him and on which he spent his thoughts when he lay down and when he got up. All that was real life. His intercourse—he did not even call it connection—with Stepanida he paid no attention to. It is true that when the wish to see her arose it came with such strength that he could think of nothing else. But this did not last long. A meeting was arranged, and he again forgot her for a week or even for a month.

In autumn Eugene often rode to town, and there became friendly with the Annenskis. They had a daughter who had just finished the Institute. And then, to Mary Pavlovna's great grief, it happened that Eugene "cheapened himself," as she expressed it, by falling in love with Liza Annenskaya and proposing to her.

From that time his relations with Stepanida ceased.

V

It is impossible to explain why Eugene chose Liza Annenskaya, as it is always impossible to explain why a man chooses this and not that woman. There were many reasons—positive and negative. One reason was that she was not a very rich heiress such as his mother sought for him, another that she was naive and to be pitied in her relations with her mother, another that she was not a beauty who attracted general attention to herself, and yet she was not bad-looking. But the chief reason was that his acquaintance with her began at the time when he was ripe for marriage. He fell in love because he knew that he would marry.

Liza Annenskaya was at first merely pleasing to Eugene, but when he decided to make her his wife his feelings for her became much stronger. He felt that he was in love.

Liza was tall, slender, and long. Everything about her was long; her face, and her nose (not prominently but downwards), and her fingers, and her feet. The color of her face was very delicate, creamy white and delicately pink; she had long, soft, and curly, light-brown hair, and beautiful eyes, clear, mild, and confiding. Those eyes especially struck Eugene, and when he thought of Liza he always saw those clear, mild, confiding eyes.

Such was she physically; he knew nothing of her spiritually, but only saw those eyes. And those eyes seemed to tell him all he needed to know. The meaning of their expression was this:

While still in the Institute, when she was fifteen, Liza used continually to fall in love with all the attractive men she met and was animated and happy only when she was in love. After leaving the Institute she continued to fall in love in just the same way with all the young men she met, and of course fell in love with Eugene as soon as she made his acquaintance. It was this being in love which gave her eyes that particular expression which so captivated Eugene. Already that winter she had been in love with two young men at one and the same time, and blushed and became excited not only when they entered the room but whenever their names were mentioned. But afterwards, when her mother hinted to her that Irtenev seemed to have serious intentions, her love for him increased so that she became almost indifferent to the two previous attractions, and when Irtenev began to come to their balls and parties and danced with her more than with others and evidently only wished to know whether she loved him, her love for him became painful. She dreamed of him in her sleep and seemed to see him when she was awake in a dark room, and everyone else vanished from her mind. But when he proposed and they were formally engaged, and when they had kissed one another and were a betrothed couple, then she had no thoughts but of him, no desire but to be with him, to love him, and to be loved by him. She was also proud of him and felt emotional about him and herself and her love, and quite melted and felt faint from love of him.

The more he got to know her the more he loved her. He had not at all expected to find such love, and it strengthened his own feeling still more.

VI

Towards spring he went to his estate at Semyonovskoye to have a look at it and to give directions about the management, and especially about the house which was being done up for his wedding.

Mary Pavlovna was dissatisfied with her son's choice, not only because the match was not as brilliant as it might have been, but also because she did not like Varvara Alexeyevna, his future mother-in-law. Whether she was good-natured or not she did not know and could not decide, but that she was not well-bred, not *comme il faut*—"not a lady" as Mary Pavlovna said to herself—she saw from their first acquaintance, and this distressed her; distressed her because she was accustomed to value breeding and knew that Eugene was sensitive to it, and she foresaw that he would suffer much annoyance on this account. But she liked the girl. Liked her chiefly because Eugene did. One could not help loving her, and Mary Pavlovna was quite sincerely ready to do so.

Eugene found his mother contented and in good spirits. She was getting everything straight in the house and preparing to go away herself as soon as he brought his young wife. Eugene persuaded her to stay for the time being, and the future remained undecided.

In the evening after tea Mary Pavlovna played patience as usual. Eugene sat by, helping her. This was the hour of their most intimate talks. Having finished one game and while preparing to begin another, she looked up at him and, with a little hesitation, began thus:

"I wanted to tell you, Jenya—of course I do not know, but in general I wanted to suggest to you—that before your wedding it is absolutely necessary to have finished with all your bachelor affairs so that nothing may disturb either you or your wife. God forbid that it should. You understand me?"

And indeed Eugene at once understood that Mary Pavlovna was hinting at his relations with Stepanida which had ended in the previous autumn, and that she attributed much more importance to those relations than they deserved, as solitary women always do. Eugene blushed, not from shame so much as from vexation that good-natured Mary Pavlovna was bothering—out of affection no doubt, but still was bothering—about matters that were not her business and that she did not and could not understand. He answered that there was nothing that needed concealment, and that he had always conducted himself so that there should be nothing to hinder his marrying.

"Well, dear, that is excellent. Only, Jenya . . . don't be vexed with me," said Mary Pavlovna, and broke off in confusion.

Eugene saw that she had not finished and had not said what she wanted to. And this was confirmed, when a little later she began to tell him how, in his absence, she had been asked to stand godmother at . . . the Pechnikovs.

Eugene flushed again, not with vexation or shame this time, but with some strange consciousness of the importance of what was about to be told him—an involuntary consciousness quite at variance with his conclusions. And what he expected happened. Mary Pavlovna, as if merely by way of conversation, mentioned that this year only boys were being born—evidently a sign of a coming war. Both at the Vasins and the Pechnikovs the young wife had a first child—at each house a boy. Mary Pavlovna wanted to say this casually, but she herself felt ashamed when she saw the color mount to her son's face and saw him nervously removing, tapping, and replacing his pince-nez and hurriedly lighting a cigarette. She became silent. He too was silent and could not think how to break that silence. So they both understood that they had understood one another.

"Yes, the chief thing is that there should be justice and no favoritism in the village—as under your grandfather."

"Mamma," said Eugene suddenly, "I know why you are saying this. You have no need to be disturbed. My future family life is so sacred to me that I should not infringe it in any case. And as to what occurred in my bachelor days, that is quite ended. I never formed any union and no one has any claims on me."

"Well, I am glad," said his mother. "I know how noble your feelings are."

Eugene accepted his mother's words as a tribute due to him, and did not reply.

Next day he drove to town thinking of his fiancee and of anything in the world except of Stepanida. But, as if purposely to remind him, on approaching the church he met people walking and driving back from it. He met old Matvey with Simon, some lads and girls, and then two women, one elderly, the other, who seemed familiar, smartly dressed and wearing a bright-red kerchief. This woman was walking lightly and boldly, carrying a child in her arms. He came up to them, and the elder woman bowed, stopping in the old-fashioned way, but the young woman with the child only bent her head, and from under the kerchief gleamed familiar, merry, smiling eyes.

Yes, this was she, but all that was over and it was no use looking at her: "and the child may be mine," flashed through his mind. No, what nonsense! There was her husband, she used to see him. He did not even consider the matter further, so settled in his mind was it that it had been necessary for his health—he had paid her money and there was no more to be said; there was, there had been, and there could be, no question of any union between them. It was not that he stifled the voice of conscience, no—his conscience simply said nothing to him. And he thought no more about her after the conversation with his mother and this meeting. Nor did he meet her again.

Eugene was married in town the week after Easter, and left at once with his young wife for his country estate. The house had been arranged as usual for a young couple. Mary Pavlovna wished to leave, but Eugene begged her to remain, and Liza still more strongly, and she only moved into a detached wing of the house.

And so a new life began for Eugene.

VII

The first year of his marriage was a hard one for Eugene. It was hard because affairs he had managed to put off during the time of his courtship now, after his marriage, all came upon him at once.

To escape from debts was impossible. An outlying part of the estate was sold and the most pressing obligations met, but others remained, and he had no money. The estate yielded a good revenue, but he had had to send payments to his brother and to spend on his own marriage, so that there was no ready money and the factory could not carry on and would have to be closed down. The only way of escape was to use his wife's money; and Liza, having realized her husband's position, insisted on this herself. Eugene agreed, but only on condition that he should give her a mortgage on half his estate, which he did. Of course this was done not for his wife's sake, who felt offended at it, but to appease his mother-in-law.

These affairs with various fluctuations of success and failure helped to poison Eugene's life that first year. Another thing was his wife's ill-health. That same first year, seven months after their marriage, a misfortune befell Liza. She was driving out to meet her husband on his return from town, and the quiet horse became rather playful and she was frightened and jumped out. Her jump was comparatively fortunate—she might have been caught by the wheel—but she was pregnant, and that same night the pains began and she had a miscarriage from which she was long in recovering. The loss of the expected child and his wife's illness, together with the disorder in his affairs, and above all the presence of his mother-in-law, who arrived as soon as Liza fell ill—all this together made the year still harder for Eugene.

But notwithstanding these difficult circumstances, towards the end of the first year Eugene felt very well. First of all his cherished hope of restoring his fallen fortune and renewing his grandfather's way of life in a new form, was approaching accomplishment, though slowly and with difficulty. There was no longer any question of having to sell the whole estate to meet the debts. The chief estate, though transferred to his wife's name, was saved, and if only the beet crop succeeded and the price kept up, by next year his position of want and stress might be replaced by one of complete prosperity. That was one thing.

Another was that however much he had expected from his wife, he had never expected to find in her what he actually found. He found not what he had expected, but something much better. Raptures of love—though he tried to produce them—did not take place or were very slight, but he discovered something quite different, namely that he was not merely more cheerful and happier but that it had become easier to live. He did not know why this should be so, but it was.

And it was so because immediately after marriage his wife decided that Eugene Irtenev was superior to anyone else in the world: wiser, purer, and nobler than they, and that therefore it was right for everyone to serve him and please him; but that as it was impossible to make everyone do this, she must do it herself to the limit of her strength. And she did; directing all her strength of mind towards learning and guessing what he liked, and then doing just that thing, whatever it was and however difficult it might be.

She had the gift which furnishes the chief delight of intercourse with a loving woman: thanks to her love of her husband she penetrated into his soul. She knew his every state and his every shade of feeling—better it seemed to him than he himself—and she behaved correspondingly and therefore never hurt his feelings, but always lessened his distresses and strengthened his joys. And she understood not only his feelings but also his joys. Things quite foreign to her—concerning the farming, the factory, or the appraisement of others—she immediately understood so that she could not merely converse with him, but could often, as he himself said, be a useful and irreplaceable counsellor. She regarded affairs and people and everything in the world only though his eyes. She loved her mother, but having seen that Eugene disliked his mother-in-law's interference in their life she immediately took her husband's side, and did so with such decision that he had to restrain her.

Besides all this she had very good taste, much tact, and above all she had repose. All that she did, she did unnoticed; only the results of what she did were observable, namely, that always and in everything there was cleanliness, order, and elegance. Liza had at once understood in what her husband's ideal of life consisted, and she tried to attain, and in the arrangement and order of the house did attain, what he wanted. Children it is true were lacking, but there was hope of that also. In winter she went to Petersburg to see a specialist and he assured them that she was quite well and could have children.

And this desire was accomplished. By the end of the year she was again pregnant.

The one thing that threatened, not to say poisoned, their happiness was her jealousy—a jealousy she restrained and did not exhibit, but from which she often suffered. Not only might Eugene not love any other woman—because there was not a woman on earth worthy of him (as to whether she herself was worthy or not she never asked herself)—but not a single woman might therefore dare to love him.

VIII

This was how they lived: he rose early, as he always had done, and went to see to the farm or the factory where work was going on, or sometimes to the fields. Towards ten o'clock he would come back for his coffee, which they had on the veranda: Mary Pavlovna, an uncle who lived with them, and Liza. After a conversation which was often very animated while they drank their coffee, they dispersed till dinnertime. At two o'clock they dined and then went for a walk or a drive. In the evening when he returned from his office they drank their evening tea and sometimes he read aloud while she worked, or when there were guests they had music or conversation. When he went away on business he wrote to his wife and received letters from her every day. Sometimes she accompanied him, and then they were particularly merry. On his name day and on hers guests assembled, and it pleased him to see how well she managed to arrange things so that everybody enjoyed coming. He saw and heard that they all admired her—the young, agreeable hostess—and he loved her still more for this.

All went excellently. She bore her pregnancy easily and, though they were afraid, they both began making plans as to how they would bring the child up. The system of education and the arrangements were all decided by Eugene, and her only wish was to carry out his desires obediently. Eugene on his part read up medical works and intended to bring the child up according to all the precepts of science. She of course agreed to everything and made preparations, making warm and also cool "envelopes," and preparing a cradle. Thus the second year of their marriage arrived and the second spring.

IX

It was just before Trinity Sunday. Liza was in her fifth month, and though careful she was still brisk and active. Both his mother and hers were living in the house, but under pretext of watching and safeguarding her only upset her by their tiffs. Eugene was specially engrossed with a new experiment for the cultivation of sugar beet on a large scale.

Just before Trinity Liza decided it was necessary to have a thorough house-cleaning as it had not been done since Easter, and she hired two women by the day to help the servants wash the floors and windows, beat the furniture and the carpets, and put covers on them. These women came early in the morning, heated the coppers, and set to work. One of the two was Stepanida, who had just weaned her baby boy and had begged for the job of washing the floors through the office clerk—whom she now carried on with. She wanted to have a good look at the new mistress. Stepanida was living by herself as formerly, her husband being away, and she was up to tricks as she had formerly been first with old Daniel (who had once caught her taking some logs of firewood), afterwards with the master, and now with the young clerk. She was not concerning herself any longer about her master. "He has a wife now," she thought. But it would be good to have a look at the lady and at her establishment: folk said it was well arranged.

Eugene had not seen her since he had met her with the child. Having a baby to attend to she had not been going out to work, and he seldom walked through the village. That morning, on the eve of Trinity Sunday, he got up at five o'clock and rode to the fallow land which was to be sprinkled with phosphates, and had left the house before the women were about, and while they were still engaged lighting the copper fires.

He returned to breakfast merry, contented, and hungry; dismounting from his mare at the gate and handing her over to the gardener. Flicking the high grass with his whip and repeating a phrase he had just uttered, as one often does, he walked towards the house. The phrase was: "phosphates justify"—what or to whom, he neither knew nor reflected.

They were beating a carpet on the grass. The furniture had been brought out.

"There now! What a house-cleaning Liza has undertaken! . . . Phosphates justify. . . .What a manageress she is! A manageress! Yes, a manageress," said he to himself, vividly imagining her in her white wrapper and with her smiling joyful face, as it nearly always was when he looked at her. "Yes, I must change my boots, or else 'phosphates justify,' that is, smell of manure, and the manageress is in such a condition. Why 'in such a condition'? Because a new little Irtenev is growing there inside her," he thought. "Yes, phosphates justify," and smiling at his thoughts he put his hand to the door of his room.

But he had not time to push the door before it opened of itself and he came face to face with a woman coming towards him carrying a pail, barefoot and with sleeves turned up high. He stepped aside to let her pass and she too stepped aside, adjusting her kerchief with a wet hand.

"Go on, go on, I won't go in, if you . . ." began Eugene and suddenly stopped, recognizing her.

She glanced merrily at him with smiling eyes, and pulling down her skirt went out at the door.

"What nonsense! . . . It is impossible," said Eugene to himself, frowning and waving his hand as though to get rid of a fly, displeased at having noticed her. He was vexed that he had noticed her and yet he could not take his eyes from her strong body, swayed by her agile strides, from her bare feet, or from her arms and shoulders, and the pleasing folds of her shirt and the handsome skirt tucked up high above her white calves.

"But why am I looking?" said he to himself, lowering his eyes so as not to see her. "And anyhow I must go in to get some other boots." And he turned back to go into his own room, but had not gone five steps before he again glanced round to have another look at her without knowing why or wherefore. She was just going round the corner and also glanced at him.

"Ah, what am I doing!" said he to himself. "She may think . . . It is even certain that she already does think . . ."

He entered his damp room. Another woman, an old and skinny one, was there, and was still washing it. Eugene passed on tiptoe across the floor, wet with dirty water, to the wall where his boots stood, and he was about to leave the room when the woman herself went out.

"This one has gone and the other, Stepanida, will come here alone," someone within him began to reflect.

"My God, what am I thinking of and what am I doing!" He seized his boots and ran out with them into the hall, put them on there, brushed himself, and went out onto the veranda where both the mammas were already drinking coffee. Liza had evidently been expecting him and came onto the veranda through another door at the same time.

"My God! If she, who considers me so honorable, pure, and inno- cent—if she only knew!"—thought he.

Liza as usual met him with shining face. But today somehow she seemed to him particularly pale, yellow, long, and weak.

X

During coffee, as often happened, a peculiarly feminine kind of conver- sation went on which had no logical sequence but which evidently was connected in some way for it went on uninterruptedly.

The two old ladies were pin-pricking one another, and Liza was skill- fully maneuvering between them.

"I am so vexed that we had not finished washing your room before you got back," she said to her husband. "But I do so want to get every- thing arranged."

"Well, did you sleep well after I got up?"

"Yes, I slept well and I feel well."

"How can a woman be well in her condition during this intolerable heat, when her windows face the sun," said Varvara Alexeyevna, her mother. "And they have no venetian blinds or awnings. I always had awnings."

"But you know we are in the shade after ten o'clock," said Mary Pavlovna.

"That's what causes fever; it comes of dampness," said Varvara Alexeyevna, not noticing that what she was saying did not agree with what she had just said. "My doctor always says that it is impossible to diagnose an illness unless one knows the patient. And he certainly knows, for he is the leading physician and we pay him a hundred rubles a visit. My late hus- band did not believe in doctors, but he did not grudge me anything."

"How can a man grudge anything to a woman when perhaps her life and the child's depend . . ."

"Yes, when she has means a wife need not depend on her husband. A good wife submits to her husband," said Varvara Alexeyevna—"only Liza is too weak after her illness."

"Oh no, mamma, I feel quite well. But why have they not brought you any boiled cream?"

"I don't want any. I can do with raw cream."

"I offered some to Varvara Alexeyevna, but she declined," said Mary Pavlovna, as if justifying herself.

"No, I don't want any today." And as if to terminate an unpleasant conversation and yield magnanimously, Varvara Alexeyevna turned to Eugene and said: "Well, and have you sprinkled the phosphates?"

Liza ran to fetch the cream.

"But I don't want it. I don't want it."

"Liza, Liza, go gently," said Mary Pavlovna. "Such rapid movements do her harm."

"Nothing does harm if one's mind is at peace," said Varvara Alexeyevna as if referring to something, though she knew that there was nothing her words could refer to.

Liza returned with the cream and Eugene drank his coffee and listened morosely. He was accustomed to these conversations, but today he was particularly annoyed by its lack of sense. He wanted to think over what had happened to him but this chatter disturbed him. Having finished her coffee Varvara Alexeyevna went away in a bad humor. Liza, Eugene, and Mary Pavlovna stayed behind, and their conversation was simple and pleasant. But Liza, being sensitive, at once noticed that something was tormenting Eugene, and she asked him whether anything unpleasant had happened. He was not prepared for this question and hesitated a little before replying that there had been nothing. This reply made Liza think all the more. That something was tormenting him, and greatly tormenting, was as evident to her as that a fly had fallen into the milk, yet he would not speak of it. What could it be?

XI

After breakfast they all dispersed. Eugene as usual went to his study, but instead of beginning to read or write his letters, he sat smoking one cigarette after another and thinking. He was terribly surprised and disturbed by the unexpected recrudescence within him of the bad feeling from which he had thought himself free since his marriage. Since then he had not once experienced that feeling, either for her—the woman he had known—or for any other woman except his wife. He had often felt glad of this emancipation, and now suddenly a chance meeting, seemingly so unimportant, revealed to him the fact that he was not free. What now tormented him was not that he was yielding to that feeling and desired her—he did not dream of so doing—but that the feeling was awake within him and he had to be on his guard against it. He had no doubt but that he would suppress it.

He had a letter to answer and a paper to write, and sat down at his writing table and began to work. Having finished it and quite forgotten what had disturbed him, he went out to go to the stables. And again as ill-luck would have it, either by unfortunate chance or intentionally, as soon as he stepped from the porch a red skirt and red kerchief appeared from round the corner, and she went past him swinging her arms and swaying her body. She not only went past him, but on passing him ran, as if playfully, to overtake her fellow servant.

Again the bright midday, the nettles, the back of Daniel's hut, and in the shade of the plane-trees her smiling face biting some leaves, rose in his imagination.

"No, it is impossible to let matters continue so," he said to himself, and waiting till the women had passed out of sight he went to the office.

It was just the dinner hour and he hoped to find the steward still there, and so it happened. The steward was just waking up from his after-dinner nap, and stretching himself and yawning was standing in the office, looking at the herdsman who was telling him something.

"Vasili Nikolayich!" said Eugene to the steward.

"What is your pleasure?"

"I want to speak to you."

"What is your pleasure?"

"Just finish what you are saying."

"Aren't you going to bring it in?" said Vasili Nikolayich to the herdsman.

"It's heavy, Vasili Nikolayich."

"What is it?" asked Eugene.

"Why, a cow has calved in the meadow. Well, all right, I'll order them to harness a horse at once. Tell Nicholas Lysukh to get out the dray cart."

The herdsman went out.

"Do you know," began Eugene, flushing and conscious that he was doing so, "do you know, Vasili Nikolayich, while I was a bachelor I went off the track a bit. . . . You may have heard . . ."

Vasili Nikolayich, evidently sorry for his master, said with smiling eyes: "Is it about Stepanida?"

"Why, yes. Look here. Please, please do not engage her to help in the house. You understand, it is very awkward for me . . ."

"Yes, it must have been Vanya the clerk who arranged it."

"Yes, please . . . and hadn't the rest of the phosphates better be strewn?" said Eugene, to hide his confusion.

"Yes, I am just going to see to it."

So the matter ended, and Eugene calmed down, hoping that as he had lived for a year without seeing her, so things would go on now. "Besides, Vasili Nikolayich will speak to Ivan the clerk; Ivan will speak to her, and she will understand that I don't want it," said Eugene to himself, and he was glad he had forced himself to speak to Vasili Nikolayich, hard as it had been to do so.

"Yes, it is better, much better, than that feeling of doubt, that feeling of shame." He shuddered at the mere remembrance of his sin in thought.

XII

The moral effort he had made to overcome his shame and speak to Vasili Nikolayich tranquillized Eugene. It seemed to him that the matter was all over now. Liza at once noticed that he was quite calm, and even happier than usual. "No doubt he was upset by our mothers pin-pricking one another. It really is disagreeable, especially for him who is so sensitive and noble, always to hear such unfriendly and ill-mannered insinuations," thought she.

The next day was Trinity Sunday. It was a beautiful day, and the peasant women, on their way into the woods to plait wreaths, came, according to custom, to the landowner's home and began to sing and dance. Mary Pavlovna and Varvara Alexeyevna came out onto the porch in smart clothes, carrying sunshades, and went up to the ring of singers. With them, in a jacket of Chinese silk, came out the uncle, a flabby libertine and drunkard, who was living that summer with Eugene.

As usual there was a bright, many-colored ring of young women and girls, the centre of everything, and around these from different sides like attendant planets that had detached themselves and were circling round, went girls hand in hand, rustling in their new print gowns; young lads giggling and running backwards and forwards after one another; full-grown lads in dark blue or black coats and caps and with red shirts, who unceasingly spat out sunflower-seed shells; and the domestic servants or other outsiders watching the dance circle from aside. Both the old ladies went close up to the ring, and Liza accompanied them in a light blue dress, with light blue ribbons on her head, and with wide sleeves under which her long white arms and angular elbows were visible.

Eugene did not wish to come out, but it was ridiculous to hide, and he too came out onto the porch smoking a cigarette, bowed to the men and lads, and talked with one of them. The women meanwhile shouted a dance song with all their might, snapping their fingers, clapping their hands, and dancing.

"They are calling for the master," said a youngster coming up to Eugene's wife, who had not noticed the call. Liza called Eugene to look at the dance and at one of the women dancers who particularly pleased her. This was Stepanida. She wore a yellow skirt, a velveteen sleeveless jacket and a silk kerchief, and was broad, energetic, ruddy, and merry. No doubt she danced well. He saw nothing.

"Yes, yes," he said, removing and replacing his pince-nez. "Yes, yes," he repeated. "So it seems I cannot be rid of her," he thought.

He did not look at her, fearing her attraction, and just on that account what his passing glance caught of her seemed to him especially attractive. Besides this he saw by her sparkling look that she saw him and saw that he admired her. He stood there as long as propriety demanded, and seeing that Varvara Alexeyevna had called her "my dear" senselessly and insincerely and was talking to her, he turned aside and went away.

He went into the house in order not to see her, but on reaching the upper story he approached the window, without knowing how or why, and as long as the women remained at the porch he stood there and looked and looked at her, feasting his eyes on her.

He ran, while there was no one to see him, and then went with quiet steps onto the veranda, and from there, smoking a cigarette, he passed through the garden as if going for a stroll, and followed the direction she had taken. He had not gone two steps along the alley before he noticed behind the trees a velveteen sleeveless jacket, with a pink and yellow skirt and a red kerchief. She was going somewhere with another woman. "Where are they going?"

And suddenly a terrible desire scorched him as though a hand were seizing his heart. As if by someone else's wish he looked round and went towards her.

"Eugene Ivanich, Eugene Ivanich! I have come to see your honor," said a voice behind him, and Eugene, seeing old Samokhin, who was digging a well for him, roused himself and turning quickly round went to meet Samokhin. While speaking with him he turned sideways and saw that she and the woman who was with her went down the slope, evidently to the well or making an excuse of the well, and having stopped there a little while ran back to the dance circle.

XIII

After talking to Samokhin, Eugene returned to the house as depressed as if he had committed a crime. In the first place she had understood him, believed that he wanted to see her, and desired it herself. Secondly that other woman, Anna Prokhorova, evidently knew of it.

Above all he felt that he was conquered, that he was not master of his own will but that there was another power moving him, that he had been saved only by good fortune, and that if not today then tomorrow or a day later, he would perish all the same.

"Yes, perish," he did not understand it otherwise: to be unfaithful to his young and loving wife with a peasant woman in the village, in the sight of everyone—what was it but to perish, perish utterly, so that it would be impossible to live? No, something must be done.

"My God, my God! What am I to do? Can it be that I shall perish like this?" said he to himself. "Is it not possible to do anything? Yet something must be done. Do not think about her"—he ordered himself. "Do not think!" and immediately he began thinking and seeing her before him, and seeing also the shade of the plane-tree.

He remembered having read of a hermit who, to avoid the temptation he felt for a woman on whom he had to lay his hand to heal her, thrust his other hand into a brazier and burnt his fingers. He called that to mind. "Yes, I am ready to burn my fingers rather than to perish." He looked round to make sure that there was no one in the room, lit a candle, and put a finger into the flame. "There, now think about her," he said to himself ironically. It hurt him and he withdrew his smoke-stained finger, threw away the match, and laughed at himself. What nonsense! That was not what had to be done. But it was necessary to do something, to avoid seeing her—either to go away himself or to send her away. Yes—send her away. Offer her husband money to remove to town or to another village. People would hear of it and would talk about it. Well, what of that? At any rate it was better than this danger. "Yes, that must be done," he said to himself, and at that very moment he was looking at her without moving his eyes. "Where is she going?" he suddenly asked himself. She, it seemed to him, had seen him at the window and now, having glanced at him and taken another woman by the hand, was going towards the garden swinging her arm briskly. Without knowing why or wherefore, merely in accord with what he had been thinking, he went to the office.

Vasili Nikolayich in holiday costume and with oiled hair was sitting at tea with his wife and a guest who was wearing an oriental kerchief.

"I want a word with you, Vasili Nikolayich!"

"Please say what you want to. We have finished tea."

"No. I'd rather you came out with me."

"Directly; only let me get my cap. Tanya, put out the samovar," said Vasili Nikolayich, stepping outside cheerfully.

It seemed to Eugene that Vasili had been drinking, but what was to be done? It might be all the better—he would sympathize with him in his difficulties the more readily.

"I have come again to speak about that same matter, Vasili

Nikolayich," said Eugene—"about that woman."

"Well, what of her? I told them not to take her again on any account."

"No, I have been thinking in general, and this is what I wanted to take your advice about. Isn't it possible to get them away, to send the whole family away?"

"Where can they be sent?" said Vasili, disapprovingly and ironically as it seemed to Eugene.

"Well, I thought of giving them money, or even some land in Koltovski—so that she should not be here."

"But how can they be sent away? Where is he to go—torn up from his roots? And why should you do it? What harm can she do you?"

"Ah, Vasili Nikolayich, you must understand that it would be dreadful for my wife to hear of it."

"But who will tell her?"

"How can I live with this dread? The whole thing is very painful for me."

"But really, why should you distress yourself? Whoever stirs up the past—out with his eye! Who is not a sinner before God and to blame before the tsar, as the saying is?"

"All the same it would be better to get rid of them. Can't you speak to the husband?"

"But it is no use speaking! Eh, Eugene Ivanich, what is the matter with you? It is all past and forgotten. All sorts of things happen. Who is there that would now say anything bad of you? Everybody sees you."

"But all the same go and have a talk with him."

"All right, I will speak to him."

Though he knew that nothing would come of it, this talk somewhat calmed Eugene. Above all, it made him feel that through excitement he had been exaggerating the danger.

Had he gone to meet her by appointment? It was impossible. He had simply gone to stroll in the garden and she had happened to run out at the same time.

XIV

After dinner that very Trinity Sunday Liza while walking from the garden to the meadow, where her husband wanted to show her the clover, took a false step and fell when crossing a little ditch. She fell gently, on her side; but she gave an exclamation, and her husband saw an expression in her face not only of fear but of pain. He was about to help her up, but she motioned him away with her hand.

"No, wait a bit, Eugene," she said, with a weak smile, and looked up guiltily as it seemed to him. "My foot only gave way under me."

"There, I always say," remarked Varvara Alexeyevna, "can anyone in her condition possibly jump over ditches?"

"But it is all right, mamma. I shall get up directly." With her husband's help she did get up, but she immediately turned pale, and looked frightened.

"Yes, I am not well!" and she whispered something to her mother.

"Oh, my God, what have you done! I said you ought not to go there," cried Varvara Alexeyevna. "Wait—I will call the servants. She must not walk. She must be carried!"

"Don't be afraid, Liza, I will carry you," said Eugene, putting his left arm round her. "Hold me by the neck. Like that." And stooping down he put his right arm under her knees and lifted her. He could never afterwards forget the suffering and yet beatific expression of her face.

"I am too heavy for you, dear," she said with a smile. "Mamma is running, tell her!" And she bent towards him and kissed him. She evidently wanted her mother to see how he was carrying her.

Eugene shouted to Varvara Alexeyevna not to hurry, and that he would carry Liza home. Varvara Alexeyevna stopped and began to shout still louder.

"You will drop her, you'll be sure to drop her. You want to destroy her. You have no conscience!"

"But I am carrying her excellently."

"I do not want to watch you killing my daughter, and I can't." And she ran round the bend in the alley.

"Never mind, it will pass," said Liza, smiling.

"Yes, If only it does not have consequences like last time."

"No. I am not speaking of that. That is all right. I mean mamma. You are tired. Rest a bit."

But though he found it heavy, Eugene carried his burden proudly and gladly to the house and did not hand her over to the housemaid and the man-cook whom Varvara Alexeyevna had found and sent to meet them. He carried her to the bedroom and put her on the bed.

"Now go away," she said, and drawing his hand to her she kissed it. "Annushka and I will manage all right."

Mary Pavlovna also ran in from her rooms in the wing. They undressed Liza and laid her on the bed. Eugene sat in the drawing room with a book in his hand, waiting. Varvara Alexeyevna went past him with such a reproachfully gloomy air that he felt alarmed.

"Well, how is it?" he asked.

"How is it? What's the good of asking? It is probably what you wanted when you made your wife jump over the ditch."

"Varvara Alexeyevna!" he cried. "This is impossible. If you want to torment people and to poison their life" (he wanted to say, "then go elsewhere to do it," but restrained himself). "How is it that it does not hurt you?"

"It is too late now." And shaking her cap in a triumphant manner she passed out by the door.

The fall had really been a bad one; Liza's foot had twisted awkwardly and there was danger of her having another miscarriage. Everyone knew that there was nothing to be done but that she must just lie quietly, yet all the same they decided to send for a doctor.

"Dear Nikolay Semyonich," wrote Eugene to the doctor, "you have always been so kind to us that I hope you will not refuse to come to my wife's assistance. She . . ." and so on. Having written the letter he went to the stables to arrange about the horses and the carriage. Horses had to be got ready to bring the doctor and others to take him back. When an estate is not run on a large scale, such things cannot be quickly decided but have to be considered. Having arranged it all and dispatched the coachman, it was past nine before he got back to the house. His wife was lying down, and said that she felt perfectly well and had no pain. But Varvara Alexeyevna was sitting with a lamp screened from Liza by some sheets of music and knitting a large red coverlet, with a mien that said that after what had happened peace was impossible, but that she at any rate would do her duty no matter what anyone else did.

Eugene noticed this, but, to appear as if he had not done so, tried to assume a cheerful and tranquil air and told how he had chosen the horses and how capitally the mare, Kabushka, had galloped as left trace-horse in the troyka.

"Yes, of course, it is just the time to exercise the horses when help is needed. Probably the doctor will also be thrown into the ditch," remarked Varvara Alexeyevna, examining her knitting from under her pince-nez and moving it close up to the lamp.

"But you know we had to send one way or another, and I made the best arrangement I could."

"Yes, I remember very well how your horses galloped with me under the arch of the gateway." This was a long-standing fancy of hers, and Eugene now was injudicious enough to remark that that was not quite what had happened.

"It is not for nothing that I have always said, and have often remarked to the prince, that it is hardest of all to live with people who are un-truthful and insincere. I can endure anything except that."

"Well, if anyone has to suffer more than another, it is certainly I," said Eugene. "But you . . ."

"Yes, it is evident."

"What?"

"Nothing, I am only counting my stitches."

Eugene was standing at the time by the bed and Liza was looking at him, and one of her moist hands outside the coverlet caught his hand and pressed it. "Bear with her for my sake. You know she cannot prevent our loving one another," was what her look said.

"I won't do so again. It's nothing," he whispered, and he kissed her damp, long hand and then her affectionate eyes, which closed while he kissed them.

"Can it be the same thing over again?" he asked. "How are you feeling?"

"I am afraid to say for fear of being mistaken, but I feel that he is alive and will live," said she, glancing at her stomach.

"Ah, it is dreadful, dreadful to think of."

Notwithstanding Liza's insistence that he should go away, Eugene spent the night with her, hardly closing an eye and ready to attend on her.

But she passed the night well, and had they not sent for the doctor she would perhaps have got up.

By dinnertime the doctor arrived and of course said that though if the symptoms recurred there might be cause for apprehension, yet actually there were no positive symptoms, but as there were also no contrary indications one might suppose on the one hand that—and on the other hand that . . . And therefore she must lie still, and that "though I do not like prescribing, yet all the same she should take this mixture and should lie quiet." Besides this, the doctor gave Varvara Alexeyevna a lecture on woman's anatomy, during which Varvara Alexeyevna nodded her head significantly. Having received his fee, as usual into the backmost part of his palm, the doctor drove away and the patient was left to lie in bed for a week.

XV

Eugene spent most of his time by his wife's bedside, talking to her, reading to her, and what was hardest of all, enduring without murmur Varvara Alexeyevna's attacks, and even contriving to turn these into jokes.

But he could not stay at home all the time. In the first place his wife sent him away, saying that he would fall ill if he always remained with her; and secondly the farming was progressing in a way that demanded his presence at every step. He could not stay at home, but had to be in the fields, in the wood, in the garden, at the thrashing floor; and everywhere he was pursued not merely by the thought but by the vivid image of Stepanida, and he only occasionally forgot her. But that would not have mattered, he could perhaps have mastered his feeling; what was worst of all was that, whereas he had previously lived for months without seeing her, he now continually came across her. She evidently understood that he wished to renew relations with her and tried to come in his way. Nothing was said either by him or by her, and therefore neither he nor she went directly to a rendezvous, but only sought opportunities of meeting.

The most possible place for them to meet was in the forest, where peasant women went with sacks to collect grass for their cows. Eugene knew this and therefore went there every day. Every day he told himself that he would not go, and every day it ended by his making his way to the forest and, on hearing the sound of voices, standing behind the bushes with sinking heart looking to see if she was there.

Why he wanted to know whether it was she who was there, he did not know. If it had been she and she had been alone, he would not have gone to her—so he believed—he would have run away; but he wanted to see her.

Once he met her. As he was entering the forest she came out of it with two other women, carrying a heavy sack full of grass on her back. A little earlier he would perhaps have met her in the forest. Now, with the other women there, she could not go back to him. But though he realized this impossibility, he stood for a long time behind a hazel bush, at the risk of attracting the other women's attention. Of course she did not return, but he stayed there a long time. And, great heavens, how delightful his imagination made her appear to him! And this not only once, but five or six times, and each time more intensely. Never had she seemed so attractive, and never had he been so completely in her power.

He felt that he had lost control of himself and had become almost insane. His strictness with himself had not weakened a jot; on the contrary he saw all the abomination of his desire and even of his action, for his going to the wood was an action. He knew that he only need come near her anywhere in the dark, and if possible touch her, and he would yield to his feelings. He knew that it was only shame before people, before her, and no doubt before himself that restrained him. And he knew too that he had sought conditions in which that shame would not be apparent— darkness or proximity—in which it would be stifled by animal passion. And therefore he knew that he was a wretched criminal, and despised and hated himself with all his soul. He hated himself because he still had not surrendered: every day he prayed God to strengthen him, to save him from perishing; every day he determined that from today onward he would not take a step to see her, and would forget her. Every day he devised means of delivering himself from this enticement, and he made use of those means.

But it was all in vain.

One of the means was continual occupation; another was intense physical work and fasting; a third was imagining to himself the shame that would fall upon him when everybody knew of it—his wife, his mother-in-law, and the folk around. He did all this and it seemed to him that he was conquering, but midday came—the hour of their former meetings and the hour when he had met her carrying the grass—and he went to the forest. Thus five days of torment passed. He only saw her from a distance, and did not once encounter her.

XVI

Liza was gradually recovering, she could move about and was only uneasy at the change that had taken place in her husband, which she did not understand.

Varvara Alexeyevna had gone away for a while, and the only visitor was Eugene's uncle. Mary Pavlovna was as usual at home.

Eugene was in his semi-insane condition when there came two days of pouring rain, as often happens after thunder in June. The rain stopped all work. They even ceased carting manure on account of the dampness and dirt. The peasants remained at home. The herdsmen wore themselves out with the cattle, and eventually drove them home. The cows and sheep wandered about in the pastureland and ran loose in the grounds. The peasant women, barefoot and wrapped in shawls, splashing through the mud, rushed about to seek the runaway cows. Streams flowed everywhere along the paths, all the leaves and all the grass were saturated with water, and streams flowed unceasingly from the spouts into the bubbling puddles.

Eugene sat at home with his wife, who was particularly wearisome that day. She questioned Eugene several times as to the cause of his discontent, and he replied with vexation that nothing was the matter. She ceased questioning him but was still distressed.

They were sitting after breakfast in the drawing room. His uncle for the hundredth time was recounting fabrications about his society acquaintances. Liza was knitting a jacket and sighed, complaining of the weather and of a pain in the small of her back. The uncle advised her to lie down, and asked for vodka for himself. It was terribly dull for Eugene in the house. Everything was weak and dull. He read a book and a magazine, but understood nothing of them.

"I must go out and look at the rasping-machine they brought yesterday," said he, and got up and went out.

"Take an umbrella with you."

"Oh, no, I have a leather coat. And I am only going as far as the boiling-room."

He put on his boots and his leather coat and went to the factory; and he had not gone twenty steps before he met her coming towards him, with her skirts tucked up high above her white calves. She was walking, holding down the shawl in which her head and shoulders were wrapped.

"Where are you going?" said he, not recognizing her the first instant. When he recognized her it was already too late. She stopped, smiling, and looked long at him.

"I am looking for a calf. Where are you off to in such weather?" said she, as if she were seeing him every day.

"Come to the shed," said he suddenly, without knowing how he said it. It was as if someone else had uttered the words.

She bit her shawl, winked, and ran in the direction which led from the garden to the shed, and he continued his path, intending to turn off beyond the lilac bush and go there too.

"Master," he heard a voice behind him. "The mistress is calling you, and wants you to come back for a minute."

This was Misha, his manservant.

"My God! This is the second time you have saved me," thought Eugene, and immediately turned back. His wife reminded him that he had promised to take some medicine at the dinner hour to a sick woman, and he had better take it with him.

While they were getting the medicine some five minutes elapsed, and then, going away with the medicine, he hesitated to go direct to the shed lest he should be seen from the house, but as soon as he was out of sight he promptly turned and made his way to it. He already saw her in imagination inside the shed smiling gaily. But she was not there, and there was nothing in the shed to show that she had been there.

He was already thinking that she had not come, had not heard or understood his words—he had muttered them through his nose as if afraid of her hearing them—or perhaps she had not wanted to come. "And why did I imagine that she would rush to me? She has her own husband; it is only I who am such a wretch as to have a wife, and a good one, and to run after another." Thus he thought sitting in the shed, the thatch of which had a leak and dripped from its straw. "But how delightful it would be if she did come—alone here in this rain. If only I could embrace her once again, then let happen what may. But I could tell if she has been here by her footprints," he reflected. He looked at the trodden ground near the shed and at the path overgrown by grass, and the fresh print of bare feet, and even of one that had slipped, was visible.

"Yes, she has been here. Well, now it is settled. Wherever I may see her I shall go straight to her. I will go to her at night." He sat for a long time in the shed and left it exhausted and crushed. He delivered the medicine, returned home, and lay down in his room to wait for dinner.

XVII

Before dinner Liza came to him and, still wondering what could be the cause of his discontent, began to say that she was afraid he did not like the idea of her going to Moscow for her confinement, and that she had decided that she would remain at home and on no account go to Moscow. He knew how she feared both her confinement itself and the risk of not having a healthy child, and therefore he could not help being touched at seeing how ready she was to sacrifice everything for his sake. All was so nice, so pleasant, so clean, in the house; and in his soul it was so dirty, despicable, and foul. The whole evening Eugene was tormented by knowing that notwithstanding his sincere repulsion at his own weakness, notwithstanding his firm intention to break off—the same thing would happen again tomorrow.

"No, this is impossible," he said to himself, walking up and down in his room. "There must be some remedy for it. My God! What am I to do?"

Someone knocked at the door as foreigners do. He knew this must be his uncle. "Come in," he said.

The uncle had come as a self-appointed ambassador from Liza.

"Do you know, I really do notice that there is a change in you," he said, "and Liza—I understand how it troubles her. I understand that it must be hard for you to leave all the business you have so excellently started, but *que veux-tu?* I should advise you to go away. It will be more satisfactory both for you and for her. And do you know, I should advise you to go to the Crimea. The climate is beautiful and there is an excellent *accoucheur* there, and you would be just in time for the best of the grape season."

"Uncle," Eugene suddenly exclaimed. "Can you keep a secret? A secret that is terrible to me, a shameful secret."

"Oh, come—do you really feel any doubt of me?"

"Uncle, you can help me. Not only help, but save me!" said Eugene. And the thought of disclosing his secret to his uncle whom he did not respect, the thought that he should show himself in the worst light and humiliate himself before him, was pleasant. He felt himself to be despicable and guilty, and wished to punish himself.

"Speak, my dear fellow, you know how fond I am of you," said the uncle, evidently well content that there was a secret and that it was a shameful one, and that it would be communicated to him, and that he could be of use.

"First of all I must tell you that I am a wretch, a good-for-nothing, a scoundrel—a real scoundrel."

"Now what are you saying . . ." began his uncle, as if he were offended.

"What! Not a wretch when I—Liza's husband, Liza's! One has only to know her purity, her love—and that I, her husband, want to be untrue to her with a peasant woman!"

"What is this? Why do you want to—you have not been unfaithful to her?"

"Yes, at least just the same as being untrue, for it did not depend on me. I was ready to do so. I was hindered, or else I should . . . now. I do not know what I should have done . . ."

"But please, explain to me . . ."

"Well, it is like this. When I was a bachelor I was stupid enough to have relations with a woman here in our village. That is to say, I used to have meetings with her in the forest, in the field . . ."

"Was she pretty?" asked his uncle.

Eugene frowned at this question, but he was in such need of external help that he made as if he did not hear it, and continued:

"Well, I thought this was just casual and that I should break it off and have done with it. And I did break it off before my marriage. For nearly a year I did not see her or think about her." It seemed strange to Eugene himself to hear the description of his own condition. "Then suddenly, I don't myself know why—really one sometimes believes in witchcraft— I saw her, and a worm crept into my heart; and it gnaws. I reproach myself, I understand the full horror of my action, that is to say, of the act I may commit any moment, and yet I myself turn to it, and if I have not committed it, it is only because God preserved me. Yesterday I was on my way to see her when Liza sent for me."

"What, in the rain?"

"Yes. I am worn out, Uncle, and have decided to confess to you and to ask your help."

"Yes, of course, it's a bad thing on your own estate. People will get to know. I understand that Liza is weak and that it is necessary to spare her, but why on your own estate?"

Again Eugene tried not to hear what his uncle was saying, and hurried on to the core of the matter.

"Yes, save me from myself. That is what I ask of you. Today I was hindered by chance. But tomorrow or next time no one will hinder me. And she knows now. Don't leave me alone."

"Yes, all right," said his uncle—"but are you really so much in love?"

"Oh, it is not that at all. It is not that, it is some kind of power that has seized me and holds me. I do not know what to do. Perhaps I shall gain strength, and then . . ."

"Well, it turns out as I suggested," said his uncle. "Let us be off to the Crimea."

"Yes, yes, let us go, and meanwhile you will be with me and will talk to me."

XVIII

The fact that Eugene had confided his secret to his uncle, and still more the sufferings of his conscience and the feeling of shame he experienced after that rainy day, sobered him. It was settled that they would start for Yalta in a week's time. During that week Eugene drove to town to get money for the journey, gave instructions from the house and from the office concerning the management of the estate, again became gay and friendly with his wife, and began to awaken morally.

So without having once seen Stepanida after that rainy day he left with his wife for the Crimea. There he spent an excellent two months. He received so many new impressions that it seemed to him that the past was obliterated from his memory. In the Crimea they met former acquaintances and became particularly friendly with them, and they also made new acquaintances. Life in the Crimea was a continual holiday for Eugene, besides being instructive and beneficial. They became friendly there with the former Marshal of the Nobility of their province, a clever and liberal-minded man who became fond of Eugene and coached him, and attracted him to his party.

At the end of August Liza gave birth to a beautiful, healthy daughter, and her confinement was unexpectedly easy.

In September they returned home, the four of them, including the baby and its wet nurse, as Liza was unable to nurse it herself. Eugene returned home entirely free from the former horrors and quite a new and happy man. Having gone through all that a husband goes through when his wife bears a child, he loved her more than ever. His feeling for the child when he took it in his arms was a funny, new, very pleasant and, as it were, a tickling feeling. Another new thing in his life now was that, besides his occupation with the estate, thanks to his acquaintance with Dumchin (the ex-Marshal) a new interest occupied his mind, that of the zemstvo[2]—partly an ambitious interest, partly a feeling of duty. In October there was to be a special assembly, at which he was to be elected. After arriving home he drove once to town and another time to Dumchin.

Of the torments of his temptation and struggle he had forgotten even to think, and could with difficulty recall them to mind. It seemed to him something like an attack of insanity he had undergone.

To such an extent did he now feel free from it that he was not even afraid to make inquiries on the first occasion when he remained alone with the steward. As he had previously spoken to him about the matter he was not ashamed to ask.

---

[2] [A provincial assembly.]

"Well, and is Sidor Pechnikov still away from home?" he inquired.

"Yes, he is still in town."

"And his wife?"

"Oh, she is a worthless woman. She is now carrying on with Zenovi. She has gone quite on the loose."

"Well, that is all right," thought Eugene. "How wonderfully indifferent to it I am! How I have changed."

XIX

All that Eugene had wished had been realized. He had obtained the property, the factory was working successfully, the beet crops were excellent, and he expected a large income; his wife had borne a child satisfactorily, his mother-in-law had left, and he had been unanimously elected to the zemstvo.

He was returning home from town after the election. He had been congratulated and had had to return thanks. He had had dinner and had drunk some five glasses of champagne. Quite new plans of life now presented themselves to him, and he was thinking about these as he drove home. It was the Indian summer: an excellent road and a hot sun. As he approached his home Eugene was thinking of how, as a result of this election, he would occupy among the people the position he had always dreamed of; that is to say, one in which he would be able to serve them not only by production, which gave employment, but also by direct influence. He imagined what his own and the other peasants would think of him in three years' time. "For instance this one," he thought, drifting just then through the village and glancing at a peasant who with a peasant woman was crossing the street in front of him carrying a full water-tub. They stopped to let his carriage pass. The peasant was old Pechnikov, and the woman was Stepanida. Eugene looked at her, recognized her, and was glad to feel that he remained quite tranquil. She was still as good-looking as ever, but this did not touch him at all. He drove home.

"Well, may we congratulate you?" said his uncle.

"Yes, I was elected."

"Capital! We must drink to it!"

Next day Eugene drove about to see to the farming which he had been neglecting. At the outlying farmstead a new thrashing machine was at work. While watching it Eugene stepped among the women, trying not to take notice of them; but try as he would he once or twice noticed the black eyes and red kerchief of Stepanida, who was carrying away the straw. Once or twice he glanced sideways at her and felt that something was happening, but could not account for it to himself. Only next day, when he again drove to the thrashing floor and spent two hours there quite unnecessarily, without ceasing to caress with his eyes the familiar, handsome figure of the young woman, did he feel that he was lost, irremediably lost. Again those torments! Again all that horror and fear, and there was no saving himself.

What he expected happened to him. The evening of the next day, without knowing how, he found himself at her backyard, by her hay shed, where in autumn they had once had a meeting. As though having a stroll, he stopped there lighting a cigarette. A neighboring peasant woman saw him, and as he turned back he heard her say to someone: "Go, he is waiting for you—on my dying word he is standing there. Go, you fool!"

He saw how a woman—she—ran to the hay shed; but as a peasant had met him it was no longer possible for him to turn back, and so he went home.

XX

When he entered the drawing room everything seemed strange and unnatural to him. He had risen that morning vigorous, determined to fling it all aside, to forget it and not allow himself to think about it. But without noticing how it occurred he had all the morning not merely not interested himself in the work, but tried to avoid it. What had formerly cheered him and been important was now insignificant. Unconsciously he tried to free himself from business. It seemed to him that he had to do so in order to think and to plan. And he freed himself and remained alone. But as soon as he was alone he began to wander about in the garden and the forest. And all those spots were besmirched in his recollection by memories that gripped him. He felt that he was walking in the garden and pretending to himself that he was thinking out something, but that really he was not thinking out anything, but insanely and unreasonably expecting her; expecting that by some miracle she would be aware that he was expecting her, and would come here at once and go somewhere where no one would see them, or would come at night when there would be no moon, and no one, not even she herself, would see—on such a night she would come and he would touch her body. . . .

"There now, talking of breaking off when I wish to," he said to himself. "Yes, and that is having a clean healthy woman for one's health's sake! No, it seems one can't play with her like that. I thought I had taken her, but it was she who took me; took me and does not let me go. Why, I thought I was free, but I was not free and was deceiving myself when I married. It was all nonsense—fraud. From the time I had her I experienced a new feeling, the real feeling of a husband. Yes, I ought to have lived with her.

"One of two lives is possible for me: that which I began with Liza: service, estate management, the child, and people's respect. If that is life, it is necessary that she, Stepanida, should not be there. She must be sent away, as I said, or destroyed so that she shall not exist. And the other life—is this: For me to take her away from her husband, pay him money, disregard the shame and disgrace, and live with her. But in that case it is necessary that Liza should not exist, nor Mimi (the baby). No, that is not so, the baby does not matter, but it is necessary that there should be no Liza—that she should go away—that she should know, curse me, and go away. That she should know that I have exchanged her for a peasant woman, that I am a deceiver and a scoundrel!—No, that is too terrible! It is impossible. But it might happen," he went on thinking—"it might happen that Liza might fall ill and die. Die, and then everything would be capital.

"Capital! Oh, scoundrel! No, if someone must die it should be Stepanida. If she were to die, how good it would be.

"Yes, that is how men come to poison or kill their wives or lovers. Take a revolver and go and call her, and instead of embracing her, shoot her in the breast and have done with it.

"Really she is—a devil. Simply a devil. She has possessed herself of me against my own will.

"Kill? Yes. There are only two ways out: to kill my wife or her. For it is impossible to live like this.[3] It is impossible! I must consider the matter and look ahead. If things remain as they are what will happen? I shall again be saying to myself that I do not wish it and that I will throw her off, but it will be merely words; in the evening I shall be at her backyard, and she will know it and will come out. And if people know of it and tell my wife, or if I tell her myself—for I can't lie—I shall not be able to live so. I cannot! People will know. They will all know—Parasha and the blacksmith. Well, is it possible to live so?

"Impossible! There are only two ways out: to kill my wife, or to kill her. Yes, or else . . . Ah, yes, there is a third way: to kill myself," said he softly, and suddenly a shudder ran over his skin. "Yes, kill myself, then I shall not need to kill them." He became frightened, for he felt that only that way was possible. He had a revolver. "Shall I really kill myself? It is something I never thought of—how strange it will be . . ."

He returned to his study and at once opened the cupboard where the revolver lay, but before he had taken it out of its case his wife entered the room.

---

[3]At this place the alternative ending, printed at the end of the story [page 122], begins.— A.M. [Aylmer Maude, the translator of this story.]

XXI

He threw a newspaper over the revolver.

"Again the same!" said she aghast when she had looked at him.

"What is the same?"

"The same terrible expression that you had before and would not explain to me. Jenya, dear one, tell me about it. I see that you are suffering. Tell me and you will feel easier. Whatever it may be, it will be better than for you to suffer so. Don't I know that it is nothing bad?"

"You know? While . . ."

"Tell me, tell me, tell me. I won't let you go."

He smiled a piteous smile.

"Shall I?—No, it is impossible. And there is nothing to tell."

Perhaps he might have told her, but at that moment the wet nurse entered to ask if she should go for a walk. Liza went out to dress the baby.

"Then you will tell me? I will be back directly."

"Yes, perhaps . . ."

She never could forget the piteous smile with which he said this. She went out.

Hurriedly, stealthily like a robber, he seized the revolver and took it out of its case. It was loaded, yes, but long ago, and one cartridge was missing.

"Well, how will it be?" He put it to his temple and hesitated a little, but as soon as he remembered Stepanida—his decision not to see her, his struggle, temptation, fall, and renewed struggle—he shuddered with horror. "No, this is better," and he pulled the trigger . . .

When Liza ran into the room—she had only had time to step down from the balcony—he was lying face downwards on the floor: black, warm blood was gushing from the wound, and his corpse was twitching.

There was an inquest. No one could understand or explain the suicide. It never even entered his uncle's head that its cause could be anything in common with the confession Eugene had made to him two months previously.

Varvara Alexeyevna assured them that she had always foreseen it. It had been evident from his way of disputing. Neither Liza nor Mary Pavlovna could at all understand why it had happened, but still they did not believe what the doctors said, namely, that he was mentally deranged—a psychopath. They were quite unable to accept this, for they knew he was saner than hundreds of their acquaintances.

And indeed if Eugene Irtenev was mentally deranged everyone is in the same case; the most mentally deranged people are certainly those who see in others indications of insanity they do not notice in themselves.

Variation of the Conclusion of "The Devil"

"To kill, yes. There are only two ways out: to kill my wife, or to kill her. For it is impossible to live like this," said he to himself, and going up to the table he took from it a revolver and, having examined it—one cartridge was wanting—he put it in his trouser pocket.

"My God! What am I doing?" he suddenly exclaimed, and folding his hands he began to pray.

"O God, help me and deliver me! Thou knowest that I do not desire evil, but by myself am powerless. Help me," said he, making the sign of the cross on his breast before the icon.

"Yes, I can control myself. I will go out, walk about and think things over."

He went to the entrance hall, put on his overcoat and went out onto the porch. Unconsciously his steps took him past the garden along the field path to the outlying farmstead. There the thrashing machine was still droning and the cries of the driver lads were heard. He entered the barn. She was there. He saw her at once. She was raking up the corn, and on seeing him she ran briskly and merrily about, with laughing eyes, raking up the scattered corn with agility. Eugene could not help watching her though he did not wish to do so. He only recollected himself when she was no longer in sight. The clerk informed him that they were now finishing thrashing the corn that had been beaten down—that was why it was going slower and the output was less. Eugene went up to the drum, which occasionally gave a knock as sheaves not evenly fed in passed under it, and he asked the clerk if there were many such sheaves of beaten-down corn.

"There will be five cartloads of it."

"Then look here . . ." began Eugene, but he did not finish the sentence. She had gone close up to the drum and was raking the corn from under it, and she scorched him with her laughing eyes. That look spoke of a merry, careless love between them, of the fact that she knew he wanted her and had come to her shed, and that she as always was ready to live and be merry with him regardless of all conditions or consequences. Eugene felt himself to be in her power but did not wish to yield.

He remembered his prayer and tried to repeat it. He began saying it to himself, but at once felt that it was useless. A single thought now engrossed him entirely: how to arrange a meeting with her so that the others should not notice it.

"If we finish this lot today, are we to start on a fresh stack or leave it till tomorrow?" asked the clerk.

"Yes, yes," replied Eugene, involuntarily following her to the heap to which with the other women she was raking the corn.

"But can I really not master myself?" said he to himself. "Have I really perished? O God! But there is no God. There is only a devil. And it is she. She has possessed me. But I won't, I won't! A devil, yes, a devil."

Again he went up to her, drew the revolver from his pocket and shot her, once, twice, thrice, in the back. She ran a few steps and fell on the heap of corn.

"My God, my God! What is that?" cried the women.

"No, it was not an accident. I killed her on purpose," cried Eugene. "Send for the police officer."

He went home and went to his study and locked himself in, without speaking to his wife.

"Do not come to me," he cried to her through the door. "You will know all about it."

An hour later he rang, and bade the manservant who answered the bell: "Go and find out whether Stepanida is alive."

The servant already knew all about it, and told him she had died an hour ago.

"Well, all right. Now leave me alone. When the police officer or the magistrate comes, let me know."

The police officer and magistrate arrived next morning, and Eugene, having bidden his wife and baby farewell, was taken to prison.

He was tried. It was during the early days of trial by jury, and the verdict was one of temporary insanity, and he was sentenced only to perform church penance.

He had been kept in prison for nine months and was then confined in a monastery for one month.

He had begun to drink while still in prison, continued to do so in the monastery, and returned home an enfeebled, irresponsible drunkard.

Varvara Alexeyevna assured them that she had always predicted this. it was, she said, evident from the way he disputed. Neither Liza nor Mary Pavlovna could understand how the affair had happened, but for all that, they did not believe what the doctors said, namely, that he was mentally deranged—a psychopath. They could not accept that, for the knew that he was saner than hundreds of their acquaintances.

And indeed, if Eugene Irtenev was mentally deranged when he committed this crime, then everyone is similarly insane. The most mentally deranged people are certainly those who see in others indications of insanity they do not notice in themselves.

Father Sergius

I

IN Petersburg in the eighteen-forties a surprising event occurred. An officer of the Cuirassier Life Guards, a handsome prince who everyone predicted would become aide-de-camp to the Emperor Nicholas I and have a brilliant career, left the service, broke off his engagement to a beautiful maid of honor, a favorite of the empress's, gave his small estate to his sister, and retired to a monastery to become a monk.

This event appeared extraordinary and inexplicable to those who did not know his inner motives, but for Prince Stepan Kasatsky himself it all occurred so naturally that he could not imagine how he could have acted otherwise.

His father, a retired colonel of the Guards, had died when Stepan was twelve, and sorry as his mother was to part from her son, she entered him at the Military College as her deceased husband had intended.

The widow herself, with her daughter, Varvara, moved to Petersburg to be near her son and have him with her for the holidays.

The boy was distinguished both by his brilliant ability and by his immense self-esteem. He was first both in his studies—especially in mathematics, of which he was particularly fond—and also in drill and in riding. Though of more than average height, he was handsome and agile, and he would have been an altogether exemplary cadet had it not been for his quick temper. He was remarkably truthful, and was neither dissipated nor addicted to drink. The only faults that marred his conduct were fits of fury to which he was subject and during which he lost control of himself and became like a wild animal. He once nearly threw out of the window another cadet who had begun to tease him about his collection of minerals. On another occasion he came almost completely to grief by flinging a whole dish of cutlets at an officer who was acting as steward, attacking him and, it was said, striking him for having broken his word and told a barefaced lie. He would certainly have been reduced

124

to the ranks had not the director of the college hushed up the whole matter and dismissed the steward.

By the time he was eighteen he had finished his college course and received a commission as lieutenant in an aristocratic regiment of the Guards.

The Emperor Nicholas Pavlovich (Nicholas I) had noticed him while he was still at the college, and continued to take notice of him in the regiment, and it was on this account that people predicted for him an appointment as aide-de-camp to the emperor. Kasatsky himself strongly desired it, not from ambition only but chiefly because since his cadet days he had been passionately devoted to Nicholas Pavlovich. The emperor had often visited the Military College and every time Kasatsky saw that tall erect figure, with breast expanded in its military overcoat, entering with brisk step, saw the cropped side-whiskers, the mustache, the aquiline nose, and heard the sonorous voice exchanging greetings with the cadets, he was seized by the same rapture that he experienced later on when he met the woman he loved. Indeed, his passionate adoration of the emperor was even stronger: he wished to sacrifice something—everything, even himself—to prove his complete devotion. And the Emperor Nicholas was conscious of evoking this rapture and deliberately aroused it. He played with the cadets, surrounded himself with them, treating them sometimes with childish simplicity, sometimes as a friend, and then again with majestic solemnity. After that affair with the officer, Nicholas Pavlovich said nothing to Kasatsky, but when the latter approached he waved him away theatrically, frowned, shook his finger at him, and afterwards when leaving, said: "Remember that I know everything. There are some things I would rather not know, but they remain here," and he pointed to his heart.

When on leaving college the cadets were received by the emperor, he did not again refer to Kasatsky's offense, but told them all, as was his custom, that they should serve him and the fatherland loyally, that he would always be their best friend, and that when necessary they might approach him direct. All the cadets were as usual greatly moved, and Kasatsky even shed tears, remembering the past, and vowed that he would serve his beloved tsar with all his soul.

When Kasatsky took up his commission his mother moved with her daughter first to Moscow and then to their country estate. Kasatsky gave half his property to his sister and kept only enough to maintain himself in the expensive regiment he had joined.

To all appearance he was just an ordinary, brilliant young officer of the Guards making a career for himself; but intense and complex strivings went on within him. From early childhood his efforts had seemed to be very varied, but essentially they were all one and the same. He tried in everything he took up to attain such success and perfection as would evoke praise and surprise. Whether it was his studies or his military exercises, he took them up and worked at them till he was praised and held up as an example to others. Mastering one subject he took up another, and obtained first place in his studies. For example, while still at college he noticed in himself an awkwardness in French conversation, and contrived to master French till he spoke it as well as Russian, and then he took up chess and became an excellent player.

Apart from his main vocation, which was the service of his tsar and the fatherland, he always set himself some particular aim, and however unimportant it was, devoted himself completely to it and lived for it until it was accomplished. And as soon as it was attained another aim would immediately present itself, replacing its predecessor. This passion for distinguishing himself, or for accomplishing something in order to distinguish himself, filled his life. On taking up his commission he set himself to acquire the utmost perfection in knowledge of the service, and very soon became a model officer, though still with the same fault of ungovernable irascibility, which here in the service again led him to commit actions inimical to his success. Then he took to reading, having once in conversation in society felt himself deficient in general education— and again achieved his purpose. Then, wishing to secure a brilliant position in high society, he learnt to dance excellently and very soon was invited to all the balls in the best circles, and to some of their evening gatherings. But this did not satisfy him: he was accustomed to being first, and in this society was far from being so.

The highest society then consisted, and I think always and everywhere does consist, of four sorts of people: rich people who are received at court, people not wealthy but born and brought up in court circles, rich people who ingratiate themselves into the court set, and people neither rich nor belonging to the court but who ingratiate themselves into the first and second sets.

Kasatsky did not belong to the first two sets, but was readily welcomed in the others. On entering society he determined to have relations with some society lady, and to his own surprise quickly accomplished this purpose. He soon realized, however, that the circles in which he moved were not the highest, and that though he was received in the highest spheres he did not belong to them. They were polite to him, but showed by their whole manner that they had their own set and that he was not of it. And Kasatsky wished to belong to that inner circle. To attain that end it would be necessary to be an aide-de-camp to the emperor—which he expected to become—or to marry into that exclusive set, which he resolved to do. And his choice fell on a beauty belonging to the court, who not merely belonged to the circle into which he wished to be accepted, but whose friendship was coveted by the very highest people and those most firmly established in that highest circle. This was Countess Korotkova. Kasatsky began to pay court to her, and not merely for the sake of his career. She was extremely attractive and he soon fell in love with her. At first she was noticeably cool towards him, but then suddenly changed and became gracious, and her mother gave him pressing invitations to visit them. Kasatsky proposed and was accepted. He was surprised at the facility with which he attained such happiness. But though he noticed something strange and unusual in the behavior towards him of both mother and daughter, he was blinded by being so deeply in love, and did not realize what almost the whole town knew—namely, that his fiancee had been the Emperor Nicholas's mistress the previous year.

Two weeks before the day arranged for the wedding, Kasatsky was at Tsarskoye Selo at his fiancee's country place. It was a hot day in May. He and his betrothed had walked about the garden and were sitting on a bench in a shady linden alley. Mary's white muslin dress suited her particularly well, and she seemed the personification of innocence and love as she sat, now bending her head, now gazing up at the very tall and handsome man who was speaking to her with particular tenderness and self-restraint, as if he feared by word or gesture to offend or sully her angelic purity.

Kasatsky belonged to those men of the eighteen-forties (they are now no longer to be found) who while deliberately and without any conscientious scruples condoning impurity in themselves, required ideal and angelic purity in their women, regarded all unmarried women of their circle as possessed of such purity, and treated them accordingly. There was much that was false and harmful in this outlook, as concerning the laxity the men permitted themselves, but in regard to the women that old-fashioned view (sharply differing from that held by young people today who see in every girl merely a female seeking a mate) was, I think, of value. The girls, perceiving such adoration, endeavored with more or less success to be goddesses.

Such was the view Kasatsky held of women, and that was how he regarded his fiancee. He was particularly in love that day, but did not experience any sensual desire for her. On the contrary he regarded her with tender adoration as something unattainable.

He rose to his full height, standing before her with both hands on his sabre.

"I have only now realized what happiness a man can experience! And it is you, my darling, who have given me this happiness," he said with a timid smile.

Endearments had not yet become usual between them, and feeling himself morally inferior he felt terrified at this stage to use them to such an angel.

"It is thanks to you that I have come to know myself. I have learnt that I am better than I thought."

"I have known that for a long time. That was why I began to love you."

Nightingales trilled near by and the fresh leafage rustled, moved by a passing breeze.

He took her hand and kissed it, and tears came into his eyes.

She understood that he was thanking her for having said she loved him. He silently took a few steps up and down, and then approached her again and sat down.

"You know . . . I have to tell you . . . I was not disinterested when I began to make love to you. I wanted to get into society; but later . . . how unimportant that became in comparison with you—when I got to know you. You are not angry with me for that?"

She did not reply but merely touched his hand. He understood that this meant: "No, I am not angry."

"You said . . ." He hesitated. It seemed too bold to say. "You said that you began to love me. I believe it—but there is something that troubles you and checks your feeling. What is it?"

"Yes—now or never!" thought she. "He is bound to know of it anyway. But now he will not forsake me. Ah, if he should, it would be terrible!" And she threw a loving glance at his tall, noble, powerful figure. She loved him now more than she had loved the tsar, and apart from the imperial dignity would not have preferred the emperor to him.

"Listen! I cannot deceive you. I have to tell you. You ask what it is? It is that I have loved before."

She again laid her hand on his with an imploring gesture. He was silent.

"You want to know who it was? It was—the emperor."

"We all love him. I can imagine you, a schoolgirl at the Institute . . ."

"No, it was later. I was infatuated, but it passed . . . I must tell you . . ."

"Well, what of it?"

"No, it was not simply—" She covered her face with her hands.

"What? You gave yourself to him?"

She was silent.

"His mistress?"

She did not answer.

He sprang up and stood before her with trembling jaws, pale as death. He now remembered how the emperor, meeting him on the Nevsky, had amiably congratulated him.

"O God, what have I done! Stiva!"

"Don't touch me! Don't touch me! Oh, how it pains!"

He turned away and went to the house. There he met her mother.

"What is the matter, Prince? I . . ." She became silent on seeing his face. The blood had suddenly rushed to his head.

"You knew it, and used me to shield them! If you weren't a woman . . . !" he cried, lifting his enormous fist, and turning aside he ran away.

Had his fiancee's lover been a private person he would have killed him, but it was his beloved tsar.

Next day he applied both for furlough and his discharge, and professing to be ill, so as to see no one, he went away to the country.

He spent the summer at his village arranging his affairs. When summer was over he did not return to Petersburg, but entered a monastery and there became a monk.

His mother wrote to try to dissuade him from this decisive step, but he replied that he felt God's call which transcended all other considerations. Only his sister, who was as proud and ambitious as he, understood him.

She understood that he had become a monk in order to be above those who considered themselves his superiors. And she understood him correctly. By becoming a monk he showed contempt for all that seemed most important to others and had seemed so to him while he was in the service, and he now ascended a height from which he could look down on those he had formerly envied. . . . But it was not this alone, as his sister Varvara supposed, that influenced him. There was also in him something else—a sincere religious feeling which Varvara did not know, which intertwined itself with the feeling of pride and the desire for preeminence, and guided him. His disillusionment with Mary, whom he had thought of angelic purity, and his sense of injury, were so strong that they brought him to despair, and the despair led him—to what? To God, to his childhood's faith which had never been destroyed in him.

II

Kasatsky entered the monastery on the feast of the Intercession of the Blessed Virgin. The abbot of that monastery was a gentleman by birth, a learned writer and a *starets,* that is, he belonged to that succession of monks originating in Walachia who each choose a director and teacher whom they implicitly obey. This superior had been a disciple of the *starets* Ambrose, who was a disciple of Makarius, who was a disciple of the *starets* Leonid, who was a disciple of Païssy Velichkovsky.

To this abbot Kasatsky submitted himself as to his chosen director. Here in the monastery, besides the feeling of ascendancy over others that such a life gave him, he felt much as he had done in the world: he found satisfaction in attaining the greatest possible perfection outwardly as well as inwardly. As in the regiment he had been not merely an irreproachable officer but had even exceeded his duties and widened the borders of perfection, so also as a monk he tried to be perfect, and was always industrious, abstemious, submissive, and meek, as well as pure both in deed and in thought, and obedient. This last quality in particular made life far easier for him. If many of the demands of life in the monastery, which was near the capital and much frequented, did not please him and were temptations to him, they were all nullified by obedience: "It is not for me to reason; my business is to do the task set me, whether it be standing beside the relics, singing in the choir, or making up accounts in the monastery guest house." All possibility of doubt about anything was silenced by obedience to the *starets.* Had it not been for this, he would have been oppressed by the length and monotony of the church services, the bustle of the many visitors, and the bad qualities of the other monks. As it was, he not only bore it all joyfully but found in it solace and support. "I don't know why it is necessary to hear the same prayers several times a day, but I know that it is necessary; and knowing this I find joy in them." His director told him that as material food is necessary for the maintenance of the life of the body, so spiritual food—the church prayers—is necessary for the maintenance of the spiritual life. He believed this, and though the church services, for which he had to get up early in the morning, were a difficulty, they certainly calmed him and gave him joy. This was the result of his consciousness of humility, and the certainty that whatever he had to do, being fixed by the *starets,* was right.

The interest of his life consisted not only in an ever greater and greater subjugation of his will, but in the attainment of all the Christian virtues, which at first seemed to him easily attainable. He had given his whole estate to his sister and did not regret it, he had no personal claims, humility towards his inferiors was not merely easy for him but afforded him pleasure. Even victory over the sins of the flesh, greed and lust, was easily attained. His director had specially warned him against the latter sin, but Kasatsky felt free from it and was glad.

One thing only tormented him—the remembrance of his fiancee; and not merely the remembrance but the vivid image of what might have been. Involuntarily he recalled a lady he knew who had been a favorite of the emperor's, but had afterwards married and become an admirable wife and mother. The husband had a high position, influence and honor, and a good and penitent wife.

In his better hours Kasatsky was not disturbed by such thoughts, and when he recalled them at such times he was merely glad to feel that the temptation was past. But there were moments when all that made up his present life suddenly grew dim before him, moments when, if he did not cease to believe in the aims he had set himself, he ceased to see them and could evoke no confidence in them but was seized by a remembrance of, and—terrible to say—a regret for, the change of life he had made.

The only thing that saved him in that state of mind was obedience and work, and the fact that the whole day was occupied by prayer. He went through the usual forms of prayer, he bowed in prayer, he even prayed more than usual, but it was lip-service only and his soul was not in it. This condition would continue for a day, or sometimes for two days, and would then pass of itself. But those days were dreadful. Kasatsky felt that he was neither in his own hands nor in God's, but was subject to something else. All he could do then was to obey the *starets*, to restrain himself, to undertake nothing, and simply to wait. In general all this time he lived not by his own will but by that of the *starets*, and in this obedience he found a special tranquillity.

So he lived in his first monastery for seven years. At the end of the third year he received the tonsure and was ordained to the priesthood by the name of Sergius. The profession was an important event in his inner life. He had previously experienced a great consolation and spiritual exaltation when receiving communion, and now when he himself officiated, the performance of the preparation filled him with ecstatic and deep emotion. But subsequently that feeling became more and more deadened, and once when he was officiating in a depressed state of mind he felt that the influence produced on him by the service would not endure. And it did in fact weaken till only the habit remained.

In general in the seventh year of his life in the monastery Sergius grew weary. He had learnt all there was to learn and had attained all there was to attain, there was nothing more to do and his spiritual drowsiness increased. During this time he heard of his mother's death and his sister Varvara's marriage, but both events were matters of indifference to him. His whole attention and his whole interest were concentrated on his inner life.

In the fourth year of his priesthood, during which the Bishop had been particularly kind to him, the *starets* told him that he ought not to decline it if he were offered an appointment to higher duties. Then monastic ambition, the very thing he had found so repulsive in other monks, arose within him. He was assigned to a monastery near the metropolis. He wished to refuse but the *starets* ordered him to accept the appointment. He did so, and took leave of the *starets* and moved to the other monastery.

The exchange into the metropolitan monastery was an important event in Sergius's life. There he encountered many temptations, and his whole willpower was concentrated on meeting them.

In the first monastery, women had not been a temptation to him, but here that temptation arose with terrible strength and even took definite shape. There was a lady known for her frivolous behavior who began to seek his favor. She talked to him and asked him to visit her. Sergius sternly declined, but was horrified by the definiteness of his desire. He was so alarmed that he wrote about it to the *starets*. And in addition, to keep himself in hand, he spoke to a young novice and, conquering his sense of shame, confessed his weakness to him, asking him to keep watch on him and not let him go anywhere except to service and to fulfil his duties.

Besides this, a great pitfall for Sergius lay in the fact of his extreme antipathy to his new abbot, a cunning worldly man who was making a career for himself in the church. Struggle with himself as he might, he could not master that feeling. He was submissive to the abbot, but in the depths of his soul he never ceased to condemn him. And in the second year of his residence at the new monastery that ill-feeling broke out.

The Vigil service was being performed in the large church on the eve of the feast of the Intercession of the Blessed Virgin, and there were many visitors. The abbot himself was conducting the service. Father Sergius was standing in his usual place and praying: that is, he was in that condition of struggle which always occupied him during the service, especially in the large church when he was not himself conducting the service. This conflict was occasioned by his irritation at the presence of fine folk, especially ladies. He tried not to see them or to notice all that went on: how a soldier conducted them, pushing the common people aside, how the ladies pointed out the monks to one another—especially himself and a monk noted for his good looks. He tried as it were to keep his mind in blinkers, to see nothing but the light of the candles on the altar screen, the icons, and those conducting the service. He tried to hear nothing but the prayers that were being chanted or read, to feel nothing but self-oblivion in consciousness of the fulfilment of duty—a feeling he always experienced when hearing or reciting in advance the prayers he had so often heard.

So he stood, crossing and prostrating himself when necessary, and struggled with himself, now giving way to cold condemnation and now to a consciously evoked obliteration of thought and feeling. Then the sacristan, Father Nicodemus—also a great stumbling-block to Sergius who involuntarily reproached him for flattering and fawning on the abbot—approached him and, bowing low, requested his presence behind the holy gates. Father Sergius straightened his mantle, put on his biretta, and went circumspectly through the crowd.

"*Lise, regarde à droite, c'est lui!*" he heard a woman's voice say.

"*Où, où? Il n'est pas tellement beau.*"[1]

He knew that they were speaking of him. He heard them and, as al-

---

[1] ["Lise, look to the right—that's him." . . . "Where? Where? He isn't so good-looking."]

ways at moments of temptation, he repeated the words, "Lead us not into temptation," and bowing his head and lowering his eyes went past the ambo and in by the north door, avoiding the canons in their cassocks who were just then passing the altar screen. On entering the sanctuary he bowed, crossing himself as usual and bending double before the icons. Then, raising his head but without turning, he glanced out of the corner of his eye at the abbot, whom he saw standing beside another glittering figure.

The abbot was standing by the wall in his vestments. Having freed his short plump hands from beneath his chasuble he had folded them over his fat body and protruding stomach, and fingering the cords of his vestments was smilingly saying something to a military man in the uniform of a general of the imperial suite, with its insignia and shoulder-knots which Father Sergius's experienced eye at once recognized. This general had been the commander of the regiment in which Sergius had served. He now evidently occupied an important position, and Father Sergius at once noticed that the abbot was aware of this and that his red face and bald head beamed with satisfaction and pleasure. This vexed and disgusted Father Sergius, the more so when he heard that the abbot had only sent for him to satisfy the general's curiosity to see a man who had formerly served with him, as he expressed it.

"Very pleased to see you in your angelic guise," said the general, holding out his hand. "I hope you have not forgotten an old comrade."

The whole thing—the abbot's red, smiling face amid its fringe of grey, the general's words, his well-cared-for face with its self-satisfied smile and the smell of wine from his breath and of cigars from his whiskers—revolted Father Sergius. He bowed again to the abbot and said:

"Your reverence deigned to send for me?"—and stopped, the whole expression of his face and eyes asking why.

"Yes, to meet the general," replied the abbot.

"Your reverence, I left the world to save myself from temptation," said Father Sergius, turning pale and with quivering lips. "Why do you expose me to it during prayers and in God's house?"

"You may go! Go!" said the abbot, flaring up and frowning.

Next day Father Sergius asked pardon of the abbot and of the brethren for his pride, but at the same time, after a night spent in prayer, he decided that he must leave this monastery, and he wrote to the *starets* begging permission to return to him. He wrote that he felt his weakness and incapacity to struggle against temptation without his help, and penitently confessed his sin of pride. By return of post came a letter from the *starets,* who wrote that Sergius's pride was the cause of all that had happened. The old man pointed out that his fits of anger were due to the fact that in refusing all clerical honors he humiliated himself not for the sake of

God but for the sake of his pride. "There now, am I not a splendid man not to want anything?" That was why he could not tolerate the abbot's action. "I have renounced everything for the glory of God, and here I am exhibited like a wild beast!" "Had you renounced vanity for God's sake you would have borne it. Worldly pride is not yet dead in you. I have thought about you, Sergius my son, and prayed also, and this is what God has suggested to me. At the Tambov hermitage the anchorite Hilary, a man of saintly life, has died. He had lived there eighteen years. The Tambov abbot is asking whether there is not a brother who would take his place. And here comes your letter. Go to Father Païssy of the Tambov Monastery. I will write to him about you, and you must ask for Hilary's cell. Not that you can replace Hilary, but you need solitude to quell your pride. May God bless you!"

Sergius obeyed the *starets,* showed his letter to the abbot, and having obtained his permission, gave up his cell, handed all his possessions over to the monastery, and set out for the Tambov hermitage.

There the abbot, an excellent manager of merchant origin, received Sergius simply and quietly and placed him in Hilary's cell, at first assigning to him a lay brother but afterwards leaving him alone, at Sergius's own request. The cell was a dual cave, dug into the hillside, and in it Hilary had been buried. In the back part was Hilary's grave, while in the front was a niche for sleeping, with a straw mattress, a small table, and a shelf with icons and books. Outside the outer door, which fastened with a hook, was another shelf on which, once a day, a monk placed food from the monastery.

And so Sergius became a hermit.

III

At carnival time, in the sixth year of Sergius's life at the hermitage, a merry company of rich people, men and women from a neighboring town, made up a troyka party, after a meal of carnival pancakes and wine. The company consisted of two lawyers, a wealthy landowner, an officer, and four ladies. One lady was the officer's wife, another the wife of the landowner, the third his sister—a young girl—and the fourth a divorcee, beautiful, rich, and eccentric, who amazed and shocked the town by her escapades.

The weather was excellent and the snow-covered road smooth as a floor. They drove some seven miles out of town, and then stopped and consulted as to whether they should turn back or drive farther.

"But where does this road lead to?" asked Makovkina, the beautiful divorcee.

"To Tambov, eight miles from here," replied one of the lawyers, who was having a flirtation with her.

"And then where?"

"Then on to L——, past the monastery."

"Where that Father Sergius lives?"

"Yes."

"Kasatsky, the handsome hermit?"

"Yes."

"*Mesdames et messieurs,* let us drive on and see Kasatsky! We can stop at Tambov and have something to eat."

"But we shouldn't get home tonight!"

"Never mind, we will stay at Kasatsky's."

"Well, there is a very good hostelry at the monastery. I stayed there when I was defending Makhin."

"No, I shall spend the night at Kasatsky's!"

"Impossible! Even your omnipotence could not accomplish that!"

"Impossible? Will you bet?"

"All right! If you spend the night with him, the stake shall be whatever you like."

"*A discrétion!*"[2]

"But on your side too!"

"Yes, of course. Let us drive on."

Vodka was handed to the drivers, and the party got out a box of pies, wine, and sweets for themselves. The ladies wrapped up in their white dogskins. The drivers disputed as to whose troyka should go ahead, and the youngest, seating himself sideways with a dashing air, swung his long knout and shouted to the horses. The troyka bells tinkled and the sledge runners squeaked over the snow.

The sledges swayed hardly at all. The shaft-horse, with his tightly bound tail under his decorated breechband, galloped smoothly and briskly; the smooth road seemed to run rapidly backwards, while the driver dashingly shook the reins. One of the lawyers and the officer sitting opposite talked nonsense to Makovkina's neighbor, but Makovkina herself sat motionless and in thought, tightly wrapped in her fur. "Always the same and always nasty! The same red shiny faces smelling of wine and cigars! The same talk, the same thoughts, and always about the same things! And they are all satisfied and confident that it should be so, and will go on living like that till they die. But I can't. It bores me. I want something that would upset it all and turn it upside down. Suppose it happened to us as to those people—at Saratov was it?—who kept on driving and froze to death. . . . What would our people do? How would they behave? Basely, for certain. Each for himself. And I too should act badly. But I at any rate have beauty. They all know it. And how about that monk?

---

[2]["Whatever I want!"; or "Unconditionally!"]

Is it possible that he has become indifferent to it? No! That is the one thing they all care for—like that cadet last autumn. What a fool he was!"

"Ivan Nikolayevich!" she said aloud.

"What are your commands?"

"How old is he?"

"Who?"

"Kasatsky."

"Over forty, I should think."

"And does he receive all visitors?"

"Yes, everybody, but not always."

"Cover up my feet. Not like that—how clumsy you are! No! More, more—like that! But you need not squeeze them!"

So they came to the forest where the cell was.

Makovkina got out of the sledge, and told them to drive on. They tried to dissuade her, but she grew irritable and ordered them to go on.

When the sledges had gone she went up the path in her white dogskin coat. The lawyer got out and stopped to watch her.

It was Father Sergius's sixth year as a recluse, and he was now forty-nine. His life in solitude was hard—not on account of the fasts and the prayers (they were no hardship to him) but on account of an inner conflict he had not at all anticipated. The sources of that conflict were two: doubts, and the lust of the flesh. And these two enemies always appeared together. It seemed to him that they were two foes, but in reality they were one and the same. As soon as doubt was gone so was the lustful desire. But thinking them to be two different fiends he fought them separately.

"O my God, my God!" thought he. "Why dost thou not grant me faith? There is lust, of course: even the saints had to fight that—Saint Anthony and others. But they had faith, while I have moments, hours, and days, when it is absent. Why does the whole world, with all its delights, exist if it is sinful and must be renounced? Why hast thou created this temptation? Temptation? Is it not rather a temptation that I wish to abandon all the joys of earth and prepare something for myself there where perhaps there is nothing?" And he became horrified and filled with disgust at himself. "Vile creature! And it is you who wish to become a saint!" he upbraided himself, and he began to pray. But as soon as he started to pray he saw himself vividly as he had been at the monastery, in a majestic post in biretta and mantle, and he shook his head. "No, that is not right. It is deception. I may deceive others, but not myself or God. I am not a majestic man, but a pitiable and ridiculous one!" And he threw back the folds of his cassock and smiled as he looked at his thin legs in their underclothing.

Then he dropped the folds of the cassock again and began reading the prayers, making the sign of the cross and prostrating himself. "Can it be that this couch will be my bier?" he read. And it seemed as if a devil whispered to him: "A solitary couch is itself a bier. Falsehood!" And in imagination he saw the shoulders of a widow with whom he had lived. He shook himself, and went on reading. Having read the precepts he took up the Gospels, opened the book, and happened on a passage he often repeated and knew by heart: "Lord, I believe. Help thou my unbelief!"—and he put away all the doubts that had arisen. As one replaces an object of insecure equilibrium, so he carefully replaced his belief on its shaky pedestal and carefully stepped back from it so as not to shake or upset it. The blinkers were adjusted again and he felt tranquillized, and repeating his childhood's prayer: "Lord, receive me, receive me!" He felt not merely at ease, but thrilled and joyful. He crossed himself and lay down on the bedding on his narrow bench, tucking his summer cassock under his head. He fell asleep at once, and in his light slumber he seemed to hear the tinkling of sledge bells. He did not know whether he was dreaming or awake, but a knock at the door aroused him. He sat up, distrusting his senses, but the knock was repeated. Yes, it was a knock close at hand, at his door, and with it the sound of a woman's voice.

"My God! Can it be true, as I have read in the *Lives of the Saints,* that the devil takes on the form of a woman? Yes—it is a woman's voice. And a tender, timid, pleasant voice. Phui!" And he spat to exorcise the devil. "No, it was only my imagination," he assured himself, and he went to the corner where his lectern stood, falling on his knees in the regular and habitual manner which of itself gave him consolation and satisfaction. He sank down, his hair hanging over his face, and pressed his head, already going bald in front, to the cold damp strip of drugget on the draughty floor. He read the psalm old Father Pimon had told him warded off temptation. He easily raised his light and emaciated body on his strong sinewy legs and tried to continue saying his prayers, but instead of doing so he involuntarily strained his hearing. He wished to hear more. All was quiet. From the corner of the roof regular drops continued to fall into the tub below. Outside was a mist and fog eating into the snow that lay on the ground. It was still, very still. And suddenly there was a rustling at the window and a voice—that same tender, timid voice, which could only belong to an attractive woman—said:

"Let me in, for Christ's sake!"

It seemed as though his blood had all rushed to his heart and settled there. He could hardly breathe. "Let God arise and let his enemies be scattered . . ."

"But I am not a devil!" It was obvious that the lips that uttered this were smiling. "I am not a devil, but only a sinful woman who has lost her way, not figuratively but literally!" She laughed. "I am frozen and beg for shelter."

He pressed his face to the window, but the little icon lamp was reflected by it and shone on the whole pane. He put his hands to both sides of his face and peered between them. Fog, mist, a tree, and—just opposite him—she herself. Yes, there, a few inches from him, was the sweet, kindly frightened face of a woman in a cap and a coat of long white fur, leaning towards him. Their eyes met with instant recognition: not that they had ever known one another, they had never met before, but by the look they exchanged they—and he particularly—felt that they knew and understood one another. After that glance to imagine her to be a devil and not a simple, kindly, sweet, timid woman, was impossible.

"Who are you? Why have you come?" he asked.

"Do please open the door!" she replied, with capricious authority. "I am frozen. I tell you I have lost my way."

"But I am a monk—a hermit."

"Oh, do please open the door—or do you wish me to freeze under your window while you say your prayers?"

"But how have you . . ."

"I shan't eat you. For God's sake let me in! I am quite frozen."

She really did feel afraid, and said this in an almost tearful voice.

He stepped back from the window and looked at an icon of the Savior in his crown of thorns. "Lord, help me! Lord, help me!" he exclaimed, crossing himself and bowing low. Then he went to the door, and opening it into the tiny porch, felt for the hook that fastened the outer door and began to lift it. He heard steps outside. She was coming from the window to the door. "Ah!" she suddenly exclaimed, and he understood that she had stepped into the puddle that the dripping from the roof had formed at the threshold. His hands trembled, and he could not raise the hook of the tightly closed door.

"Oh, what are you doing? Let me in! I am all wet. I am frozen! You are thinking about saving your soul and are letting me freeze to death . . ."

He jerked the door towards him, raised the hook, and without considering what he was doing, pushed it open with such force that it struck her.

"Oh—*pardon!*" he suddenly exclaimed, reverting completely to his old manner with ladies.

She smiled on hearing that *pardon*. "He is not quite so terrible, after all," she thought. "It's all right. It is you who must pardon me," she said, stepping past him. "I should never have ventured, but such an extraordinary circumstance . . ."

"If you please!" he uttered, and stood aside to let her pass him. A strong smell of fine scent, which he had long not encountered, struck him. She went through the little porch into the cell where he lived. He closed the outer door without fastening the hook, and stepped in after her.

"Lord Jesus Christ, Son of God, have mercy on me a sinner! Lord, have mercy on me a sinner!" he prayed unceasingly, not merely to himself but involuntarily moving his lips. "If you please!" he said to her again. She stood in the middle of the room, moisture dripping from her to the floor as she looked him over. Her eyes were laughing.

"Forgive me for having disturbed your solitude. But you see what a position I am in. It all came about from our starting from town for a sledge drive, and my making a bet that I would walk back by myself from the Vorobyovka to the town. But then I lost my way, and if I had not happened to come upon your cell . . ." She began lying, but his face confused her so that she could not continue, but became silent. She had not expected him to be at all such as he was. He was not as handsome as she had imagined, but was nevertheless beautiful in her eyes: his greyish hair and beard, slightly curling, his fine, regular nose, and his eyes like glowing coal when he looked at her, made a strong impression on her.

He saw that she was lying.

"Yes . . . so," said he, looking at her and again lowering his eyes. "I will go in there, and this place is at your disposal."

And taking down the little lamp, he lit a candle, and bowing low to her went into the small cell beyond the partition, and she heard him begin to move something about there. "Probably he is barricading himself in from me!" she thought with a smile, and throwing off her white dogskin cloak she tried to take off her cap, which had become entangled in her hair and in the woven kerchief she was wearing under it. She had not got at all wet when standing under the window, and had said so only as a pretext to get him to let her in. But she really had stepped into the puddle at the door, and her left foot was wet up to the ankle and her overshoe full of water. She sat down on his bed—a bench only covered by a bit of carpet—and began to take off her boots. The little cell seemed to her charming. The narrow little room, some seven feet by nine, was as clean as glass. There was nothing in it but the bench on which she was sitting, the book-shelf above it, and a lectern in the corner. A sheepskin coat and a cassock hung on nails by the door. Above the lectern was the little lamp and an icon of Christ in his crown of thorns. The room smelt strangely of perspiration and of earth. It all pleased her—even that smell. Her wet feet, especially one of them, were uncomfortable, and she quickly began to take off her boots and stockings without ceasing to smile, pleased not so much at having achieved her object as because she perceived that she had abashed that charming, strange, striking, and attractive man. "He did not respond, but what of that?" she said to herself.

"Father Sergius! Father Sergius! Or how does one call you?"

"What do you want?" replied a quiet voice.

"Please forgive me for disturbing your solitude, but really I could not help it. I should simply have fallen ill. And I don't know that I shan't now. I am all wet and my feet are like ice."

"Pardon me," replied the quiet voice. "I cannot be of any assistance to you."

"I would not have disturbed you if I could have helped it. I am only here till daybreak."

He did not reply and she heard him muttering something, probably his prayers.

"You will not be coming in here?" she asked, smiling. "For I must undress to dry myself."

He did not reply, but continued to read his prayers.

"Yes, that is a man!" thought she, getting her dripping boot off with difficulty. She tugged at it, but could not get it off. The absurdity of it struck her and she began to laugh almost inaudibly. But knowing that he would hear her laughter and would be moved by it just as she wished him to be, she laughed louder, and her laughter—gay, natural, and kindly—really acted on him just in the way she wished.

"Yes, I could love a man like that—such eyes and such a simple noble face, and passionate too despite all the prayers he mutters!" thought she. "You can't deceive a woman in these things. As soon as he put his face to the window and saw me, he understood and knew. The glimmer of it was in his eyes and remained there. He began to love me and desired me. Yes—desired!" said she, getting her overshoe and her boot off at last and starting to take off her stockings. To remove those long stockings fastened with elastic it was necessary to raise her skirts. She felt embarrassed and said:

"Don't come in!"

But there was no reply from the other side of the wall. The steady muttering continued and also a sound of moving.

"He is prostrating himself to the ground, no doubt," thought she. "But he won't bow himself out of it. He is thinking of me just as I am thinking of him. He is thinking of these feet of mine with the same feeling that I have!" And she pulled off her wet stockings and put her feet up on the bench, pressing them under her. She sat a while like that with her arms round her knees and looking pensively before her. "But it is a desert, here in this silence. No one would ever know. . . ."

She rose, took her stockings over to the stove, and hung them on the damper. It was a queer damper, and she turned it about, and then, stepping lightly on her bare feet, returned to the bench and sat down there again with her feet up.

There was complete silence on the other side of the partition. She looked at the tiny watch that hung round her neck. It was two o'clock. "Our party should return about three!" She had not more than an hour before her. "Well, am I to sit like this all alone? What nonsense! I don't want to. I will call him at once."

"Father Sergius, Father Sergius! Sergey Dmitrich! Prince Kasatsky!"

Beyond the partition all was silent.

"Listen! This is cruel. I would not call you if it were not necessary. I am ill. I don't know what is the matter with me!" she exclaimed in a tone of suffering. "Oh! Oh!" she groaned, falling back on the bench. And strange to say she really felt that her strength was failing, that she was becoming faint, that everything in her ached, and that she was shivering with fever.

"Listen! Help me! I don't know what is the matter with me. Oh! Oh!" She unfastened her dress, exposing her breast, and lifted her arms, bare to the elbow. "Oh! Oh!"

All this time he stood on the other side of the partition and prayed. Having finished all the evening prayers, he now stood motionless, his eyes looking at the end of his nose, and mentally repeated with all his soul: "Lord Jesus Christ, Son of God, have mercy upon me!"

But he had heard everything. He had heard how the silk rustled when she took off her dress, how she stepped with bare feet on the floor, and had heard how she rubbed her feet with her hand. He felt his own weakness, and that he might be lost at any moment. That was why he prayed unceasingly. He felt rather as the hero in the fairy tale must have felt when he had to go on and on without looking round. So Sergius heard and felt that danger and destruction were there, hovering above and around him, and that he could only save himself by not looking in that direction for an instant. But suddenly the desire to look seized him. At the same instant she said:

"This is inhuman. I may die. . . ."

"Yes, I will go to her, but like the saint who laid one hand on the adulteress and thrust his other into the brazier. But there is no brazier here." He looked round. The lamp! He put his finger over the flame and frowned, preparing himself to suffer. And for a rather long time, as it seemed to him, there was no sensation, but suddenly—he had not yet decided whether it was painful enough—he writhed all over, jerked his hand away, and waved it in the air. "No, I can't stand that!"

"For God's sake come to me! I am dying! Oh!"

"Well," he thought, "shall I perish? No, not so!"

"I will come to you directly," he said, and having opened his door, he went without looking at her through the cell into the porch where he used to chop wood. There he felt for the block and for an axe which leant against the wall.

"Immediately!" he said, and taking up the axe with his right hand he laid the forefinger of his left hand on the block, swung the axe, and struck with it below the second joint. The finger flew off more lightly than a stick of similar thickness, and bounding up, turned over on the edge of the block and then fell to the floor.

He heard it fall before he felt any pain, but before he had time to be surprised he felt a burning pain and the warmth of flowing blood. He hastily wrapped the stump in the skirt of his cassock, and pressing it to his hip went back into the room, and standing in front of the woman, lowered his eyes and asked in a low voice: "What do you want?"

She looked at his pale face and his quivering left cheek, and suddenly felt ashamed. She jumped up, seized her fur cloak, and throwing it round her shoulders, wrapped herself up in it.

"I was in pain . . . I have caught cold . . . I . . . Father Sergius . . . I . . ."

He let his eyes, shining with a quiet light of joy, rest upon her, and said:

"Dear sister, why did you wish to ruin your immortal soul? Temptations must come into the world, but woe to him by whom temptation comes. Pray that God may forgive us!"

She listened and looked at him. Suddenly she heard the sound of something dripping. She looked down and saw that blood was flowing from his hand and down his cassock.

"What have you done to your hand?" She remembered the sound she had heard, and seizing the little lamp ran out into the porch. There on the floor she saw the bloody finger. She returned with her face paler than his and was about to speak to him, but he silently passed into the back cell and fastened the door.

"Forgive me!" she said. "How can I atone for my sin?"

"Go away."

"Let me tie up your hand."

"Go away from here."

She dressed hurriedly and silently, and when ready sat waiting in her furs. The sledge bells were heard outside.

"Father Sergius, forgive me!"

"Go away. God will forgive."

"Father Sergius! I will change my life. Do not forsake me!"

"Go away."

"Forgive me—and give me your blessing!"

"In the name of the Father and of the Son and of the Holy Ghost!"— she heard his voice from behind the partition. "Go!"

She burst into sobs and left the cell. The lawyer came forward to meet her.

"Well, I see I have lost the bet. It can't be helped. Where will you sit?"

"It is all the same to me."

She took a seat in the sledge, and did not utter a word all the way home.

A year later she entered a convent as a novice, and lived a strict life under the direction of the hermit Arseny, who wrote letters to her at long intervals.

IV

Father Sergius lived as a recluse for another seven years.

At first he accepted much of what people brought him—tea, sugar, white bread, milk, clothing, and firewood. But as time went on he led a more and more austere life, refusing everything superfluous, and finally he accepted nothing but rye bread once a week. Everything else that was brought to him he gave to the poor who came to him. He spent his entire time in his cell, in prayer or in conversation with callers, who became more and more numerous as time went on. Only three times a year did he go out to church, and when necessary he went out to fetch water and wood.

The episode with Makovkina had occurred after five years of his hermit life. That occurrence soon became generally known—her nocturnal visit, the change she underwent, and her entry into a convent. From that time Father Sergius's fame increased. More and more visitors came to see him, other monks settled down near his cell, and a church was erected there and also a hostelry. His fame, as usual exaggerating his feats, spread ever more and more widely. People began to come to him from a distance, and began bringing invalids to him whom they declared he cured.

His first cure occurred in the eighth year of his life as a hermit. It was the healing of a fourteen-year-old boy, whose mother brought him to Father Sergius insisting that he should lay his hand on the child's head. It had never occurred to Father Sergius that he could cure the sick. He would have regarded such a thought as a great sin of pride; but the mother who brought the boy implored him insistently, falling at his feet and saying: "Why do you, who heal others, refuse to help my son?" She besought him in Christ's name. When Father Sergius assured her that only God could heal the sick, she replied that she only wanted him to lay his hands on the boy and pray for him. Father Sergius refused and returned to his cell. But next day (it was in autumn and the nights were already cold) on going out for water he saw the same mother with her son, a pale boy of fourteen, and was met by the same petition.

He remembered the parable of the unjust judge, and though he had previously felt sure that he ought to refuse, he now began to hesitate and, having hesitated, took to prayer and prayed until a decision formed itself in his soul. This decision was, that he ought to accede to the woman's request and that her faith might save her son. As for himself, he would in this case be but an insignificant instrument chosen by God.

And going out to the mother he did what she asked—laid his hand on the boy's head and prayed.

The mother left with her son, and a month later the boy recovered, and the fame of the holy healing power of the *starets* Sergius (as they now called him) spread throughout the whole district. After that, not a week passed without sick people coming, riding or on foot, to Father Sergius; and having acceded to one petition he could not refuse others, and he laid his hands on many and prayed. Many recovered, and his fame spread more and more.

So seven years passed in the monastery and thirteen in his hermit's cell. He now had the appearance of an old man: his beard was long and grey, but his hair, though thin, was still black and curly.

V

For some weeks Father Sergius had been living with one persistent thought: whether he was right in accepting the position in which he had not so much placed himself as been placed by the archimandrite and the abbot. That position had begun after the recovery of the fourteen-year-old boy. From that time, with each month, week, and day that passed, Sergius felt his own inner life wasting away and being replaced by external life. It was as if he had been turned inside out.

Sergius saw that he was a means of attracting visitors and contributions to the monastery, and that therefore the authorities arranged matters in such a way as to make as much use of him as possible. For instance, they rendered it impossible for him to do any manual work. He was supplied with everything he could want, and they only demanded of him that he should not refuse his blessing to those who came to seek it. For his convenience they appointed days when he would receive. They arranged a reception room for men, and a place was railed in so that he should not be pushed over by the crowds of women visitors, and so that he could conveniently bless those who came.

They told him that people needed him, and that fulfilling Christ's law of love he could not refuse their demand to see him, and that to avoid them would be cruel. He could not but agree with this, but the more he gave himself up to such a life the more he felt that what was internal became external, and that the fount of living water within him dried up, and that what he did now was done more and more for men and less and less for God.

Whether he admonished people, or simply blessed them, or prayed for the sick, or advised people about their lives, or listened to expressions of gratitude from those he had helped by precepts, or alms, or healing (as they assured him)—he could not help being pleased at it, and could not be indifferent to the results of his activity and to the influence he exerted. He thought himself a shining light, and the more he felt this the more was he conscious of a weakening, a dying down of the divine light of truth that shone within him.

"In how far is what I do for God and in how far is it for men?" That was the question that insistently tormented him and to which he was not so much unable to give himself an answer as unable to face the answer.

In the depth of his soul he felt that the devil had substituted an activity for men in place of his former activity for God. He felt this because, just as it had formerly been hard for him to be torn from his solitude so now that solitude itself was hard for him. He was oppressed and wearied by visitors, but at the bottom of his heart he was glad of their presence and glad of the praise they heaped upon him.

There was a time when he decided to go away and hide. He even planned all that was necessary for that purpose. He prepared for himself a peasant's shirt, trousers, coat, and cap. He explained that he wanted these to give to those who asked. And he kept these clothes in his cell, planning how he would put them on, cut his hair short, and go away. First he would go some three hundred versts by train, then he would leave the train and walk from village to village. He asked an old man who had been a soldier how he tramped: what people gave him, and what shelter they allowed him. The soldier told him where people were most charitable, and where they would take a wanderer in for the night, and Father Sergius intended to avail himself of this information. He even put on those clothes one night in his desire to go, but he could not decide what was best—to remain or to escape. At first he was in doubt, but afterwards this indecision passed. He submitted to custom and yielded to the devil, and only the peasant garb reminded him of the thought and feeling he had had.

Every day more and more people flocked to him and less and less time was left him for prayer and for renewing his spiritual strength. Sometimes in lucid moments he thought he was like a place where there had once been a spring. "There used to be a feeble spring of living water which flowed quietly from me and through me. That was true life, the time when she tempted me!" (He always thought with ecstasy of that night and of her who was now Mother Agnes.) She had tasted of that pure water, but since then there had not been time for it to collect before thirsty people came crowding in and pushing one another aside. And they had trampled everything down and nothing was left but mud.

So he thought in rare moments of lucidity, but his usual state of mind was one of weariness and a tender pity for himself because of that weariness.

It was in spring, on the eve of the mid-Pentecostal feast. Father Sergius was officiating at the Vigil Service in his hermitage church, where the congregation was as large as the little church could hold—about twenty people. They were all well-to-do proprietors or merchants. Father Sergius admitted anyone, but a selection was made by the monk in attendance and by an assistant who was sent to the hermitage every day from the monastery. A crowd of some eighty people—pilgrims and peasants, and especially peasant women—stood outside waiting for Father Sergius to come out and bless them. Meanwhile he conducted the service, but at the point at which he went out to the tomb of his predecessor, he staggered and would have fallen had he not been caught by a merchant standing behind him and by the monk acting as deacon.

"What is the matter, Father Sergius? Dear man! O Lord!" exclaimed the women. "He is as white as a sheet!"

But Father Sergius recovered immediately, and though very pale, he waved the merchant and the deacon aside and continued to chant the service.

Father Seraphim, the deacon, the acolytes, and Sofya Ivanovna, a lady who always lived near the hermitage and tended Father Sergius, begged him to bring the service to an end.

"No, there's nothing the matter," said Father Sergius, slightly smiling from beneath his mustache and continuing the service. "Yes, that is the way the saints behaved!" thought he.

"A holy man—an angel of God!" he heard just then the voice of Sofya Ivanovna behind him, and also of the merchant who had supported him. He did not heed their entreaties, but went on with the service. Again crowding together they all made their way by the narrow passages back into the little church, and there, though abbreviating it slightly, Father Sergius completed vespers.

Immediately after the service Father Sergius, having pronounced the benediction on those present, went over to the bench under the elm tree at the entrance to the cave. He wished to rest and breathe the fresh air—he felt in need of it. But as soon as he left the church the crowd of people rushed to him soliciting his blessing, his advice, and his help. There were pilgrims who constantly tramped from one holy place to another and from one *starets* to another, and were always entranced by every shrine and every *starets*. Father Sergius knew this common, cold, conventional, and most irreligious type. There were pilgrims, for the most part discharged soldiers, unaccustomed to a settled life, poverty-stricken, and many of them drunken old men, who tramped from monastery to monastery merely to be fed. And there were rough peasants and peasant-women who had come with their selfish requirements, seeking cures or to have doubts about quite practical affairs solved for them: about marrying off a daughter, or hiring a shop, or buying a bit of land, or how to atone for having overlaid a child or having an illegitimate one.

All this was an old story and not in the least interesting to him. He knew he would hear nothing new from these folk, that they would arouse no religious emotion in him; but he liked to see the crowd to which his blessing and advice was necessary and precious, so while that crowd oppressed him it also pleased him. Father Seraphim began to drive them away, saying that Father Sergius was tired. But Father Sergius, remembering the words of the Gospel: "Forbid them" (children) "not to come unto me," and feeling tenderly towards himself at this recollection, said they should be allowed to approach.

He rose, went to the railing beyond which the crowd had gathered, and began blessing them and answering their questions, but in a voice so weak that he was touched with pity for himself. Yet despite his wish to receive them all he could not do it. Things again grew dark before his eyes, and he staggered and grasped the railings. He felt a rush of blood to his head and first went pale and then suddenly flushed.

"I must leave the rest till tomorrow. I cannot do more today," and, pronouncing a general benediction, he returned to the bench. The merchant again supported him, and leading him by the arm helped him to be seated.

"Father!" came voices from the crowd. "Dear Father! Do not forsake us. Without you we are lost!"

The merchant, having seated Father Sergius on the bench under the elm, took on himself police duties and drove the people off very resolutely. It is true that he spoke in a low voice so that Father Sergius might not hear him, but his words were incisive and angry.

"Be off, be off! He has blessed you, and what more do you want? Get along with you, or I'll wring your necks! Move on there! Get along, you old woman with your dirty leg-bands! Go, go! Where are you shoving to? You've been told that it is finished. Tomorrow will be as God wills, but for today he has finished!"

"Father! Only let my eyes have a glimpse of his dear face!" said an old woman.

"I'll glimpse you! Where are you shoving to?"

Father Sergius noticed that the merchant seemed to be acting roughly, and in a feeble voice told the attendant that the people should not be driven away. He knew that they would be driven away all the same, and he much desired to be left alone and to rest, but he sent the attendant with that message to produce an impression.

"All right, all right! I am not driving them away. I am only remonstrating with them," replied the merchant. "You know they wouldn't hesitate to drive a man to death. They have no pity, they only consider themselves. . . . You've been told you cannot see him. Go away! Tomorrow!" And he got rid of them all.

He took all these pains because he liked order and liked to domineer and drive the people away, but chiefly because he wanted to have Father Sergius to himself. He was a widower with an only daughter who was an invalid and unmarried, and whom he had brought fourteen hundred versts[3] to Father Sergius to be healed. For two years past he had been taking her to different places to be cured: first to the university clinic in the chief town of the province, but that did no good; then to a peasant in the province of Samara, where she got a little better; then to a doctor in Moscow to whom he paid much money, but this did no good at all. Now he had been told that Father Sergius wrought cures, and had brought her to him. So when all the people had been driven away he approached Father Sergius, and suddenly falling on his knees loudly exclaimed:

"Holy Father! Bless my afflicted offspring that she may be healed of her malady. I venture to prostrate myself at your holy feet."

And he placed one hand on the other, cup-wise. He said and did all this as if he were doing something clearly and firmly appointed by law and usage—as if one must and should ask for a daughter to be cured in just this way and no other. He did it with such conviction that it seemed even to Father Sergius that it should be said and done in just that way, but nevertheless he bade him rise and tell him what the trouble was. The merchant said that his daughter, a girl of twenty-two, had fallen ill two years ago, after her mother's sudden death. She had moaned (as he expressed it) and since then had not been herself. And now he had brought her fourteen hundred versts and she was waiting in the hostelry till Father Sergius should give orders to bring her. She did not go out during the day, being afraid of the light, and could only come after sunset.

"Is she very weak?" asked Father Sergius.

"No, she has no particular weakness. She is quite plump, and is only 'nerastenic' the doctors say. If you will only let me bring her this evening, Father Sergius, I'll fly like a spirit to fetch her. Holy Father! Revive a parent's heart, restore his line, save his afflicted daughter by your prayers!" And the merchant again threw himself on his knees and bending sideways, with his head resting on his clenched fists, remained stock still.

---

[3] [A verst is approximately one kilometer, or two-thirds of a mile.]

Father Sergius again told him to get up, and thinking how heavy his activities were and how he went through with them patiently notwithstanding, he sighed heavily and after a few seconds of silence, said:

"Well, bring her this evening. I will pray for her, but now I am tired . . ." and he closed his eyes. "I will send for you."

The merchant went away, stepping on tiptoe, which only made his boots creak the louder, and Father Sergius remained alone.

His whole life was filled by Church services and by people who came to see him, but today had been a particularly difficult one. In the morning an important official had arrived and had had a long conversation with him; after that a lady had come with her son. This son was a sceptical young professor whom the mother, an ardent believer and devoted to Father Sergius, had brought that he might talk to him. The conversation had been very trying. The young man, evidently not wishing to have a controversy with a monk, had agreed with him in everything as with someone who was mentally inferior. Father Sergius saw that the young man did not believe but yet was satisfied, tranquil, and at ease, and the memory of that conversation now disquieted him.

"Have something to eat, Father," said the attendant.

"All right, bring me something."

The attendant went to a hut that had been arranged some ten paces from the cave, and Father Sergius remained alone.

The time was long past when he had lived alone doing everything for himself and eating only rye bread, or rolls prepared for the church. He had been advised long since that he had no right to neglect his health, and he was given wholesome, though Lenten, food. He ate sparingly, though much more than he had done, and often he ate with much pleasure, and not as formerly with aversion and a sense of guilt. So it was now. He had some gruel, drank a cup of tea, and ate half a white roll.

The attendant went away, and Father Sergius remained alone under the elm tree.

It was a wonderful May evening, when the birches, aspens, elms, wild cherries, and oaks, had just burst into foliage.

The bush of wild cherries behind the elm tree was in full bloom and had not yet begun to shed its blossoms, and the nightingales—one quite near at hand and two or three others in the bushes down by the river—burst into full song after some preliminary twitters. From the river came the far-off songs of peasants returning, no doubt, from their work. The sun was setting behind the forest, its last rays glowing through the leaves. All that side was brilliant green, the other side with the elm tree was dark. The cockchafers flew clumsily about, falling to the ground when they collided with anything.

After supper Father Sergius began to repeat a silent prayer: "O Lord

Jesus Christ, Son of God, have mercy upon us!" and then he read a psalm, and suddenly in the middle of the psalm a sparrow flew out from the bush, alighted on the ground, and hopped towards him chirping as it came, but then it took fright at something and flew away. He said a prayer which referred to his abandonment of the world, and hastened to finish it in order to send for the merchant with the sick daughter. She interested him in that she presented a distraction, and because both she and her father considered him a saint whose prayers were efficacious. Outwardly he disavowed that idea, but in the depths of his soul he considered it to be true.

He was often amazed that this had happened, that he, Stepan Kasatsky, had come to be such an extraordinary saint and even a worker of miracles, but of the fact that he was such there could not be the least doubt. He could not fail to believe in the miracles he himself witnessed, beginning with the sick boy and ending with the old woman who had recovered her sight when he had prayed for her.

Strange as it might be, it was so. Accordingly the merchant's daughter interested him as a new individual who had faith in him, and also as a fresh opportunity to confirm his healing powers and enhance his fame. "They bring people a thousand versts and write about it in the papers. The emperor knows of it, and they know of it in Europe, in unbelieving Europe"—thought he. And suddenly he felt ashamed of his vanity and again began to pray. "Lord, King of Heaven, Comforter, Soul of Truth! Come and enter into me and cleanse me from all sin and save and bless my soul. Cleanse me from the sin of worldly vanity that troubles me!" he repeated, and he remembered how often he had prayed about this and how vain till now his prayers had been in that respect. His prayers worked miracles for others, but in his own case God had not granted him liberation from this petty passion.

He remembered his prayers at the commencement of his life at the hermitage, when he prayed for purity, humility, and love, and how it seemed to him then that God heard his prayers. He had retained his purity and had chopped off his finger. And he lifted the shrivelled stump of that finger to his lips and kissed it. It seemed to him now that he had been humble then when he had always seemed loathsome to himself on account of his sinfulness; and when he remembered the tender feelings with which he had then met an old man who was bringing a drunken soldier to him to ask alms; and how he had received *her,* it seemed to him that he had then possessed love also. But now? And he asked himself whether he loved anyone, whether he loved Sofya Ivanovna, or Father Seraphim, whether he had any feeling of love for all who had come to him that day—for that learned young man with whom he had had that instructive discussion in which he was concerned only to show off his own intelligence and that he had not lagged behind the times in knowledge. He wanted and needed their love, but felt none towards them. He now had neither love nor humility nor purity.

He was pleased to know that the merchant's daughter was twenty-two, and he wondered whether she was good-looking. When he inquired whether she was weak, he really wanted to know if she had feminine charm.

"Can I have fallen so low?" he thought. "Lord, help me! Restore me, my Lord and God!" And he clasped his hands and began to pray.

The nightingales burst into song, a cockchafer knocked against him and crept up the back of his neck. He brushed it off. "But does he exist? What if I am knocking at a door fastened from outside? The bar is on the door for all to see. Nature—the nightingales and the cockchafers—is that bar. Perhaps the young man was right." And he began to pray aloud. He prayed for a long time till these thoughts vanished and he again felt calm and confident. He rang the bell and told the attendant to say that the merchant might bring his daughter to him now.

The merchant came, leading his daughter by the arm. He led her into the cell and immediately left her.

She was a very fair girl, plump and very short, with a pale, frightened, childish face and a much developed feminine figure. Father Sergius remained seated on the bench at the entrance and when she was passing and stopped beside him for his blessing he was aghast at himself for the way he looked at her figure. As she passed by him he was acutely conscious of her femininity, though he saw by her face that she was sensual and feeble-minded. He rose and went into the cell. She was sitting on a stool waiting for him, and when he entered she rose.

"I want to go back to Papa," she said.

"Don't be afraid," he replied. "What are you suffering from?"

"I am in pain all over," she said, and suddenly her face lit up with a smile.

"You will be well," said he. "Pray!"

"What is the use of praying? I have prayed and it does no good"—and she continued to smile. "I want you to pray for me and lay your hands on me. I saw you in a dream."

"How did you see me?"

"I saw you put your hands on my breast like that." She took his hand and pressed it to her breast. "Just here."

He yielded his right hand to her.

"What is your name?" he asked, trembling all over and feeling that he was overcome and that his desire had already passed beyond control.

"Marie. Why?"

She took his hand and kissed it, and then put her arm round his waist and pressed him to herself.

"What are you doing?" he said. "Marie, you are a devil!"

"Oh, perhaps. What does it matter?"

And embracing him she sat down with him on the bed.

At dawn he went out into the porch.

"Can this all have happened? Her father will come and she will tell him everything. She is a devil! What am I to do? Here is the axe with which I chopped off my finger." He snatched up the axe and moved back towards the cell.

The attendant came up.

"Do you want some wood chopped? Let me have the axe."

Sergius yielded up the axe and entered the cell. She was lying there asleep. He looked at her with horror, and passed on beyond the partition, where he took down the peasant clothes and put them on. Then he seized a pair of scissors, cut off his long hair, and went out along the path down the hill to the river, where he had not been for more than three years.

A road ran beside the river and he went along it and walked till noon. Then he went into a field of rye and lay down there. Towards evening he approached a village, but without entering it went towards the cliff that overhung the river. There he again lay down to rest.

It was early morning, half an hour before sunrise. All was damp and gloomy and a cold early wind was blowing from the west. "Yes, I must end it all. There is no God. But how am I to end it? Throw myself into the river? I can swim and should not drown. Hang myself? Yes, just throw this sash over a branch." This seemed so feasible and so easy that he felt horrified. As usual at moments of despair he felt the need of prayer. But there was no one to pray to. There was no God. He lay down resting on his arm, and suddenly such a longing for sleep overcame him that he could no longer support his head on his hand, but stretched out his arm, laid his head upon it, and fell asleep. But that sleep lasted only for a moment. He woke up immediately and began not to dream but to remember.

He saw himself as a child in his mother's home in the country. A carriage drives up, and out of it steps Uncle Nicholas Sergeyevich, with his long, spade-shaped, black beard, and with him Pashenka, a thin little girl with large mild eyes and a timid pathetic face. And into their company of boys Pashenka is brought and they have to play with her, but it is dull. She is silly, and it ends by their making fun of her and forcing her to show how she can swim. She lies down on the floor and shows them, and they all laugh and make a fool of her. She sees this and blushes red in patches and becomes more pitiable than before, so pitiable that he feels ashamed and can never forget that crooked, kindly, submissive smile. And

Sergius remembered having seen her since then. Long after, just before he became a monk, she had married a landowner who squandered all her fortune and was in the habit of beating her. She had had two children, a son and a daughter, but the son had died while still young. And Sergius remembered having seen her very wretched. Then again he had seen her in the monastery when she was a widow. She had been still the same, not exactly stupid, but insipid, insignificant, and pitiable. She had come with her daughter and her daughter's fiance. They were already poor at that time and later on he had heard that she was living in a small provincial town and was very poor.

"Why am I thinking about her?" he asked himself, but he could not cease doing so. "Where is she? How is she getting on? Is she still as unhappy as she was then when she had to show us how to swim on the floor? But why should I think about her? What am I doing? I must put an end to myself."

And again he felt afraid, and again, to escape from that thought, he went on thinking about Pashenka.

So he lay for a long time, thinking now of his unavoidable end and now of Pashenka. She presented herself to him as a means of salvation. At last he fell asleep, and in his sleep he saw an angel who came to him and said: "Go to Pashenka and learn from her what you have to do, what your sin is, and wherein lies your salvation."

He awoke, and having decided that this was a vision sent by God, he felt glad, and resolved to do what had been told him in the vision. He knew the town where she lived. It was some three hundred versts away, and he set out to walk there.

VI

Pashenka had already long ceased to be Pashenka and had become old, withered, wrinkled Praskovya Mikhaylovna, mother-in-law of that failure, the drunken official Mavrikyev. She was living in the country town where he had had his last appointment, and there she was supporting the family: her daughter, her ailing neurasthenic son-in-law, and her five grandchildren. She did this by giving music lessons to tradesmen's daughters, giving four and sometimes five lessons a day of an hour each, and earning in this way some sixty rubles a month. So they lived for the present, in expectation of another appointment. She had sent letters to all her relations and acquaintances asking them to obtain a post for her son-in-law, and among the rest she had written to Sergius, but that letter had not reached him.

It was a Saturday, and Praskovya Mikhaylovna was herself mixing dough for currant bread such as the serf-cook on her father's estate used to make so well. She wished to give her grandchildren a treat on the Sunday.

Masha, her daughter, was nursing her youngest child, the eldest boy and girl were at school, and her son-in-law was asleep, not having slept during the night. Praskovya Mikhaylovna had remained awake too for a great part of the night, trying to soften her daughter's anger against her husband.

She saw that it was impossible for her son-in-law, a weak creature, to be other than he was, and realized that his wife's reproaches could do no good—so she used all her efforts to soften those reproaches and to avoid recrimination and anger. Unkindly relations between people caused her actual physical suffering. It was so clear to her that bitter feelings do not make anything better, but only make everything worse. She did not in fact think about this: she simply suffered at the sight of anger as she would from a bad smell, a harsh noise, or from blows on her body.

She had—with a feeling of self-satisfaction—just taught Lukerya how to mix the dough, when her six-year-old grandson Misha, wearing an apron and with darned stockings on his crooked little legs, ran into the kitchen with a frightened face.

"Grandma, a dreadful old man wants to see you."

Lukerya looked out at the door.

"There is a pilgrim of some kind, a man . . ."

Praskovya Mikhaylovna rubbed her thin elbows against one another, wiped her hands on her apron and went upstairs to get a five-kopek piece out of her purse for him, but remembering that she had nothing less than a ten-kopek piece she decided to give him some bread instead. She returned to the cupboard, but suddenly blushed at the thought of having grudged the ten-kopek piece, and telling Lukerya to cut a slice of bread, went upstairs again to fetch it. "It serves you right," she said to herself. "You must now give twice over."

She gave both the bread and the money to the pilgrim, and when doing so—far from being proud of her generosity—she excused herself for giving so little. The man had such an imposing appearance.

Though he had tramped two hundred versts as a beggar, though he was tattered and had grown thin and weatherbeaten, though he had cropped his long hair and was wearing a peasant's cap and boots, and though he bowed very humbly, Sergius still had the impressive appearance that made him so attractive. But Praskovya Mikhaylovna did not recognize him. She could hardly do so, not having seen him for almost twenty years.

"Don't think ill of me, Father. Perhaps you want something to eat?"

He took the bread and the money, and Praskovya Mikhaylovna was surprised that he did not go, but stood looking at her.

"Pashenka, I have come to you! Take me in . . ."

His beautiful black eyes, shining with the tears that started in them, were fixed on her with imploring insistence. And under his greyish mustache his lips quivered piteously.

Praskovya Mikhaylovna pressed her hands to her withered breast, opened her mouth, and stood petrified, staring at the pilgrim with dilated eyes.

"It can't be! Styopa! Sergey! Father Sergius!"

"Yes, it is I," said Sergius in a low voice. "Only not Sergius, or Father Sergius, but a great sinner, Stepan Kasatsky—a great and lost sinner. Take me in and help me!"

"It's impossible! How have you so humbled yourself? But come in."

She reached out her hand, but he did not take it and only followed her in.

But where was she to take him? The lodging was a small one. Formerly she had had a tiny room, almost a closet, for herself, but later she had given it up to her daughter, and Masha was now sitting there rocking the baby.

"Sit here for the present," she said to Sergius, pointing to a bench in the kitchen.

He sat down at once, and with an evidently accustomed movement slipped the straps of his wallet first off one shoulder and then off the other.

"My God, my God! How you have humbled yourself, Father! Such great fame, and now like this . . ."

Sergius did not reply, but only smiled meekly, placing his wallet under the bench on which he sat.

"Masha, do you know who this is?"—And in a whisper Praskovya Mikhaylovna told her daughter who he was, and together they then carried the bed and the cradle out of the tiny room and cleared it for Sergius.

Praskovya Mikhaylovna led him into it.

"Here you can rest. Don't take offense . . . but I must go out."

"Where to?"

"I have to go to a lesson. I am ashamed to tell you, but I teach music!"

"Music? But that is good. Only just one thing, Praskovya Mikhaylovna, I have come to you with a definite object. When can I have a talk with you?"

"I shall be very glad. Will this evening do?"

"Yes. But one thing more. Don't speak about me, or say who I am. I have revealed myself only to you. No one knows where I have gone to. It must be so."

"Oh, but I have told my daughter."

"Well, ask her not to mention it."

And Sergius took off his boots, lay down, and at once fell asleep after a sleepless night and a walk of nearly thirty miles.

When Praskovya Mikhaylovna returned, Sergius was sitting in the little room waiting for her. He did not come out for dinner, but had some soup and gruel which Lukerya brought him.

"How is it that you have come back earlier than you said?" asked Sergius. "Can I speak to you now?"

"How is it that I have the happiness to receive such a guest? I have missed one of my lessons. That can wait . . . I had always been planning to go to see you. I wrote to you, and now this good fortune has come."

"Pashenka, please listen to what I am going to tell you as to a confession made to God at my last hour. Pashenka, I am not a holy man, I am not even as good as a simple ordinary man; I am a loathsome, vile, and proud sinner who has gone astray, and who, if not worse than everyone else, is at least worse than most very bad people."

Pashenka looked at him at first with staring eyes. But she believed what he said, and when she had quite grasped it she touched his hand, smiling pityingly, and said:

"Perhaps you exaggerate, Stiva?"

"No, Pashenka. I am an adulterer, a murderer, a blasphemer, and a deceiver."

"My God! How is that?" exclaimed Praskovya Mikhaylovna.

"But I must go on living. And I, who thought I knew everything, who taught others how to live—I know nothing and ask you to teach me."

"What are you saying, Stiva? You are laughing at me. Why do you always make fun of me?"

"Well, if you think I am jesting you must have it as you please. But tell me all the same how you live, and how you have lived your life."

"I? I have lived a very nasty, horrible life, and now God is punishing me as I deserve. I live so wretchedly, so wretchedly . . ."

"How was it with your marriage? How did you live with your husband?"

"It was all bad. I married because I fell in love in the nastiest way. Papa did not approve. But I would not listen to anything and just got married. Then instead of helping my husband I tormented him by my jealousy, which I could not restrain."

"I heard that he drank . . ."

"Yes, but I did not give him any peace. I always reproached him, though you know it is a disease! He could not refrain from it. I now remember how I tried to prevent his having it, and the frightful scenes we had!"

And she looked at Kasatsky with beautiful eyes, suffering from the remembrance.

Kasatsky remembered how he had been told that Pashenka's husband used to beat her, and now, looking at her thin withered neck with prominent veins behind her ears, and her scanty coil of hair, half grey half auburn, he seemed to see just how it had occurred.

"Then I was left with two children and no means at all."

"But you had an estate!"

"Oh, we sold that while Vasya was still alive, and the money was all spent. We had to live, and like all our young ladies I did not know how to earn anything. I was particularly useless and helpless. So we spent all we had. I taught the children and improved my own education a little. And then Mitya fell ill when he was already in the fourth form, and God took him. Masha fell in love with Vanya, my son-in-law. And—well, he is well-meaning but unfortunate. He is ill."

"Mamma!"—her daughter's voice interrupted her—"Take Mitya! I can't be in two places at once."

Praskovya Mikhaylovna shuddered, but rose and went out of the room, stepping quickly in her patched shoes. She soon came back with a boy of two in her arms, who threw himself backwards and grabbed at her shawl with his little hands.

"Where was I? Oh yes, he had a good appointment here, and his chief was a kind man too. But Vanya could not go on, and had to give up his position."

"What is the matter with him?"

"Neurasthenia—it is a dreadful complaint. We consulted a doctor, who told us he ought to go away, but we had no means. . . . I always hope it will pass of itself. He has no particular pain, but . . ."

"Lukerya!" cried an angry and feeble voice. "She is always sent away when I want her. Mamma . . ."

"I'm coming!" Praskovya Mikhaylovna again interrupted herself. "He has not had his dinner yet. He can't eat with us."

She went out and arranged something, and came back wiping her thin dark hands.

"So that is how I live. I always complain and am always dissatisfied, but thank God the grandchildren are all nice and healthy, and we can still live. But why talk about me?"

"But what do you live on?"

"Well, I earn a little. How I used to dislike music, but how useful it is to me now!" Her small hand lay on the chest of drawers beside which she was sitting, and she drummed an exercise with her thin fingers.

"How much do you get for a lesson?"

"Sometimes a ruble, sometimes fifty kopeks, or sometimes thirty. They are all so kind to me."

"And do your pupils get on well?" asked Kasatsky with a slight smile.

Praskovya Mikhaylovna did not at first believe that he was asking seriously, and looked inquiringly into his eyes.

"Some of them do. One of them is a splendid girl—the butcher's daughter—such a good kind girl! If I were a clever woman I ought, of course, with the connections Papa had, to be able to get an appointment for my son-in-law. But as it is I have not been able to do anything, and have brought them all to this—as you see."

"Yes, yes," said Kasatsky, lowering his head. "And how is it, Pashenka—do you take part in church life?"

"Oh, don't speak of it. I am so bad that way, and have neglected it so! I keep the fasts with the children and sometimes go to church, and then again sometimes I don't go for months. I only send the children."

"But why don't you go yourself?"

"To tell the truth" (she blushed) "I am ashamed, for my daughter's sake and the children's, to go there in tattered clothes, and I haven't anything else. Besides, I am just lazy."

"And do you pray at home?"

"I do. But what sort of prayer is it? Only mechanical. I know it should not be like that, but I lack real religious feeling. The only thing is that I know how bad I am . . ."

"Yes, yes, that's right!" said Kasatsky, as if approvingly.

"I'm coming! I'm coming!" she replied to a call from her son-in-law, and tidying her scanty plait she left the room.

But this time it was long before she returned. When she came back, Kasatsky was sitting in the same position, his elbows resting on his knees and his head bowed. But his wallet was strapped on his back.

When she came in, carrying a small tin lamp without a shade, he raised his fine weary eyes and sighed very deeply.

"I did not tell them who you are," she began timidly. "I only said that you are a pilgrim, a nobleman, and that I used to know you. Come into the dining room for tea."

"No . . ."

"Well then, I'll bring some to you here."

"No, I don't want anything. God bless you, Pashenka! I am going now. If you pity me, don't tell anyone that you have seen me. For the love of God don't tell anyone. Thank you. I would bow to your feet but I know it would make you feel awkward. Thank you, and forgive me for Christ's sake!"

"Give me your blessing."

"God bless you! Forgive me for Christ's sake!"

He rose, but she would not let him go until she had given him bread and butter and rusks. He took it all and went away.

It was dark, and before he had passed the second house he was lost to sight. She only knew he was there because the dog at the priest's house was barking.

"So that is what my dream meant! Pashenka is what I ought to have been but failed to be. I lived for men on the pretext of living for God, while she lived for God imagining that she lives for men. Yes, one good deed—a cup of water given without thought of reward—is worth more than any benefit I imagined I was bestowing on people. But after all was there not some share of sincere desire to serve God?" he asked himself, and the answer was: "Yes, there was, but it was all soiled and overgrown by desire for human praise. Yes, there is no God for the man who lives, as I did, for human praise. I will now seek him!"

And he walked from village to village as he had done on his way to Pashenka, meeting and parting from other pilgrims, men and women, and asking for bread and a night's rest in Christ's name. Occasionally some angry housewife scolded him, or a drunken peasant reviled him, but for the most part he was given food and drink and even something to take with him. His noble bearing disposed some people in his favor, while others on the contrary seemed pleased at the sight of a gentleman who had come to beggary.

But his gentleness prevailed with everyone.

Often, finding a copy of the Gospels in a hut he would read it aloud, and when they heard him the people were always touched and surprised, as at something new yet familiar.

When he succeeded in helping people, either by advice, or by his knowledge of reading and writing, or by settling some quarrel, he did not wait to see their gratitude but went away directly afterwards. And little by little God began to reveal himself within him.

Once he was walking along with two old women and a soldier. They were stopped by a party consisting of a lady and gentleman in a gig and another lady and gentleman on horseback. The husband was on horse-back with his daughter, while in the gig his wife was driving with a Frenchman, evidently a traveller.

The party stopped to let the Frenchman see the pilgrims who, in accord with a popular Russian superstition, tramped about from place to place instead of working.

They spoke French, thinking that the others would not understand them.

"*Demandez-leur,*" said the Frenchman, "*s'ils sont bien sûr de ce que leur pèlerinage est agréable à Dieu.*"[4]

---

[4]["Ask them if they're certain that their pilgrimage is pleasing to God."]

The question was asked, and one old woman replied:

"As God takes it. Our feet have reached the holy places, but our hearts may not have done so."

They asked the soldier. He said that he was alone in the world and had nowhere else to go.

They asked Kasatsky who he was.

"A servant of God."

"*Qu'est-ce qu'il dit? Il ne répond pas.*"

"*Il dit qu'il est un serviteur de Dieu. Cela doit être un fils de prêtre. Il a de la race. Avez-vous de la petite monnaie?*"[5]

The Frenchman found some small change and gave twenty kopeks to each of the pilgrims.

"*Mais dites-leur que ce n'est pas pour les cierges que je leur donne, mais pour qu'ils se régalent de thé. Chay, chay pour vous, mon vieux!*"[6] he said with a smile. And he patted Kasatsky on the shoulder with his gloved hand.

"May Christ bless you," replied Kasatsky without replacing his cap and bowing his bald head.

He rejoiced particularly at this meeting, because he had disregarded the opinion of men and had done the simplest, easiest thing—humbly accepted twenty kopeks and given them to his comrade, a blind beggar. The less importance he attached to the opinion of men the more did he feel the presence of God within him.

For eight months Kasatsky tramped on in this manner, and in the ninth month he was arrested for not having a passport. This happened at a night refuge in a provincial town where he had passed the night with some pilgrims. He was taken to the police station, and when asked who he was and where was his passport, he replied that he had no passport and that he was a servant of God. He was classed as a tramp, sentenced, and sent to live in Siberia.

In Siberia he has settled down as the hired man of a well-to-do peasant, in which capacity he works in the kitchen garden, teaches children, and attends to the sick.

---

[5] ["What does he say? He doesn't answer." "He says he's a servant of God. He must be a minister's son. He's got an aristocratic bearing. Do you have any change?"]

[6] ["But tell them we're not giving it to them for candles, but so they can enjoy themselves with tea. Tea, tea for you, my friend!"]

Master and Man

I

It happened in the 'seventies in winter, on the day after St. Nicholas's Day. There was a fête in the parish and the innkeeper, Vasili Andreyevich Brekhunov, a Second Guild merchant, being a church elder had to go to church, and had also to entertain his relatives and friends at home.

But when the last of them had gone he at once began to prepare to drive over to see a neighboring proprietor about a grove which he had been bargaining over for a long time. He was now in a hurry to start, lest buyers from the town might forestall him in making a profitable purchase.

The youthful landowner was asking ten thousand rubles for the grove simply because Vasili Andreyevich was offering seven thousand. Seven thousand was, however, only a third of its real value. Vasili Andreyevich might perhaps have got it down to his own price, for the woods were in his district and he had a long-standing agreement with the other village dealers that no one should run up the price in another's district, but he had now learnt that some timber dealers from town meant to bid for the Goryachkin grove, and he resolved to go at once and get the matter settled. So as soon as the feast was over, he took seven hundred rubles from his strong box, added to them two thousand three hundred rubles of church money he had in his keeping, so as to make up the sum to three thousand; carefully counted the notes, and having put them into his pocketbook made haste to start.

Nikita, the only one of Vasili Andreyevich's laborers who was not drunk that day, ran to harness the horse. Nikita, though an habitual drunkard, was not drunk that day because since the last day before the fast, when he had drunk his coat and leather boots, he had sworn off drink and had kept his vow for two months, and was still keeping it despite the temptation of the vodka that had been drunk everywhere during the first two days of the feast.

Nikita was a peasant of about fifty from a neighboring village, "not a

161

manager" as the peasants said of him, meaning that he was not the thrifty head of a household but lived most of his time away from home as a laborer. He was valued everywhere for his industry, dexterity, and strength at work, and still more for his kindly and pleasant temper. But he never settled down anywhere for long because about twice a year, or even oftener, he had a drinking bout, and then besides spending all his clothes on drink he became turbulent and quarrelsome. Vasili Andreyevich himself had turned him away several times, but had afterwards taken him back again—valuing his honesty, his kindness to animals, and especially his cheapness. Vasili Andreyevich did not pay Nikita the eighty rubles a year such a man was worth, but only about forty, which he gave him haphazard, in small sums, and even that mostly not in cash but in goods from his own shop and at high prices.

Nikita's wife Martha, who had once been a handsome vigorous woman, managed the homestead with the help of her son and two daughters, and did not urge Nikita to live at home: first because she had been living for some twenty years already with a cooper, a peasant from another village who lodged in their house; and secondly because though she managed her husband as she pleased when he was sober, she feared him like fire when he was drunk. Once when he had got drunk at home, Nikita, probably to make up for his submissiveness when sober, broke open her box, took out her best clothes, snatched up an axe, and chopped all her undergarments and dresses to bits. All the wages Nikita earned went to his wife, and he raised no objection to that. So now, two days before the holiday, Martha had been twice to see Vasili Andreyevich and had got from him wheat flour, tea, sugar, and a quart of vodka, the lot costing three rubles, and also five rubles in cash, for which she thanked him as for a special favor, though he owed Nikita at least twenty rubles.

"What agreement did we ever draw up with you?" said Vasili Andreyevich to Nikita. "If you need anything, take it; you will work it off. I'm not like others to keep you waiting, and making up accounts and reckoning fines. We deal straightforwardly. You serve me and I don't neglect you."

And when saying this Vasili Andreyevich was honestly convinced that he was Nikita's benefactor, and he knew how to put it so plausibly that all those who depended on him for their money, beginning with Nikita, confirmed him in the conviction that he was their benefactor and did not overreach them.

"Yes, I understand, Vasili Andreyevich. You know that I serve you and take as much pains as I would for my own father. I understand very well!" Nikita would reply. He was quite aware that Vasili Andreyevich was cheating him, but at the same time he felt that it was useless to try to clear up his accounts with him or explain his side of the matter, and that as long as he had nowhere to go he must accept what he could get.

Now, having heard his master's order to harness, he went as usual cheerfully and willingly to the shed, stepping briskly and easily on his rather turned-in feet; took down from a nail the heavy tasselled leather bridle, and jingling the rings of the bit went to the closed stable where the horse he was to harness was standing by himself.

"What, feeling lonely, feeling lonely, little silly?" said Nikita in answer to the low whinny with which he was greeted by the good-tempered, medium-sized bay stallion, with a rather slanting crupper, who stood alone in the shed. "Now then, now then, there's time enough. Let me water you first," he went on, speaking to the horse just as to someone who understood the words he was using, and having whisked the dusty, grooved back of the well-fed young stallion with the skirt of his coat, he put a bridle on his handsome head, straightened his ears and forelock, and having taken off his halter led him out to water.

Picking his way out of the dung-strewn stable, Mukhorty frisked, and making play with his hind leg pretended that he meant to kick Nikita, who was running at a trot beside him to the pump.

"Now then, now then, you rascal!" Nikita called out, well knowing how carefully Mukhorty threw out his hind leg just to touch his greasy sheepskin coat but not to strike him—a trick Nikita much appreciated.

After a drink of the cold water the horse sighed, moving his strong wet lips, from the hairs of which transparent drops fell into the trough; then standing still as if in thought, he suddenly gave a loud snort.

"If you don't want any more, you needn't. But don't go asking for any later," said Nikita quite seriously and fully explaining his conduct to Mukhorty. Then he ran back to the shed pulling the playful young horse, who wanted to gambol all over the yard, by the rein.

There was no one else in the yard except a stranger, the cook's husband, who had come for the holiday.

"Go and ask which sledge is to be harnessed—the wide one or the small one—there's a good fellow!"

The cook's husband went into the house, which stood on an iron foundation and was iron-roofed, and soon returned saying that the little one was to be harnessed. By that time Nikita had put the collar and brass-studded belly band on Mukhorty and, carrying a light, painted shaft bow in one hand, was leading the horse with the other up to two sledges that stood in the shed.

"All right, let it be the little one!" he said, backing the intelligent horse, which all the time kept pretending to bite him, into the shafts, and with the aid of the cook's husband he proceeded to harness. When everything was nearly ready and only the reins had to be adjusted, Nikita sent the other man to the shed for some straw and to the barn for a drugget.

"There, that's all right! Now, now, don't bristle up!" said Nikita, pressing down into the sledge the freshly threshed oat straw the cook's husband had brought. "And now let's spread the sacking like this, and the drugget over it. There, like that it will be comfortable sitting," he went on, suiting the action to the words and tucking the drugget all round over the straw to make a seat.

"Thank you, dear man. Things always go quicker with two working at it!" he added. And gathering up the leather reins fastened together by a brass ring, Nikita took the driver's seat and started the impatient horse over the frozen manure which lay in the yard, towards the gate.

"Uncle Nikita! I say, Uncle, Uncle!" a high-pitched voice shouted, and a seven-year-old boy in a black sheepskin coat, new white felt boots, and a warm cap, ran hurriedly out of the house into the yard. "Take me with you!" he cried, fastening up his coat as he ran.

"All right, come along, darling!" said Nikita, and stopping the sledge he picked up the master's pale thin little son, radiant with joy, and drove out into the road.

It was past two o'clock and the day was windy, dull, and cold, with more than twenty degrees Fahrenheit of frost. Half the sky was hidden by a lowering dark cloud. In the yard it was quiet, but in the street the wind was felt more keenly. The snow swept down from a neighboring shed and whirled about in the corner near the bathhouse.

Hardly had Nikita driven out of the yard and turned the horse's head to the house, before Vasili Andreyevich emerged from the high porch in front of the house with a cigarette in his mouth and wearing a cloth-covered sheepskin coat tightly girdled low at his waist, and stepped onto the hard-trodden snow which squeaked under the leather soles of his felt boots, and stopped. Taking a last whiff of his cigarette he threw it down, stepped on it, and letting the smoke escape through his mustache and looking askance at the horse that was coming up, began to tuck in his sheepskin collar on both sides of his ruddy face, clean-shaven except for the mustache, so that his breath should not moisten the collar.

"See now! The young scamp is there already!" he exclaimed when he saw his little son in the sledge. Vasili Andreyevich was excited by the vodka he had drunk with his visitors, and so he was even more pleased than usual with everything that was his and all that he did. The sight of his son, whom he always thought of as his heir, now gave him great satisfaction. He looked at him, screwing up his eyes and showing his long teeth.

His wife—pregnant, thin, and pale, with her head and shoulders wrapped in a shawl so that nothing of her face could be seen but her eyes—stood behind him in the vestibule to see him off.

"Now really, you ought to take Nikita with you," she said timidly, stepping out from the doorway.

Vasili Andreyevich did not answer. Her words evidently annoyed him and he frowned angrily and spat.

"You have money on you," she continued in the same plaintive voice. "What if the weather gets worse! Do take him, for goodness' sake!"

"Why? Don't I know the road that I must needs take a guide?" exclaimed Vasili Andreyevich, uttering every word very distinctly and compressing his lips unnaturally, as he usually did when speaking to buyers and sellers.

"Really you ought to take him. I beg you in God's name!" his wife repeated, wrapping her shawl more closely round her head.

"There, she sticks to it like a leech! . . . Where am I to take him?"

"I'm quite ready to go with you, Vasili Andreyevich," said Nikita cheerfully. "But they must feed the horses while I am away," he added, turning to his master's wife.

"I'll look after them, Nikita dear. I'll tell Simon," replied the mistress.

"Well, Vasili Andreyevich, am I to come with you?" said Nikita, awaiting a decision.

"It seems I must humor my old woman. But if you're coming you'd better put on a warmer cloak," said Vasili Andreyevich, smiling again as he winked at Nikita's short sheepskin coat, which was torn under the arms and at the back, was greasy and out of shape, frayed to a fringe round the skirt, and had endured many things in its lifetime.

"Hey, dear man, come and hold the horse!" shouted Nikita to the cook's husband, who was still in the yard.

"No, I will myself, I will myself!" shrieked the little boy, pulling his hands, red with cold, out of his pockets, and seizing the cold leather reins.

"Only don't be too long dressing yourself up. Look alive!" shouted Vasili Andreyevich, grinning at Nikita.

"Only a moment, Father, Vasili Andreyevich!" replied Nikita, and running quickly with his inturned toes in his felt boots with their soles patched with felt, he hurried across the yard and into the workmen's hut.

"Arinushka! Get my coat down from the stove. I'm going with the master," he said, as he ran into the hut and took down his girdle from the nail on which it hung.

The workmen's cook, who had had a sleep after dinner and was now getting the samovar ready for her husband, turned cheerfully to Nikita, and infected by his hurry began to move as quickly as he did, got down his miserable worn-out cloth coat from the stove where it was drying, and began hurriedly shaking it out and smoothing it down.

"There now, you'll have a chance of a holiday with your good man," said Nikita, who from kindhearted politeness always said something to anyone he was alone with.

Then, drawing his worn narrow girdle round him, he drew in his breath, pulling in his lean stomach still more, and girdled himself as tightly as he could over his sheepskin.

"There now," he said addressing himself no longer to the cook but the girdle, as he tucked the ends in at the waist, "now you won't come un-done!" And working his shoulders up and down to free his arms, he put the coat over his sheepskin, arched his back more strongly to ease his arms, poked himself under the armpits, and took down his leather-covered mittens from the shelf. "Now we're all right!"

"You ought to wrap your feet up, Nikita. Your boots are very bad."

Nikita stopped as if he had suddenly realized this.

"Yes, I ought to. . . . But they'll do like this. It isn't far!" and he ran out into the yard.

"Won't you be cold, Nikita?" said the mistress as he came up to the sledge.

"Cold? No, I'm quite warm," answered Nikita as he pushed some straw up to the forepart of the sledge so that it should cover his feet, and stowed away the whip, which the good horse would not need, at the bottom of the sledge.

Vasili Andreyevich, who was wearing two fur-lined coats one over the other, was already in the sledge, his broad back filling nearly its whole rounded width, and taking the reins he immediately touched the horse. Nikita jumped in just as the sledge started, and seated himself in front on the left side, with one leg hanging over the edge.

II

The good stallion took the sledge along at a brisk pace over the smooth-frozen road through the village, the runners squeaking slightly as they went.

"Look at him hanging on there! Hand me the whip, Nikita!" shouted Vasili Andreyevich, evidently enjoying the sight of his "heir," who stand-ing on the runners was hanging on at the back of the sledge. "I'll give it you! Be off to mamma, you dog!"

The boy jumped down. The horse increased his amble and, suddenly changing foot, broke into a fast trot.

The Crosses, the village where Vasili Andreyevich lived, consisted of six houses. As soon as they had passed the blacksmith's hut, the last in the village, they realized that the wind was much stronger than they had thought. The road could hardly be seen. The tracks left by the sledge runners were immediately covered by snow and the road was only dis-tinguished by the fact that it was higher than the rest of the ground. There was a whirl of snow over the fields and the line where sky and earth met could not be seen. The Telyatin forest, usually clearly visible, now only loomed up occasionally and dimly through the driving snowy dust. The wind came from the left, insistently blowing over to one side the mane on Mukhorty's sleek neck and carrying aside even his fluffy tail, which was tied in a simple knot. Nikita's wide coat-collar, as he sat on the windy side, pressed close to his cheek and nose.

"This road doesn't give him a chance—it's too snowy," said Vasili Andreyevich, who prided himself on his good horse. "I once drove to Pashutino with him in half an hour."

"What?" asked Nikita, who could not hear on account of his collar.

"I say I once went to Pashutino in half an hour," shouted Vasili Andreyevich.

"It goes without saying that he's a good horse," replied Nikita.

They were silent for a while. But Vasili Andreyevich wished to talk.

"Well, did you tell your wife not to give the cooper any vodka?" he began in the same loud tone, quite convinced that Nikita must feel flattered to be talking with so clever and important a person as himself, and he was so pleased with his jest that it did not enter his head that the remark might be unpleasant to Nikita.

The wind again prevented Nikita's hearing his master's words.

Vasili Andreyevich repeated the jest about the cooper in his loud, clear voice.

"That's their business, Vasili Andreyevich. I don't pry into their affairs. As long as she doesn't ill-treat our boy—God be with them."

"That's so," said Vasili Andreyevich. "Well, and will you be buying a horse in spring?" he went on, changing the subject.

"Yes, I can't avoid it," answered Nikita, turning down his collar and leaning back towards his master.

The conversation now became interesting to him and he did not wish to lose a word.

"The lad's growing up. He must begin to plough for himself, but till now we've always had to hire someone," he said.

"Well, why not have the lean-cruppered one. I won't charge much for it," shouted Vasili Andreyevich, feeling animated, and consequently starting on his favorite occupation—that of horse dealing—which absorbed all his mental powers.

"Or you might let me have fifteen rubles and I'll buy one at the horse market," said Nikita, who knew that the horse Vasili Andreyevich wanted to sell him would be dear at seven rubles, but that if he took it from him it would be charged at twenty-five, and then he would be unable to draw any money for half a year.

"It's a good horse. I think of your interest as of my own—according to conscience. Brekhunov isn't a man to wrong anyone. Let the loss be mine. I'm not like others. Honestly!" he shouted in the voice in which he hypnotized his customers and dealers. "It's a real good horse."

"Quite so!" said Nikita with a sigh, and convinced that there was nothing more to listen to, he again released his collar, which immediately covered his ear and face.

They drove on in silence for about half an hour. The wind blew sharply onto Nikita's side and arm where his sheepskin was torn.

He huddled up and breathed into the collar which covered his mouth, and was not wholly cold.

"What do you think—shall we go through Karamyshevo or by the straight road?" asked Vasili Andreyevich.

The road through Karamyshevo was more frequented and was well marked with a double row of high stakes. The straight road was nearer but little used and had no stakes, or only poor ones covered with snow.

Nikita thought awhile.

"Though Karamyshevo is farther, it is better going," he said.

"But by the straight road, when once we get through the hollow by the forest, it's good going—sheltered," said Vasili Andreyevich, who wished to go the nearest way.

"Just as you please," said Nikita, and again let go of his collar.

Vasili Andreyevich did as he had said, and having gone about half a verst came to a tall oak stake which had a few dry leaves still dangling on it, and there he turned to the left.

On turning they faced directly against the wind, and snow was beginning to fall. Vasili Andreyevich, who was driving, inflated his cheeks, blowing the breath out through his mustache. Nikita dozed.

So they went on in silence for about ten minutes. Suddenly Vasili Andreyevich began saying something.

"Eh, what?" asked Nikita, opening his eyes.

Vasili Andreyevich did not answer, but bent over, looking behind them and then ahead of the horse. The sweat had curled Mukhorty's coat between his legs and on his neck. He went at a walk.

"What is it?" Nikita asked again.

"What is it? What is it?" Vasili Andreyevich mimicked him angrily. "There are no stakes to be seen! We must have got off the road!"

"Well, pull up then, and I'll look for it," said Nikita, and jumping down lightly from the sledge and taking the whip from under the straw, he went off to the left from his own side of the sledge.

The snow was not deep that year, so that it was possible to walk anywhere, but still in places it was knee-deep and got into Nikita's boots. He went about feeling the ground with his feet and the whip, but could not find the road anywhere.

"Well, how is it?" asked Vasili Andreyevich when Nikita came back to the sledge.

"There is no road this side. I must go to the other side and try there," said Nikita.

"There's something there in front. Go and have a look."

Nikita went to what had appeared dark, but found that it was earth which the wind had blown from the bare fields of winter oats and had strewn over the snow, colouring it. Having searched to the right also, he returned to the sledge, brushed the snow from his coat, shook it out of his boots, and seated himself once more.

"We must go to the right," he said decidedly. "The wind was blowing on our left before, but now it is straight in my face. Drive to the right," he repeated with decision.

Vasili Andreyevich took his advice and turned to the right, but still there was no road. They went on in that direction for some time. The wind was as fierce as ever and it was snowing lightly.

"It seems, Vasili Andreyevich, that we have gone quite astray," Nikita suddenly remarked, as if it were a pleasant thing. "What is that?" he added, pointing to some potato vines that showed up from under the snow.

Vasili Andreyevich stopped the perspiring horse, whose deep sides were heaving heavily.

"What is it?"

"Why, we are on the Zakharov lands. See where we've got to!"

"Nonsense!" retorted Vasili Andreyevich.

"It's not nonsense, Vasili Andreyevich. It's the truth," replied Nikita. "You can feel that the sledge is going over a potato-field, and there are the heaps of vines which have been carted here. It's the Zakharov factory land."

"Dear me, how we have gone astray!" said Vasili Andreyevich. "What are we to do now?"

"We must go straight on, that's all. We shall come out somewhere—if not at Zakharova, then at the proprietor's farm," said Nikita.

Vasili Andreyevich agreed, and drove as Nikita had indicated. So they went on for a considerable time. At times they came onto bare fields and the sledge runners rattled over frozen lumps of earth. Sometimes they got onto a winter-rye field, or a fallow field on which they could see stalks of wormwood, and straws sticking up through the snow and swaying in the wind; sometimes they came onto deep and even white snow, above which nothing was to be seen.

The snow was falling from above and sometimes rose from below. The horse was evidently exhausted, his hair had all curled up from sweat and was covered with hoarfrost, and he went at a walk. Suddenly he stumbled and sat down in a ditch or water-course. Vasili Andreyevich wanted to stop, but Nikita cried to him:

"Why stop? We've got in and must get out. Hey, pet! Hey, darling! Gee up, old fellow!" he shouted in a cheerful tone to the horse, jumping out of the sledge and himself getting stuck in the ditch.

The horse gave a start and quickly climbed out onto the frozen bank. It was evidently a ditch that had been dug there.

"Where are we now?" asked Vasili Andreyevich.

"We'll soon find out!" Nikita replied. "Go on, we'll get somewhere."

"Why, this must be the Goryachkin forest!" said Vasili Andreyevich, pointing to something dark that appeared amid the snow in front of them.

"We'll see what forest it is when we get there," said Nikita.

He saw that beside the black thing they had noticed, dry, oblong willow leaves were fluttering, and so he knew it was not a forest but a settlement, but he did not wish to say so. And in fact they had not gone twenty-five yards beyond the ditch before something in front of them, evidently trees, showed up black, and they heard a new and melancholy sound. Nikita had guessed right: it was not a wood, but a row of tall willows with a few leaves still fluttering on them here and there. They had evidently been planted along the ditch round a threshing floor. Coming up to the willows, which moaned sadly in the wind, the horse suddenly planted his forelegs above the height of the sledge, drew up his hind legs also, pulling the sledge onto higher ground, and turned to the left, no longer sinking up to his knees in snow. They were back on a road.

"Well, here we are, but heaven only knows where!" said Nikita.

The horse kept straight along the road through the drifted snow, and before they had gone another hundred yards the straight line of the dark wattle wall of a barn showed up black before them, its roof heavily covered with snow which poured down from it. After passing the barn the road turned to the wind and they drove into a snowdrift. But ahead of them was a lane with houses on either side, so evidently the snow had been blown across the road and they had to drive through the drift. And so in fact it was. Having driven through the snow they came out into a street. At the end house of the village some frozen clothes hanging on a line—shirts, one red and one white, trousers, leg-bands, and a petticoat—fluttered wildly in the wind. The white shirt in particular struggled desperately, waving its sleeves about.

"There now, either a lazy woman or a dead one has not taken her clothes down before the holiday," remarked Nikita, looking at the fluttering shirts.

III

At the entrance to the street the wind still raged and the road was thickly covered with snow, but well within the village it was calm, warm, and cheerful. At one house a dog was barking, at another a woman, covering her head with her coat, came running from somewhere and entered the door of a hut, stopping on the threshold to have a look at the passing sledge. In the middle of the village girls could be heard singing.

Here in the village there seemed to be less wind and snow, and the frost was less keen.

"Why, this is Grishkino," said Vasili Andreyevich.

"So it is," responded Nikita.

It really was Grishkino, which meant that they had gone too far to the left and had travelled some six miles, not quite in the direction they aimed at, but towards their destination for all that.

From Grishkino to Goryachkin was about another four miles.

In the middle of the village they almost ran into a tall man walking down the middle of the street.

"Who are you?" shouted the man, stopping the horse, and recognizing Vasili Andreyevich he immediately took hold of the shaft, went along it hand over hand till he reached the sledge, and placed himself on the driver's seat.

He was Isay, a peasant of Vasili Andreyevich's acquaintance, and well known as the principal horse thief in the district.

"Ah, Vasili Andreyevich! Where are you off to?" said Isay, enveloping Nikita in the odor of the vodka he had drunk.

"We were going to Goryachkin."

"And look where you've got to! You should have gone through Molchanovka."

"Should have, but didn't manage it," said Vasili Andreyevich, holding in the horse.

"That's a good horse," said Isay, with a shrewd glance at Mukhorty, and with a practiced hand he tightened the loosened knot high in the horse's bushy tail.

"Are you going to stay the night?"

"No, friend. I must get on."

"Your business must be pressing. And who is this? Ah, Nikita Stepanych!"

"Who else?" replied Nikita. "But I say, good friend, how are we to avoid going astray again?"

"Where can you go astray here? Turn back straight down the street and then when you come out keep straight on. Don't take to the left. You will come out onto the high road, and then turn to the right."

"And where do we turn off the high road? As in summer, or the winter way?" asked Nikita.

"The winter way. As soon as you turn off you'll see some bushes, and opposite them there is a way mark—a large oak, one with branches—and that's the way."

Vasili Andreyevich turned the horse back and drove through the outskirts of the village.

"Why not stay the night?" Isay shouted after them.

But Vasili Andreyevich did not answer and touched up the horse. Four miles of good road, two of which lay through the forest, seemed easy to manage, especially as the wind was apparently quieter and the snow had stopped.

Having driven along the trodden village street, darkened here and there by fresh manure, past the yard where the clothes hung out and where the white shirt had broken loose and was now attached only by one frozen sleeve, they again came within sound of the weird moan of the willows, and again emerged on the open fields. The storm, far from ceasing, seemed to have grown yet stronger. The road was completely covered with drifting snow, and only the stakes showed that they had not lost their way. But even the stakes ahead of them were not easy to see, since the wind blew in their faces.

Vasili Andreyevich screwed up his eyes, bent down his head, and looked out for the way-marks, but trusted mainly to the horse's sagacity, letting it take its own way. And the horse really did not lose the road but followed its windings, turning now to the right and now to the left and sensing it under his feet, so that though the snow fell thicker and the wind strengthened they still continued to see way-marks now to the left and now to the right of them.

So they travelled on for about ten minutes, when suddenly, through the slanting screen of wind-driven snow, something black showed up which moved in front of the horse.

This was another sledge with fellow travellers. Mukhorty overtook them, and struck his hoofs against the back of the sledge in front of them.

"Pass on . . . hey there . . . get in front!" cried voices from the sledge.

Vasili Andreyevich swerved aside to pass the other sledge. In it sat three men and a woman, evidently visitors returning from a feast. One peasant was whacking the snow-covered croup of their little horse with a long switch, and the other two sitting in front waved their arms and shouted something. The woman, completely wrapped up and covered with snow, sat drowsing and bumping at the back.

"Who are you?" shouted Vasili Andreyevich.

"From A-a-a . . ." was all that could be heard.

"I say, where are you from?"

"From A-a-a-a!" one of the peasants shouted with all his might, but still it was impossible to make out who they were.

"Get along! Keep up!" shouted another, ceaselessly beating his horse with the switch.

"So you're from a feast, it seems?"

"Go on, go on! Faster, Simon! Get in front! Faster!"

The wings of the sledges bumped against one another, almost got jammed but managed to separate, and the peasants' sledge began to fall behind.

Their shaggy, big-bellied horse, all covered with snow, breathed heavily under the low shaft-bow and, evidently using the last of its strength, vainly endeavored to escape from the switch, hobbling with its short legs through the deep snow which it threw up under itself.

Its muzzle, young-looking, with the nether lip drawn up like that of a fish, nostrils distended and ears pressed back from fear, kept up for a few seconds near Nikita's shoulder and then began to fall behind.

"Just see what liquor does!" said Nikita. "They've tired that little horse to death. What pagans!"

For a few minutes they heard the panting of the tired little horse and the drunken shouting of the peasants. Then the panting and the shouts died away, and around them nothing could be heard but the whistling of the wind in their ears and now and then the squeak of their sledge runners over a windswept part of the road.

This encounter cheered and enlivened Vasili Andreyevich, and he drove on more boldly without examining the way marks, urging on the horse and trusting to him.

Nikita had nothing to do, and as usual in such circumstances he drowsed, making up for much sleepless time. Suddenly the horse stopped and Nikita nearly fell forward onto his nose.

"You know we're off the track again!" said Vasili Andreyevich.

"How's that?"

"Why, there are no way marks to be seen. We must have got off the road again."

"Well, if we've lost the road we must find it," said Nikita curtly, and getting out and stepping lightly on his pigeon-toed feet he started once more going about on the snow.

He walked about for a long time, now disappearing and now reappearing, and finally he came back.

"There is no road here. There may be farther on," he said, getting into the sledge.

It was already growing dark. The snowstorm had not increased but had also not subsided.

"If we could only hear those peasants!" said Vasili Andreyevich.

"Well they haven't caught us up. We must have gone far astray. Or maybe they have lost their way too."

"Where are we to go then?" asked Vasili Andreyevich.

"Why, we must let the horse take its own way," said Nikita. "He will take us right. Let me have the reins."

Vasili Andreyevich gave him the reins, the more willingly because his hands were beginning to feel frozen in his thick gloves.

Nikita took the reins, but only held them, trying not to shake them and rejoicing at his favorite's sagacity. And indeed the clever horse, turning first one ear and then the other now to one side and then to the other, began to wheel round.

"The one thing he can't do is to talk," Nikita kept saying. "See what he is doing! Go on, go on! You know best. That's it, that's it!"

The wind was now blowing from behind and it felt warmer.

"Yes, he's clever," Nikita continued, admiring the horse. "A Kirgiz horse is strong but stupid. But this one—just see what he's doing with his ears! He doesn't need any telegraph. He can scent a mile off."

Before another half-hour had passed they saw something dark ahead of them—a wood or a village—and stakes again appeared to the right. They had evidently come out onto the road.

"Why, that's Grishkino again!" Nikita suddenly exclaimed.

And indeed, there on their left was that same barn with the snow flying from it, and farther on the same line with the frozen washing, shirts and trousers, which still fluttered desperately in the wind.

Again they drove into the street and again it grew quiet, warm, and cheerful, and again they could see the manure-stained street and hear voices and songs and the barking of a dog. It was already so dark that there were lights in some of the windows.

Halfway through the village Vasili Andreyevich turned the horse towards a large double-fronted brick house and stopped at the porch.

Nikita went to the lighted snow-covered window, in the rays of which flying snowflakes glittered, and knocked at it with his whip.

"Who is there?" a voice replied to his knock.

"From Kresty, the Brekhunovs, dear fellow," answered Nikita. "Just come out for a minute."

Someone moved from the window, and a minute or two later there was the sound of the passage door as it came unstuck, then the latch of the outside door clicked and a tall white-bearded peasant, with a sheepskin coat thrown over his white holiday shirt, pushed his way out holding the door firmly against the wind, followed by a lad in a red shirt and high leather boots.

"Is that you, Andreyevich?" asked the old man.

"Yes, friend, we've gone astray," said Vasili Andreyevich. "We wanted to get to Goryachkin but found ourselves here. We went a second time but lost our way again."

"Just see how you have gone astray!" said the old man. "Petrushka, go and open the gate!" he added, turning to the lad in the red shirt.

"All right," said the lad in a cheerful voice, and ran back into the passage.

"But we're not staying the night," said Vasili Andreyevich.

"Where will you go in the night? You'd better stay!"

"I'd be glad to, but I must go on. It's business, and it can't be helped."

"Well, warm yourself at least. The samovar is just ready."

"Warm myself? Yes, I'll do that," said Vasili Andreyevich. "It won't get darker. The moon will rise and it will be lighter. Let's go in and warm ourselves, Nikita."

"Well, why not? Let us warm ourselves," replied Nikita, who was stiff with cold and anxious to warm his frozen limbs.

Vasili Andreyevich went into the room with the old man, and Nikita drove through the gate opened for him by Petrushka, by whose advice he backed the horse under the penthouse. The ground was covered with manure and the tall bow over the horse's head caught against the beam. The hens and the cock had already settled to roost there, and clucked peevishly, clinging to the beam with their claws. The disturbed sheep shied and rushed aside trampling the frozen manure with their hooves. The dog yelped desperately with fright and anger and then burst out barking like a puppy at the stranger.

Nikita talked to them all, excused himself to the fowls and assured them that he would not disturb them again, rebuked the sheep for being frightened without knowing why, and kept soothing the dog, while he tied up the horse.

"Now that will be all right," he said, knocking the snow off his clothes. "Just hear how he barks!" he added, turning to the dog. "Be quiet, stupid! Be quiet. You are only troubling yourself for nothing. We're not thieves, we're friends. . . ."

"And these are, it's said, the three domestic counsellors," remarked the lad, and with his strong arms he pushed under the pent-roof the sledge that had remained outside.

"Why counsellors?" asked Nikita.

"That's what is printed in Paulson. A thief creeps to a house—the dog barks, that means 'Be on your guard!' The cock crows, that means, 'Get up!' The cat licks herself—that means, 'A welcome guest is coming. Get ready to receive him!'" said the lad with a smile.

Petrushka could read and write and knew Paulson's primer, his only book, almost by heart, and he was fond of quoting sayings from it that he thought suited the occasion, especially when he had had something to drink, as today.

"That's so," said Nikita.

"You must be chilled through and through," said Petrushka.

"Yes, I am rather," said Nikita, and they went across the yard and the passage into the house.

IV

The household to which Vasili Andreyevich had come was one of the richest in the village. The family had five allotments, besides renting other land. They had six horses, three cows, two calves, and some twenty sheep. There were twenty-two members belonging to the homestead: four married sons, six grandchildren (one of whom, Petrushka, was married), two great-grandchildren, three orphans, and four daughters-in-law with their babies. It was one of the few homesteads that remained still undivided, but even here the dull internal work of disintegration which would inevitably lead to separation had already begun, starting as usual among the women. Two sons were living in Moscow as water-carriers, and one was in the army. At home now were the old man and his wife, their second son who managed the homestead, the eldest who had come from Moscow for the holiday, and all the women and children. Besides these members of the family there was a visitor, a neighbor who was godfather to one of the children.

Over the table in the room hung a lamp with a shade, which brightly lit up the tea things, a bottle of vodka, and some refreshments, besides illuminating the brick walls, which in the far corner were hung with icons on both sides of which were pictures. At the head of the table sat Vasili Andreyevich in a black sheepskin coat, sucking his frozen mustache and observing the room and the people around him with his prominent hawklike eyes. With him sat the old, bald, white-bearded master of the house in a white homespun shirt, and next him the son home from Moscow for the holiday—a man with a sturdy back and powerful shoulders and clad in a thin print shirt—then the second son, also broad-shouldered, who acted as head of the house, and then a lean red-haired peasant—the neighbor.

Having had a drink of vodka and something to eat, they were about to take tea, and the samovar standing on the floor beside the brick oven was already humming. The children could be seen in the top bunks and on the top of the oven. A woman sat on a lower bunk with a cradle beside her. The old housewife, her face covered with wrinkles which wrinkled even her lips, was waiting on Vasili Andreyevich.

As Nikita entered the house she was offering her guest a small tumbler of thick glass which she had just filled with vodka.

"Don't refuse, Vasili Andreyevich, you mustn't! Wish us a merry feast. Drink it, dear!" she said.

The sight and smell of vodka, especially now when he was chilled through and tired out, much disturbed Nikita's mind. He frowned, and having shaken the snow off his cap and coat, stopped in front of the icons as if not seeing anyone, crossed himself three times, and bowed to the icons. Then, turning to the old master of the house and bowing first to him, then to all those at table, then to the women who stood by the oven, and muttering: "A merry holiday!" he began taking off his outer things without looking at the table.

"Why, you're all covered with hoarfrost, old fellow!" said the eldest brother, looking at Nikita's snow-covered face, eyes, and beard.

Nikita took off his coat, shook it again, hung it up beside the oven, and came up to the table. He too was offered vodka. He went through a moment of painful hesitation and nearly took up the glass and emptied the clear fragrant liquid down his throat, but he glanced at Vasili Andreyevich, remembered his oath and the boots that he had sold for drink, recalled the cooper, remembered his son for whom he had promised to buy a horse by spring, sighed, and declined it.

"I don't drink, thank you kindly," he said frowning, and sat down on a bench near the second window.

"How's that?" asked the eldest brother.

"I just don't drink," replied Nikita without lifting his eyes but looking askance at his scanty beard and mustache and getting the icicles out of them.

"It's not good for him," said Vasili Andreyevich, munching a cracknel after emptying his glass.

"Well, then, have some tea," said the kindly old hostess. "You must be chilled through, good soul. Why are you women dawdling so with the samovar?"

"It is ready," said one of the young women, and after flicking with her apron the top of the samovar which was now boiling over, she carried it with an effort to the table, raised it, and set it down with a thud.

Meanwhile Vasili Andreyevich was telling how he had lost his way, how they had come back twice to this same village, and how they had gone astray and had met some drunken peasants. Their hosts were surprised, explained where and why they had missed their way, said who the tipsy people they had met were, and told them how they ought to go.

"A little child could find the way to Molchanovka from here. All you have to do is to take the right turning from the high road. There's a bush you can see just there. But you didn't even get that far!" said the neighbor.

"You'd better stay the night. The women will make up beds for you," said the old woman persuasively.

"You could go on in the morning and it would be pleasanter," said the old man, confirming what his wife had said.

"I can't, friend. Business!" said Vasili Andreyevich. "Lose an hour and you can't catch it up in a year," he added, remembering the grove and the dealers who might snatch that deal from him. "We shall get there, shan't we?" he said, turning to Nikita.

Nikita did not answer for some time, apparently still intent on thawing out his beard and mustache.

"If only we don't go astray again," he replied gloomily.

He was gloomy because he passionately longed for some vodka, and the only thing that could assuage that longing was tea and he had not yet been offered any.

"But we have only to reach the turning and then we shan't go wrong. The road will be through the forest the whole way," said Vasili Andreyevich.

"It's just as you please, Vasili Andreyevich. If we're to go, let us go," said Nikita, taking the glass of tea he was offered.

"We'll drink our tea and be off."

Nikita said nothing but only shook his head, and carefully pouring some tea into his saucer began warming his hands, the fingers of which were always swollen with hard work, over the steam. Then, biting off a tiny bit of sugar, he bowed to his hosts, said, "Your health!" and drew in the steaming liquid.

"If somebody would see us as far as the turning," said Vasili Andreyevich.

"Well, we can do that," said the eldest son. "Petrushka will harness and go that far with you."

"Well, then, put in the horse, lad, and I shall be thankful to you for it."

"Oh, what for, dear man?" said the kindly old woman. "We are heartily glad to do it."

"Petrushka, go and put in the mare," said the eldest brother.

"All right," replied Petrushka with a smile, and promptly snatching his cap down from a nail he ran away to harness.

While the horse was being harnessed the talk returned to the point at which it had stopped when Vasili Andreyevich drove up to the window. The old man had been complaining to his neighbor, the village elder, about his third son who had not sent him anything for the holiday though he had sent a French shawl to his wife.

"The young people are getting out of hand," said the old man.

"And how they do!" said the neighbor. "There's no managing them! They know too much. There's Demochkin now, who broke his father's arm. It's all from being too clever, it seems."

Nikita listened, watched their faces, and evidently would have liked to share in the conversation, but he was too busy drinking his tea and only nodded his head approvingly. He emptied one tumbler after another and grew warmer and warmer and more and more comfortable. The talk continued on the same subject for a long time—the harmfulness of a household dividing up—and it was clearly not an abstract discussion but

concerned the question of a separation in that house; a separation demanded by the second son who sat there morosely silent.

It was evidently a sore subject and absorbed them all, but out of propriety they did not discuss their private affairs before strangers. At last,
however, the old man could not restrain himself, and with tears in his
eyes declared that he would not consent to a breakup of the family during his lifetime, that his house was prospering, thank God, but that if they
separated they would all have to go begging.

"Just like the Matveevs," said the neighbour. "They used to have a
proper house, but now they've split up none of them has anything."

"And that is what you want to happen to us," said the old man, turning to his son.

The son made no reply and there was an awkward pause. The silence
was broken by Petrushka, who having harnessed the horse had returned
to the hut a few minutes before this and had been listening all the time
with a smile.

"There's a fable about that in Paulson," he said. "A father gave his sons
a broom to break. At first they could not break it, but when they took it
twig by twig they broke it easily. And it's the same here," and he gave a
broad smile. "I'm ready!" he added.

"If you're ready, let's go," said Vasili Andreyevich. "And as to sepa-
rating, don't you allow it, Grandfather. You got everything together and
you're the master. Go to the justice of the peace. He'll say how things
should be done."

"He carries on so, carries on so," the old man continued in a whining
tone. "There's no doing anything with him. It's as if the devil possessed
him."

Nikita having meanwhile finished his fifth tumbler of tea laid it on its
side instead of turning it upside down, hoping to be offered a sixth glass.
But there was no more water in the samovar, so the hostess did not fill it
up for him. Besides, Vasili Andreyevich was putting his things on, so
there was nothing for it but for Nikita to get up too, put back into the
sugar-basin the lump of sugar he had nibbled all round, wipe his perspiring face with the skirt of his sheepskin, and go to put on his overcoat.

Having put it on he sighed deeply, thanked his hosts, said good-
bye, and went out of the warm bright room into the cold dark passage, through which the wind was howling and where snow was
blowing through the cracks of the shaking door, and from there into
the yard.

Petrushka stood in his sheepskin in the middle of the yard by his
horse, repeating some lines from Paulson's primer. He said with a
smile:

"Storms with mist the sky conceal,
Snowy circles wheeling wild.
Now like savage beast 'twill howl,
And now 'tis wailing like a child."

Nikita nodded approvingly as he arranged the reins.

The old man, seeing Vasili Andreyevich off, brought a lantern into the passage to show him a light, but it was blown out at once. And even in the yard it was evident that the snowstorm had become more violent.

"Well, this is weather!" thought Vasili Andreyevich. "Perhaps we may not get there after all. But there is nothing to be done. Business! Besides, we have got ready, our host's horse has been harnessed, and we'll get there with God's help!"

Their aged host also thought they ought not to go, but he had already tried to persuade them to stay and had not been listened to.

"It's no use asking them again. Maybe my age makes me timid. They'll get there all right, and at least we shall get to bed in good time and without any fuss," he thought.

Petrushka did not think of danger. He knew the road and the whole district so well, and the lines about "snowy circles wheeling wild" described what was happening outside so aptly that it cheered him up. Nikita did not wish to go at all, but he had been accustomed not to have his own way and to serve others for so long that there was no one to hinder the departing travellers.

V

Vasili Andreyevich went over to his sledge, found it with difficulty in the darkness, climbed in and took the reins.

"Go on in front!" he cried.

Petrushka kneeling in his low sledge started his horse. Mukhorty, who had been neighing for some time past, now scenting a mare ahead of him started after her, and they drove out into the street. They drove again through the outskirts of the village and along the same road, past the yard where the frozen linen had hung (which, however, was no longer to be seen), past the same barn, which was now snowed up almost to the roof and from which the snow was still endlessly pouring past the same dismally moaning, whistling, and swaying willows, and again entered into the sea of blustering snow raging from above and below. The wind was so strong that when it blew from the side and the travellers steered against it, it tilted the sledges and turned the horses to one side. Petrushka drove his good mare in front at a brisk trot and kept shouting lustily. Mukhorty pressed after her.

After travelling so for about ten minutes, Petrushka turned round and shouted something. Neither Vasili Andreyevich nor Nikita could hear anything because of the wind, but they guessed that they had arrived at the turning. In fact Petrushka had turned to the right, and now the wind that had blown from the side blew straight in their faces, and through the snow they saw something dark on their right. It was the bush at the turning.

"Well now, God speed you!"

"Thank you, Petrushka!"

"Storms with mist the sky conceal!" shouted Petrushka as he disappeared.

"There's a poet for you!" muttered Vasili Andreyevich, pulling at the reins.

"Yes, a fine lad—a true peasant," said Nikita.

They drove on.

Nikita, wrapping his coat closely about him and pressing his head down so close to his shoulders that his short beard covered his throat, sat silently, trying not to lose the warmth he had obtained while drinking tea in the house. Before him he saw the straight lines of the shafts which constantly deceived him into thinking they were on a well-travelled road, and the horse's swaying crupper with his knotted tail blown to one side, and farther ahead the high shaft-bow and the swaying head and neck of the horse with its waving mane. Now and then he caught sight of a way sign, so that he knew they were still on a road and that there was nothing for him to be concerned about.

Vasili Andreyevich drove on, leaving it to the horse to keep to the road. But Mukhorty, though he had had a breathing space in the village, ran reluctantly, and seemed now and then to get off the road, so that Vasili Andreyevich had repeatedly to correct him.

"Here's a stake to the right, and another, and here's a third," Vasili Andreyevich counted, "and here in front is the forest," thought he, as he looked at something dark in front of him. But what had seemed to him a forest was only a bush. They passed the bush and drove on for another hundred yards but there was no fourth way mark nor any forest.

"We must reach the forest soon," thought Vasili Andreyevich, and animated by the vodka and the tea he did not stop but shook the reins, and the good obedient horse responded, now ambling, now slowly trotting in the direction in which he was sent, though he knew that he was not going the right way. Ten minutes went by, but there was still no forest.

"There now, we must be astray again," said Vasili Andreyevich, pulling up.

Nikita silently got out of the sledge and holding his coat, which the wind now wrapped closely about him and now almost tore off, started to feel about in the snow, going first to one side and then to the other.

Three or four times he was completely lost to sight. At last he returned and took the reins from Vasili Andreyevich's hand.

"We must go to the right," he said sternly and peremptorily, as he turned the horse.

"Well, if it's to the right, go to the right," said Vasili Andreyevich, yielding up the reins to Nikita and thrusting his freezing hands into his sleeves.

Nikita did not reply.

"Now then, friend, stir yourself!" he shouted to the horse, but in spite of the shake of the reins Mukhorty moved only at a walk.

The snow in places was up to his knees, and the sledge moved by fits and starts with his every movement.

Nikita took the whip that hung over the front of the sledge and struck him once. The good horse, unused to the whip, sprang forward and moved at a trot, but immediately fell back into an amble and then to a walk. So they went on for five minutes. It was dark and the snow whirled from above and rose from below, so that sometimes the shaft-bow could not be seen. At times the sledge seemed to stand still and the field to run backwards. Suddenly the horse stopped abruptly, evidently aware of something close in front of him. Nikita again sprang lightly out, throwing down the reins, and went ahead to see what had brought him to a standstill, but hardly had he made a step in front of the horse before his feet slipped and he went rolling down an incline.

"Whoa, whoa, whoa!" he said to himself as he fell, and he tried to stop his fall but could not, and only stopped when his feet plunged into a thick layer of snow that had drifted to the bottom of the hollow.

The fringe of a drift of snow that hung on the edge of the hollow, disturbed by Nikita's fall, showered down on him and got inside his collar.

"What a thing to do!" said Nikita reproachfully, addressing the drift and the hollow and shaking the snow from under his collar.

"Nikita! Hey, Nikita!" shouted Vasili Andreyevich from above.

But Nikita did not reply. He was too occupied in shaking out the snow and searching for the whip he had dropped when rolling down the incline. Having found the whip he tried to climb straight up the bank where he had rolled down, but it was impossible to do so: he kept rolling down again, and so he had to go along at the foot of the hollow to find a way up. About seven yards farther on he managed with difficulty to crawl up the incline on all fours, then he followed the edge of the hollow back to the place where the horse should have been. He could not see either horse or sledge, but as he walked against the wind he heard Vasili Andreyevich's shouts and Mukhorty's neighing, calling him.

"I'm coming! I'm coming! What are you cackling for?" he muttered.

Only when he had come up to the sledge could he make out the horse, and Vasili Andreyevich standing beside it and looking gigantic.

"Where the devil did you vanish to? We must go back, if only to Grishkino," he began reproaching Nikita.

"I'd be glad to get back, Vasili Andreyevich, but which way are we to go? There is such a ravine here that if we once get in it we shan't get out again. I got stuck so fast there myself that I could hardly get out."

"What shall we do, then? We can't stay here! We must go somewhere!" said Vasili Andreyevich.

Nikita said nothing. He seated himself in the sledge with his back to the wind, took off his boots, shook out the snow that had got into them, and taking some straw from the bottom of the sledge, carefully plugged with it a hole in his left boot.

Vasili Andreyevich remained silent, as though now leaving everything to Nikita. Having put his boots on again, Nikita drew his feet into the sledge, put on his mittens and took up the reins, and directed the horse along the side of the ravine. But they had not gone a hundred yards before the horse again stopped short. The ravine was in front of him again.

Nikita again climbed out and again trudged about in the snow. He did this for a considerable time and at last appeared from the opposite side to that from which he had started.

"Vasili Andreyevich, are you alive?" he called out.

"Here!" replied Vasili Andreyevich. "Well, what now?"

"I can't make anything out. It's too dark. There's nothing but ravines. We must drive against the wind again."

They set off once more. Again Nikita went stumbling through the snow, again he fell in, again climbed out and trudged about, and at last quite out of breath he sat down beside the sledge.

"Well, how now?" asked Vasili Andreyevich.

"Why, I am quite worn out and the horse won't go."

"Then what's to be done?"

"Why, wait a minute."

Nikita went away again but soon returned.

"Follow me!" he said, going in front of the horse.

Vasili Andreyevich no longer gave orders but implicitly did what Nikita told him.

"Here, follow me!" Nikita shouted, stepping quickly to the right, and seizing the rein he led Mukhorty down towards a snowdrift.

At first the horse held back, then he jerked forward, hoping to leap the drift, but he had not the strength and sank into it up to his collar.

"Get out!" Nikita called to Vasili Andreyevich, who still sat in the sledge, and taking hold of one shaft he moved the sledge closer to the horse. "It's hard, brother!" he said to Mukhorty, "but it can't be helped. Make an effort! Now, now, just a little one!" he shouted.

The horse gave a tug, then another, but failed to clear himself and settled down again as if considering something.

"Now, brother, this won't do!" Nikita admonished him. "Now once
more!"

Again Nikita tugged at the shaft on his side, and Vasili Andreyevich
did the same on the other.

Mukhorty lifted his head and then gave a sudden jerk.

"That's it! That's it!" cried Nikita. "Don't be afraid—you won't sink!"

One plunge, another, and a third, and at last Mukhorty was out of the
snowdrift, and stood still, breathing heavily and shaking the snow off
himself. Nikita wished to lead him farther, but Vasili Andreyevich, in his
two fur coats, was so out of breath that he could not walk farther and
dropped into the sledge.

"Let me get my breath!" he said, unfastening the kerchief with which
he had tied the collar of his fur coat at the village.

"It's all right here. You lie there," said Nikita. "I will lead him along."
And with Vasili Andreyevich in the sledge he led the horse by the bridle about ten paces down and then up a slight rise, and stopped.

The place where Nikita had stopped was not completely in the
hollow where the snow sweeping down from the hillocks might have
buried them altogether, but still it was partly sheltered from the wind
by the side of the ravine. There were moments when the wind
seemed to abate a little, but that did not last long and as if to make
up for that respite the storm swept down with tenfold vigor and tore
and whirled the more fiercely. Such a gust struck them at the moment
when Vasili Andreyevich, having recovered his breath, got out of the
sledge and went up to Nikita to consult him as to what they should
do. They both bent down involuntarily and waited till the violence
of the squall should have passed. Mukhorty too laid back his ears and
shook his head discontentedly. As soon as the violence of the blast
had abated a little, Nikita took off his mittens, stuck them into his
belt, breathed onto his hands, and began to undo the straps of the
shaft-bow.

"What's that you are doing there?" asked Vasili Andreyevich.

"Unharnessing. What else is there to do? I have no strength left," said
Nikita as though excusing himself.

"Can't we drive somewhere?"

"No, we can't. We shall only kill the horse. Why, the poor beast is not
himself now," said Nikita, pointing to the horse, which was standing sub-
missively waiting for what might come, with his steep wet sides heaving
heavily. "We shall have to stay the night here," he said, as if preparing to
spend the night at an inn, and he proceeded to unfasten the collar straps.
The buckles came undone.

"But shan't we be frozen?" remarked Vasili Andreyevich.

"Well, if we are we can't help it," said Nikita.

VI

Although Vasili Andreyevich felt quite warm in his two fur coats, especially after struggling in the snowdrift, a cold shiver ran down his back on realizing that he must really spend the night where they were. To calm himself he sat down in the sledge and got out his cigarettes and matches.

Nikita meanwhile unharnessed Mukhorty. He unstrapped the bellyband and the back band, took away the reins, loosened the collar strap, and removed the shaft-bow, talking to him all the time to encourage him. "Now come out! come out!" he said, leading him clear of the shafts. "Now we'll tie you up here and I'll put down some straw and take off your bridle. When you've had a bite you'll feel more cheerful."

But Mukhorty was restless and evidently not comforted by Nikita's remarks. He stepped now on one foot and now on another, and pressed close against the sledge, turning his back to the wind and rubbing his head on Nikita's sleeve. Then, as if not to pain Nikita by refusing his offer of the straw he put before him, he hurriedly snatched a wisp out of the sledge, but immediately decided that it was now no time to think of straw and threw it down, and the wind instantly scattered it, carried it away, and covered it with snow.

"Now we will set up a signal," said Nikita, and turning the front of the sledge to the wind he tied the shafts together with a strap and set them up on end in front of the sledge. "There now, when the snow covers us up, good folk will see the shafts and dig us out," he said, slapping his mittens together and putting them on. "That's what the old folk taught us!"

Vasili Andreyevich meanwhile had unfastened his coat, and holding its skirts up for shelter, struck one sulphur match after another on the steel box. But his hands trembled, and one match after another either did not kindle or was blown out by the wind just as he was lifting it to the cigarette. At last a match did burn up, and its flame lit up for a moment the fur of his coat, his hand with the gold ring on the bent forefinger, and the snow-sprinkled oat straw that stuck out from under the drugget. The cigarette lighted, he eagerly took a whiff or two, inhaled the smoke, let it out through his mustache, and would have inhaled again, but the wind tore off the burning tobacco and whirled it away as it had done the straw.

But even these few puffs had cheered him.

"If we must spend the night here, we must!" he said with decision. "Wait a bit, I'll arrange a flag as well," he added, picking up the kerchief which he had thrown down in the sledge after taking it from round his collar, and drawing off his gloves and standing up on the front of the sledge and stretching himself to reach the strap, he tied the handkerchief to it with a tight knot.

The kerchief immediately began to flutter wildly, now clinging round the shaft, now suddenly streaming out, stretching and flapping.

"Just see what a fine flag!" said Vasili Andreyevich, admiring his handiwork and letting himself down into the sledge. "We should be warmer together, but there's not room enough for two," he added.

"I'll find a place," said Nikita. "But I must cover up the horse first— he sweated so, poor thing. Let go!" he added, drawing the drugget from under Vasili Andreyevich.

Having got the drugget he folded it in two, and after taking off the breechband and pad, covered Mukhorty with it.

"Anyhow it will be warmer, silly!" he said, putting back the breechband and the pad on the horse over the drugget. Then having finished that business he returned to the sledge, and addressing Vasili Andreyevich, said: "You won't need the sackcloth, will you? And let me have some straw."

And having taken these things from under Vasili Andreyevich, Nikita went behind the sledge, dug out a hole for himself in the snow, put straw into it, wrapped his coat well round him, covered himself with the sackcloth, and pulling his cap well down seated himself on the straw he had spread, and leant against the wooden back of the sledge to shelter himself from the wind and the snow.

Vasili Andreyevich shook his head disapprovingly at what Nikita was doing, as in general he disapproved of the peasant's stupidity and lack of education, and he began to settle himself down for the night.

He smoothed the remaining straw over the bottom of the sledge, putting more of it under his side. Then he thrust his hands into his sleeves and settled down, sheltering his head in the corner of the sledge from the wind in front.

He did not wish to sleep. He lay and thought: thought ever of the one thing that constituted the sole aim, meaning, pleasure, and pride of his life—of how much money he had made and might still make, of how much other people he knew had made and possessed, and of how those others had made and were making it, and how he, like them, might still make much more. The purchase of the Goryachkin grove was a matter of immense importance to him. By that one deal he hoped to make perhaps ten thousand rubles. He began mentally to reckon the value of the wood he had inspected in autumn, and on five acres of which he had counted all the trees.

"The oaks will go for sledge runners. The undergrowth will take care of itself, and there'll still be some thirty sazhens[1] of firewood left on each desyatin," said he to himself. "That means there will be at least two hundred and twenty-five rubles' worth left on each desyatin. Fifty-six desyatins means fifty-six hundreds, and fifty-six hundreds, and fifty-six tens, and another fifty-six tens, and then fifty-six fives...." He saw that it came out to more than twelve thousand rubles, but could not reckon it up exactly without a counting-frame. "But I won't give ten thousand, anyhow. I'll give about eight thousand with a deduction on account of the glades. I'll grease the surveyor's palm—give him a hundred rubles, or a hundred and fifty, and he'll reckon that there are some five desyatins of glade to be deducted. And he'll let it go for eight thousand. Three thousand cash down. That'll move him, no fear!" he thought, and he pressed his pocketbook with his forearm.

"God only knows how we missed the turning. The forest ought to be there, and a watchman's hut, and dogs barking. But the damned things don't bark when they're wanted." He turned his collar down from his ear and listened, but as before only the whistling of the wind could be heard, the flapping and fluttering of the kerchief tied to the shafts, and the pelting of the snow against the woodwork of the sledge. He again covered up his ear.

"If I had known I would have stayed the night. Well, no matter, we'll get there tomorrow. It's only one day lost. And the others won't travel in such weather." Then he remembered that on the 9th he had to receive payment from the butcher for his oxen. "He meant to come himself, but he won't find me, and my wife won't know how to receive the money. She doesn't know the right way of doing things," he thought, recalling how at their party the day before she had not known how to treat the police officer who was their guest. "Of course she's only a woman! Where could she have seen anything? In my father's time what was our house like? Just a rich peasant's house: just an oat mill and an inn—that was the whole property. But what have I done in these fifteen years? A shop, two taverns, a flour mill, a grain store, two farms leased out, and a house with an iron-roofed barn," he thought proudly. "Not as it was in Father's time! Who is talked of in the whole district now? Brekhunov! And why? Because I stick to business. I take trouble, not like others who lie abed or waste their time on foolishness while I don't sleep of nights. Blizzard or no blizzard I start out. So business gets done. They think money-making is a joke. No, take pains and rack your brains! You get overtaken out of doors at night, like this, or keep awake night after night till the thoughts whirling in your head make the pillow turn," he meditated with pride. "They think people get on through luck. After all, the

---

[1][A sazhen' is a Russian measure of length, equivalent to about seven feet.]

Mironovs are now millionaires. And why? Take pains and God gives. If only he grants me health!"

The thought that he might himself be a millionaire like Mironov, who began with nothing, so excited Vasili Andreyevich that he felt the need of talking to somebody. But there was no one to talk to. . . . If only he could have reached Goryachkin he would have talked to the landlord and shown him a thing or two.

"Just see how it blows! It will snow us up so deep that we shan't be able to get out in the morning!" he thought, listening to a gust of wind that blew against the front of the sledge, bending it and lashing the snow against it. He raised himself and looked round. All he could see through the whirling darkness was Mukhorty's dark head, his back covered by the fluttering drugget, and his thick knotted tail; while all round, in front and behind, was the same fluctuating whity darkness, sometimes seeming to get a little lighter and sometimes growing denser still.

"A pity I listened to Nikita," he thought. "We ought to have driven on. We should have come out somewhere, if only back to Grishkino and stayed the night at Taras's. As it is we must sit here all night. But what was I thinking about? Yes, that God gives to those who take trouble, but not to loafers, lie-abeds, or fools. I must have a smoke!"

He sat down again, got out his cigarette case, and stretched himself flat on his stomach, screening the matches with the skirt of his coat. But the wind found its way in and put out match after match. At last he got one to burn and lit a cigarette. He was very glad that he had managed to do what he wanted, and though the wind smoked more of the cigarette than he did, he still got two or three puffs and felt more cheerful. He again leant back, wrapped himself up, started reflecting and remembering, and suddenly and quite unexpectedly lost consciousness and fell asleep.

Suddenly something seemed to give him a push and awoke him. Whether it was Mukhorty who had pulled some straw from under him, or whether something within him had startled him, at all events it woke him, and his heart began to beat faster and faster so that the sledge seemed to tremble under him. He opened his eyes. Everything around him was just as before. "It looks lighter," he thought. "I expect it won't be long before dawn." But he at once remembered that it was lighter because the moon had risen. He sat up and looked first at the horse. Mukhorty still stood with his back to the wind, shivering all over. One side of the drugget, which was completely covered with snow, had been blown back, the breeching had slipped down and the snow-covered head with its waving forelock and mane were now more visible. Vasili Andreyevich leant over the back of the sledge and looked behind. Nikita still sat in the same position in which he had settled himself. The sack-

ing with which he was covered, and his legs, were thickly covered with
snow.

"If only that peasant doesn't freeze to death! His clothes are so
wretched. I may be held responsible for him. What shiftless people they
are—such a want of education," thought Vasili Andreyevich, and he felt
like taking the drugget off the horse and putting it over Nikita, but it
would be very cold to get out and move about and, moreover, the horse
might freeze to death. "Why did I bring him with me? It was all her stupidity!" he thought, recalling his unloved wife, and he rolled over into
his old place at the front part of the sledge. "My uncle once spent a
whole night like this," he reflected, "and was all right." But another case
came at once to his mind. "But when they dug Sebastian out he was
dead—stiff like a frozen carcass. If I'd only stopped the night in
Grishkino all this would not have happened!"

And wrapping his coat carefully round him so that none of the
warmth of the fur should be wasted but should warm him all over, neck,
knees, and feet, he shut his eyes and tried to sleep again. But try as he
would he could not get drowsy, on the contrary he felt wide awake and
animated. Again he began counting his gains and the debts due to him,
again he began bragging to himself and feeling pleased with himself and
his position, but all this was continually disturbed by a stealthily approaching fear and by the unpleasant regret that he had not remained in
Grishkino.

"How different it would be to be lying warm on a bench!" He turned
over several times in his attempts to get into a more comfortable position
more sheltered from the wind, he wrapped up his legs closer, shut his
eyes, and lay still. But either his legs in their strong felt boots began to
ache from being bent in one position, or the wind blew in somewhere,
and after lying still for a short time he again began to recall the disturbing fact that he might now have been lying quietly in the warm hut at
Grishkino. He again sat up, turned about, muffled himself up, and settled
down once more.

Once he fancied that he heard a distant cockcrow. He felt glad, turned
down his coat collar and listened with strained attention, but in spite of
all his efforts nothing could be heard but the wind whistling between the
shafts, the flapping of the kerchief, and the snow pelting against the frame
of the sledge.

Nikita sat just as he had done all the time, not moving and not even
answering Vasili Andreyevich who had addressed him a couple of times.
"He doesn't care a bit—he's probably asleep!" thought Vasili
Andreyevich with vexation, looking behind the sledge at Nikita, who
was covered with a thick layer of snow.

Vasili Andreyevich got up and lay down again some twenty times. It seemed to him that the night would never end. "It must be getting near morning," he thought, getting up and looking around. "Let's have a look at my watch. It will be cold to unbutton, but if I only know that it's getting near morning I shall at any rate feel more cheerful. We could begin harnessing."

In the depth of his heart Vasili Andreyevich knew that it could not yet be near morning, but he was growing more and more afraid, and wished both to get to know and yet to deceive himself. He carefully undid the fastening of his sheepskin, pushed in his hand, and felt about for a long time before he got to his waistcoat. With great difficulty he managed to draw out his silver watch with its enamelled flower design, and tried to make out the time. He could not see anything without a light. Again he went down on his knees and elbows as he had done when he lighted a cigarette, got out his matches, and proceeded to strike one. This time he went to work more carefully, and feeling with his fingers for a match with the largest head and the greatest amount of phosphorus, lit it at the first try. Bringing the face of the watch under the light he could hardly believe his eyes. . . . It was only ten minutes past twelve. Almost the whole night was still before him.

"Oh, how long the night is!" he thought, feeling a cold shudder run down his back, and having fastened his fur coats again and wrapped himself up, he snuggled into a corner of the sledge intending to wait patiently. Suddenly, above the monotonous roar of the wind, he clearly distinguished another new and living sound. It steadily strengthened, and having become quite clear diminished just as gradually. Beyond all doubt it was a wolf, and he was so near that the movement of his jaws as he changed his cry was brought down the wind. Vasili Andreyevich turned back the collar of his coat and listened attentively. Mukhorty too strained to listen, moving his ears, and when the wolf had ceased its howling he shifted from foot to foot and gave a warning snort. After this Vasili Andreyevich could not fall asleep again or even calm himself. The more he tried to think of his accounts, his business, his reputation, his worth and his wealth, the more and more was he mastered by fear, and regrets that he had not stayed the night at Grishkino dominated and mingled in all his thoughts.

"Devil take the forest! Things were all right without it, thank God. Ah, if we had only put up for the night!" he said to himself. "They say it's drunkards that freeze," he thought, "and I have had some drink." And observing his sensations he noticed that he was beginning to shiver, without knowing whether it was from cold or from fear. He tried to wrap himself up and lie down as before, but could no longer do so. He could not stay in one position. He wanted to get up, to do something to master the gathering fear that was rising in him and against which he felt himself powerless. He again got out his cigarettes and matches, but only three matches were left and they were bad ones. The phosphorus rubbed off them all without lighting.

"The devil take you! Damned thing! Curse you!" he muttered, not knowing whom or what he was cursing, and he flung away the crushed cigarette. He was about to throw away the matchbox too, but checked the movement of his hand and put the box in his pocket instead. He was seized with such unrest that he could no longer remain in one spot. He climbed out of the sledge and standing with his back to the wind began to shift his belt again, fastening it lower down in the waist and tightening it.

"What's the use of lying and waiting for death? Better mount the horse and get away!" The thought suddenly occurred to him. "The horse will move when he has someone on his back. As for him," he thought of Nikita—"it's all the same to him whether he lives or dies. What is his life worth? He won't grudge his life, but I have something to live for, thank God."

He untied the horse, threw the reins over his neck and tried to mount, but his coats and boots were so heavy that he failed. Then he clambered up in the sledge and tried to mount from there, but the sledge tilted under his weight, and he failed again. At last he drew Mukhorty nearer to the sledge, cautiously balanced on one side of it, and managed to lie on his stomach across the horse's back. After lying like that for a while he shifted forward once and again, threw a leg over, and finally seated himself, supporting his feet on the loose breeching-straps. The shaking of the sledge awoke Nikita. He raised himself, and it seemed to Vasili Andreyevich that he said something.

"Listen to such fools as you! Am I to die like this for nothing?" exclaimed Vasili Andreyevich. And tucking the loose skirts of his fur coat in under his knees, he turned the horse and rode away from the sledge in the direction in which he thought the forest and the forester's hut must be.

VII

From the time he had covered himself with the sackcloth and seated himself behind the sledge, Nikita had not stirred. Like all those who live in touch with nature and have known want, he was patient and could wait for hours, even days, without growing restless or irritable. He heard his master call him, but did not answer because he did not want to move or talk. Though he still felt some warmth from the tea he had drunk and from his energetic struggle when clambering about in the snow-drift, he knew that this warmth would not last long and that he had no

strength left to warm himself again by moving about, for he felt as tired
as a horse when it stops and refuses to go further in spite of the whip,
and its master sees that it must be fed before it can work again. The foot
in the boot with a hole in it had already grown numb, and he could no
longer feel his big toe. Besides that, his whole body began to feel colder
and colder.

The thought that he might, and very probably would, die that night
occurred to him, but did not seem particularly unpleasant or dreadful. It
did not seem particularly unpleasant, because his whole life had been not
a continual holiday, but on the contrary an unceasing round of toil of
which he was beginning to feel weary. And it did not seem particularly
dreadful, because besides the masters he had served here, like Vasili
Andreyevich, he always felt himself dependent on the Chief Master, who
had sent him into this life, and he knew that when dying he would still
be in that Master's power and would not be ill-used by him. "It seems a
pity to give up what one is used to and accustomed to. But there's nothing to be done, I shall get used to the new things."

"Sins?" he thought, and remembered his drunkenness, the money that
had gone on drink, how he had offended his wife, his cursing, his neglect
of church and of the fasts, and all the things the priest blamed him for at
confession. "Of course they are sins. But then, did I take them on of myself? That's evidently how God made me. Well, and the sins? Where am
I to escape to?"

So at first he thought of what might happen to him that night, and
then did not return to such thoughts but gave himself up to whatever
recollections came into his head of themselves. Now he thought of
Martha's arrival, of the drunkenness among the workers and his own re-
nunciation of drink, then of their present journey and of Taras's house
and the talk about the breaking up of the family, then of his own lad, and
of Mukhorty now sheltered under the drugget, and then of his master
who made the sledge creak as he tossed about in it. "I expect you're sorry
yourself that you started out, dear man," he thought. "It would seem hard
to leave a life such as his! It's not like the likes of us."

Then all these recollections began to grow confused and got mixed in
his head, and he fell asleep.

But when Vasili Andreyevich, getting on the horse, jerked the sledge,
against the back of which Nikita was leaning, and it shifted away and hit
him in the back with one of its runners, he awoke and had to change his
position whether he liked it or not. Straightening his legs with difficulty
and shaking the snow off them he got up, and an agonizing cold immediately penetrated his whole body. On making out what was happening
he called to Vasili Andreyevich to leave him the drugget which the horse
no longer needed, so that he might wrap himself in it.

But Vasili Andreyevich did not stop, but disappeared amid the powdery snow.

Left alone, Nikita considered for a moment what he should do. He felt that he had not the strength to go off in search of a house. It was no longer possible to sit down in his old place—it was by now all filled with snow. He felt that he could not get warmer in the sledge either, for there was nothing to cover himself with, and his coat and sheepskin no longer warmed him at all. He felt as cold as though he had nothing on but a shirt. He became frightened. "Lord, heavenly Father!" he muttered, and was comforted by the consciousness that he was not alone but that there was One who heard him and would not abandon him. He gave a deep sigh, and keeping the sackcloth over his head he got inside the sledge and lay down in the place where his master had been.

But he could not get warm in the sledge either. At first he shivered all over, then the shivering ceased and little by little he began to lose consciousness. He did not know whether he was dying or falling asleep, but felt equally prepared for the one as for the other.

VIII

Meanwhile Vasili Andreyevich, with his feet and the ends of the reins, urged the horse on in the direction in which for some reason he expected the forest and forester's hut to be. The snow covered his eyes and the wind seemed intent on stopping him, but bending forward and constantly lapping his coat over and pushing it between himself and the cold harness pad which prevented him from sitting properly, he kept urging the horse on. Mukhorty ambled on obediently though with difficulty, in the direction in which he was driven.

Vasili Andreyevich rode for about five minutes straight ahead, as he thought, seeing nothing but the horse's head and the white waste, and hearing only the whistle of the wind about the horse's ears and his coat collar.

Suddenly a dark patch showed up in front of him. His heart beat with joy, and he rode towards the object, already seeing in imagination the walls of village houses. But the dark patch was not stationary, it kept moving; and it was not a village but some tall stalks of wormwood sticking up through the snow on the boundary between two fields, and desperately tossing about under the pressure of the wind which beat it all to one side and whistled through it. The sight of that wormwood tormented by the pitiless wind made Vasili Andreyevich shudder, he knew not why, and he hurriedly began urging the horse on, not noticing that when riding up to the wormwood he had quite changed his direction and was now heading the opposite way, though still imagining that he was riding towards where the hut should be. But the horse kept making towards the right, and Vasili Andreyevich kept guiding it to the left. Again something dark appeared in front of him. Again he rejoiced, convinced that now it was certainly a village. But once more it was the same boundary line overgrown with wormwood, once more the same wormwood desperately tossed by the wind and carrying unreasoning terror to his heart. But its being the same wormwood was not all, for beside it there was a horse's track partly snowed over. Vasili Andreyevich stopped, stooped down, and looked carefully. It was a horse track only partially covered with snow, and could be none but his own horse's hoof-prints. He had evidently gone round in a small circle. "I shall perish like that!" he thought, and not to give way to his terror he urged on the horse still more, peering into the snowy darkness in which he saw only flitting and fitful points of light. Once he thought he heard the barking of dogs or the howling of wolves, but the sounds were so faint and indistinct that he did not know whether he heard them or merely imagined them, and he stopped and began to listen intently.

Suddenly some terrible, deafening cry resounded near his ears, and everything shivered and shook under him. He seized Mukhorty's neck, but that too was shaking all over and the terrible cry grew still more frightful. For some seconds Vasili Andreyevich could not collect himself or understand what was happening. It was only that Mukhorty, whether to encourage himself or to call for help, had neighed loudly and reso-nantly. "Ugh, you wretch! How you frightened me, damn you!" thought Vasili Andreyevich. But even when he understood the cause of his ter-ror he could not shake it off.

"I must calm myself and think things over," he said to himself, but yet he could not stop, and continued to urge the horse on, without noticing that he was now going with the wind instead of against it. His body, es-pecially between his legs where it touched the pad of the harness and was not covered by his overcoats, was getting painfully cold, especially when the horse walked slowly. His legs and arms trembled and his breathing came fast. He saw himself perishing amid this dreadful snowy waste, and could see no means of escape.

Suddenly the horse under him tumbled into something and, sinking into a snowdrift, began to plunge and fell on his side. Vasili Andreyevich jumped off, and in so doing dragged to one side the breechband on which his foot was resting, and twisted round the pad to which he held as he dismounted. As soon as he had jumped off, the horse struggled to his feet, plunged forward, gave one leap and another, neighed again, and dragging the drugget and the breechband after him, disappeared, leaving Vasili Andreyevich alone on the snowdrift.

The latter pressed on after the horse, but the snow lay so deep and his coats were so heavy that, sinking above his knees at each step, he stopped breathless after taking not more than twenty steps. "The copse, the oxen, the leasehold, the shop, the tavern, the house with the iron-roofed barn, and my heir," thought he. "How can I leave all that? What does this mean? It cannot be!" These thoughts flashed through his mind. Then he thought of the wormwood tossed by the wind, which he had twice ridden past, and he was seized with such terror that he did not believe in the reality of what was happening to him. "Can this be a dream?" he thought, and tried to wake up but could not. It was real snow that lashed his face and covered him and chilled his right hand from which he had lost the glove, and this was a real desert in which he was now left alone like that wormwood, awaiting an inevitable, speedy, and meaningless death.

"Queen of Heaven! Holy Father Nicholas, teacher of temperance!" he thought, recalling the service of the day before and the holy icon with its black face and gilt frame, and the tapers which he sold to be set before that icon and which were almost immediately brought back to him scarcely burnt at all, and which he put away in the store-chest. He began to pray to that same Nicholas the Wonder-Worker to save him, promising him a thanksgiving service and some candles. But he clearly and indubitably realized that the icon, its frame, the candles, the priest, and the thanksgiving service, though very important and necessary in church, could do nothing for him here, and that there was and could be no connection between those candles and services and his present disastrous plight. "I must not despair," he thought. "I must follow the horse's track before it is snowed under. He will lead me out, or I may even catch him. Only I must not hurry, or I shall stick fast and be more lost than ever."

But in spite of his resolution to go quietly, he rushed forward and even ran, continually falling, getting up and falling again. The horse's track was already hardly visible in places where the snow did not lie deep. "I am lost!" thought Vasili Andreyevich. "I shall lose the track and not catch the horse." But at that moment he saw something black. It was Mukhorty, and not only Mukhorty, but the sledge with the shafts and the kerchief. Mukhorty, with the sacking and the breechband twisted round to one side, was standing not in his former place but nearer to the shafts, shaking his head which the reins he was stepping on drew downwards. It turned out that Vasili Andreyevich had sunk in the same ravine Nikita had previously fallen into, and that Mukhorty had been bringing him back to the sledge and he had got off his back no more than fifty paces from where the sledge was.

IX

Having stumbled back to the sledge Vasili Andreyevich caught hold of it and for a long time stood motionless, trying to calm himself and recover his breath. Nikita was not in his former place, but something, already covered with snow, was lying in the sledge, and Vasili Andreyevich concluded that this was Nikita. His terror had now quite left him, and if he felt any fear it was lest the dreadful terror should return that he had experienced when on the horse and especially when he was left alone in the snowdrift. At any cost he had to avoid that terror, and to keep it away he must do something—occupy himself with something. And the first thing he did was to turn his back to the wind and open his fur coat. Then, as soon as he recovered his breath a little, he shook the snow out of his boots and out of his left-hand glove (the right-hand glove was hopelessly lost and by this time probably lying somewhere under a dozen inches of snow); then as was his custom when going out of his shop to buy grain from the peasants, he pulled his girdle low down and tightened it and prepared for action. The first thing that occurred to him was to free Mukhorty's leg from the rein. Having done that, and tethered him to the iron cramp at the front of the sledge where he had been before, he was going round the horse's quarters to put the breechband and pad straight and cover him with the cloth, but at that moment he noticed that something was moving in the sledge and Nikita's head rose up out of the snow that covered it. Nikita, who was half frozen, rose with great difficulty and sat up, moving his hand before his nose in a strange manner just as if he were driving away flies. He waved his hand and said something, and seemed to Vasili Andreyevich to be calling him. Vasili Andreyevich left the cloth unadjusted and went up to the sledge.

"What is it?" he asked. "What are you saying?"

"I'm dy . . . ing, that's what," said Nikita brokenly and with difficulty. "Give what is owing to me to my lad, or to my wife, no matter."

"Why, are you really frozen?" asked Vasili Andreyevich.

"I feel it's my death. Forgive me for Christ's sake . . ." said Nikita in a tearful voice, continuing to wave his hand before his face as if driving away flies.

Vasili Andreyevich stood silent and motionless for half a minute. Then suddenly, with the same resolution with which he used to strike hands when making a good purchase, he took a step back and turning up his sleeves began raking the snow off Nikita and out of the sledge. Having done this he hurriedly undid his girdle, opened out his fur coat, and having pushed Nikita down, lay down on top of him, covering him not only with his fur coat but with the whole of his body, which glowed with warmth. After pushing the skirts of his coat between Nikita and the sides of the sledge, and holding down its hem with his knees, Vasili Andreyevich lay like that face down, with his head pressed against the front of the sledge. Here he no longer heard the horse's movements or the whistling of the wind, but only Nikita's breathing. At first and for a long time Nikita lay motionless, then he sighed deeply and moved.

"There, and you say you are dying! Lie still and get warm, that's our way . . ." began Vasili Andreyevich.

But to his great surprise he could say no more, for tears came to his eyes and his lower jaw began to quiver rapidly. He stopped speaking and only gulped down the risings in his throat. "Seems I was badly frightened and have gone quite weak," he thought. But this weakness was not only not unpleasant, but gave him a peculiar joy such as he had never felt before.

"That's our way!" he said to himself, experiencing a strange and solemn tenderness. He lay like that for a long time, wiping his eyes on the fur of his coat and tucking under his knee the right skirt, which the wind kept turning up.

But he longed so passionately to tell somebody of his joyful condition that he said: "Nikita!"

"It's comfortable, warm!" came a voice from beneath.

"There, you see, friend, I was going to perish. And you would have been frozen, and I should have . . ."

But again his jaws began to quiver and his eyes to fill with tears, and he could say no more.

"Well, never mind," he thought. "I know about myself what I know."

He remained silent and lay like that for a long time.

Nikita kept him warm from below and his fur coats from above. Only his hands, with which he kept his coat-skirts down round Nikita's sides, and his legs which the wind kept uncovering, began to freeze, especially his right hand which had no glove. But he did not think of his legs or of his hands but only of how to warm the peasant who was lying under him. He looked out several times at Mukhorty and could see that his back was uncovered and the drugget and breeching lying on the snow, and that he ought to get up and cover him, but he could not bring himself to leave Nikita and disturb even for a moment the joyous condition he was in. He no longer felt any kind of terror.

"No fear, we shan't lose him this time!" he said to himself, referring to his getting the peasant warm with the same boastfulness with which he spoke of his buying and selling.

Vasili Andreyevich lay in that way for one hour, another, and a third, but he was unconscious of the passage of time. At first impressions of the snowstorm, the sledge shafts, and the horse with the shaft bow shaking before his eyes, kept passing through his mind, then he remembered Nikita lying under him, then recollections of the festival, his wife, the police officer, and the box of candles, began to mingle with these; then again Nikita, this time lying under that box, then the peasants, customers and traders, and the white walls of his house with its iron roof with Nikita lying underneath, presented themselves to his imagination.

Afterwards all these impressions blended into one nothingness. As the colors of the rainbow unite into one white light, so all these different impressions mingled into one, and he fell asleep.

For a long time he slept without dreaming, but just before dawn the visions recommenced. It seemed to him that he was standing by the box of tapers and that Tikhon's wife was asking for a five-kopek taper for the Church fête. He wished to take one out and give it to her, but his hands would not lift, being held tight in his pockets. He wanted to walk round the box but his feet would not move and his new clean galoshes had grown to the stone floor, and he could neither lift them nor get his feet out of the galoshes. Then the taper box was no longer a box but a bed, and suddenly Vasili Andreyevich saw himself lying in his bed at home. He was lying in his bed and could not get up. Yet it was necessary for him to get up because Ivan Matveyich, the police officer, would soon call for him and he had to go with him—either to bargain for the forest or to put Mukhorty's breeching straight.

He asked his wife: "Nikolayevna, hasn't he come yet?" "No, he hasn't," she replied. He heard someone drive up to the front steps. "It must be him." "No, he's gone past." "Nikolayevna! I say, Nikolayevna, isn't he here yet?" "No." He was still lying on his bed and could not get up, but was always waiting. And this waiting was uncanny and yet joyful. Then suddenly his joy was completed. He whom he was expecting came; not Ivan Matveyich the police officer, but someone else—yet it was he whom he had been waiting for. He came and called him; and it was he who had called him and told him to lie down on Nikita. And Vasili Andreyevich was glad that that one had come for him.

"I'm coming!" he cried joyfully, and that cry awoke him, but woke him up not at all the same person he had been when he fell asleep. He tried to get up but could not, tried to move his arm and could not, to move his leg and also could not, to turn his head and could not. He was surprised but not at all disturbed by this. He understood that this was death, and was not at all disturbed by that either. He remembered that Nikita was lying under him and that he had got warm and was alive, and it seemed to him that he was Nikita and Nikita was he, and that his life was not in himself but in Nikita. He strained his ears and heard Nikita breathing and even slightly snoring. "Nikita is alive, so I too am alive!" he said to himself triumphantly.

And he remembered his money, his shop, his house, the buying and selling, and Mironov's millions, and it was hard for him to understand why that man, called Vasili Brekhunov, had troubled himself with all those things with which he had been troubled.

"Well, it was because he did not know what the real thing was," he thought, concerning that Vasili Brekhunov. "He did not know, but now

I know and know for sure. Now I know!" And again he heard the voice of the one who had called him before. "I'm coming! Coming!" he responded gladly, and his whole being was filled with joyful emotion. He felt himself free and that nothing could hold him back any longer.

After that Vasili Andreyevich neither saw, heard, nor felt anything more in this world.

All around the snow still eddied. The same whirlwinds of snow circled about, covering the dead Vasili Andreyevich's fur coat, the shivering Mukhorty, the sledge, now scarcely to be seen, and Nikita lying at the bottom of it, kept warm beneath his dead master.

X

Nikita awoke before daybreak. He was aroused by the cold that had begun to creep down his back. He had dreamt that he was coming from the mill with a load of his master's flour and when crossing the stream had missed the bridge and let the cart get stuck. And he saw that he had crawled under the cart and was trying to lift it by arching his back. But strange to say the cart did not move, it stuck to his back and he could neither lift it nor get out from under it. It was crushing the whole of his loins. And how cold it felt! Evidently he must crawl out. "Have done!" he exclaimed to whoever was pressing the cart down on him. "Take out the sacks!" But the cart pressed down colder and colder, and then he heard a strange knocking, awoke completely, and remembered everything. The cold cart was his dead and frozen master lying upon him. And the knock was produced by Mukhorty, who had twice struck the sledge with his hoof.

"Andreyevich! Eh, Andreyevich!" Nikita called cautiously, beginning to realize the truth, and straightening his back. But Vasili Andreyevich did not answer and his stomach and legs were stiff and cold and heavy like iron weights.

"He must have died! May the Kingdom of Heaven be his!" thought Nikita.

He turned his head, dug with his hand through the snow about him and opened his eyes. It was daylight; the wind was whistling as before between the shafts, and the snow was falling in the same way, except that it was no longer driving against the frame of the sledge but silently covered both sledge and horse deeper and deeper, and neither the horse's movements nor his breathing were any longer to be heard.

"He must have frozen too," thought Nikita of Mukhorty, and indeed those hoof knocks against the sledge, which had awakened Nikita, were the last efforts the already numbed Mukhorty had made to keep on his feet before dying.

"O Lord God, it seems Thou art calling me too!" said Nikita. "Thy Holy Will be done. But it's uncanny. . . . Still, a man can't die twice and must die once. If only it would come soon!"

And he again drew in his head, closed his eyes, and became unconscious, fully convinced that now he was certainly and finally dying.

It was not till noon that day that peasants dug Vasili Andreyevich and Nikita out of the snow with their shovels, not more than seventy yards from the road and less than half a mile from the village.

The snow had hidden the sledge, but the shafts and the kerchief tied to them were still visible. Mukhorty, buried up to his belly in snow, with the breeching and drugget hanging down, stood all white, his dead head pressed against his frozen throat: icicles hung from his nostrils, his eyes were covered with hoarfrost as though filled with tears, and he had grown so thin in that one night that he was nothing but skin and bone.

Vasili Andreyevich was stiff as a frozen carcass, and when they rolled him off Nikita his legs remained apart and his arms stretched out as they had been. His bulging hawk eyes were frozen, and his open mouth under his clipped mustache was full of snow. But Nikita though chilled through was still alive. When he had been brought to, he felt sure that he was already dead and that what was taking place with him was no longer happening in this world but in the next. When he heard the peasants shouting as they dug him out and rolled the frozen body of Vasili Andreyevich from off him, he was at first surprised that in the other world peasants should be shouting in the same old way and had the same kind of body, and then when he realized that he was still in this world he was sorry rather than glad, especially when he found that the toes on both his feet were frozen.

Nikita lay in hospital for two months. They cut off three of his toes, but the others recovered so that he was still able to work and went on living for another twenty years, first as a farm laborer, then in his old age as a watchman. He died at home as he had wished, only this year, under the icons with a lighted taper in his hands. Before he died he asked his wife's forgiveness and forgave her for the cooper. He also took leave of his son and grandchildren, and died sincerely glad that he was relieving his son and daughter-in-law of the burden of having to feed him, and that he was now really passing from this life of which he was weary into that other life which every year and every hour grew clearer and more desirable to him. Whether he is better or worse off there where he awoke after his death, whether he was disappointed or found there what he expected, we shall all soon learn.